A
THOUSAND
SUNS

A RULON HURT NOVEL

A THOUSAND SUNS

A RULON HURT NOVEL

JIM HABERKORN

BONNEVILLE BOOKS
AN IMPRINT OF CEDAR FORT, INC.
SPRINGVILLE, UTAH

ISBN 13: 978-1-4621-1185-5

Published by Bonneville Books, an imprint of Cedar Fort, Inc.
2373 W. 700 S., Springville, UT, 84663
Distributed by Cedar Fort, Inc., www.cedarfort.com

Library of Congress Cataloging-in-Publication Data on File

Cover design by Angela D. Olsen
Cover design © 2013 by Lyle Mortimer
Edited and typeset by Melissa J. Caldwell

Printed in the United States of America

10 9 8 7 6 5 4 3 2 1

— TO MY MOTHER AND FATHER —

their stalwart natures and love of reading were my inheritance

CHAPTER 1

In the bowels of the Kremlin, two hundred yards from Lenin's tomb, a guard made his rounds late at night, the click of his boots echoing in the dark and deserted hallways. Checking each door, he came to one and saw the fractured luminescence of a small green lamp through the frosted glass. This one he knew to avoid and moved on. The echoes of his passing faded down the hall.

Inside the room, the lamp's soft glow dropped a dim circle of light on a gray metal desk, leaving an old man's hollow eyes and hawklike face securely in the shadows. He sat in a wooden roller chair talking quietly into a speakerphone. The voice on the other end was male, mid-thirties, insistent.

"Reconsider, sir. Please."

"Why?" the thin man asked.

"The Serbians are demanding revenge," the younger voice said.

"As they have since Kosovo Fields," said the old man impatiently, referring to the 1389 battle with the Ottomans.

"Please reconsider, sir. Except for this, I have never asked for anything twice."

"And that is why you are still around to annoy me," said the old man sharply. Instant silence. Then with more patience to his protégé, "I said there would be no retaliation. I did not say we would do nothing." The old man pressed a button, ending the call but not his dilemma. He sat thinking, slowly stroking the chair's left arm, buffed smooth by decades of hard decisions. Both he and the chair

1

were old comrades-in-arms, he liked to joke—both relics of the siege of Stalingrad. He tapped his finger on his laptop touchpad. For the fifth time that night, he clicked "Play," closed his eyes, and listened to the DVD from CERN.

The camera had been knocked over when the American cowboy broke free, giving only an angled, distorted picture of a table leg, a confusion of booted feet, and the cowboy's black loafers. The audio came through perfectly, however—an unintelligible, bellowing roar. *And they say we Russians are brutes*. Yells of alarm. Thudding, hammering blows. Two explosions: gunshots three seconds apart—an eternity in that room. Now screams from the dying, sounds impossible to interpret unless you saw the bodies, which the thin man had. An image of the cowboy with his hammer appeared. The old man tried recalling an expression he once heard. It came to him . . . *anger management problem*. He smiled grimly. *The Americans and their euphemisms.*

The thin man ejected the DVD, returned it to its plastic case, and resumed stroking the chair. After a few minutes, he reached into his top drawer, pulled out a file, and laid it on the desk. Flipping through the tabbed sections, he came to a picture of a man and woman taken in a stairwell by a CERN surveillance camera: Rulon Hurt, cowboy from America, and Yohaba Meleksen, Swiss citizen, his woman. He picked up the photo and studied the girl closely. A smart girl, he'd been told, and quite lovely. Yes, the Cowboy had his reasons.

He carefully replaced the photo in the file. Yes, the Cowboy would live. There would be no hollow-point bullet in the face from close range. No camouflaged sniper in the hills above the ranch in Idaho. No poison-tipped umbrella. No booby-trapped cell phone.

Neither mercy nor romanticism played a part in the thin man's decision. In fact, any suggestion of either would have only made him laugh. Having ordered in his lifetime the deaths of many enemies and more than a few comrades, he no longer felt intoxicated by the power of life and death or the need to wield it indiscriminately. An execution was but a tool, and he understood its limitations. And while he did not believe in God, he did believe in martyrs.

The Cowboy would not be executed. The dead men had disobeyed orders. The Cowboy had meted out . . . a proportional response. But something would have to be done. Something.

THIRTY MONTHS LATER

IT WAS THE first Karaoke Wednesday after Graduation Day, and the Rockin' Rooster Saloon in Twin Falls, Idaho, was bursting at the seams. People sat at tables around the karaoke stage, and others crowded around the bar, some on stools, some standing sideways in the gaps, talking and bobbing to the music. As usual, there was old Gilly serving drinks between the bar and the long, ornately framed mirror behind it, his bald head barely visible through the crowd. Normally, there were five small tables set up in a half-circle in front of the stage. Tonight, in expectation of an extra large crowd, there was double that number, leaving hardly any room for those who came to dance. Most people, though, had come for a different reason.

The tables were full, three or four people around each, except for the table tucked around the far corner of the stage and half hidden in the dark. There, a single, dark, brooding giant of a man sat quietly by himself in the shadows with his back to the wall and a clear view of the entrance. He was about thirty years old with a stone block for a face, massive cheek and brow bones, and a three-day growth of black sandpaper. His face said "hard miles"—and lots of them. He'd been sitting there for two hours and was now on his third Jack Daniels. Which felt about right to him. Three drinks in two hours, still alert, feeling good despite the jet lag—just the right amount of reckless. No one bothered him, though he attracted a lot of looks. People knew why he was there. First Karaoke Wednesday after Graduation Day. Somebody like him always showed up.

A short, blonde woman wearing the uniform of the day—cowboy hat, jeans, and boots—stood on stage nervously gripping a microphone and singing the old Garth Brooks song "Friends in Low Places." She finished to polite applause and curtsied to the room. No one got up to take her place, and the DJ let the music play through the rest of the album.

The room was a swirling buzz of commotion and conversation. *Stretched tight like a wire*, thought Gilly. It was a symphony of discordant sounds—raucous chatter of fifty voices, the clinking of glasses and frequent bursts of laughter mingled with the sliding of chairs, boots, and stools against the wood floor. A couple walked in the front door; all heads turned, and the bar collectively held its breath . . . then went back to their drinks and nachos. The buzzing paused and then started up again every time the door swung open, the disappointment so obvious in the faces of the crowd that even the brute in the corner knew what was happening. His adrenaline surged each time.

"Hey, Gilly," said a man at the bar. "How come the place is so crowded tonight?" The speaker was about fifty with a loosened tie, a crumpled suit jacket over the back of his stool, and a dingy white shirt with sleeves rolled up to his elbows. Everything about him said "traveling salesman." Plumbing supplies, maybe fertilizer. Weary. Eighty thousand miles a year in a Ford F-series. Probably knew every bar and bartender between Winnemucca and Missoula.

Gilly slid a beer expertly down the bar and immediately reached behind him for another glass. Without looking up, he said, "Karaoke Wednesday, Ted. Can't believe you didn't know that." Not missing a beat, Gilly filled the next glass and sent that one sliding in the same direction as the first. This was going to be a record night. Probably pull in ten times more than the restaurant.

"Baloney," said Ted. "Remember, I was here last Wednesday too."

Gilly did a quick scan down the bar just to make sure everyone was served, then placed both hands on the bar and said squarely to the salesman, "It's a fight. That's all. See all the women? Nothing brings the women out better'n a fight. I thought everybody knew that. You ever see a bar where there's almost as many women as men, well, either Dwight Yoakam's showing up or there's gonna be a fight. Just sit there."

"Who's fighting?" asked Ted.

Gilly took a rag out of his signature Dagwood apron and began polishing the bar's dark mahogany surface. "See that guy over there," he said, nodding at the giant in the corner. "The guy with the crew cut and black jacket. Doesn't fit in, does he?"

Ted turned in his stool and noticed the man for the first time. "Where's Godzilla from?" he asked.

"Moscow," Gilly said.

"Played for the Vandals, did he? What's his story?"

"Not Moscow, Idaho. I'm talking Moscow, Russia," Gilly said with a laugh. "That there boy's from a Russian *clan-des-tine* organization. He's the pick of the litter. The graduating class valedictorian, I imagine. Every six months when another class graduates, they pick the toughest hombre and send him here to fight one of the local boys."

"Makes perfect sense," said Ted, not taking the conversation seriously. "I'm sure the same thing's happening in bars all over the country right now. Who gets to fight him? Do you have some kinda lottery system?"

"You don't believe me, do you? That's all right. Stick around. Fact is the Rooskies do the choosin'. Always the same cowboy— Rulon Hurt. Been that way for the past two, three years. Every six months like clockwork, ever since Rulon came back from overseas somewheres. Anyway, a monster Rooskie always shows up first Karaoke Wednesday after Graduation Day. That's the way it is."

Ted looked around. Sounded crazy, but something sure was up. "A fistfight, you say. No weapons?"

"Nope. Rulon says the Russians have a code. Says their government lies all the time, but their spy agencies stick to their deals. Rulon, though, doesn't like to fight. Always tries to talk 'em out of it first."

"What happens then?"

"Oh," Gilly said, half distracted by a yell for more beer from the other end of the bar. "They always fight. Rulon couldn't talk his way out of a taffy pull. Not with Yohaba around." Just then the place hushed for about the tenth time as the front door swung open, but this time the hush continued for an extra beat. Gilly looked over and saw the guest of honor.

"Well, look who's here," Gilly said, "and you've got a ring-side seat."

Ted, still clutching his beer, swiveled on his stool to look. "Which one?"

"See the galoot in the brown cowboy hat with the tall, good-looking gal? That's him." When Ted didn't say anything but just focused on Yohaba, Gilly said, a bit irritated, "The fella we're talking about is on her right."

"Oh, yeah," Ted said. "You mean the guy with the checkered shirt? The chubby fella?"

"Yeah, but I'd keep the chubby part to myself if I was you. And I wouldn't stare at the girl."

RULON AND YOHABA stood in the doorway, Yohaba chattering like a magpie and Rulon mostly ignoring her as he scanned the room. The Russian wasn't hard to spot. Rulon gently nudged Yohaba, then nodded toward the lone table in the corner.

Yohaba flipped her long auburn hair out of her face, piped down for a few seconds of concentrated gazing, and then said, "Geez, Cowboy, he looks like a genetic experiment."

"I see a glint of compassion in his eyes," Rulon said.

"Yeah, the one in the middle."

"Don't start," Rulon growled. He grabbed her arm and together they wove through the crowd to the bar, ignoring the exuberant greetings from half-drunk cowboys.

"How's it going, Rulon?"

"Howdy, Yohaba."

"Looking good, you two."

"How's it hangin', buddy?"

"Ready to rumble, Rul?"

Rulon and Yohaba knew most of the faces but were annoyed to see more than the usual number of drunken, good-ole-boy strangers there. Even more disturbing, there was a gaggle of sullen skinheads with white T-shirts stretched tight over their prison-molded physiques.

What rock did they crawl out from under? thought Rulon.

The first Karaoke Wednesday after Graduation Day had been drawing a progressively bigger, drunker, and more motley crowd over the years. This was the part Rulon hated most. He'd just as soon settle it on a dirt patch somewhere in the hills, but the Russians insisted it be in a public place with no weapons. They trusted Rulon even less than he trusted them. He had no choice but to agree. It was the price for the Russians not just saying the heck with it and sending in a seventy-year-old bag lady with a silenced .22.

Rulon and Yohaba pushed their way to the bar, and folks made room for them to squeeze in. Gilly came over with a big smile, the sweat glistening on his bald head. He was working hard tonight.

"Shoot, man," Rulon said, in a bad mood from all the fuss. "I oughta be getting a cut of this."

"Proceeds from demon rum? Doesn't sound like you," Gilly said. "But if I was to do that, to be fair, I'd have to give him a share too." He glanced at the Russian. Then he added as he wiped down the bar, "He's the biggest one yet. And light on his feet. Like a boxer. I'd say they brought in a ringer this time. I told you they'd get tired of you wompin' on their boys." Rulon snorted. Gilly looked at Yohaba. "Why don't you take him home, darlin'?"

"Afraid they'll bust up the place?" Yohaba asked.

"Not particularly. Same as always. The Rooskie gave me a credit card and a note saying he was good for the damage. But, all the same, why don't you and Rulon just go home?" Gilly looked the crowd over. "Heck, there's twenty guys in here would love to fight him for you." He laughed. "All at once, I mean."

"I would never think of depriving Rulon of this," Yohaba said. "He protests a lot, but he'd sooner miss Christmas. But, hey, who's the bartender around here? How about a couple of the usuals?"

Rulon leaned on the bar and appraised the big Russian in the reflection of the mirror. The Russian sat at his table as straight and stoic as a war memorial. "Make that three," Rulon said.

Gilly reached behind him into a half-height fridge and brought out three cans of Sprite. "Knock yourselves out. It's on the house. It's the least I can do. Man, I'm gonna run out of beer tonight at this rate. Tell the Rooskies I'll pay their way over if they come every month." When Rulon and Yohaba gave him a dirty look, he laughed and went back to working the rest of the bar.

Rulon and Yohaba popped open their Sprites, turned around, and leaned back against the bar, sipping their drinks. Rulon occasionally touched his can to the rim of his hat to acknowledge a passerby's greeting. A few times, a friend stopped to chat for a minute.

"I'd rather see you fighting some of those yobs," Yohaba said in between visits, referring to the skinheads. She'd been living in Idaho for over two years now and had a good handle on the local vernacular.

"Night's still young," Rulon said.

"Shouldn't they be home watching *Prison Break* or something?" Yohaba said, eyeing the supremacists suspiciously.

"Do you think he's bigger than me? I think he's bigger than me," Rulon said, changing the subject. Rulon was six foot and 290 pounds; a little big for a cowboy but just right for a former collegiate hammer thrower and Greco-Roman wrestler. Up until two and half years ago, he worked indirectly for the US State Department in Switzerland as an agent for a rough and tumble outfit called OCD— Office Crimes Division. That's where he ran afoul of the Russians. They'd been on his case ever since.

"I never thought it possible, but, yeah, I think he's bigger than you. I wonder how he got through the door." She blew a strand of hair out of her face, then glanced at Rulon. "Not too late to change tactics."

"How's your Russian?"

"I don't think you're talking your way out of this one, Cowboy. But what the heck. Let's give it a try." Rulon grabbed the extra Sprite, and then he and Yohaba pushed off the bar and wove their way around the cluster of tables, heading straight for the Russian. The noise and rhythm of the place never varied, but every eye in the saloon was on them.

When they got to the table, Rulon stood there for a moment and let the Russian size him up. Rulon moved well for a big man: massive shoulders and back, neck muscles popping out, huge hands, and big-boned. He had a chiseled jaw that belied his ample girth and was more muscular than he first appeared. He had kind eyes and a mellow, amiable expression, and wore dusty jeans, boots, and a black hat. Except for looking like he rode in on a Clydesdale, Rulon was just another cowboy.

And Yohaba was just another cowgirl, if you concentrated only on the boots and tight jeans. The first time Rulon saw her picture in an OCD case file, her oval face and green eyes made him wonder if there was a dash of Oriental in the recipe. But in real life she looked more regal, more Russian. She had long, auburn hair hanging loose past her shoulders and a pert nose. She rarely smiled big but had an expression that grabbed you all the same—a look that asked, "Are you as interesting as me?" On the left side of her neck, just above the collar of her way-too-tight Offspring concert T-shirt, was a four-inch-wide spider web tattoo. Wouldn't have drawn a second look in Zurich, but well, this was a cowboy bar in Twin Falls, Idaho. Less obvious was the tiny scar where her nose ring used to loop.

Rulon took off his hat, looked around at all the gawkers, frowned, and then wiped his sweaty forehead with his sleeve.

"Mind if we sit down?" Rulon asked pleasantly as he put his hat back on. Yohaba translated. The Russian answered in a voice like a grinding transaxle. Yohaba said something in reply and reached for a chair. Rulon followed her lead and sat next to her, across from the Russian.

Rulon opened the extra Sprite and set it down in front of his adversary. He started to say something, but the Russian cut him short by swiping the can off the table with the back of his hand. The place went quiet except for the Garth Brooks song in the background. Rulon looked the Russian up and down. *Big hands like mine*, he thought. *Mushed up right ear. Confident. Big as a house. They keep sending upgrades.*

"Don't worry about it. The soda was free," Rulon said cheerfully. When Yohaba continued to sit there quietly, Rulon said out of the corner of his mouth, "Go on. Translate for heaven's sake."

"Oh, yeah," Yohaba said. Then speaking in Russian, she said, "Rulon says if you do that again he's going to use you to wipe up the floor."

Figuring that Yohaba had patched things up, Rulon quickly interjected, "You remind me of someone." Yohaba translated, but the Russian didn't respond, just fixed Rulon with a glare. "Me," said Rulon after a long pause.

The Russian finished off the rest of his whiskey, slowly put the glass down on the table, and then said to Yohaba, "You speak excellent Russian. Tell him that after tonight there will be no more of us coming to visit."

"What? Are you out of Russians already?" Yohaba asked. "Did

Rulon go through that many? I'd lost count."

"What did he say?" Rulon asked. "Tell him I don't want to fight. Tell him this is ridiculous."

"Shhh, darling," Yohaba said. "I'm handling this." Just then the sounds of "Back in the USSR" blared over the sound system. Rulon looked down, rubbed the bridge of his nose, and sighed.

"Darling, could you please tell Frank that we've got a situation here. Thank you."

Yohaba excused herself and got up, leaving Rulon and Boris to stare at each other. She pushed through the crowd to the karaoke machine on the other side of the stage, where Frank, its grizzled, white-haired, eighty-year-old operator was fiddling with the buttons.

"Howdy, Yohaba," Frank said cheerfully. "How's it going over there? I can crank this baby up louder if you want."

"Ah . . . Frank. Thanks, but Rulon's a mite touchy right now. Do you mind?"

"Oh. Sorry, Yohaba." He fumbled for the controls. "Just trying to help. You know. Get the place revved up."

Yohaba looked over the crowd standing ten feet behind Rulon, the front row straining to keep the others back. "Frank. It's already like the killing of the fascists in *For Whom the Bell Tolls*."

"What?"

"Never mind." Yohaba started to turn away and stopped. She looked around. "Wednesday night. Big crowd. What do you think? Maybe a little Mellencamp for the main event? Can you queue something up?"

"You got it," said Frank.

Yohaba returned to the table and sat down. "Where were we?" she asked in Russian.

"My name is Boris," said the big Russian.

"And my name is Natasha," Yohaba replied. "Oh, yeah. I suggest you take your ugly mug out of here before Rulon stuffs you in a diplomatic bag back to Siberia."

"Would you mind telling me what's going on?" Rulon asked.

"We're negotiating, dear," Yohaba said. Just then, four drunken cowboys walked up and asked Rulon if he needed any help.

"Scram," said Rulon, without turning his head. One of the

cowboys started to say something, but his more sober friends pulled him away.

"You can make your jokes," the Russian said, "but in the end he will have to fight. You think this is funny? They told me what your husband did at CERN. It is a mystery to me why we are letting him live. But after tonight he'll think a bullet was the easy way out. I won't be finishing him off quickly. I'm going to take my time."

Rulon jumped in before Yohaba could answer. "Tell him I just want to be friends. Invite him out to the ranch for a late supper. Tell him we have a spare room. He's welcome to stay a few days. Ask him if he likes horses. I'll take him out for a ride tomorrow and show him the ranch. He can go back to Moscow and tell his buddies he beat me to a pulp. I'll walk around with a fake splint for a few weeks. No one will ever know." Rulon said all this with as big a smile as he could fake, trying his best to seem friendly and unassuming. He jerked his head in the direction of the door as a way of emphasizing the invitation. "C'mon, we can all fit in my pickup."

"What did he say?" the Russian asked. "And why is he grinning like an idiot?"

"He said he's picturing you with his boot up your kazoo," Yohaba said. "And he's going to throw you through the front door and run over you with his truck." She turned to Rulon, "I don't think he's buying it, honey. This one's a real hard case."

Boris said, "I will break him. I was my country's super-heavyweight mixed martial arts champion, recruited by the Russian SVR just for this. I grew up in the boomtowns of Siberia, street fighting with oil riggers every day since I was fifteen. Tell him. Go ahead and tell him."

Yohaba translated.

Rulon said, "Tell him those are mighty impressive credentials. Tell him he is way out of my league and that I forfeit. Wish him a pleasant trip back to Moscow. Ask him if he needs a ride to the airport. Tell him I'll drive him all the way back to Boise. Or even to Salt Lake if that's where he flew in."

Yohaba said, "Rulon says you're awfully strong, but smell's not everything. He says he's willing to let you go back to Russia peacefully, but first you have to crawl out of this saloon on your belly."

"Enough of these insults," snarled the now red-faced Boris. "We fight. Here. Now. No more talk. I will break him in half. He used to ride bulls, eh? Tell him after this, he'll ride a wheelchair."

"What do you think? Is he buying any of this?" Rulon asked, leaning in close to Yohaba but keeping his eyes on the brute. "By the way, I really appreciate this. If I didn't have you to translate, I'd really be up a creek."

"Thanks, darling. But I don't know what more to say," Yohaba said. "He's unbelievably stubborn."

"Try again," Rulon said. "Offer to make him one of your omelets."

"Okay, my love, but I don't know how much good it's going to do." She leaned over the table and looked the Russian square in the eyes. "Rulon says that he's going to break you like an egg and scramble your brains."

The big Russian stood up, rising like a mountain and knocking over his chair. He cupped one massive fist in his other hand and cracked his battle-scarred knuckles. Rulon and Yohaba stood up too.

Rulon asked, "What do you think? I don't think it's working."

"I think he's pretty determined. It would be humiliating for him to go back without even a black eye. Cowboy, I think you've got it to do."

The Russian said, "Why is he stalling? He knows why I'm here. He knows what will happen if he doesn't fight."

"My husband says you're wasting his time. Go back to Russia and tell them to send a real man next time. He says there's only one thing you can say to make him fight a wimp like you." When she saw him hesitating, she said, "C'mon, C'mon. I'm sure they told you."

With that, the huge Russian reached into an inside jacket pocket and pulled out an index card. He studied it carefully, then licked his lips and haltingly pronounced the words in heavily accented English: "I am going to kick your butt . . ." He paused, struggling with the last word, his native Russian tongue having trouble with the "h" sound ". . . haystack."

Yohaba looked at Rulon, then shrugged and stepped away from

the table. "I tried," she said, holding her palms up as she backed away.

Like a mirage, Rulon's amiable demeanor dissipated. Even Yohaba shuddered and took another step back. Rulon's eyes went hard and bored into the Russian's like a pile driver. For the first time, the Russian understood. They'd told him Rulon was easy to underestimate, but even so, he'd been lulled. This Rulon had killed an entire Spetsnaz team with a hammer. Meeting him for the first time, seemingly overweight and dressed like a caricature of the Marlboro Man, it was impossible to take him seriously. But the way those other men had backed away when Rulon spoke . . . it should have registered.

Boris looked around, and the thought struck him how much this place reminded him of the bars in Khanty-Mansiysk and Tyumen. Filled with rough men and women. Heavy drinkers. Always spoiling for a fight. The women too. These were Boris's kind of people, yet they treated Rulon with deference, much like the people back home treated Boris.

Boris looked past Rulon at the unruly crowd. There was a commotion as the skinheads, moving like a pack of Siberian wolves, pushed their way to the front. *Maybe this isn't such a joke?* he thought. He looked at Yohaba and she was smiling. *What?* And then he realized he'd been had. He looked at Rulon and braced himself for the fight of his life. *Da budet tak. So be it.* Boris grabbed the heavy wooden table between them and with one hand flung it against the far wall. The crowd jumped back and let out a collective "Aaaahhhh . . ."

Rulon stood rooted like an oak, knees slightly bent, feet spaced wide, his hands hanging loose at his sides like a gunslinger waiting to draw. He unconsciously rolled his shoulders to loosen up. The Russian had been warned about that too.

Boris's expression hardened. He stared warily at Rulon while slowly dropping into a martial arts stance: one foot forward, knee bent, left fist high in front of his face, the right cocked low by his hip. He circled Rulon, like a predator, careful, looking for an opening, but staying away from the crowd. Rulon turned in place to face him, slowly—no fear, no hurry.

Boris faked a snap kick, but Rulon didn't move, didn't even flinch. The Russian then circled back the other way, took a quick step in, and threw a lazy jab. Again Rulon hardly reacted, just swayed back, not even raising his hands to block, and the punch fell short. A frustrated Boris stepped back and waved a paw at Rulon, as if to say "c'mon."

Without taking his eyes off his adversary, Rulon took off his hat and flipped it like a Frisbee to Yohaba, who was standing off to the side near the karaoke machine. She caught the hat with one hand and said to Frank, "Time to fire up the puppy." Frank hit a button and the raucous, driving sound of "Small Town" blared from the speakers.

Immediately the rapt and silent crowd came back to life, again shoving to get a better view. The semicircle closed tighter, front row straining to hold everyone back. Four cowboys sitting on the bar drinking beer began to sing along and the crowd joined in, all except the snarling skinheads.

> *Well, I was born in a small town*
> *And I live in a small town*
> *Prob'ly die in a small town*
> *Oh, those small communities*

As Boris circled to his right, Rulon focused on the center of Boris's chest, watching the whole man but mostly looking for subtle shifts in his center of gravity. Boris stepped around a chair and, once clear, moved in closer to Rulon, then backed out, then quickly moved in again, and snapped his leg up for a roundhouse kick—an unexpected move for a man so big. But in a flash, faster than Boris had ever seen a big man move, as fast as any flyweight, Rulon, with all the quickness of his hammer-thrower days, was on him, coming in strong—totally committed to his move.

Boris reacted with amazing athleticism himself, recalling the kick in midair and snapping a punch at the oncoming freight train that was Rulon. But Rulon saw it coming, dropped his head, and charged just as Boris's punch slid across the top of his scalp. Boris tried bringing his knee up for another kick, but Rulon was too close and smothered the move, still coming in like a bull.

The big Russian, off balance, awkwardly punched at Rulon with his other hand, but Rulon drove his head straight into his chest, dead center in his solar plexus, and sent the air exploding from his lungs. Like he'd been hit with a wrecking ball, Boris twisted as he went down, unable to breathe, and crashed to the floor on his stomach. He shook his head to clear it, but Rulon was on him in an instant, wrapping his huge arms around Boris's waist and locking his hands together.

Boris struggled and fought back to his feet, twisting like a cat and almost breaking free, but Rulon, grunting with the effort, held on and spun with him. Boris, knowing something bad was coming, tried desperately to catch Rulon with a flurry of elbows, but Rulon, dodging a few and catching a few, grimly hung on. The Russian then violently threw his head back, hoping to butt Rulon in the face. But Rulon anticipated the move and had his head to the side, continuing to tighten his grip. Boris next stomped down with his heavy shoes trying to break Rulon's foot, but it was an instant too late. Rulon was arching backward with all his strength, lifting Boris clear off the ground. The crowd stopped singing and held its collective breath as the music played on.

But I've seen it all in a small town
Had myself a ball in a small town

The big cowboy continued arching backward, his arms wrapped around Boris like a python. He lifted Boris up and up, the huge Russian still struggling like a madman to break free. With a mighty bellow, Rulon completed the move, throwing himself completely backward, and brought Boris over the top, head over heels, controlling the Russian all the way to the floor to smash him headfirst through a chair, where he bounced once and collapsed in a heap.

Boris rolled over on his back and lay still. Rulon had nimbly danced out of the way just as he released Boris, and he turned quick as a cat to see the effect. He was all warmed up, having taken a few shots, and was eager to mix it up some more. But Boris wasn't moving.

Rulon dropped his hands, moved closer, and nudged him cautiously with the toe of his boot. No reaction. He bent over and lifted up one of Boris's arms by the wrist. He let go, and it dropped limply to the floor. Kneeling down, he placed his hand over Boris's heart and snorted. He was alive. Then he lifted up Boris's right eyelid and checked the pupil's reaction to light.

Yohaba walked over and handed Rulon his hat just as he stood up. By then the crowd had pressed in closer but still maintained a respectful distance. Rulon kicked away the broken chair and turned Boris onto his side so his windpipe would stay clear while he recovered. Yohaba signaled to Frank to turn off the music.

When it was quiet, Rulon said in a voice loud enough for everyone to hear, "It was a fair fight. No tricks. This guy's okay in my book."

Someone from the crowd asked, "Is he dead?"

"Nah. He's just knocked out," Rulon said. "He'll be all right." He looked around at the silent, gawping crowd. Extreme violence tends to have that effect on people. "Go on now," Rulon said. "Go have some fun. See ya'll in six months, huh?"

The crowd slowly dispersed, half of them heading for the door, the other half for the bar. Gilly was again hustling like a one-armed paperhanger but still had time to catch Rulon's eye and give him a wink and a smile.

Once the crowd cleared, Rulon turned to Yohaba and started to say something but was interrupted by an arrogant, dismissive voice from behind. "We'll take it from here, cowpoke." Rulon and Yohaba turned. The four skinheads were facing them, a cruel eagerness playing across their faces. The biggest one, a brute with tattoos covering his arms and neck, nodded toward Boris to make his intentions clear and said, "You can head home now. We'll take the garbage out." His three buddies chuckled, impressed with his cleverness.

Rulon handed Yohaba back his hat and said, "I'm thinking 'Born in the U.S.A.' for this one, darlin'."

"I'll tell Frank," Yohaba replied as she quickly backed away.

CHAPTER 2

The French port city of Marseilles was settled in 600 BC by Greeks sailing from Phocaea in Asia Minor. The story goes that the Greek captain Protis sailed into the harbor on the very day that the local Ligurian chieftain's daughter was about to choose her husband the old-fashioned way. After a banquet attended by the warrior-suitors, she was to stride into the room and hand the lucky man a cup of wine. Her name was Gyptis and she was reported to be very beautiful.

Protis was invited to the ceremony, and it doesn't take too much imagination to picture him stumbling into the room, flicking his Adonis-like locks out of his Greek-god face, and the girl then trampling over the other suitors to get to him. Her dowry was the nearby piece of land now called Garde Hill. The newlyweds settled there and founded the town of Massalia, which eventually became Marseilles.

Under the early influence of the intrepid Greek sailors, the city steadily grew in significance to eventually become the primary port of call for North African goods, services, and immigrants, including, in AD 543, a shipload of small, furry ones carrying fleas infested with bubonic plague. The death toll from that first plague was relatively low, only because there weren't many people around to kill. But the second incursion in 1346 spread throughout the continent and killed twenty-five million people, a quarter of Europe's population. The third plague, in 1720, killed far fewer, though it wreaked havoc in the whole of Provence.

No wonder, then, that one of the world's foremost centers for disease control was the University of the Mediterranean on Boulevard Charles Livon in Marseilles. Generations of city fathers had had a personal interest in viruses, bacteria, and plagues, and the university's primary medical vault contained a murderer's row of each—for research purposes. They were guarded. Safe. But not as safe as, say, the US nuclear arsenal at Nellis Air Force Base in Nevada, though possibly just as deadly.

It was an honor to work at the university. Researchers from all over the world vied for the privilege. A fact not lost on the university's directors; hence, salaries were not particularly competitive. French taxes were an additional strain. If supply and demand is the first immutable law of wealth, both legal and illegal, then greed is the second, the chink in the armor of every security system.

It was greed in 1720 that unleashed the third great plague. A ship arrived at Marseilles carrying the plague and was immediately quarantined. But it also carried a cargo of silks that the local merchants dearly wanted. They put pressure on the port authorities to lift the quarantine, and within two years half the city was dead—thirty thousand in the first three months. That is why, even to this day, the streets and sidewalks of Marseilles are swept and washed daily.

"PESTE IS COMING," said Figeli quietly into the microphone velcroed to his lapel. He swept the gutter with desultory strokes, head down.

"Describe him," Helmut commanded.

Figeli paused in his sweeping and casually brushed the dust from his street cleaner's yellow uniform. He made a show of yawning and sneaked a clear look at the target. "Six foot, thin, thick black mustache. Looks about fifty. Walks bent over as if his back was hurting. Thick glasses. *Mon dieu*. His code name should be *lunettes*."

"He sits all night peering into a microscope. Worst thing you can do for your eyes and back. What is he wearing?"

"A brown beret and a gray overcoat down to his knees. As instructed. The coat is unbuttoned, and I can see his university ID badge. It's him."

"Is he holding anything?"

"A silver metal case. Looks heavy."

"Good. Any sign of a tail?"

"No."

"Keep watching," Helmut ordered. He looked at his watch— 7:14 a.m. *So he came after all. Life is full of surprises.*

The team was in place: eleven members each precisely positioned in this Marseilles neighborhood of sand-colored buildings glittering in the morning sun. The epicenter of their activity was Le David, a café with a second-story outdoor terrace overlooking the Promenade Georges Pompidou. Across the street were the La Prodo beaches, quiet and empty except for the timeless lapping of small waves and seagulls pecking in the sand. Nearby was the famous statue of David.

The café had just opened for the day. A few quiet customers, some in suits, some in overalls, were already sitting on the terrace sipping their petite, brutally strong coffees and reading *La Provence,* the daily paper.

Helmut—stocky, mid-forties, shaved head, gray closely trimmed beard, scarred knuckles, and a perfect surgically repaired nose—sat tucked in a corner of the terrace. He wore a dark gray Ermenegildo Zegna suit with a white shirt and a plain navy-blue tie. He wished to appear something he wasn't; that is, legitimate, corporate, and nonviolent.

His cell phone lay on the table next to his coffee. A cord with a dangling microphone ran to his ear, but it was only for show. When he spoke, his conversations were intended instead for a dis- creetly placed throat mike and hidden earpiece attached to a small Brickhouse Security two-way radio clipped to his belt.

The members of his team were similarly equipped, and they kept him apprised of Peste's progress. There were two women on roofs looking for tails. Six heavily armed men close to the café watched for police. Figeli the street sweeper. Two others like Figeli, one posing as a newspaper vendor, the other as a tired worker sitting on a bench. An entire cell plus Figeli and his two other companions on loan from Corsica's Brise de Mer gang. Enough to do a proper surveillance and countersurveillance commensurate with the risk of the operation.

This was Helmut's second attempt at breaching the university's security. The first one had resulted in an unexpected sabbatical at La Sante prison.

If caught a second time, the French judicial system would lock the cell door behind him and swallow the key. France no longer sent its special criminals to Devil's Island. It didn't have to. *Maison d'arret de la Sante* in Paris—or simply, La Sante—was hell enough. Helmut had just spent three years there, fighting during the day alongside his neo-Nazi brothers against the other gangs, and at night, pushing towels or whatever else he could find into the cracks of his cell to keep out the rats. La Sante was for the hard cases. Toward the end of Helmut's tour, Manuel Noriega, the ex-Panamanian dictator, moved into the same cellblock.

Helmut stood up, stretched, and let the wind strike him full in the face. Overhead, seagulls circled and squawked like nagging consciences, but Helmut was oblivious. The titanium rod in his left leg throbbed constantly and made it difficult for him to sit for long periods. The thing felt just like . . . well, like a rod in his leg. The doctors had said the pain would eventually go away. That was four years ago.

Every second was a teeth-gritting reminder of why it was there. The fat American from Zurich. The rumor was the fat man had killed a few Russians with the same hammer he'd used on Helmut. Now he was in hiding. Helmut's associates had been unsuccessful in locating the fat man while Helmut was in prison, and Helmut couldn't find him either once he was out. It was like the man had dropped off the face of the earth. When this job was over, Helmut would hunt him again. He owed him. Helmut sat back down and rubbed his leg.

Peste was three blocks away and heading farther from the restaurant. He hadn't been told his final destination, just knew to keep walking a specified route until contacted. He also knew to take three different taxis on his way from the university to the statue of David, the starting point for the walking phase of the operation. Helmut was taking no chances.

Helmut sipped his coffee and listened to the team's chatter. Figeli reported that Peste was resting on a bench. Helmut did a quick double check with the team to verify that all was clear. He drummed his fingers on the table for a few beats and then gave the word.

Figeli walked over to Peste.

CODENAMED "PESTE"—THE PLAGUE—Professor Langemier from the University of the Mediterranean's Department of Communicable Diseases sat on the worn wooden bench and massaged his hand. He was tired and his hand had cramped while carrying the heavy Ermetico bio-carrier anodized aluminum case.

What am I doing? he asked himself for the thousandth time. A seagull landed at his feet, then flew off with something in its mouth. The professor watched it rejoin the circling flock. Up until now, the professor had placated his conscience with the fiction that he was a man fighting institutionalized injustice. Paid far below his imagined worth, he was practically forced by his employer to take steps to supplement his income.

Maintaining this illusion was difficult, but the professor was up to the task. He managed this feat by focusing single-mindedly on the assurances of his anonymous benefactors that progress was too slow in the medical community and that a reclusive billionaire needed certain specimens for his own highly-accelerated research program—all for the betterment of mankind. Why this philanthropist needed both the bubonic plague virus and the giant mimivirus from the university's bio-specimen vault was not as clearly explained. The messengers, after all, were not scientists themselves and could hardly be expected to articulate the full picture.

The mimivirus was first discovered in 1992, existing, as viruses are wont to do, as a parasite attached to a living organism; in this case, to a batch of amoeba in a water tower in Bradford, England. What made the mimivirus unique was not just its size—ten times larger than most viruses—but its resistance to classification. While it is generally acknowledged that viruses are not living, the mimivirus contained genes for amino acid synthesis, a feat beyond the ability of even some bacteria.

Why bubonic plague and the virus? Professor Langemier had no idea, his normal scientific curiosity being swallowed up by the allure of money. Perhaps it was to develop a super vaccine. Perhaps the viruses were for two unrelated experiments. If he had known the true nature of the people he was dealing with, his guesses would have been more murderous but closer to the truth

The professor rested on the bench and tried to regain his

composure. *Why all this cloak and dagger business? This is juvenile.* He took off his glasses and mopped his brow with a handkerchief. The fools insisted he wear a heavy coat. It was hot and uncomfortable and made movement difficult. He sighed and was momentarily distracted by the shimmering sea. *How peaceful.* He counted thirteen small boats bobbing in the water. *Such a simple life.* As a young boy, he had fished in a different part of this sea with his grandfather, baiting hooks and helping to reel in the fish. It wasn't hard. The fish weren't very smart. It was simply a matter of finding the right bait. *Oh, if only I had a boat and could simply sail away.*

On some level he knew he was in danger. But from which direction? *What if this is a police sting?* In such situations, men of his station have committed suicide. The professor looked up and saw a street sweeper approaching. *An undercover policeman?* The professor froze.

Figeli walked up to the professor. "Excuse me, sir. I need to sweep under your feet."

The professor looked up and saw a short man of about forty, olive skinned, with a narrow face and nose, and jet-black hair. Figeli leaned forward and in a quieter, more cheerful voice said, "Bonjour, Professor. Did my little disguise fool you? I am with the director. He sends his greetings."

Langemier stood up quickly. "This is not what I expected. We should do this another day."

"Nonsense, Professor," Figeli said soothingly. "All is going perfectly well. The director has the money with him now. He is waiting for you. In a few minutes you will be a rich man. You've come this far. Just a little further. What can it hurt?"

"No, this is all wrong. I have to go now."

"Wrong? There is no wrong. This is business," Figeli said. "Just business. This is new for you, but we do this all the time for clients who wish to remain discreet. This is the way these things are done."

"I've changed my mind," the professor said. "I really need to go." He turned and walked awkwardly away, the metal case banging against his knee with every frantic step.

Figeli watched him go and spoke into his mike. "Hey, Capo.

He's not cooperating. He's walking away. What do you want me to do?"

"That's the problem with professors. They think too much," Helmut said. "Reel him back in. Offer him more money. Remind him what a greedy pig he is. Tell him we have other offers. I don't care what you say—just don't let him get in a cab. Do you understand me?"

Figeli acknowledged and went briskly after the professor.

"Hey," he said. "Hey." Figeli came up alongside the professor and matched his stride. He half twisted as he walked so he could see the professor's face. "The director is waiting for you on the terrace of Le David. You passed it a few blocks back. Did you notice it?"

The professor nodded.

Figeli continued. "What? Do you think we won't pay you? Is that it?"

"No, that's not it," mumbled the professor as he hurried along.

"What then? You don't like money anymore? Did you win the lottery? Is that it?"

Sweat dripped from the professor's face and clouded his glasses. "No, that's not it. Please, just leave me alone. If you keep following me, I'll have to call the police."

"I wouldn't do that if I were you, professor. Not with that thing you're carrying. I think they would take you away and tell me to get back to work." Figeli waited for him to smile at the joke. When he didn't, Figeli continued. "The director is wearing a dark gray suit. His head is shaved. He's got a gray beard like St. Nicholas, but shorter. You can't miss him. He is waiting alone. Do you believe in St. Nicholas? Don't quit now. You've come all this way. Think about the money. Think about your miserable employer. You are a champion of justice. They will think twice about swindling professors after this. Think how good it will feel when you quit. Picture the looks when you laugh in their faces and tell them you are buying a home in Provence."

The professor struggled with the weight of the case but kept on. An inspiration came to Figeli. He remembered the expression on the professor's face as he sat on the bench gazing at the sea.

"With the money you'll have, you can buy a boat if you want and get away from everything. Just sail off over the horizon." Figeli saw the professor's countenance change from fear to a wistful hope as the words evoked that original memory.

"I will need more money," the professor said cautiously. His gait slowed.

"Don't we all," Figeli said, laughing. "Whenever we do this, they always want more money. We've come to expect it. Don't worry. We're prepared to close the deal. It's just business. In a just world, our expenses would be tax deductible." This time the professor and Figeli laughed together. "I shouldn't be telling you this, but I'll let you in on a little secret about the director. He is a terrible negotiator. Tell him you want more money. Tell him you insist on it. He knows you are holding all the cards. And besides, it's not his money, so he doesn't care. He will give in. I promise you. This is the time to be greedy."

Figeli continued to encourage the professor until the end of the block and finally got him turned around and going in the right direction. They walked together for half a block more; then, with a final hearty slap on the back, Figeli sent him to Helmut.

The professor, slightly bent, tilting to one side to compensate for the weight of the case, kept walking—a sad character in a formless gray coat like a faceless dark figure in a Van Gogh painting.

Figeli watched him for a few seconds, then spoke into the mike. "He's on his way. I hope he makes it. Maybe I should go with him."

Helmut, who had been listening in all along, said, "A well-dressed man with a metal case walking with a street sweeper in a fluorescent yellow jacket. Yes, *very* unobtrusive. No. The team will track him. You did well, by the way." Helmut opened up his mike to the entire team. "Peste is heading to the nest. Make sure he gets here."

"*Bonjour*, PROFESSOR," HELMUT said with a warm smile, rising to shake hands as the professor walked up to the table. "At last we meet. This is a great honor. Did you have a hard time getting here? Were you working all night? You look tired. Please, don't sit just yet, I first must search you."

"What?" asked the professor, startled.

Helmut maneuvered his body so the search would be blocked from the view of nearby tables. "Just relax." He stood close to the professor, speaking calmly while his hands worked deftly. "Aren't you glad you are dealing with professionals? It's a necessary precaution in our business. You can search me too, if you want. Professionals understand these things. There. See, there is nothing to it."

"What? Why would I do that?" the professor asked, too bewildered to react.

"Please, sit down," Helmut said. The procedure took less than ten seconds. "I'd order you something, but unfortunately I must leave almost immediately."

"Yes. Let's do this quickly," the professor said, still unsettled from the frisking. He sat down with the metal case against his leg. "Did you bring the money?" He twisted in his chair as he spoke and scanned the restaurant nervously. "Do you have people here? Am I safe?" Then before Helmut could answer, he said, "I would like more money."

Helmut played along and haggled convincingly. Emboldened, the professor proposed an outrageously high figure and managed to stutter, "I insist on it." Helmut eventually capitulated, leaving the professor beaming with triumph.

Helmut said, "We will have to take a short drive together for the rest of the money. A small sacrifice that we are happy to make. It is not far. You are a rich man, professor. A very rich man. How we all envy you. How much were your taxi fares?" The professor told him and Helmut placed a hundred-euro note on a saucer and slid it across the table.

"Keep the change, my friend," he said.

"You swear this is for medical research?" Langemier asked. Despite the breeze on the terrace, he was still sweating. "Yersinia Pestis is almost 100 percent lethal. I hope your people know what they're doing."

Helmut went rigid. "What is that? Did we not make ourselves clear? We required the plague and the mimivirus. That was the agreement. We discussed nothing by any other name."

"No, no. That is the plague. It's the Latin name. I have both viruses. Do not worry. You're sure this is for medical research?"

"Of course. What else would it be for?" Helmut asked, relaxing. "We're as concerned as you are about the plight of third-world countries. We are both driven by our humanitarian goals. It is a crime how long it takes to find cures. Smallpox is wiped out, but still the plague exists among the poorest of the poor. It is not right."

"But there are less than three thousand plague cases in the world each year," said the professor. "Why the plague? Why not cure malaria? Why not—"

Helmut cut the professor off. "Wasn't that explained? Our benefactor lost a brother to the plague in Madagascar while on a mission for his church. Surely you were told." The professor was starting to annoy Helmut. *Crime is not so easy, is it, my greedy little weasel? You know, don't you? Deep down you know. Or at least you suspect.*

"Yes, yes. I just want to be reassured. And your people, they are experts, yes? They understand what they are handling?"

"Yes."

"And you know you only have five days. The viruses can only last five days in this carrier. You understand that?"

"Yes. It will be in a lab by the end of today. If we leave now."

Helmut believed that men had a dormant instinct, a sixth sense that told them when they were being hunted or watched. Whether those feelings were precipitated by auras or some metaphysical vibration, he had no idea. But he knew that nothing triggered the instinct more than being in the presence of something seeking your life. He had trained himself over the years to control his vibrations so as not to set off these instincts in others. But that skill was more art than science. The two men inadvertently locked eyes, and Helmut felt his aura expanding, like a cobra spreading its hood. Quickly, he looked away and started talking.

He said, "You should see the lab. It is magnificent. State of the art. It is a good sign that you worry so much about the health of others. You are a true humanitarian."

Beads of sweat broke out on the professor's forehead. His breathing intensified. His eyes shifted to the exit. Helmut leaned forward and grabbed his wrist. "Think of the thousands you will be saving. They will write songs about you. Syringes with the cure will be labeled with your name. You will be immortal." Helmut released his grip. The professor did not move or make eye contact. "I salute you, brave soul," Helmut said.

Helmut leaned back and studied his face. He fancied himself a good judge of people, and thought, *The hook is not yet set. This can go either way.*

Helmut absently tapped the table as he waited. He was just about to resign himself to the more messy Plan B, when the professor reached down, heaved up the bio-carrier, and set it on the table.

"Here. Let's do what we must do quickly. I'm tired of carrying this. You carry it. Let us go. Protis and Gyptis. As we agreed."

"How clever," Helmut said. "You know your Marseilles history. Which one is which?"

"Protis is the mimivirus," said the professor. "They are labeled."

Helmut dropped ten euros on the table, and he and the professor left together side by side at a brisk walk. Helmut carried the briefcase in one hand, and with the other, gently guided the professor toward the exit, then down the stairs to the street. Along the way, Helmut chatted enthusiastically about his experiences among the poor in southeast Asia and how much suffering would be eliminated by the professor's initiative.

Once on the sidewalk, they headed for a black Mercedes parked by itself half a block away. At the car, Helmut opened the back door and stepped aside. Figeli was in the driver's seat, now dressed in a brown leather jacket. He nodded and beamed at the professor.

Helmut cleared his throat. "Please get in."

"Why is the backseat covered in plastic?" asked the professor in a voice like ashes.

"It is necessary to protect the new leather," Helmut said. Figeli stifled a laugh. "Now, get in," Helmut said harshly. "I am a busy man."

CHAPTER 3

Rulon and Yohaba raced down highway 93 in Rulon's 1983 Chevrolet Scottsdale with both windows rolled down, liking the dryness and smell of the fresh high-plains air after the stuffiness of the Rockin' Rooster. It was 11:57 p.m. mountain daylight time, Wednesday, and at that exact moment, in Marseilles at 7:57 a.m. central European time, Thursday, Helmut was wiping his knife blade on Professor Langemier's trousers leg and retrieving his hundred-euro note from the professor's dead body in the backseat of the Mercedes. The plastic had done its job.

Rulon had his arm around Yohaba, holding her tight against him on the bench seat. The Norah Jones song "Broken" blared through the speakers. The two of them were recounting the events of the evening and laughing so hard that Rulon almost swerved off the road. They were about ten miles out of town with another twenty to go in the pitch black under the stars before they reached the ranch.

"Tell me the truth," Rulon said when he finally quit laughing. "You set me up again, didn't you? Tell the truth. I won't be mad." He sneaked a peek at her snuggled up tight against him.

Yohaba pulled away and sat up straight. "You're a wuss, you know that? When it comes to psychological warfare, you're a big wuss. You stink at it. You owe me, Cowboy. By the time I was done with him, he was totally discombobulated. I was the picador setting up the bull for the matador."

"Yeah, yeah, but remind me again, which one am I? The bull or the matador? I forget."

Yohaba reached over with both hands and rubbed his ears. "Why, darling, sometimes, I'm happy to say, you're a little of both. But let me look at you." She turned his face.

"Ouch," Rulon said. "Watch it. I've had a rough night, remember?"

"Sorry. Turn your head more." Rulon obeyed while straining to keep one eye on the road. Yohaba changed position and flipped on the dome light so she could see better. "Swelling's already started. Rulon Hurt, what am I going to do with you? Are you okay? Tell me the truth."

She let go of his face and felt his arms and ribs. "Does that hurt? Does that hurt?" When he winced at every squeeze, she said, "Geez, Cowboy. If I find a place that doesn't hurt, will you tell me? You're such a baby." Then she thought of something else. "Let me see your knuckles." One at a time, Rulon dutifully showed her his unmarred hands. Having run out of things to nag him about, Yohaba sat fuming with her arms crossed.

"See," he said. "I told you. Body blows. Always go for the body. Saves the hands every time." When Yohaba just huffed rather than replying, he said, "Don't be mad. There were three of 'em. I was doing the best I could."

Yohaba slammed her hand on the dashboard. "Try blocking the punches with something other than your face sometime, will ya? And stop with the jokes. All right? I'm serious. Are you okay? And, by the way, there were four of them."

"One guy was under the size limit. I couldn't legally count him." Rulon let out a big guffaw. When Yohaba didn't laugh along, he continued, "I'm fine. Lighten up, woman."

Yohaba shook her head and settled back in her seat. "I never realized you hated skinheads so much. Gosh, you slapped them around worse than you did old Boris."

"Yeah, well. You know my motto. The fight's not over till the Nazis quit groaning." He let out another big laugh and then reached over and scooped up Yohaba in his arms.

She didn't resist. Despite the jokes, Yohaba wasn't fooled. She knew Rulon always felt guilty after a fight. Less so since CERN. But he still had to deal with things. Tomorrow he'd be quiet most of the day. Probably get up early and go shoot tin cans or throw the hammer for an hour just to settle himself down.

After a few minutes, Yohaba asked seriously, "What was that killer move you used on him? I never saw you use it before."

"Did you like it?" Rulon asked, feeling chuffed that she noticed. "It's called a Karelin reverse body lift. Ironically, it was developed by a Russian, a Greco-Roman wrestler named Alexander Karelin. Now that guy was one scary dude. He'd get a guy in the right position so they knew what was coming, and sometimes they'd just go limp and let themselves be pinned. Big guys aren't used to being lifted off their feet. It scares 'em."

"But Boris almost got away from you."

"Yeah, my left hand's still not what it used to be. But he was quick for his size. I'm not making excuses."

"But that was an awesome move, Cowboy," Yohaba said, excited again and facing him. "He never had a chance. How come with a move like that you weren't a better wrestler in college?"

"Ah, baby, I'd never use that in college. I could hurt someone." Just then Rulon sensed the truck bed moving and looked in the rear view mirror. "Frankenstein's awake. You're going to have to talk to him and explain what happened."

Yohaba turned and looked. "I think you better pull over. He's on his knees. Man, I'll bet he thinks he's been kidnapped by aliens. Welcome to Idaho, my friend."

Rulon angled off the road and rolled to a stop. He turned around and slid open the cab's small rear window.

"Hey," he yelled. "Yeah, you. You okay? You wanna ride up front? C'mon. I won't bite."

They felt the truck rocking in the dark, telling them that Boris was on the move.

"Hey, genius," Yohaba said to Rulon. "Remember, he doesn't speak English." Then she yelled through the window in Russian, "Hey, no hard feelings. Ride up here with us. C'mon, Boris, or what-ever your name is." She closed the window and turned to Rulon. "I hope you know what you're doing bringing him home with us."

"Relax. It's all part of the master plan. We'll be his friend and see what happens. This could be a way out."

"Cowboy," Yohaba said, "your naïveté is exceeded only by your waistline."

The truck rocked violently, and then they heard the crunch of Boris's heavy shoes on gravel. Yohaba slid closer to Rulon to make room. Boris fumbled with the door latch for a few seconds, then tumbled into the seat next to Yohaba.

"Close the door, will you?" Yohaba said. When Boris didn't respond, she said it louder. In an obvious daze, Boris closed the door, then touched the back of his head and winced.

"What happened?" he asked in Russian, speaking slowly and carefully, as if every word was an effort.

"Do you want the short story or the long story?" Yohaba asked. "Well, actually, there's only a short story."

"Just tell me what happened."

"How much do you remember?"

"I don't remember the fight at all."

"Well, don't feel too bad, buckeroo," Yohaba said with a wink at Rulon, which Rulon didn't understand. "There wasn't much to remember. My husband threw you with a Karelin reverse body lift. It was over in fifteen seconds. I couldn't believe you fell for it. Oldest trick in the book. You almost broke free with a nifty little spin move, but he lifted you up and over, and then you smacked your head on the corner of a chair and it was lights out, amigo." The Russian looked confused and introspective. Yohaba added, "We can help you come up with a better story if it's going to get you in trouble."

"Why was I in the truck?"

"You've got nothing to be ashamed of. Honest. You didn't do as good as number two, but number two was sneaky. He had a blade in his shoe. But, hey, that spin move really impressed Rulon. Right, Cowboy?" She gave Rulon an elbow and he nodded back, not knowing what he was agreeing to. "Anyway, some of the locals felt cheated. Remember those skinheads? They tried to stomp you when you were out, and Rulon here had to settle them down."

"But why was I in the truck?"

"I'm getting to that," Yohaba said. "It was for protection. We didn't think it safe to leave you. On account of the yobs."

Rulon coughed. "Do you mind?" he said. "A little English now and again wouldn't hurt."

For the rest of the ride back to the ranch, the three of them kept up an awkward and complicated communication with Yohaba as the middleman. Boris's things were back in his motel room, and he had a flight to catch the next day, but Yohaba convinced him it was better if he stayed with them for the night.

"You can't trust skinheads," she said. "Fighting them is like playing 'whack-a-mole.' Another one always pops up. We can pick up your things in the morning. I assume you're flying out of Joslin Field," she said, referring to the small local airport.

Too muddle-headed to argue, Boris nodded and went along with the plan. Yohaba pulled his credit card wrapped in a receipt out of her shirt pocket and made him grip it. He stared down at his hand.

"I had to sign for you," Yohaba said. "Hope you don't mind. All you had to pay for was a table and chair, three drinks, a broken glass, and a Sprite. See, there's an upside to having a short fight. Yeah, I know what you're thinking: we said the Sprite was free. But it wasn't our call. The bartender wasn't happy with that little swipey thing you did."

Boris grunted and Yohaba took that as understanding.

They pulled into the driveway a little after midnight. Gus, a German Shepherd mix, and Molly, a huge white Great Pyrenees, came bounding off the porch, barking up a storm. Rulon and Yohaba quieted them down with a few ear scratches and got their tails wagging. All Boris got were two deep growls that said "stay away." He didn't need a translation.

The house was quiet and the lights were out. Rulon's father's bedroom door was closed. Rulon almost knocked but decided explanations could wait until morning.

Rulon showed Boris to his room, handed him a towel, and pointed him in the direction of the shower. While both men were cleaning up, Yohaba retreated to the kitchen.

Fifteen minutes later, they were all around the kitchen table with the mini-feast Yohaba had prepared: a stack of roast beef sandwiches on a platter in the center of the table, half a chocolate cake, an overflowing salad bowl, and two liters of Sprite.

Rulon said a blessing while Boris sat there with his eyes open, not knowing what to do. Yohaba opened her eyes to peek at Boris and their eyes met. She gave a little smile, as if to say, "That's okay. It's just our way."

When Rulon finished, he dived into the food. Boris hung back. Yohaba urged him to eat but Rulon, his mouth full, cut her off. "Let him be. He's probably nauseous after being knocked out." Eventually, Boris had a bite of everything, chewing slow and easy like he had a toothache.

When he'd had enough, Boris carried everyone's plate, glass, and silverware to the sink and started to wash them until Yohaba came up behind, gently pulled him away, and told him to sit down. Next, out came the medical supplies. Yohaba made both men stay at the kitchen table while she tended first to Rulon's bruises and small cuts and then, armed with a damp cloth, antibiotic ointment, and an ice pack, went to work on the back of Boris's head.

When done, she stepped back and surveyed her work. "What a pair," she said.

When Boris looked at her quizzically, she translated, and got him to smile. The first one.

Boris asked, "What happened to your husband's face? Was it the skinheads?" He used a Russian vulgarity when he said "skinheads" and Yolanda had to straighten him out about the swearing. He mumbled an apology.

"Yeah, it was the skinheads," she answered.

"What happened?"

"Just yobs being yobs."

"But what happened?"

"Just Rulon being Rulon," she said. When Boris looked puzzled, she smiled and said, "Same as you eventually."

Boris was woozy, and Rulon was dealing with his usual post-combat blues. Except for Yohaba, no one felt like talking. A little after one, the conversation died off, and Boris went off to his room.

Rulon stayed behind to help Yohaba with the kitchen, but when he broke a dish and she saw his hands trembling, she told him to take the night off.

He went outside and stood on the porch. The night was cool and smelled of musty barn and animals. A few small clouds drifted past the full moon, breaking up the shadows in the yard. Rulon walked over to the barn and checked the door, then went over to the corral gates. Next he saw to the horses and milk cows. Everything was right in his little world except him.

This always happens, he said to himself. He'd get pushed into a corner where there was only one thing he could do, and then he'd do it and feel worried and guilty afterward. He wandered back to the porch and sat on the top step, looking out over the yard. He mentally kicked himself. Yohaba came out and sat down next to him as close as she could.

"I wish I was as smart as you," he said after a minute.

"We fill gaps," Yohaba said. "I can calculate the trajectory of colliding meteors, and you can lift heavy things." She waited for Rulon to say something sarcastic or at least bite on the obvious *Rocky* reference. When he didn't, she knew he was worried. "When we're together," she said, "it's both of us working on the same problem."

Rulon gave a small smile. "I know, baby." He got up and helped Yohaba to her feet.

That night in bed, with the lights out and the house quiet, Yohaba asked Rulon if he wasn't just a little afraid Boris was going to kill them all in their sleep.

"No," Rulon said. "When I said that he reminded me of me, I wasn't kidding. I've got a good sense for people. He's got a code."

"So what? He's got a code. Maybe his code is to sneak up on people in the dark and hack them to death with an ax." Yohaba was lying on her side as she talked, absently playing with Rulon's ear.

"Nope. If we ever fight again, it'll be straight up. It's the people without a code you gotta watch. They're unpredictable. Even they don't know what they're going to do. Now me, I have a code. I'm predictable. Guess what my code's telling me to do right now?"

"Don't tell me," Yohaba said with a dramatized groan. "It's that post-combat Viking thing you're always warning me about."

"War is heck, darling," Rulon said as he grabbed her around the waist and pulled her closer.

Later, when Rulon was asleep, Yohaba slipped out of bed, went over to the bedroom desk, and took her laptop out of hibernation. She checked her email. There was one from her grandfather, a director at CERN, the huge European Nuclear Research complex near Geneva, Switzerland.

Dear Yohaba,

I hope you and Rulon are well. I'm sure your great-great-grandfather is chuckling to himself right now at having proved me wrong again. Yes, another asteroid is bearing down on 182 Elsa. And, yes (please don't gloat) his projected date looks correct, as well—June 4th. I suspect you are not surprised. This only gives us two days. My numbers in the attached file say there won't be an actual collision, but only a close pass. I need you to double-check. It's so good of you to assist. I would like to keep my staff working on their current projects for as long as possible.
Love,
Leonard

Yohaba opened the file and went to work. She patched into her grandfather's computer network and accessed the cluster of HP computers sitting underground at CERN's Meyrin site. Two hours later, she completed her calculations and sent back her report. Her grandfather's calculations looked correct.

WHEN YOHABA OPENED up Leonard's attachment in Idaho, it was 10:30 a.m. in France on Thursday morning, and Helmut and Figeli were driving toward the Mediterranean port of Toulon with the professor's body rolled in plastic in the trunk.

Helmut always started every mission with five throwaway cell phones. Special numbers known only to a special few. Use once. Throw away. Layers of security. While Figeli drove, Helmut fished cell phone number one out of his jacket pocket and placed a call.

"It's me," he said when the other side picked up. "It's a sunny day and we're heading for the beach. We packed a picnic basket."

"Well done. Stay in touch."

Helmut ended the call and removed the battery and SIM card from the phone. He bent the SIM card in half and threw it out the window. The cell phone and battery he threw in the backseat.

Figeli watched him out of the corner of his eye. When Helmut was finished, he asked, "You think someone is out there listening to everything you say?"

"Yes," Helmut answered.

CHAPTER 4

IDAHO, THURSDAY MORNING, 8:00 A.M.

Yohaba awoke late. It was already light. She rolled over and lay on her back for a few moments, collecting herself. The window was open, and a gentle, early morning breeze rustled the curtains. The men were outside talking, but she couldn't make out the words. She could hear Rulon getting frustrated and Boris saying something in Russian, when suddenly the morning calm was broken by a man's gut-wrenching scream. In a flash she was up, rushing to the window and grabbing Rulon's Colt automatic off the nightstand.

As she moved the curtains out of the way, she heard Rulon's father order, "Extend your arms more."

Rulon, his father, and Boris were fifty feet away by the corral.

I don't believe this, she thought. There was Rulon doing a couple of slow turns without a hammer on the hammer throw circle he'd built between the corral and the barn.

"You're not fully extending your arms," said Rulon's dad.

Rulon finished his turns and then began to coach Boris through it. Now he was on his knees in the cement ring, pushing the dogs away with one hand while trying to move Boris's feet into the right position with the other. Rulon's father—lean, deeply tanned, and tough as woodpecker lips—stood against the fence with one foot on the lower rail.

Next to him, draped over the top fence rail, were three Polanik

36

sixteen-pound hammers, their stainless steel balls glinting in the early morning sun. Rulon owned four. Yohaba correctly deduced that the earlier scream was him heaving one of them out into the west pasture.

She turned from the window, ejected the magazine from the Colt, and then ejected the bullet left in the chamber, catching it deftly in her right hand as it flew out of the breech. She then replaced the bullet in the magazine and slammed the magazine back in the well. On her way to the shower, she put the pistol on safe and returned it to the nightstand.

After the Serb had busted up Rulon's hand during the clash at CERN, it had been a long, painful rehabilitation to get the hand healed and working properly. As a way of gauging his progress, Rulon had taken up hammer throwing again and built himself a regulation seven-foot ring next to the barn. When he was stressed out, it was a toss-up whether he'd be out there plunking tin cans with the Colt or throwing the hammer. Both did the trick. Rulon swore his hand never would have healed up as well as it did if it weren't for the hammer. The doctors thought he was nuts.

After her shower, Yohaba made breakfast. She worked away, cracking eggs and mixing waffle batter, sounds of the local rock station intermixing with the occasional whir of a blender or a war cry from one of the boys. In between checking on how things were cooking, she stood out on the porch and watched.

Boris was dressed same as the previous night, except without the leather jacket. The old man, with two hours of work already under his belt, wore his usual bib overalls and beat-up brown Stetson. Rulon wore jeans and a denim vest over a blue Levi's shirt. His black hat perched on one of the corral fence posts. He looked like the cowboy he was, except for the pair of old Nike Zoom Rotational IV hammer shoes on his feet and the throwing glove on his left hand, as befitted a right-handed thrower.

One time, Boris accidentally released the hammer at the wrong point in the spin and it skidded up the barn roof, tearing off a few shingles before launching off into the north paddock. It sent the three grazing milk cows scattering, barely missing one of them. Rulon's father was grumpy about it, but Rulon couldn't stop laughing and almost did the same thing himself on his next throw.

Ten minutes later, breakfast was ready. Just for fun, even though she was only thirty feet away, Yohaba clanged the antique chuck wagon bell hanging on the porch.

Rulon looked at her with a big grin. "Watch this."

He motioned Boris away and, while Rulon's father held the dogs, swung the hammer using only his arms, making slow, easy turns until the weight settled. Then he rode the momentum with his entire body, spinning like a top, his footwork intricate and unbelievably fast. One, two, three turns, then to Yohaba's surprise, a fourth turn that took him a foot out of the ring. A precisely timed release, and then a mighty roar.

He stood there, arms outstretched, holding his form like a golfer after a swing, following the ball with the trailing wire and handle jerking behind—way, way out there, past the stand of spruces and clear over the west paddock. All three men stood unblinking, following the arc, seeing it land and stick in the soft earth, and hearing the thud of the landing. The moment held for a few beats. Boris whistled and Rulon smiled.

Then the elder Mr. Hurt said, "You died a little on the fourth turn. You need to keep pushing all the way through," and walked away into the barn with the dogs trailing behind.

By the time breakfast was over, Boris was over his fuddle-headedness from the previous night and felt like talking. Out on the porch, Rulon asked him about the Russian SVR, the spy agency he worked for. Boris told him about their training and admission standards. Sounded a lot like what Rulon had gone through with OCD. Rulon also wanted to know about the thin man.

"What is there to say?" said Boris through Yohaba. "I'm sure you have people exactly like him. He is old. Fought in Stalingrad when he was twelve. Makes fools suffer. Even Putin fears him. Probably has a file on Putin to protect against . . . accidents. I will tell you something. I met him. He is a scary old man. Much blood on his hands. They took me to see him before I came here. He told me personally what you did in CERN. It made no sense that they let you live. He told me that teams were already assembling to go after you when he gave the order to stand down. He said he decided you were too useful to be killed. He said you were to be his mountain man, his Jeremiah Johnson. Do you understand the reference?"

"Nope," Rulon said after Yohaba translated. "Unless he meant that I look like Robert Redford," referring to the 1972 movie. "What do you think, honey? Could that be it?"

Yohaba looked away angrily and wouldn't answer.

"I think that means no," Rulon said, embarrassed by her reaction but knowing they'd be discussing this later. "I didn't think so either. Hey, ask our friend here what the thin man told him about CERN. I'm really curious."

The story was that Rulon had kidnapped Yohaba from the Russians who were trying to protect her, and when a highly decorated Spetsnaz team went to her rescue, Rulon ambushed them.

"Why did I marry him then?" Yohaba asked.

"Stockholm syndrome," Boris answered seriously.

"Give me a break!" Yohaba said in Russian without pausing to translate for Rulon. "You're supposed to be some kind of secret agent man. Didn't they teach you to think?"

"Parts of it did not make sense," Boris said in his gravelly voice, "but that does not make us bad guys."

"I got news for you: you *are* bad guys," Yohaba said. "They strapped Rulon's hand down and smashed it with a hammer. I'll show you."

With that, Yohaba jumped up and ran into the house. Rulon and Boris waited in their rocking chairs. A minute later, she was back with Rulon's SaeboFlex dynamic hand splint. She walked up to Boris and held it in front of his face, letting it dangle by a strap, then dropping it onto his lap.

"Rulon had to have four operations and wear this for eight months after CERN. Had to fight your first guy with it still on his hand." She switched to English and said to Rulon, "Show him the scars, Cowboy. Go on."

Rulon shook his head and waved her off, but she made him show Boris his hand; in particular, the long ugly scar running from the base of the fingers, along the back of the hand, and six inches past the wrist.

Yohaba told Boris how they met and was about to launch into the story of Einstein's trunk when suddenly Rulon got up to stand next to one of the porch pillars. He looked out over the hills to the east, his mouth a grim line and his eyes focused somewhere past the horizon. Watching him, Yohaba's expression slowly softened into tender empathy, and she drifted into silence.

"G-14b," Rulon said to no one. Then he turned around and faced Boris. "It happened in room G-14b eighty meters underground in CERN. They were hunting us because Yohaba is Einstein's great-great-granddaughter, and they thought she could help them crack a riddle."

Rulon told him, through Yohaba, what really happened, taking Boris through the fights with the Russians in the Zurich luggage store and the Desperado restaurant. He took him through the deadly car chase on Regensdorferstrasse after the Serbs had kidnapped Yohaba and then what happened with the one Serbian and the Spetsnaz team at CERN. He told him a little about Leonard Steenberg, Yohaba's grandfather, and Einstein's trunk but left out any mention of Einstein's doomsday prediction that two asteroids were going to collide in deep space and send one of them hurtling toward earth. At one point, Yohaba started crying, but Rulon made her finish the translation.

When Rulon was done, he looked Boris in the eye and nodded as if to say, "There it is. Believe what you want." Then he looked away, embarrassed at talking so much, and absently scraped some mud off his boot on one of the porch steps.

"Too much talking. Let's go," he said when he was done. "Or Boris here is gonna miss his plane."

On the way to the airport, they stopped at Boris's motel room so he could pick up the rest of his things. Rulon and Yohaba waited in the truck while Boris packed and settled the bill.

"You're their Jeremiah Johnson," Yohaba said once they were alone.

"Yeah," said Rulon. "I heard it."

"You understood the reference then, didn't you?" Yohaba said angrily.

"Yeah."

"Dang, Rulon, I don't like this one bit. Using you as some kind of mythic training dummy for their men. So what are they going to do? Keep sending someone here every six months until you're seventy years old?"

"No. If I keep winning, they'll get tired of it and change the rules. They probably didn't think it would go this long. Let's drop it."

"Why don't you let the next one win?" Yohaba asked.

"I said drop it."

Yohaba sat there slowly twirling a strand of red hair around her finger. After a minute, she said, "I think you're right. He's not a bad guy. And he's not dumb. Maybe you can't tell because I'm translating, but he's actually pretty smart. He's got a good vocabulary. Think we should ask him to put in a good word for us?"

"No," Rulon said, speaking firmly at first and then with a rising sense of frustration. "If he comes up with it on his own, fine, but I can't ask. It's not just pride. I can't show weakness with these people. If I stop being their Jeremiah Johnson, then maybe I'm no more use to them. I'm telling you, this is as good as it gets. If the thin man dies, his replacement could order me dead the next day. I've gone over this from every angle. I don't know these people. I don't know their real motivations. I don't know whether if I refused to fight, they'd just forget the whole thing. I don't know if this is the only thing keeping me alive. Or even if it's just me they want. I've thought about that. Maybe you're a target too. I honestly don't have any answers right now."

Rulon's grabbed the steering wheel with both hands and shook it violently. He rested his head against it and said softly, "I'm not sure what to do, but I'll think of something."

Yohaba threw her arms around him and stroked his head. "Oh, my love. I know. I know. What a tangled mess. What have I gotten you into? I am so sorry, so very sorry. Please, this time, can we go to the authorities?"

"I'm not sorry," Rulon said, sitting up. "Not one bit." He reached around her and pulled her close. "And no, I've told you. Unless we want to run for the rest of our lives and give up everything we have and make every family member a target for them to draw us out, no. I have to take care of this myself."

They kicked around their options for a few more minutes. When Boris came out, they were just pulling apart from a kiss.

Boris had changed into a dark blue suit and was looking, if you could get past his size and imposing demeanor, like any other smartly dressed European traveler. He threw the suitcase into the back and jumped into the cab next to Yohaba.

"Looking sharp," Yohaba said. "Almost didn't recognize you."

They drove twenty minutes to the airport in silence.

When Boris stepped out, Rulon and Yohaba both got out of the truck to say good-bye. They were in a drop-off zone, so they couldn't hang around. No hugs, no teary farewells. Handshakes all around, then they were back in the truck, with a last friendly wave. Rulon started to let out the clutch when Yohaba suddenly yelled, "Stop!"

Boris, fifteen feet away and just about to step through the terminal door, turned around.

While half-leaning out the window, Yohaba said, "So here's something else for you to think about on your way back to Siberia. There's a guy on your side named Dmitri something. About forty-five. He was in Zurich a couple of years ago. Spent time in a hospital there, thanks to Rulon. Has a wife and an eighteen-year-old daughter. If you don't believe us, ask him the story about Einstein's trunk. Then ask yourself who the heck you're working for when you come after Rulon. Figure that one out, and I'll buy you an ice cream cone next time you're in Twin Falls."

Boris looked puzzled, but he waved once more—a friendly wave.

Yohaba waved back and, as Rulon was driving off, leaned further out the window and yelled, "See ya . . . and watch out for those reverse body lifts."

CHAPTER 5

THE RANCH, THURSDAY, 2:00 P.M.

Later that afternoon, Rulon was on the roof of the barn, fixing the shingles torn off by Boris's mistimed hammer throw. It was an unseasonably hot day for this early in June, and he sat there when he was done, thirty feet off the ground and halfway up the roof slope, sweating with his tool belt on and a hammer in his hand. A breeze came up from the north, and the weather vane squeaked as it shifted direction.

So much work to do, thought Rulon. *Frittered away the whole morning with Boris.*

Yohaba had received another email from her grandfather and was inside, curled up on her bed, working on another one of his assignments. She looked up from her laptop, rubbed her eyes, and decided to take a break and change the sheets in Boris's room.

Up on the roof, Rulon could hear the tractor going. The weather was changing—one of those late spring storms. He wished he had the oil can. The squeak from the vane was annoying. Just then Yohaba came out of the house holding something in her hand. "Guess what I found, Cowboy?" she yelled up at Rulon.

"What?" he yelled back.

"Frankenstein left his passport. Can you believe it?" She waved the little booklet in the air. "Think he has two of them?"

"No."

"Guess what? His name really is Boris. Boris Zorg. I thought he was putting us on."

"It's probably not his real name. Hold on." Rulon threw the broken shingles to the ground, then scuttled feetfirst with his tools to the edge of the roof and climbed down the ladder.

"Let me see," Rulon said once he was down. Yohaba handed him the passport.

While he was reading, Yohaba said, "Check it out. He's six-five and weighs 357 pounds. I didn't think he weighed that much. Man, how did you lift him?"

"Muscle is denser than fat," Rulon said, only half listening. "Makes him look smaller than he is." He looked up. "He's not getting on an airplane without this." Rulon looked in the direction of town and could see a plume of dust about five miles away coming up the dirt road to the house. "I'll bet that's him. The idiot missed his plane." He slapped the passport against his leg. "Dang it!"

Rulon slipped the passport into his vest pocket. While he and Yohaba waited for Boris, Rulon's father, with the two dogs trotting behind him, came rumbling around the corner in the tractor. He parked in front of the barn door and turned off the engine. The dogs followed him into the barn.

Standing in the barnyard, Yohaba said, "I need to do some shopping. Want to come?"

Rulon started to say something but felt, and then immediately heard, the bullet whizzing past his head. Before the crack of the rifle reached his ears, he was already moving.

He roared, "Incoming!" and ran with Yohaba to the house just as another bullet from a different-sounding rifle hit the dirt twenty feet away. The thought came, *Two shooters*. They leaped up the porch stairs hand in hand. Rulon pushed her through the front door and yelled, "Get in the basement!"

In quick succession came three bullets: one hit the house, another clanged off the tractor, and the third punctured the pickup's driver-side front tire. On his stomach, Rulon pulled the Colt from his small-of-back holster and peered through the slots in the porch railing, trying to spot the gunmen. Nothing moved on the hills in front of him. He couldn't see a target, and they were out of range even if he did.

When he and Yohaba first came back to the ranch almost two and a half years earlier, the first thing he did, just as a precaution against the Russians, was to scout out the area around the house to identify likely places of concealment. He even moved some dead wood around and did some spade work to make a few of the places especially inviting. From the direction of the bullets, he knew which hill the shooters were on and had a good guess where they might be hunkered down. He fired off three quick shots at the likely spot, three hundred yards away. An impossible shot with a pistol, but some people just don't like being shot at even if the odds of being hit were low. No reaction.

Yohaba yelled at him from the house. He yelled back for her to stay down and get in the basement.

He picked the next most likely spot a little further up the hill and fired two more shots. Four poorly aimed shots came back in return. Rulon had his answer; all he needed now was a rifle. The car on the road was three miles away, the driver oblivious. If Boris, or whoever it was, drove into the yard, he'd be right in the middle of things.

A rifle blast sounded from the direction of the barn. Rulon looked over, and there was his dad behind the tractor with his rifle pointing over the top of the engine. The old man fired again. Three hundred and fifty yards away, two men got up and ran over the hill out of sight.

Rulon fired off two shots of his own, then jumped off the porch and ran to his father behind the tractor.

"Dad, way to go!" he said, huffing when he got there. He crouched down next to his father and peered over the top of the tractor. "That got 'em running."

"Shhh . . ." Rulon's father said.

Rulon watched as his dad rolled his chin in one of his quirky mannerisms, then settled down behind the sight of his rifle. He slightly altered the angle.

"If I figured right, they should be showing up about now. Must have snuck up using the old mill road." He waited. "There," he said.

He pulled the trigger, and the Winchester 30-30 lever action bucked and cracked. Rulon's father stood up straight and pumped five more rounds in the same direction. "Hit something, I reckon," he snorted.

"Wow, Dad. If you did, that was mighty fine shooting." Five hundred yards away there was a cleft between two hills. It was the only place where the mill road was visible. There was some dust. Maybe from a vehicle. *Dang, the old man has good eyes.* Rulon could hear the faraway sound of a revving truck engine.

"What d'ya do to stir up the skinheads?" asked his father while squinting toward the hills.

"How'd ya know it was skinheads?

"'Cause I got eyes, that's how." Rulon's dad walked around the tractor to check where the bullet hit. "We got lucky. Tractor's okay. So, what'd ya do?"

"Had to slap a few of them around last night."

"Sore losers. Where at?"

"Around town."

"Where at?"

"The Rooster."

"What the heck were ya doing there?" Rulon's father asked angrily.

"Karaoke Wednesday, Dad. Yohaba and I like to sing there sometimes."

"Singing in a bar? No wonder they were trying to shoot ya."

"Dad, we have to call the cops."

"Check on the girl," Rulon's father said. Rulon called for Yohaba, and she came cautiously out of the house with two rifles, a rifle case, and her shirt bulging with magazines.

When he saw she was okay, Rulon's father growled at his son, "Take care of this," and walked back into the barn.

Yohaba jumped off the porch and bobbed and weaved across the yard in a half crouch as if evading enemy fire. She got down behind the tractor's big tire breathing heavily. "Are they gone? Is everyone all right? Dang, Rulon, anything else you wanna tell me about Idaho?"

"You can stand up," Rulon said, ignoring her Idaho jibe. "They're gone." Rulon noted where the bullets had hit. "Actually, they weren't trying to hit us. Just scare us." He laid his automatic on the hood, took the rifles and case from her, and stacked them against the trac-tor. She'd brought the Colt AR-15, the SIG SR 553 Commando carbine, and the case with the Remington model 700 VTR and Leupold scope.

That's my girl, thought Rulon.

"How do you know that? Maybe they were just bad shots," she said, talking fast as she handed him the extra magazines from her pockets and shirt. "I hope you're planning to call the police. This is clearly a police matter. I'll bet it was the yobs."

"Yeah, skinheads. Dad saw 'em. No point calling the police, though. What would we say? My seventy-five-year-old dad recog-nized them while they were three hundred and fifty yards away run-ning like jackrabbits?"

"Does sound a bit lame," Yohaba admitted.

"Dad wants me to take care of this. They were just trying to scare us. They hit the tire. That was a pretty good shot."

"Just another day in paradise then, is that it, Rulon? The wind could've kicked up. They could've sneezed while pulling the trigger. With a gun, all it takes is one mistake. Call the police. We could've been killed. Why are we even talking about this?"

"Don't worry about it. I'll take care of it. I knew this was going to happen. It always turns out the same."

"Violence begets violence," Yohaba said, flicking her head to get her hair out of her face. "Hey, we know that, don't we?"

"Yep. Every time. What did that last guy say to me?"

"What are you talking about?"

"The fight. You know. What did that one guy say?"

"You mean the last guy? Last night? I think it was 'Get away from me, you monster.'"

"No. Before that."

"'Don't leave me, guys!'"

"No. After that."

"Rulon, I don't know what he said. It was crazy in there. Why don't you get it out of second gear and just tell me? What did he say?"

"He said, 'There's people after you.'"

"You mean after me?" Yohaba asked. She stood up and brushed herself off.

"No," Rulon said, frustrated. "He meant me."

"That doesn't make sense. The Russians already know where you live."

"Yeah. I think he meant someone else is looking for me. I'd been thinking about it. I had a run-in with some Nazis in a bar in Marseilles a few years back. Did I ever tell you that story? It was when I first hooked up with Freya."

"No, I think you forgot to tell me. Oh, this ought to be a good one."

Just as Rulon was about to launch into the story, the car they'd seen coming down the road pulled into the yard. "I'll tell ya later," Rulon said.

It was Boris. Still wearing his suit. Big smile. Then his expression changed when he saw the rifles resting against the tractor and the looks on everyone's faces.

Looking uncertain, Boris got out of the brown Ford SUV. As he walked toward them, he said in Russian, "I forgot the passport. I tried to call but you have an unlisted number." Then he noticed the truck's flat tire. He did a quick calculation and looked past Rulon and Yohaba toward the hills.

"Well, Boris," Yohaba said in Russian, "good thing you were in that car or you'd be a prime suspect right now."

Those remarks stopped Boris in his tracks, or maybe it was Rulon lifting his automatic off the tractor hood. When Rulon continued in the same motion to replace the empty magazine and reach behind his back to reholster the Colt, Boris continued his advance. When he got within five feet, he stopped, and Rulon tossed him his passport.

Boris caught it cleanly. "What happened?"

Before answering, Yohaba turned to Rulon. "He wants to know what happened. What do you want me to say? Do I blow him off?"

Rulon looked at the flat tire and rubbed his chin with his massive hand. He looked at Boris's SUV. Then his watch. "Tell him we're having a little local trouble. Ask him if I can borrow his rig for a few hours."

Yohaba translated. Boris said no.

"Ah . . . that's a negative, Cowboy," Yohaba said. "He says you're not listed as a driver. He wants to know what's going on."

It wouldn't take long to change the tire on the truck, thought Rulon. *That is, if I had a spare.*

"I've got a flat tire, and I ain't got no spare," Rulon said.

"Bonnie and Clyde. Dub Taylor. Oh, circa 1967, if I'm not mistaken," Yohaba said.

Rulon gave her a sidelong glance, annoyed that she'd gotten that one right. He continued. "I can't believe I'm doing this." He took off his hat and ran his hand over his brown, buzz-cut hair. "Ask him if it's too late to catch his plane."

Yohaba asked and the answer came back affirmative.

Rulon asked, "Has he booked another return flight?" Yohaba checked, and the answer was no. "Okay," Rulon said. "Now ask him if he wants to go for a drive."

CHAPTER 6

Even thirty miles per hour on the rutted dirt roads through the sage-covered hills was hard on a car . . . and the passengers. Boris was doing fifty. Despite being seat-belted, Rulon's head hit the roof again.

Boris had the seat back as far as possible but was still cramped. He hunched over the steering wheel, roaring with laughter every time they went airborne. Rulon braced himself as best he could. He had the AR-15 between his legs and his now-crushed cowboy hat resting on his lap. The SIG Commando and the Remington varmint rifle in its case were in the luggage space in back. Yohaba sat in the rear seat, wincing every time they landed.

"Howzit going back there, babe?" Rulon asked between bounces.

"It's not the take-offs," Yohaba said, "it's the—" The car hit another bump and she paused momentarily as it hung in midair then bounded several times before settling. "—it's the reentries, darling. I'll be all right."

Originally, Rulon wouldn't let Yohaba come because of the danger, but after rushing off with Boris and leaving her fuming in the yard, he had a change of heart less than a mile down the road. Using hand signals and talking extra loud, he tried explaining to Boris in English that he wanted to track down the Nazis and talk some sense into them. When Boris nodded seriously and drew a finger across his throat in reply, Rulon decided to go back for Yohaba.

When they pulled into the yard, she was sitting on the porch in her rocking chair with the AR-15 across her lap. "If you want to come, give me the rifle and get in," yelled Rulon. In a flash she was in the backseat.

Rulon had a pretty good guess where the Nazis were headed. There was an Aryan Nation Covenant of the Chosen compound out near Carey, about eighty miles away. He knew a route through the hills that offered the chance of intercepting them before they reached the main highway. That would be the cleanest option. Take out one of their tires and then talk. But they'd have to hurry. He looked at his watch. Might have lost his chance when he went back for Yohaba.

Rulon said, "Tell him what happened back at the ranch. Tell him I'm just going to talk to the skinheads and work this out. He's to stay out of it."

Yohaba told Boris, and he replied in Russian, "I can make it look like an accident."

Yohaba's eyes widened as she translated.

Rulon said casually, "Darlin', ask him what he meant, will ya?"

When she had her answer, she turned to Rulon. "He was serious. Now he wants to know if we have some plastic and a chain saw. He said getting rid of the bodies should be easy in this country, but their vehicle will be more difficult. Hey, Cowboy, I'm starting to like this guy."

"Darlin', listen. Do not joke with him about this. Do not joke with this man ever. You have no idea how he will take it. We lost three hundred thousand fighting the Nazis in World War II. The Russians lost twenty-seven million. You have no idea what he thinks of Germans and Nazis. Tell him as clearly as you can that we are a peaceful people and that this is not the way we handle things in this country."

"I thought you said you trusted him," Yohaba said.

"I do," Rulon said. "Don't ask me why, but I do. I think he and I are kindred spirits in a way. But I still think he's incredibly dangerous."

"I don't feel those vibes from him," Yohaba said. "He doesn't have the same look as that Spetsnaz team. Those guys were devils.

Did I ever tell you that I could smell something that day? It was strange. It was as if I could smell their rotten souls. Isn't that weird?"

"Not really. Don't talk about it."

"But you think Boris is dangerous?"

"Yeah, but not to us. Now, go on, tell him how peaceful we are."

Yohaba translated. Boris laughed and said something in Russian. She said, "He asked, 'Are you making his leg long?' What's that mean, Cowboy?"

"He's asking if I'm pulling his leg."

"Oh, right. He wants to know how many guns we own. Hey, that's a good question. How many guns do we own?"

"Well, it depends what you're including. Ask him if he's including handguns. No, forget that. If I include all the handguns, he'll think we're gun nuts. Tell him that if we're talking only about military-grade assault rifles, then it's just four. If you count the sniper rifles, you have to add three more. Tell him I don't count hunting rifles, shotguns, or handguns. So, really, it's only seven. Of course, if you include Dad's guns, then the number is much higher. Ask him what his point is."

Yohaba translated, and Boris roared with laughter again and repeatedly hit the steering wheel with the flat of his hand. When he was done, he said something, and Yohaba translated.

"He says that he admires your support of the second amendment. Hey, Cowboy, I told you this guy wasn't stupid."

Ten minutes later they were parked on a sandy, boulder- and bush-covered hill. The interstate was a ribbon of dark asphalt three miles to the east. Boris and Yohaba were sitting on a rock, talking, while Rulon was over by the SUV, his elbows on the hood to steady his binoculars. He scanned the dirt road below as it snaked up the valley. No skinheads.

After a few minutes, Rulon walked over and said, "Must have missed them. No problem. We'll do plan B." The day had turned warm. Boris had taken off his tie and suit jacket and rolled up the sleeves of his white shirt.

He has forearms like Popeye. No, like Bluto, thought Rulon. Black hairy forearms with tattoos. And then the thought came, *Maybe he left the passport on purpose. He doesn't want to go back a loser.* Rulon pondered that for a few beats. *It'll be a straight-up fight when it comes, but he's not done with me yet.*

"What's plan B, Cowboy?" Yohaba asked.

"We're heading for the compound. I want this done and dusted today. Tell Bluto that this is not his fight, that I'm going to settle this without violence. Tell him if he watches closely, he may learn something about handling interpersonal conflicts. Tell him from now on his name is Bluto."

"Rulon!" Yohaba said. "That's insulting. I'm not calling him Bluto."

"Okay, but tell him what I told ya, please."

When she finished translating, she said. "Look, Cowboy, I don't know how to say this, but every time you try talking your way out of a fight, it's like waving a red flag in front of a bull. You just irritate people."

"You have nothing to base that on but the past," Rulon said. "Let's saddle up,"

An hour later they were on the crest of another sandy, wind-swept, rock- and brush-covered hill looking down on the Covenant of the Chosen compound four hundred yards away. Rulon lay on his stomach peering through the binoculars. Yohaba and Boris were stretched out prone on either side of him. The sun was on its downward arc but getting hotter. The car was out of sight over the crest. To their left, a branch cracked and a jackrabbit did a broken field run across their line of sight.

"How's it looking?" Yohaba asked.

"Bingo," Rulon said. He lifted his eyes from the binoculars. "There's a truck down there with a cracked windshield. Wanna bet from one of Dad's bullets? I'm gonna check it out. Dang, my old man can shoot."

"Rulon, listen to me," Yohaba said, turning on her side so she could face him. "I'm having second thoughts about this. First you beat them up, then they're shooting at us, and next we're here. This is what's called throwing gasoline on a fire. This is the classic escalation pattern. We keep this up, people are going to be shooting each other by the time this is over. Mark my words. What are we doing? You don't know these guys. They probably became Nazis in prison.

Probably all their buddies are still there. Going back to prison would be like returning to Valhalla. Don't get in fights with people who have nothing to lose. Why are we doing this? Just call the police. Let them do their jobs. Our tax dollars at work. C'mon, I'm making sense here."

"This isn't going to get out of control. And I can't just call the police. If I bring in the police, they'll just be sneakier about it next time. Probably poison the cattle or shoot the dogs. It's better to just talk to them. Let everyone see the humanity in each other's eyes. We have to live together, whether we like it or not. We just have to establish a mutual respect."

"Cowboy, you beat the living daylights out of four of them last night. How much more mutual respect are we talking about?"

"More."

"I knew that was it," Yohaba said. "This is nothing more than stubborn male pride. Think for a second, will you? Those are Nazis down there. World War II really did happen, and *they* think the Nazis were the good guys. You can't reason with them. Their paradigm is so screwed up, they can't see straight anymore. Let them win this round. Who cares?"

Rulon looked like he was seriously considering her words. "Maybe you're right. I'll think about it, but as long as I'm here, I should at least go down there and talk to them."

He didn't tell her, but he had a knot in his stomach. There was too much firepower, too much anger, and, she was right, too much pride on all sides. He felt like he was being sucked into something, and he didn't have an exit strategy. He couldn't even picture what a win would look like. He just knew he had to confront them.

The three of them reverse-crawled down the far side of the hill a few feet. When out of view, they stood up and brushed off their clothes. Boris's blue suit pants and white shirt were soaked in sweat and nicked from dust and grit, but he didn't seem to care.

Must be on an expense account, thought Rulon. Boris stood there with his hands at his side, silently watching the two of them.

Rulon handed Yohaba the binoculars. "Remind Boris again that he is to stay out of this no matter what. Tell him thanks for driving me. And one more thing . . ." Rulon looked down and scuffed in the dirt with the toe of his boot. "You got your cell phone with you?" She nodded. "On the completely off chance that something were to happen, call the police. Nothing will, but just in case. They can be here in twenty minutes if they step on it." He frowned and looked at her. "If this is gonna have a chance of working out, this is the best way. Don't fret. Just stay here and talk to Bluto. I'll be back in fifteen at the most." He looked at Boris, then back at her. "Hey, I feel okay leaving you alone with him. Are you okay with that?"

"I told you. I like the guy," Yohaba said. She stole a look at Boris. "He reminds me of you. I'm sure one of his tattoos says 'Mother.'"

"Okay then."

"Okay."

Rulon gave Yohaba a quick kiss, nodded good-bye to Boris, then walked over the hill toward the compound.

Yohaba hesitated, then ran to the crest and watched him weave down the hill through the mesquite. She shouted after him, "I don't like this," but he just waved her off.

Over his shoulder, Rulon shouted back at her, "Don't let Bluto get involved, no matter what. And keep your head down."

She watched Rulon slide a few feet, then gain control, slide a few feet, then gain control, all the way down the hill.

Get a grip, girl, thought Yohaba. *This is nothing compared to what happened at CERN.*

The compound was the size of a football field and completely enclosed in a chain-link fence topped with a loosely coiled roll of military-grade concertina wire. The thirty-foot entrance had two chain-link gates. One was closed; the other flung wide open. Rulon had deliberately hidden from Yohaba how angry he was. He hoped, after what he was about to do, that getting out would be as easy as getting in.

Inside the compound were four buildings clustered around a yard a hundred feet across. In the middle was a thirty-foot flagpole sporting a red flag with a black swastika.

What a fun life, thought Rulon.

The largest structure was a Quonset hut, fifteen yards long by five yards wide, with a rounded roof and the sun glaring off its metal surface. Next to it was a rancher's two-story home with a porch.

Must have come with the property.

Next to that was a barn. The fourth building was a perfectly square cinder-block structure, twenty feet on a side, flat roof, with gun slits every five feet along the sides.

The Keep for the last stand, no doubt, thought Rulon with a disbelieving shake of his head.

In the yard between the buildings were three pickup trucks, a black Humvee, and a blue Dodge Intrepid. During the time Rulon had watched through the binoculars, he saw only one person. That man had walked across the yard from the home to the Quonset Hut—a big guy, tattoos covering one arm, wearing the Fourth Reich uniform of the day: white T-shirt and jeans.

First the vehicles, thought Rulon.

Up on the hill, Yohaba and Boris were on their bellies watching the compound. Yohaba had the binoculars. She saw Rulon stop to check out the fence and then walk through the gate. She lost sight of him as he went behind the cinder-block fort, but he quickly appeared again, now with the Colt in his right hand.

"Uh-oh," Yohaba said in English. "What's he up to?" She watched Rulon walk over to the truck with the cracked windshield, lean over the hood, and touch the glass. After a brief inspection, he stepped back and pointed his gun at the truck. Dust exploded off a tire. Then the sound of a pistol shot reached her ears, and she saw the truck sag to one side. She watched as Rulon moved quickly, shooting a tire out of each vehicle in succession, each sagging the same way, the sound coming about a half second later.

Yohaba stood up and refocused the binoculars. Boris stood up beside her. Two men came running out of the hut. Rulon pointed his pistol at them, and Yohaba saw the men get down on their stomachs with their hands behind their heads. Two more men ran out, one with a rifle. Rulon got the drop on them too. The one man lowered his weapon, and Rulon quickly had them on the ground just like the others. He bent over and searched them in turn, found a couple of weapons and tossed them away. She watched as he walked slowly around his four prone captives, his gun waving slightly as he used his hands to talk.

"Rulon, Rulon, Rulon," muttered Yohaba. "What are you doing? I hope you're not quoting from the Bible."

Suddenly, Boris said something and pointed. Yohaba redirected the binoculars and saw three men in white T-shirts inching their way along the side of the cinder-block building. They had their backs against the wall with their pistols drawn. Yohaba put down the binoculars and yelled a warning, but her voice was lost in the wind.

She watched through the binoculars again as the three men continued creeping along the wall until the one in the lead could peer around the corner. He took a quick look, then pulled back and pressed flat against the wall, legs bent, and his pistol in a two-handed grip pointing downward. Yohaba could see him breathing hard, scared. The three men paused to confer. Yohaba watched as they each chambered a round and got ready to spring. She sensed them counting, "One, two, three." They jumped out together. The faint sound of yelling reached her ears. Rulon then had his hands up, with the Colt dangling over his head by the trigger guard. As Yohaba watched, she kept up a running commentary to Boris, oblivious that in her surging fear she had slipped into English.

The four men on the ground stood up. One of them took the pistol from Rulon's outstretched hand, then stepped back. Yohaba could tell he and Rulon were jawing at each other, then watched in distress as the man reared back and launched a haymaker at Rulon's face. Rulon's head snapped back at the impact, but the man bent over and turned away from Rulon, grabbing his own hand in obvious pain.

"Oh, they're punching him, Boris," Yohaba said in horror. One of the three men with pistols came over and punched Rulon in the stomach. "Boris, we have to do something," she cried.

Rulon held his ground under the pummeling until a man buffaloed him from behind with a pistol, and he dropped to one knee. Four of them tried manhandling him into the hut, but he resisted. A gun in his face settled Rulon down. He disappeared through the door with his hands behind his head.

"Oh, Rulon. Oh, Rulon, what have you gotten yourself into?" she moaned. She turned to Boris and said calmly in English, "Boris, if you have any ideas, now would be the time." When he didn't react, she released the binoculars, letting them hang from her neck by the strap, grabbed him by the lapels of his shirt, and shook him.

"Time to earn your waffles, comrade," she yelled, her eyes wild and brimming with angry, fearful tears. "Time for the Seventh Cavalry. C'mon, I can't do it alone." She beat him on the chest with her fists. He didn't move. She grabbed his shirt and shook him again, pleading, "You have to help me."

Boris looked blankly at her, then, like removing a mask, his expression changed to one of recognition. Towering over her, he grabbed her hands and slowly pried them away.

In reasonably good English, he replied, "They shot in direction of his woman. That's what he thinking." He held her at arm's length, and said, "You stay. I will help."

"I'm going too," Yohaba said fiercely as she struggled to break free of his grip. "You can't stop me."

Boris looked at her and then looked down at the compound. Every second counted. "Okay. I will get vehicle."

He let go of her hands and ran down the opposite side of the hill to the SUV. Yohaba wiped her face and peered through the binoculars again. While she was watching the compound, Boris came roaring up over the crest and stopped alongside her in a cloud of dust.

The SIG Commando and AR-15 were leaning across the passenger seat. Boris lowered the window. "Don't call police. Olive Oil stays here." He laughed that axle-grinding laugh of his. "Bluto will now save Popeye." Before Yohaba could react, he hit the gas.

She ran a few steps after him, but he was gone. She yelled, "Bring him back, you hear me? You bring him back, mister!" For some reason, her words sounded strange to her. Then, with a start, she realized, *We've been speaking English.*

She watched Boris drive off, ripping through bushes and bounding over rocks. The Ford landed on its front wheels, once almost flipping end over end. Somehow, Boris got to the bottom in one piece and floored it toward the gate.

Yohaba was on the binoculars again. She watched him tear through the gate and then do a K-turn in the yard and drive backward at a controlled twenty miles per hour, straight past the disabled vehicles and into the door of the Quonset hut, knocking it clear off its hinges. The SUV didn't stop there but crashed right through the doorway, the light metal of the hut shearing loose from the

58

foundation bolts and easily giving way. For a second, she lost sight of the Ford, but then it surged back out and stopped just outside the widened doorway.

Boris got out with the AR-15 in one hand and the SIG Commando in the other and plunged back through the opening. Immediately, rippling up the hill on the wind, came the sounds of multiple three-shot bursts of automatic gunfire.

Like the police station scene in the first Terminator *movie*, she thought.

The gunfire died off. A few seconds later, a big man in a white T-shirt came sailing out the Quonset hut window and lay motionless on the ground. Another man tried climbing through the same window but got pulled back in, clawing at the frame. Unable to stand it any longer, Yohaba slid down the hill. The gunfire started up again, sporadic single shots. She got to the bottom and ran, but she had only gone a few steps before the banged-up Ford Escape came barreling out the gate with Boris driving and Rulon sitting in the passenger seat, half hanging out the window, looking back with the Colt in his hand.

They drove up to Yohaba, and Rulon, an ugly gash along his left cheek and one eye almost swelled shut, said sternly, "Don't say a word. Not one word."

Yohaba rushed to the car window with a pained expression. "Rulon, my baby! My poor baby." She tenderly held his battered face as her eyes welled with tears.

"Okay, you can say that if you want to," he said.

"Déjà vu all over again," she said. "What am I going to do with you? Are you all right? Tell me what happened." She stopped rubbing his ears and wiped her eyes with the back of her sleeve. She sniffed back a few tears. "I forgot to call the police. Do you still want me to?" Before Rulon could answer, she started up again. "Why do you do these things? You know I couldn't live without you. Why are you such an idiot? What were you trying to prove?"

Rulon let her talk, only half listening, his attention more focused on who might be coming out of the Quonset hut door with a gun.

Yohaba suddenly stopped in midsentence and bent over to look in the window at Boris. "Are you okay?" Boris was also looking behind him and didn't immediately answer. She yelled, "Talk to me! Somebody talk to me!"

Rulon held his hand up for her to quiet down. "Hold it. We have to go back. I left my hat."

Boris laughed, but Yohaba got angry. "Are you crazy? Are you really that crazy?"

Rulon turned to Boris and pointed at his head. Speaking loud and slow, he said, "Hat for head. Must go back. Understand, big fella?"

In heavily accented English, Boris replied, "Look in backseat. I save you *and* your fat American hat. Yohaba, get in. We must leave. *Davaj seichas.* Do it now."

Rulon stared at Boris in astonishment, then slowly reached over his shoulder, grabbed the hat, and set it firmly on his head. He eyed Boris suspiciously, then glanced back behind him. There were men limping out of the Quonset hut, some supported by their friends.

Rulon said to Yohaba, "Better do what he says. But you"—he pointed at Boris—"you and I have lots to discuss."

Yohaba scrambled into the backseat, and they drove off in a cloud of dust.

EIGHT TIME ZONES away, Figeli was speeding along with one hand on the steering wheel of a rented Jeanneau Cap Camarat 715 speedboat and one hand on the throttle. The waves were choppy and the boat jarred with every bounce. It had been a beautiful day, but now they were jetting along on a dark, moonless night, and something was bugging him.

"What was that word you used?" he asked, yelling into the wind.

"What word?" Helmut asked. He was standing behind Figeli, holding firmly to the boat's handrail and gazing out over the black waves of an empty Mediterranean.

"It had something to do with his feet," Figeli said.

"Oh, you mean 'galoshes,' I said 'cement galoshes.' It's an American expression from the thirties. Galoshes are rubber shoes you put over your good shoes when it rains."

"Oh. Now I get it," Figeli said.

When they pulled into port at Toulon, Helmut and Figeli

gathered up the empty cement bags they'd stuck under the seats, threw them in the trash along with the plastic from the car, then hosed down the boat. The French rental companies were murder on you if you returned a boat dirty.

Once back in the Mercedes they headed straight for Nice, where Figeli had a late-night flight back to Corsica. Figeli drove, and Helmut sat in the passenger seat with the aluminum case on the floor between his feet.

At the airport, Figeli got out and Helmut slipped into the driver's seat. He nodded good-bye and Figeli, leaning over to look in the window, stroked his index finger across his nose in return.

"It was a good sting, yes?" Figeli said.

"Yes," Helmut said. "It was a good sting. Here, take this." Helmut gave Figeli the hundred-euro note he'd taken from the professor's body. "A bonus. You earned it."

Figeli held the bill up to the light. "This is counterfeit," he said.

"Consider it a souvenir then," Helmut said. He put the Mercedes in gear and raised his right hand in a familiar salute. "Heil Hitler."

Helmet drove off, heading for Boblingen, Germany, just south of Stuttgart, where the lab was located. It was less than four hundred miles, but he would be taking a more circuitous route. Force of habit. Always assume you are being followed. Layers of security. It should take eleven hours unless he hit traffic in Zurich. He reached down and rubbed his leg. It was throbbing again. The fat American.

Ten miles down the road, he pulled out cell phone number two and made another call.

CHAPTER 7

It was fifteen miles to the highway. Rulon concentrated on directing Boris through the labyrinth of dirt roads that crisscrossed the hills. Yohaba knelt on the backseat, keeping an eye out for a posse. Boris was doing twenty miles per hour too fast. The road wasn't badly rutted, but sixty was pushing it. The car fishtailed around turns, just staying under control.

A man of many talents, thought Rulon approvingly. He was driving fast enough to discourage conversation, but not so fast that Yohaba couldn't lean over the seat and use her blue bandana to staunch the cut on Rulon's cheek—caused by a ring on a fist.

"This reminds me of my OCD days," Rulon said after they pulled out of one particularly tight turn. "Once I was on assignment—"

Boris interrupted. "OCD? What's that stand for?"

"Obsessive compulsive disorder," Yohaba quickly answered as she dabbed at Rulon's cheek.

"Office Crimes Division," Rulon said, ignoring her remark. "I was subcontracted out to the US State Department back then. Boy, we had some wild times."

After twenty minutes of breakneck driving, Boris came flying out of the hills into a half-mile-wide valley. They cut into the main road at right angles, where he swerved onto the blacktop, settled the car down, checked his mirrors, accelerated up to sixty, and kept it

62

there. Everyone breathed a sigh of relief in the brief moment before Yohaba laid into Rulon.

"What happened back there? And don't give me any of that self-deprecating cowboy 'ah shucks it weren't nuttin, ma'am' nonsense. C'mon, out with it. By the way, I'm retiring as translator. I think you figured out that Boris here speaks English. On second thought, Boris, let's start with you. What the heck is going on? You came here to beat up Rulon. Okay, that I can understand. But why the trick?"

Boris cleared his throat and then said in English, "You never suspected that I was . . . how you say, how you say . . ."

"A phony?" suggested Yohaba.

". . . a charlatan," Boris said with a sly smile. "It is better to be underestimated. It is not trick. This is to survive. Because of my size, most people think I'm dumb as oil drum. And that is good for me. It is difficult to do, to not answer to language you know. Sometimes it's my only . . . my only . . ."

"Edge?" Yohaba suggested.

". . . advantage," Boris said, "for people to think I'm not intelligent. I am excellent chess player, by the way. But really? I fooled Rulon?"

"Yes, you did. But don't get conceited about it, that's not as tough as you might think." Yohaba now focused on Rulon. "Gosh, Cowboy, you are such an idiot. Why did you shoot out their tires? What were you thinking?"

"I was thinking they shot out my tire. But mostly I was thinking they endangered my wife. Though, I still think they were just trying to scare us."

"Well, if that was their goal, it worked. Now tell me."

"I had everything under control. I had four of them on the ground, and I was trying to talk some sense into them—"

"Yes, yes, we know. I saw all that. What were you saying to them? Were you quoting from the Bible?"

"Maybe."

"Geez, you are pathetic without me around. You should have been quoting from *Mein Kampf.*"

"Anyway, three of them snuck up behind me—"

"We saw all that. What happened in the hut? This is like pulling teeth. Boris, feel free to jump in anytime."

Rulon and Boris looked at each other as if to say, *You tell her.*

When Rulon made no effort to speak, Boris said, "The woman is your woman."

Rulon relented. "There's really not much to tell. They were working me over; Boris showed up and made them stop. Now we're here."

At that, Yohaba went ballistic.

"Okay, okay." Rulon relented. He launched into a fifty-word version of the story, a little more detailed than before. It was like putting a second coat of paint on a fence. Yohaba was still not satisfied.

"How did you get your shiner?" she asked. "Let's start with that."

"Okay, that part's funny. This one big guy takes off his shirt and his whole upper body is covered in tattoos. You might be right about the prison thing. Anyway, they have me on a chair in the middle of the hut. They've got a couple of guns on me, so I can't move. Well, this guy hauls off and punches me right in the face. I laugh and say, 'I've been hit harder by girls,' and the guy goes berserk. A minute later Boris shows up. Okay, I'm talked out. Let him tell you the rest."

Boris took up the story. "I crash the Nazi party," he said with a laugh and several vulgarities. He noticed the look on Yohaba's face. "Sorry. No swearing. Yes, I remember. Where was I? Oh, yes. They stand there with mouths down to here." Boris laughed and held his hand down by his knees. "I shoot first. I really like the SIG. The Swiss make more than chocolate, eh."

Boris paused while he and Rulon both went silent, reliving the moment in their minds: bullets whizzing by, everything in slow motion, no sound except the faraway booms, faces contorted, fear. It was uglier than they'd ever admit to Yohaba.

Grown men in a large, open room, thinking they were in a fight for their lives. Boris shooting up the place. The Nazis shooting back until cowed by Boris's firepower. Some on the floor. A few trying for the window. Boris spraying the place with bullets to keep their heads down, stomping around and roaring, "Fashisty. Fashisty." Rulon settling the score with the tattooed brute, throwing him through the window. Another one trying to escape. Boris dragging him back and feeding him to Rulon.

But all Boris said was, "They drop their guns and we fight like men. Then your man annoys everyone with speech. Annoys me too. We back through the door and tell them don't move for long time. That is it."

"There, you got your novel," Rulon said. "Now, can we drop it?" Despite the glibness, he and Boris were both trembling as their bodies reabsorbed the excess adrenaline. Yohaba recognized the signs. She was feeling it too and didn't push.

"Fine. I don't care. I'll get the story out of Rulon tonight in bed."

"Trouble up ahead," Boris said.

The highway ran straight as an arrow. The Ford Escape was starting its descent down a long, sweeping hill that bottomed out after a mile, ran flat for three miles, and then began a gradual two-mile climb up to another crest. Just coming into view over that faraway ridge was a line of five pickup trucks running suspiciously close together—a convoy. Rulon and Yohaba stared straight ahead, quiet, not quite sure what to make of it. But it didn't feel right.

"Darlin'. Hand me the binocs, will ya?" Rulon said, reaching behind him without taking his eyes off the trucks. He took the binoculars and slowly unwrapped the strap. Next he blew on the lenses to clear off the dust. He held the binoculars up to his eyes and adjusted the focus. The convoy was now four miles away. "It looks like a chapter of the follicly-challenged big galoot society heading off to an NRA meeting."

"Huh?" Boris said.

"Heavily armed skinheads," Yohaba said. "Fat ones."

"Take a right up here," Rulon said.

Boris skidded off the highway onto a dirt road.

"Now slow down, and let's hope they go by."

Boris slowed to thirty—just another local having fun in his four-wheel drive. Yohaba and Rulon turned in their seats to watch the road. The trucks were still coming. Same speed as before. Maybe two miles away.

"We're doing fine," Rulon said. "Got anything to drink?" He traded Yohaba the binoculars for a bottle of water. He took a swig and passed it to Boris. "How about another one, babe?"

"How's it looking?" Boris asked after he drained his bottle.

The trucks were a mile away from the dirt road turnoff. Same speed.

"No change. Just keep driving."

"What'll we do if they come after us?" Yohaba asked. "Is there ever a time we can call the police?"

"You can try now," Rulon said, "but I'm pretty sure we're in a dead zone."

Yohaba tried. No luck. There were no other vehicles on the road. Just the line of trucks. They passed the turnoff for the dirt road.

Rulon let out a sigh, faced front, and said to Boris, "Okay, let's keep going for another minute then turn around."

"Uh-oh," Yohaba said.

Rulon quickly turned. The trucks were a mile away, stopped dead on the road about two hundred yards past the turnoff. Five trucks. There were men in the cabs and several in the beds.

Yohaba said, "I'll bet they're wondering how many brown Ford Escapes can be driving around today. Shoot, Rulon. I've got a bad feeling."

"Control your vibes, everyone," Rulon said. "Boris, try driving more relaxed."

"How do I do that?"

"I don't know. Drive with one hand. Breathe from your diaphragm. Do something."

Everyone was quiet. Rulon and Yohaba watched the trucks. Boris adjusted his mirror so he could see.

Suddenly, the lead truck spun around and raced back to the dirt road, the others right behind.

"Not yet," Rulon said. "Wait till he turns. Wait. Wait."

They watched as the lead truck reached the side road going fast, then it turned sharply onto the dirt, sending up a plume of dust, the others following closely.

"Dang," Rulon said. "Go. Go. Go!"

Boris hit the gas.

Yohaba gripped the back of Rulon's seat. "What's your plan?" she asked. Rulon didn't answer. "What's your plan, Cowboy?" she repeated louder.

Rulon's eyes looked down and to the right as he calculated. He rubbed his chin. Boris continued to accelerate. They went airborne, came down hard, and then rattled over a cattle guard. Yohaba saw the odometer blow past eighty.

"I need you to get some distance between us and them," Rulon said finally.

"*Da*," Boris said.

"But don't kill us."

"*Da*."

They reached the hills and began to climb. Now they were winding through the hills and the trucks were lost from view. Boris slowed to fifty—still alarmingly fast for the conditions. The truck swerved through a hairpin, and Boris steered in the direction of the skid, the rear wheels locking. They came out of it and were immediately up to fifty again, driving up a valley on a narrow dirt road that followed the twisting path of a small creek intermittently lined with trees.

A mile further on there was no sign of the trucks, but the road was so windy their pursuers could have been catching up and they'd never know it.

Betting Boris had increased their lead, Rulon pointed up ahead to a steep hundred-foot hill. "Up there."

"Ah . . . there's no road," Boris said.

"Roads? Where we're going, we don't need roads," Yohaba said absently, without looking up from reloading the rifles.

"*Back to the Future*, 1985, Dr. Emmett Brown," Boris said.

"Yeah, but who was the actor? Be careful," Rulon said as Boris swerved around a juniper tree.

"I don't know."

"That would be Christopher Lloyd," Yohaba said. "But Boris, that was amazing for a Rooskie."

"To repeat," Boris said, "there is still no road."

"Just do it," Rulon said.

Boris slowed slightly, then careened off the dirt track, downshifted, and bounded up the hill. The rear bumper, already loose from crashing through the Quonset hut, fell off, but Boris kept his foot on the gas, needing all the power and every bit of the four-wheel drive to make it to the top. With the wheels slipping during the last steep part, they arched over the hill and parked on the other side, out of sight from the road.

They all jumped out, and Yohaba and Boris immediately ran back to the ridge to watch. They lay down in the cheat grass so they wouldn't be seen.

Rulon went around the van, opened the back, and pulled out a long, rectangular rifle case that was wedged between the rear seat and the van's internal wall. He laid the case in the cargo area, unlatched it, and took out the Remington 700 AcuSport VTR .308 caliber rifle. Desert Recon model, camouflaged stock. *For varmints*, thought Rulon. *Just the ticket*. 5-R rifling, just like the US army's M24 sniper rifle.

"Darlin', where'd you put the shells?" he asked as he checked the sight and worked the bolt.

But Yohaba was talking to Boris and didn't hear him.

Despite the bouncing, the Remington was in pretty good shape. Rulon dry-fired the rifle and sniffed. He reached into the case, pulled out a screwdriver, and adjusted a small set screw near the trigger.

"Anyone coming?" he asked as he worked.

"No," Boris said.

He dry-fired again. Trigger pull about three and a half pounds. *Perfect*. He asked again, "Darlin', where'd you put the shells?"

This time she heard him. "Under the rear seat, babe."

"Thanks."

He stretched across the cargo area and retrieved the box, flicked open the top of the Buffalo Bore Ultra Match Sniper ammo, and shook out ten shells. He loaded four shells into the magazine and put the rest in his Levi's vest pocket.

One deep breath and a quick look up at the clouds. He shifted his gaze to the nearby willows and Russian olive trees and studied the movement of their branches. Then the grass. Wind was picking up, shifting. He picked up some dirt, crumbled it in his fingers, then threw it in the air to watch it blow away. In the distance he could hear the trucks coming. Boris watched the road, but Yohaba was watching Rulon.

"The boy can shoot," Yohaba said to Boris. "He used to be an instructor at a place called Front Sight. He could have been a sniper."

"We know," Boris said. "The Serbian. The one he left alive told us how he killed his brother in the Hönggerberg forest."

"I was there," Yohaba said. "At the time I didn't know anything about shooting. I didn't know it was an impossible shot."

"He was driving. How fast?"

"About one twenty."

"Kilometers?"

"Nope, miles per hour."

"Not possible."

"Possible," Yohaba said. "I wouldn't be here if it wasn't."

"They said Serbian was shot between eyes. Impossible."

"Possible."

Just then, Rulon lay down beside Yohaba with the Remington. "Talking about me?" he asked.

"No. Only a totally self-absorbed oaf would even ask the question," Yohaba said.

"Yes," Boris answered.

Rulon winked at both of them.

Rulon wove his left arm through the Remington's sling and settled into a solid shooting position. He looked through the scope and adjusted the focus.

"Boris, my fine furry friend, this here's a Remington 700. Do you understand? How good is your English? Do you understand American idioms like 'my fine furry friend'?"

"Yes, I understand very well, mister lard belly," Boris said.

Rulon and Yohaba looked at each other and burst out laughing. Rulon then got down to business.

"With this baby and a Luepold Mark 4 8-25 power scope like I've got here, I've done what I call a 4-2-4. That's four shots within two inches at four hundred yards. Wind's a mite tricky today, though, and I'll be shooting downhill."

"What crazy country you have where civilians can own such gun. You Americans are the most crazy. In Russia, the police would not go outside if population could own this."

"If Russians owned this in the thirties," said Rulon, "they wouldn't have gone walking off to the Gulags like sheep."

"Maybe they still go," said Boris. "My people are strange people.

My great-grandfather was shot at Kolyma in 1937 when Stalin purged military. His brother was captured by Germans near Kiev in July 1941. His own people freed him in counterattack but then shot him for surrendering and sent my great-grandmother to Gulag for two years. Stalin's order number 227—not one step backward and no surrendering or you get shot and family get punished too." Boris spat down the hill. "Stalin was a pig, but he was consistent. He did the same thing to his own daughter-in-law when his son was captured at Vetebsk. Hitler or Stalin, I don't know which one worse."

"Nothing that a sniper with one of these babies couldn't have sorted out," Rulon said.

A three-quarter ton Chevy truck came tearing around a bend below them four hundred yards away. It climbed steadily up the narrow valley along the dirt road winding alongside the creek. In the truck bed were three men in white T-shirts. One was standing, looking over the cab, rifle resting on the hood. Two were sitting with their backs against the sidewalls, rifles upright between their legs. Ar-15s. Two men were in the cab.

The gruppenfuhrers, surmised Rulon with an amused snort and a shake of his head. Ouch, his jaw hurt. *But what luck*, thought Rulon. It was his left eye that had swollen shut. He didn't even have to close his eye to aim.

The first truck was past their hill and out of sight before four more trucks appeared, coming slower, more cautious. Rulon waited until all four trucks were within range.

"Cover your ears," he said. The Remington bucked, and the last truck in line swerved and stopped, sagging—the front right tire gone.

"Why did you take out the last one, Cowboy?" Yohaba asked. "Why not the first one? I would have taken out the first one. Maybe blocked the road."

Rulon didn't answer.

"Cover your ears," he said. The rifle bucked, and the next to last truck sagged and stopped again—the front right tire.

"Now that doesn't make any sense whatsoever," Yohaba said.

"Cover your ears," Rulon said. Boom. Next truck. Swerve. Stop. Sag.

"Cover your ears," Rulon said. *Boom*. Now the last remaining truck, the closest one to them, sagged and stopped. Rulon talked as he quickly reloaded. "Always shoot the last turkey in the flock. Keeps the rest coming. The old Sergeant York tactic." Down below, men jumped from their trucks, rifles in hand. They crouched down, eyes searching, unable to tell where the shots came from because the echoes of Rulon's gunshots were still bouncing around the hills.

Their cell phones wouldn't do them any good. Dead zone. No chance of warning the first truck—the sounds of its engine carrying on the wind as it continued to speed away unawares.

Rulon left the rifle on the ground, stood up, waved his hat at the skinheads, and yelled, "Hey! Hey! You down there. Hey!"

"What are you doing?" Yohaba asked as she tugged at his pants leg. "Are you crazy? Get back down here."

Now Rulon waved both arms overhead. "Hey!" he yelled again.

Down below, the band of immobilized Nazis looked up and spotted him, curious. Nobody lifted a rifle. Rulon cupped his hands like a megaphone.

"Hey! Get away from the trucks. Step away, will ya?" He motioned vigorously with his hand. "Go back, go back into the creek. Get back, please." The dozen or so men turned to each other, puzzled. Then a few moved toward the creek. The rest, looking confused, just took a few steps back and continued to look up at Rulon.

"Thank you," Rulon yelled.

He got back down and set the Remington against his shoulder. "Cover your ears," he said. Four more shots in quick succession. At the first shot, the men below all jumped into the creek. When Rulon was done, there were now four trucks with two flat tires each.

"That should do it," Rulon said. He propped himself up on his elbows and yelled again at the Nazis. "Use the good tires. Make two good trucks. Swap tires."

Down by the creek, some of the skinheads were yelling back.

"Don't listen to them, honey," Rulon said when he heard what they were saying. "C'mon. Let's go."

The three of them reverse-crawled down the opposite side of the hill until they were out of sight enough to stand up.

"Having fun?" Yohaba asked. "You don't think they would've

figured it out on their own? To use the good tires from two of the trucks to fix the others?"

"If they were smart, they wouldn't be Nazis," Rulon said. "I was just trying to help. Probably didn't even bring water with them. But, hey, your old man's still got it. That last truck in line was almost four hundred yards away. What d'ya think?"

"Excellent, considering the wind and the angle," Boris said.

"Ya really think so?" Rulon asked, pleased. "Yeah, not bad. Now where did those gruppenfuhrers run off to?"

CHAPTER 8

They came off the hill on the reverse side and swung around to catch the dirt road again higher up the valley. Rulon figured the lead truck with the *gruppenfuhrers* would be coming back pretty soon, wondering where everyone was.

"I just want to talk to them," Rulon said.

"Yeah, me too," Boris said. "I want to ask them about Stalingrad and the human soap factories they set up in western Russia."

"That was almost seventy years ago," Rulon offered quietly. "At some point, you've gotta let go."

"Where does it say that?" Boris asked. "Do you have any idea what those monsters did in my country?"

"Your soul counts too," Rulon said. "You can't carry the hate and grudge with you three generations later. It makes their atrocities doubly effective."

Boris made no reply, just sat there with that Russian war memorial expression on his face.

Yohaba changed the subject. "Hey, Cowboy. How come those guys didn't shoot at you when you stood up? They had guns."

"Yeah, but I didn't think they would use them. An unarmed man stands up and asks them to move away from the trucks. You don't just shoot him. Besides, no one's been shot so far. We can beat up each other and shoot out tires all day and most likely just

73

keep it between ourselves. But if someone gets shot, then someone's going to jail, and who do you think that would be? Let's see.
Jury of our peers. Let's get twelve ranchers sitting on a jury and
see which one of us goes to IMSI. Even the skinheads can figure
that one out."

"IMSI?" Boris asked.

"Idaho Maximum Security Institute, near Kuna, southeast
of Boise," Yohaba said. And then to Rulon, "Yeah, but these guys
don't think straight. You were taking a chance. You're dealing with
cretins."

"Not totally, darlin'," Rulon said. "Theirs is a peasant cunning."

That broke through Boris's stoic demeanor, and he let out a huge
laugh.

"Dang it, you two," Yohaba said. "This is all a big joke to you,
isn't it, Rulon?"

"Darlin'," Rulon said. "Just what would you have me do? Should
I go to the police then? Should I do nothing? What's gonna settle
this? Should I invite them to church?"

"Compared to the ones in Germany," Boris said, "these Nazis
are babies."

"There's no Nazis in Germany," Yohaba said. "They've been out-
lawed there."

"Actually," Rulon said, "there's something that exists today called
the Nationalist Socialist Underground that does a pretty good imitation of a Nazi. I think that's what Boris is talking about. Right?"

"No," Boris said. "Worse. Real Nazis. Still there. Waiting. They'd
do it all over again. They think they lost because Hitler too soft."

"He never should have declared war on America," Yohaba said.
"That's what did him in."

"No," Boris said. "His big mistake was declaring war on Russia.
Eighty percent of all German combat deaths came on the Eastern
Front. It was Russian blood that defeated Hitler."

Yohaba started to argue, but Rulon cut her off. "He's right, baby.
We Americans whumped the Japanese pretty much on our own, but
Boris has a point. The Russians and Germans had battles no one ever
heard of that were bigger than D-Day."

"*Da,*" Boris said. "Operation Bagration. June 22, 1944. Two weeks after your D-Day. We came out of the Northern Pripet Marshes and destroyed Hitler's Army Group Center—four hundred thousand fashisty killed, another five hundred thousand wounded or captured. Our losses too terrible to speak, but we crush them. That was battle. And no one in West even know it. You westerners still talk of Flanders Field. You have no idea." Boris shook his head. "No idea."

They continued to climb steadily as they talked, the road still winding up the valley. After a couple of miles, they came upon a stand of spruce trees that spread out on both sides of the road and across the creek on the left. There was shade on the road where it took a sharp right.

"What'd'ya think?" Rulon asked Boris. "Does this work for you?"

"Sure," Boris said. He slowed and parked the Escape so it blocked enough of the road that no vehicle could get by.

"But if this does not work," Boris said, "we will be trapped between them."

"Nah," Rulon said. "There's lots of ways outta here if you've got four-wheel drive."

The three of them got out. Boris had the SIG Commando, and Rulon, despite Yohaba's protests, kept both the Remington and the AR-15. Rulon wiped his forehead. Even though the high desert sun was just a few hours from setting, it was still getting hotter.

He said to Yohaba. "You're watching from the bleachers." She started to argue but stopped herself. Rulon was easygoing, but when it came to protecting her, there was no give.

Ten minutes later, Rulon was by the creek getting a drink when they heard the sounds of a truck coming back down the valley. He came running up the ten-foot embankment to the road where Boris and Yohaba were waiting by the SUV. Rulon had his hat in one hand and a soaking wet red bandana in the other.

"All right. Battle stations, everyone," Rulon said. He put on his hat and tied the dripping bandana around his neck. "You all know what to do, right? Which is to say, do nothing, right?"

"Remember, you're just gonna talk," Yohaba said.

"Darlin', it's me. Don't worry. These guys don't want to go to jail. They want to end this just as much as we do. If they went to jail they'd miss their paint ball war games. Now skedaddle."

"Okay," Yohaba said, "but remember, don't do all the talking. Nobody likes a blabbermouth. Listen to what they have to say. And don't be afraid to make a concession. Offer to pay for half the tires you shot out. We can afford it. This is getting out of control."

"Yes, ma'am," Rulon said. "Now, git."

Yohaba stood at attention, clicked her heels, saluted, then gave Rulon a quick kiss and took off up the hill with that odd Charlie Chaplin splayed-foot walk of hers. When she'd gone a hundred feet, she turned around and looked back at Rulon for approval.

"Farther!" he yelled. He vigorously pointed to a group of Russian olives another hundred feet up. "A lot farther. Behind those trees up there. Go on. Go." When she reached the trees, she sat down in the shade, stuck a blade of cheat grass in her mouth, and leaned back to ruminate and wait.

Rulon turned to Boris. He was fiddling with the Commando, blowing dust off the bullets and reinserting them into the clip.

"Ah . . . are we going to be able to control ourselves?" Rulon asked.

"Maybe," Boris said without looking up. He slammed the magazine back in the rifle. "Maybe not."

"Well, just in case you have ideas, let me tell you how it works in this country. If you shoot someone, you won't be leaving the country for a long time. And you'll have a choice: Either change your skin color or become a Nazi yourself. Do you see where I'm going with this? You will be doing serious time in a penitentiary where Russian is not the flavor of the month. Of course, they'll put me and maybe Yohaba in jail too, as accomplices and for being stupid enough to give you an illegal assault rifle in the first place. When we get out, we'll come visit you, though, since we'll get out years before you do." Rulon looked hard at Boris. "I'm trusting you."

"I am not stupid," Boris said. "Did you not see with your eyes that no one got shot before? Or what do you think, I'm just very bad marksman?"

"Sorry," Rulon said. "But all the same, maybe you should hide behind a tree. You can be my ace in the hole." Boris slung the rifle over his shoulder and trudged up the hill to hunker down behind a fifty-year-old spruce.

Rulon laid the Remington and AR-15 out of sight on the vehicle's seat, closed the door, and waited for the Nazis. He removed the Colt from his small-of-back holster, chambered a round, and replaced it. Next, he reached through the open window and grabbed a bottle of warm water.

Rulon sipped the water and listened. He judged he had about five minutes, when suddenly the truck turned the corner right in front of him and stopped in a swirl of dust. *Darn hills*, thought Rulon. He finished his drink, placed the bottle on the hood, and leaned casually against the SUV.

In front of him was a black, late-model Dodge Ram with three guys standing in the bed holding rifles and peering at him over the top of the cab. The sun was behind Rulon and in their eyes. The glare off the Ram's windshield obscured the faces of the two men inside.

"Which one of you is Adolf junior?" Rulon asked.

Someone from the truck bed laughed, put down his rifle, and shaded his eyes with his free hand. "Dang, Rulon. You are a royal pain, man. Ya know?"

"Who is that?" Rulon asked. "Is that you, Ed? Ed Ryerson? I thought you got all the nonsense beat outta you in high school. What the heck are you doing with these clowns?"

"Yeah, it's me," Ed said with an ear-to-ear grin. "Guess I'm a slow learner." He was tall and as lanky as a flamingo compared to the muscle-heads on either side of him. With his sunny smile, he didn't seem to quite fit in, even though he was dressed like the others, with a white T-shirt, jeans, red armband, black swastika, and tattoos running up and down his arms.

"When did you become a mouseketeer?" Rulon asked.

"You need to show a little more respect," Ed said. "Not everyone appreciates your sense of humor. These boys take themselves mighty seriously."

A middle-aged man with a flaming red goatee stuck his head out the driver's window and said in an odd, lilting, tent-revival rhythm, "You will know when the end is near. When we rise up, the traitors to the white race will be singing a different tune. We will know our own. The Reverend won't forget. If your name's not written in the Book of Life, there will be no mercy."

From up on the hill Yohaba yelled down, "You guys couldn't organize a piss-up at a brewery. If real Nazis were around, you'd be the first ones gassed."

"Darlin'," Rulon yelled, "I think I can handle this. Do you mind?"

The man with the goatee retreated back into the cab.

"Hey, Ed," Rulon said. "What is it with you guys? Why'd ya shoot up my place this morning?"

"It was 'cause of last night, Rul. But the guys were acting on their own. Unauthorized military incursion. They were gonna be disciplined. You should have just walked in and complained to the Reverend. He would have meted out justice."

"My wife was there. There were bullets flying all around."

"They were idiots," Ed said. "We're sorry. What can I say? Nazis aren't perfect."

"Oh, sure they are," Yohaba yelled. "THEY'RE *PERFECT* IDIOTS."

"Yohaba!" Rulon yelled, this time looking up the hill. "Please! I'm trying to calm things down here. Do you mind?"

A contrite "Sorry, honey" came back in return.

Rulon turned back to the truck just as the red goatee stepped out. Mr. Goatee came around the front, opened up the passenger door, stood back, and came to attention.

A boot emerged, then a leg. Then the Reverend Reichsfuhrer in full uniform, complete with puffy pant legs and riding crop. He drew himself up to his full six-foot, three-inch height and scanned the scene, his eyes unreadable behind his reflector sunglasses. He wore the obligatory tan uniform, jackboots, and red armband with white disk and black swastika. The Reichsfuhrer readjusted his visored cap and smoothed the lapels of his jacket.

Mr. Goatee and the three men in the back all gave a Nazi salute and yelled, "Heil Hitler." From up on the hill, Yohaba let out a huge guffaw.

Rulon had never seen the Reverend in person before except on the TV news, usually in the same tan uniform, pounding a pulpit, spittle flying, red-faced, head jerking, gnashing his words like Hitler on the balcony of the Reichstag, whipping his minions into a maniacal fury—all twenty of them. The Reverend Reichsfuhrer Tyrone R. Bernbailer—the only Nazi in America taken seriously by the hardcore bitter-enders in Europe.

The Reverend was in his early fifties, blond with a touch of gray around the temples, like a pilot you could trust. He had a square jaw, full lips, and was tanned, with high cheekbones. Ramrod straight, clean-shaven, muscular. Rulon had to admit, he didn't look bad. The Reverend took off his sunglasses and met Rulon's stare with an unwavering gaze from his piercing green eyes. No lines, no dark circles. But something about them wasn't right. There was this weird light shining in them like the guy had spent a week on a coffee IV drip. Or maybe that was just the look of a "true believer."

His flat, tan hat with its small, highly polished black visor didn't help much against the sun, and the Reverend had to shield his eyes to look at Rulon.

The Reverend turned to Mr. Goatee and in a deep, penetrating voice said, "Gruppenfuhrer, tell the men to stand down. There won't be any need for weapons. Mr. Hurt is unarmed." The Reverend fixed Rulon with a glare. "Isn't that right, Mr. Hurt?"

Rulon held up two empty hands for all to see.

Mr. Goatee clicked his heels and shouted, "Yes, sir." Then turning to his men, he said, "You heard the Reverend, boys. At ease."

Ed and the other two men lowered their rifles and climbed out of the truck.

"Mr. Hurt," the Reverend said. "I believe we have something to discuss."

"Yep," Rulon replied.

"Do I have your permission to approach?" the Reverend asked.

"Yes, but please, no goose-stepping. It stirs up the dust."

Over by the truck, Ed let out a laugh and got slapped across the back of his head by the man behind him.

"Certainly, Mr. Hurt, but please, no boot licking when I get there. Your Zionist puppet masters will be jealous."

The Reverend advanced and stopped in the shade just out

of Rulon's reach. "Your eye looks painful, Mr. Hurt. How did it happen? Did you step on a rake?"

"No, it happened the usual Nazi way. Seven against one. Guns pointed at my head. Me unarmed and one sadistic brute swinging away."

"A team effort then. Excellent! Sometimes we wonder if our training is taking effect."

"After today, your team could have used more first aid training," said Rulon dryly.

The Reverend crinkled the corners of his mouth into a forced smile. "I heard what some of my men did at your ranch this morning. You have to understand, we Aryans are fiercely loyal. It is part of our genetic, Teutonic heritage. Those men you pummeled last night were their friends. But I'd like to apologize. They were out of order." As he talked, he occasionally smacked his thigh with the riding crop.

"Apology accepted," Rulon said. He took his foot off the bumper and stood up straight. "They were butting in where they didn't belong—trying to stomp a knocked-out Russian. Not very sporting."

"Yes, old habits die hard, eh, Mr. Hurt? Operation Barbarossa lives on. It's in their racial DNA." And then raising his voice to oratorical levels, he said, "Mankind has grown strong in eternal struggle, and only in eternal peace does it perish." He brought his voice back to normal and continued. "Recognize those words? They came from the lips of the Fuhrer himself. You should study his writings. You would find them most enlightening. Nothing like they are portrayed in the Zionist controlled media."

"I'd rather rewatch *Saving Private Ryan*. Great movie. Ever seen it?"

"No. Propaganda of the worst kind. Wouldn't waste my time. If memory serves me, lost the 1999 Best Picture Oscar to *Shakespeare in Love*. Need I say more?"

Drat, good comeback, thought Rulon. "A terrible injustice," was all he could mutter in response.

The Reverend waved Rulon off. "But enough of this nonsense. You think you were noble defending the Slav, don't you? And perhaps from your perspective you were. But I wouldn't expect any gratitude from him, if I were you. He'll turn on you first chance he gets.

Those people have no loyalty. Not even to their own kind. Think of the Gulags under Stalin. Who would do that to their own people?"

"Many of the Jews your heroes gassed were German citizens who fought for Germany in World War I," Rulon said. "So there's your answer. Nazis would do that."

"I can see you know your Holocaust propaganda. Hitler was a supremacist with the purest ideology. We are separatists. A less radical form."

"Yeah, separatists." Rulon laughed. "We've all heard that one before. Let's see now, we'll take the fertile land and you get the dunghill in the malarial swamp."

A visible wave of annoyance passed over the Reverend's face. He flexed his riding crop obsessively, and for a second Rulon thought he was going to lose it like Lawrence Olivier in *Spartacus* when he screamed and struck Kirk Douglas. But instead, he broke eye contact, took his cap off, and polished the visor with his sleeve. After a few seconds, he took a deep breath and put the cap back on with a sharp tug.

Calmly he said, "You may have friends here you don't realize, Mr. Hurt. Don't burn your bridges. You're white. You're smart. I'm told you have British ancestors. Did you know, Hitler never wanted to fight the British? He respected them. That's why he let them escape at Dunkirk. You have talents we could use. My sources tell me you used to be a security expert. There could be a spot for you in our organization."

"Organization? What organization? You don't have an organization," said Rulon. "You have Ed from the video store and a bunch of lost souls." Rulon called over to Ed, "Hey, no offense, Ed. Just making a point."

"None taken," Ed shouted back, sitting on the tailgate, wearily waving a hand holding a beer. "Take your time."

"And you," Rulon said, "have you ever read even one book on World War II? If so, how on earth can you stand there with a swastika on your arm after what the Nazis did? If you have even a shred of human decency, you'll rip off that armband and spend more time with your grandchildren."

"History books are written by the winners," the Reverend said. "There is far more to the story."

"Yeah, and lucky for you most people don't know it. This isn't about your beliefs, as twisted as they are, this is about the hate in your heart. If you were living in Russia in the thirties you'd be part of the NKVD. If you lived in Afghanistan in the nineties, you'd be lopping off hands. The one thing I could never figure out about you guys is how you ever got to the point where this garbage started sounding right. Were you abused as a child or something?"

"Mr. Hurt, you're treading dangerously close to being a traitor to your white race. Someday you will remember this conversation with deep shame and regret. In your stupor you are doing nothing to help all those children who will grow up ruled by the Zionists and the mongrel races, enslaved by them. And by the way, did it ever occur to you that you have no proof about the shooting at your place this morning, but that we could have you arrested for what you did today at the compound?"

"Yeah, but you won't, will you? That's one of the drawbacks of being the master race. Can't just pick up a phone and call on the enforcement arm of the Zionist conspiracy for protection. Wouldn't seem quite Aryan, would it?"

The Reverend Reichsfuhrer moved closer to Rulon and lowered his voice. "Correct, Mr. Hurt. We are the warriors of the white revolution. When it comes to self-defense, we believe in cutting out the middleman. Instead of calling the police, what would you say if we called on one of our friends in Marseilles? Oh, don't look so surprised, Mr. Hurt. We know they've been looking for you, and we've not turned you in . . . yet. But don't push us. We may be restrained by the law and its hired traitors, but after what you did to them, our mutual friends from Marseilles will have no such inhibitions. Did you know they have a bounty out on you? It would more than cover the damage you did today at the compound."

Rulon said, "Those maniacs were up to something nasty. They had to be stopped. But listen. You apologized for your guys shooting up my place. Fine. I accept that. For my part, I might have over-reacted a bit at your compound. My wife says I should pay for half the tires I shot out. If I do that, does that settle things between us?"

"Sure, Mr. Hurt. How many tires are we talking about?"

Rulon looked away and did some quick figuring. He looked up. "That would be six."

"Sure, Mr. Hurt. You pay for three and we'll pay for three."

"Ah . . . no, not exactly. There was twelve total. I meant I pay for six, you pay for six."

Bernbailer looked away, struggled to control his anger, then turned back to Rulon. "I see. We shoot one of your tires. You shoot twelve of ours. Not exactly a proportional response, Mr. Hurt."

"It wasn't about the tire. My wife was standing near me when the bullets whizzed by."

"I'm told she is Swiss. A neutral. Have you ever heard anything so ridiculous? But, yes, that was an error—to endanger the woman. It makes your Aryan blood boil, doesn't it? Come, we will split the cost and make an alliance of peace. You see, Mr. Hurt, we are reasonable people."

"I guess that's it then," Rulon said without offering his hand. He stood waiting for the Reverend to leave. When he didn't move, Rulon said, "I'll move my rig."

The Reverend got the hint and turned to go, hesitated, then leveled a menacing stare at Rulon. He said loudly enough for everyone to hear, "Don't play games with us again, Mr. Hurt. 'We will not capitulate—no, never! We may be destroyed, but if we are, we shall drag a world with us—a world in flames.' That, too, is one of the Fuhrer's quotes. Remember it."

This isn't over, thought Rulon as he looked into Bernbailer's eyes. *Hitler broke his treaty with Russia. What did he say about alliances? Any alliance whose purpose is not the intention to wage war is senseless and useless.*

Rulon and the Reichsfuhrer held eye contact for a long second, when suddenly, over the Reverend's right shoulder, Rulon saw a puff of dust explode off the Ram's front right tire, followed immediately by the crack of a gunshot. Instantly, Rulon whipped out the Colt from his holster and dropped into a crouch. In slow motion he saw the Reverend turn, scream a soundless shout, and point up the hill. Then Rulon noticed the Dodge sagging to one side. In that instant his hearing came back, and he heard Boris roar, "Touch a gun, Fashisty, and you die!" More shots rang out, and the truck sagged again. Men hit the ground. Another tire shot. Boris strode down the hill, the SIG in his shoulder, firing off single shots.

Aw, heck, thought Rulon.

RULON, YOHABA, AND BORIS rode home in silence. Boris was driving and Yohaba was in the back with her legs and arms crossed, staring out the window. When they were ten miles from the ranch, Rulon spoke up.

"Whether we pay for six or eight tires—"

Yohaba angrily cut him off. "You mean six or nine tires. You guys shot out seventeen tires altogether. You should pay for the odd one."

Rulon sighed and started over. "Whether we pay for six or nine tires, what difference does it make in the scheme of things?"

"You shouldn't have done what you did to that guy in the uniform," Yohaba said.

"Call him Reichsfuhrer," said Rulon.

Boris cracked up for an instant, then went quiet under Yohaba's glare.

Yohaba continued. "He could have had a heart attack in the stream. I'm sure the water was freezing. Where does it come from?"

"I think all the way from the Sawtooths. But, hey, why are you picking on me? Talk to Boris here. He started it."

"Boris is hopeless," she said.

"I told you. One was reaching for gun," Boris said. "I couldn't take chance."

They drove the rest of the way in silence.

REVEREND REICHSFUHRER BERNBAILER sat on the tailgate of his truck with its four flattened tires, trying to dry off. The sun was sinking behind the hills. In a few minutes the truck would be in the shade, and he'd have to move if he wanted to keep drying. He'd sent one of the men to go find the others or get to a place where a cell phone would work.

Ed should have gone, but the Reichsfuhrer didn't trust him anymore. Ed was the only one besides Bernbailer who could walk without pain. In the melee, Rulon had pulled the Russian brute off Ed before any real damage was done. The other men hadn't put up much of a fight, though. In a fistfight, Rulon was a known quantity in this part of the state, and the Russian was just plain scary. There didn't seem much point in contesting the issue.

Actually, the truck had five flats. The Russian had even shot the spare under the truck bed.

"Gruppenfuhrer, front and center!" the Reverend yelled after a half hour's deliberation. Mr. Goatee stood up slowly from where he sat against a tree, wiggled his swollen jaw to make sure it still worked, and walked over. Ed got up and followed.

"Yes, my Reichsfuhrer," Mr. Goatee said.

Before the Reverend could answer, Ed stepped in and blurted out, "Permission to speak, sir."

The Gruppenfuhrer started to cut him off, but the Reverend raised a hand. "Let him speak. Go ahead, Corporal."

"You don't want to do this. There's nothing wrong with this Rulon guy. He's not a talker. He's never bragged about anything in his life. No one will ever hear about this from him. Let it go. His family goes back generations in this valley, since the days of Brigham Young. If you take him on unfairly, the people here will drive us out. He won. So what? We're now just part of a long list of people who wish they'd never tangled with the guy. Nothing permanent got broke. Heck, the guys were shooting near his wife. We had it coming. I think it would be best if we just let it go."

"Thank you, Mr. Ryerson," the Reverend said. "We'll take it under advisement. Would you leave us now?"

Ed backed away respectfully.

When he was out of earshot, the Reverend asked, "And what do you think? Do you agree with him?"

"Seriously?"

"Seriously."

"No. If you don't do something all the men will be gone in a year. It'll be you and me." He jerked his head in the direction of Ed. "And him."

The Reverend nodded slowly and ran his hand through his hair. "It seems Mr. Hurt, our reckless Zog lover, has backed me into a corner then. He's made it a matter of pride—for the cause."

"Survival actually."

The Reverend nodded. "Maybe we should include the Ivan too?"

"No. We can't explain two deaths. Besides, the Russian will be gone in a day. We won't have time." The two men locked eyes. "I've heard the Cowboy fancies himself a peaceful man deep down," said the Gruppenfuhrer. "I find that funny."

"Do you know what I find funny?" Bernbailer said. "That we'll make money on this. The Marseilles cell is run by a maniac named Helmut von Bock, a regular one-man Einsatzgruppe. And he has a reward out on Mr. Hurt. I'd say that seals it." Bernbailer's eyes got that strange light in them again. "Let slip the dogs of war, Gruppenfuhrer."

CHAPTER 9

They drove into the ranch yard just after six o'clock, and before the Ford's tires stopped spinning, Rulon was jumping out and rushing into the house. He came out a minute later holding a bag of frozen peas over his swollen eye and clutching a bag of leftover sandwiches. A quick kiss for Yohaba, then he and Boris rushed off in the pickup with its shiny new tire. There were a couple of quarter-mile-long irrigation wheel lines and three hundred feet of irrigation pipes that needed moving. Said they'd be back in a couple of hours.

Yohaba field stripped and cleaned the guns before getting dinner ready. When the boys took longer than expected, she killed time by plunking cans off the fence with her Smith and Wesson snub-nosed .38 revolver—a gift from Rulon's father when she earned her concealed weapons permit. After firing off a box of shells, she went inside and checked her email. There was another message from her grandfather.

Dear Yohaba,

I appreciate all your work and quick responses. Again, I feel moved to offer, if you ever return to Switzerland there is a position waiting for you at CERN.

At this point, I'm predicting the asteroids will pass each other and not collide. Your calculations support my conclusion. But because we are talking about your great-great-grandfather

*Einstein, there is still an element of doubt. We will know for
sure in two days.*

*I have pulled some strings and enlisted the HARPS instru-
ment on the 3.6-meter telescope at the La Silla observatory in
Chile. This has required that I extend our circle of conspirators
to include four others. I'm sure you understand. Perhaps, in the
end, I may also have to enlist a billiards champion to solve the
riddle. I will stay in touch.*
Your devoted grandfather,

Leonard

Yohaba reread the letter several times. Ever since she first met
him two and a half years ago, they had kept in close correspondence.
She knew her grandfather was Jesuit trained, brilliant, ascetic, dedi-
cated in the extreme, but especially sparing with words. Not that he
was taciturn, but when he spoke every word counted. She pondered
his reference to billiards.

Einstein had first plotted the trajectory of 182 Elsa on a billiard
table in 1955, and it was his photographs of billiard balls arranged
in star patterns that first alerted them to his apocalyptic prediction.
Also, according to the Russian agent who recorded her conversation
with Einstein in the hospital in Princeton, New Jersey, just before
he died, he had asked her if she knew that a slow massé shot curves
sooner, even though a harder shot spins faster.

Yohaba knew that Leonard, just like herself, was plagued by a
nagging sense that somehow there was a connection between the
riddle of 182 Elsa and Einstein's fascination with billiards. Well, they
would know in two days.

THE MEN CAME back around 8:30, just before dark, hit the showers,
and changed into clean clothes. Yohaba had showered earlier and
changed into tight jeans and a Grateful Dead T-shirt. As usual, her
hair hung long and loose around her shoulders, partially obscuring
the spiderweb tattoo on her neck.

Rulon's father said the blessing on the food. When he was done,
Rulon and Yohaba said "Amen," followed a split second later by

Boris, who was starting to get the hang of it. The table came to life and everyone reached across each other for the food.

In between bites, Rulon told Boris, "Everything you eat here, we grow ourselves. It's probably all organic even though we don't think of it that way. It's just food to us. But that's why it tastes so good. We let the beef graze free on the range. We own about six hundred acres, but graze the cattle for most of the year on about forty thousand acres of government land next to our property on the west. The vegetables were canned last year by me and Yohaba. If the world economy fell apart, we'd still make do. That's what I call freedom."

"In Russia the food's not so good," Boris said. "I think it is Yohaba's cooking."

Rulon laughed at the obvious flattery, but Yohaba took it at face value. "That's nice of you to say so. I can never tell with Rulon. He always compliments my cooking, but he and Dad would eat anything."

"Did you take care of it?" asked Rulon's father softly, looking down at his plate.

"What?" Rulon said.

"I asked if you took care of that skinhead business," he said sharply.

"Yeah."

"So, you called the police then?" said the old man.

"No," Rulon said. "You told me to take care of it, so I paid them a visit."

"You what!" Rulon's father snapped. "I told you to take care of it. What did you think I meant? So that's what happened to your face. I thought you'd been kicked by a steer. Jiminy Christmas. I just wanted you to call the police." He threw his napkin on his plate. "I'm checking on the horses. Thanks, Yohaba. It was a great meal as always." He got up, rinsed his plate at the sink, and left.

After he was gone, Boris said, "He never talks to me. Is he angry I am here?"

"No, not at all," Yohaba said. "He's checking you out. It's just too soon for talking. Give it a few days. You'll only get on his bad side if you don't work or don't go to church on Sunday."

It was 2:00 a.m. and Rulon couldn't sleep. He lay in bed staring at the ceiling in the dark. It had stopped raining just a few minutes ago, a quick, hard burst, and the fresh smell of wet, kicked-up dust wafted in through the open bedroom window. The night had turned cool, and he pulled the comforter over him and Yohaba. Now, as he lay there, he sensed she might be awake.

"Are you awake?" he asked.

"Of course not, Cowboy," Yohaba said. "I'm sleeping like a baby. Why should I be worried about humiliated Nazis burning the house down in the middle of the night?"

Rulon ignored her comment and turned on his side to face her. "I'm feeling like I did when we first met in Zurich. Remember? When everything was spinning out of control. I was just doing my job and all of a sudden things were taking weird turns. In all the years I lived in Zurich, I never had a physical confrontation with anyone, and then—"

"You mean never within the city limits."

"Yes, yes, never in the city limits," Rulon repeated, annoyed at being corrected. "Anyway, I get in a fight with your boss, then the Russians in the store, then Dmitri in your apartment, and the Russians again in the Desperado—all in one day. I'm feeling the same way now. This whole thing is spiraling out of control, but I really don't know what I could have done differently. I guess I should have just walked away and let them stomp Boris. Then I'd have two problems solved."

"No, you did the right thing," Yohaba said. "You had to do it." They lay there silent for a minute before Rulon spoke again.

"D'ya know what I miss right now? I miss Zurich."

Yohaba rolled on her side so she could see Rulon's face in the moonlight. "Me too," she said, sounding so enthusiastic that Rulon wondered if she wanted to go back. "What do you miss most?"

"I miss walking down the Bahnhofstrasse on a dark, cloudy day and stopping in the Honold bakery for some of their chocolate-covered orange slices."

"Dark or light chocolate?"

"Dark, of course."

"Then what?

"Then I'd weave my way around the winding, cobblestoned side streets to the Storchen Hotel and sit in the downstairs tearoom and have one of their expensive hot chocolates. Maybe two. I'd watch the tour boats go by on the river and the shoppers and trams on the other side. Just sit there. No hurry."

"I'm detecting a definite theme here."

"What?"

"Chocolate. But keep going. Where would you have dinner?"

"Well, that's a no-brainer. Either the Desperado or Tres Kilos, of course. Depending on where I was when the urge hit. A fajita plate. No, no, it would be a chicken tostada with a nacho plate appetizer and a liter of Sprite."

"Dessert? Let me guess. Chocolate cake topped with a dollop of Gruyère cream."

"Bingo."

"You are so predictable. But only you would reminisce about Zurich and want to go to a Mexican restaurant."

"I admit it sounds funny."

"Yeah, but just answer me one thing," Yohaba said. "Do you love me?"

"Uh-oh. What'd I do?"

"I gave up my nose ring for you."

"Hey, don't even go there. I never made a thing about your nose ring. I only said that people around here might mistake you for a bull if you wore one. That's all. It was your decision."

"Ha, my decision! I took off the ring as a symbol of my new life . . . and so you wouldn't brand me come roundup time."

Rulon touched the scar where her nose ring used to be. "You did sacrifice a lot," he said, bemused.

"You never take me seriously!" She slapped his hand away and Rulon chuckled. "You think this is a joke?" asked Yohaba. Without warning she jumped on Rulon and wrestled his hands down until she had him pinned. "Say 'Uncle,'" she ordered. "Say it."

He struggled unsuccessfully and gave up. "Uncle," he said.

Yohaba threw her head back and laughed victoriously.

After her laughter had subsided into a loving smile, she looked down at him in the dark, her long auburn hair forming a little tunnel around their faces. "Darlin', I find you *immensely* attractive."

"I'm not sure how I should take that," Rulon said, "but I refuse to quibble at a time like this." Yohaba rolled off and Rulon turned on his side to face her. They cuddled as close as Rulon's physique would allow.

"Darlin'," he said. "The day I married you was the happiest day of my life. You were made for me. God couldn't have picked me out a better wife. Yeah, I love you." He put his arm around her and Yohaba snuggled up close, wrapping her leg over his under the blanket, while they exchanged a long passionate kiss.

"There," said Yohaba when they pulled apart, "now that that's settled, let's get down to business. Tell me about Marseilles. What happened there? You said that's where you first met Freya. And I want to know what really happened back at the compound today as well. There was a lot of shooting going on. What the heck happened?"

"Which do you want first?"

"Oh, give me the compound. But wait, first I have to say, Cowboy, I was proud of you the way you gave it back to old Reichsfuhrer today. You had him on his heels with all that World War II history. If it had been a presidential debate, I would have voted for you."

"Nazis are so discredited, no one takes them seriously. It's easy to out-debate a Nazi."

"Yeah, the problem is their rhetorical tactics live on."

"What do you mean?" Rulon asked.

"All the fear. The scapegoats. Defining the enemy as trying to take away all that is decent. 'The Republicans are going to destroy the American way of life!' Or is it the Democrats? I forget sometimes. That kind of stuff. That all came from Hitler. He was brilliant at brand marketing. But let's not get sidetracked. What I really want to know is how come nobody got shot today at the compound? Those guys were shooting back too. And there were more of them than you. Right? How come you didn't get blown to smithereens? Explain that."

Rulon thought about it for a few moments. "Well, for starters, nobody got shot because Boris didn't shoot anyone. He's not dumb. But, darlin', I've told you before. Forget the movies and books. It's never like that. In real life most people are so scared in these situations, especially when they're caught by surprise, it's like they're in a different dimension. Their senses don't work right. Hearing disappears; they get tunnel vision; they freeze up; the brain overloads. They can't shoot straight. They forget to reload. They're so scared they get crazy. Boris knows the game. He's got a war face on him like you wouldn't believe. Almost as good as mine."

"Show me," Yohaba said. "Show me your war face."

"You saw it at CERN," Rulon said. "That's enough." Yohaba kept urging him, so he said, "Okay. Get ready." He put an index finger in each side of his mouth and pulled his cheeks apart. "There, that's my war face."

"You're no fun," Yohaba said.

"Anyway, those guys today weren't trained; they were just tough guys. It's different when bullets are flying and you got a psycho stomping around who you think just might be crazy enough to kill everyone and not care about the consequences. Which, by the way, is a pretty good description of Boris when he gets riled up." Rulon's speech picked up as his words rekindled the memory. "You have to be trained or else, at the very least, guns going off will make you flinch and not aim. The military has done studies and about a third of new soldiers in combat never fire their guns. For most people, it takes training and experience to overcome it."

"So, were you ever that scared?"

"Sure, lots of times, but for some reason I never got it as bad as some guys. I think it comes from my bull-riding days. Once you've ridden bulls for a living, you'd have to be strapped to a nuclear bomb to get the same effect. I mean, man, those bulls weren't just big, they were two-thousand-pound psychopaths."

"Bet you were really scared the first time."

"Nah, the first time I was too stupid to be scared. But, the second time, yeah, that's the one that had me digging deep."

"Okay, so why not make bull riding part of soldier training? Train guys that way."

"There'd be too few survivors, darlin', that's why."

Yohaba, playfully punched Rulon in the nose. "You think you're so macho. Now tell me about Freya and Marseilles."

Rulon rolled onto his back, interlocked his fingers behind his head, and took a deep breath. "There's not much to tell, really. Some Nazi thugs were up to something. It was Marseilles, so at first we figured it was drugs. But they were trying to infiltrate the university there, throwing money around. Somebody in the company got wind of it, and they sent me in."

"What was it?"

"Never did find out exactly. Most people assumed it was drugs, but I was never convinced. These guys had a heavy-duty ideology that was scary. Everything was going fine until our last meeting. We were in a sleazy bar and somehow they'd caught onto me."

Yohaba interrupted. "When they offered to buy you a drink, did you by any chance tell them it was against your religion?"

"No, of course not."

"Did they challenge you to a swearing contest and the best you could say was 'dang'?"

"No. They were all smoking, and I kept holding my breath." When Yohaba nodded as if taking him seriously, Rulon said, "No, no, no. I was ratted out by someone in the local police. Geez, woman. Can't you tell when I'm joking?"

Yohaba laughed. "I won't interrupt again. Now tell me."

Rulon continued, "I don't tell you these things because I don't like to scare you. Okay, this gets a little serious. There were four of us around a table and we're all talking calmly, and then a guy I didn't see comes up behind me with a garrote. Fortunately I had my jacket collar up, and he mostly caught that with the wire, but he knew what he was doing, and I was in big trouble. I remember the three guys at the table jumping clear of my kicking feet, and I'm seeing everybody's face real clear, even the customers', and no one seemed surprised or upset. Even the bartender didn't do anything, just stood there drying glasses."

"You probably weren't the first murder that day. But how'd you get out of it? I'll bet you were scared then?"

"Well, the adrenaline came on like opening the gates to Valhalla. But, no, I wouldn't say I was scared. Just amazingly focused. I got out of it by picking up the table and smashing it over my own head to get to the guy behind me. Luckily he was taller than me. The table broke in pieces, and he was knocked out." Rulon chuckled at the memory. "I was dazed but okay. I still had to deal with the others, though. You should have seen the looks on their faces. Boy, were they surprised when I got out of that one.

"To make a long story short, they all had knives. I tried fighting them off with chairs and tables and anything that wasn't nailed down. Just started throwing stuff. Even threw the bartender at them. They eventually had me cornered behind the bar. It wasn't going too good, but then I looked down and saw a toolbox. I picked it up to throw it, and the thing opened and Freya fell out. A short-handled Wilton Demolition sledgehammer. It was the happiest moment of my life."

"Really?" asked Yohaba. "The happiest?"

"Well, not the happiest ever. Just the happiest up till that point, darling. Now don't be a troublemaker."

"Got yourself out of that one, mister. Keep going."

"The neat thing about the hammer is that it breaks bones and people can't stand up or hold things no matter how much adrenaline they've got in their system. Once I had Freya, I cleared a path straight to the door and didn't look back. Oh, I got arrested, but the American Consulate bailed me out and patched things up. That's it."

"Was it like CERN? Was it bad like CERN? Did you . . . ?"

"No, babe. I didn't kill anyone. CERN was in a class by itself. Let's drop it."

After a long silence, Yohaba said, "I assume those guys are still in jail."

"No. They only got three years. All we could prove was conspiracy to commit some vague crime. We couldn't even make attempted murder stick. Everyone in the bar swore I started it. Anyway, if they didn't misbehave, they're back on the street by now."

"If that's what Nazi-boy was referring to, then you're in deep kimshi. Geez, Cowboy. What are we gonna do?"

"I don't think we have to worry," said Rulon. "I don't think they could even get through immigration. Heck, they assaulted a federal contractor. It's got to be on a record somewhere. And old Bernbailer is a nut case, but even he's not crazy enough to sell me out to foreigners. His own people would turn on him. Ed would warn me. There's nothing to worry about." With that, Rulon kissed Yohaba good night and rolled over to get some sleep.

Yohaba lay next to him on her back. After a long silence, she asked, "How much do they hate you?"

Half asleep, without opening his eyes, Rulon mumbled, "Oh . . . I'd say with the heat of a thousand suns. Yeah, that sounds about right . . ."

After a few minutes, Yohaba propped herself up on one elbow and looked at Rulon sleeping like a baby. Moonlight breaking through the clouds streamed in the window and made moving shadows on Rulon's face. Her love for him stirred and her heart gave a leap. She looked around the room and up at the ceiling trying to focus on something, anything, to keep from crying. She managed all right except for a single tear that ran down her face into the corner of her mouth.

The salty tear mixed with the lingering feel of Rulon's lips and, like an Oracle's potion, set her mind to racing and conjuring memories of their life together, the love and violence they had shared so far in equal doses, as if a cosmic scale needed to stay in balance. Yohaba gasped, suddenly overwhelmed with a portent of the future—this would not end well. She knew it without a doubt: there would be blood.

The moment of realization quickly passed and was replaced with a terrible calm. Looking down at Rulon's kindly face, she whispered, "What a coincidence. A thousand suns. That's exactly how much I love you, Cowboy." She rolled over onto her side away from Rulon and the moon shadows spilled across her face as she rested on her pillow. "But mine burn hotter," she said into the night.

CHAPTER 10

At the same time Rulon and Yohaba finally fell asleep, Helmut's cell phone number two rang as he was stuck in traffic coming into Zurich from the south.

That's odd, he thought. Only a few people knew his number, and the ones that did, also knew he was on a mission and had instructions not to call. He looked at the phone sitting on the passenger seat, listened to it ring, and debated whether to pick it up. The ringing stopped before he could make up his mind. Problem solved. What he craved most after a mission was anonymity.

He went back to being annoyed by the traffic, but only for a moment. The phone rang again. He hesitated briefly, looked at the number, didn't recognize it, then with an aggravated snatch, answered it anyway. It was a member of the brotherhood from Marseilles.

"I know this is not a good time, but there is someone you wish to speak to. He has been cleared. He's an American. A brother in arms. I think you know each other. He only speaks English. Stay on the line." A few clicks later, the Reverend Bernbailer came on.

"Do you recognize my voice?" Bernbailer asked.

"Yes," Helmut said.

"I hear you are looking for a fat American."

"Those are easy to find," Helmut said. "I'm looking for a particular kind of fat American."

"His name is Rulon Hurt, and he lives just outside Twin Falls, Idaho."

Idaho, thought Helmut. *No wonder we couldn't find him. He really was a cowboy.* He listened for five minutes, then hung up without agreeing to come.

In twenty minutes he'd be out of Zurich, heading toward the German border crossing near Schaffhausen. Another two hours and he'd be in Boblingen. Mission accomplished. The case on the floor pulled at his attention. He looked at his watch and calculated the flying time. If he remembered correctly, there was a 12:55 p.m. flight from Zurich to Chicago on Swiss Air.

It had been a four-year wait for Mr. Hurt. Twin Falls. Helmut never even heard of it. At least two flights to get there, maybe three. No. Can't do it now. Helmut smacked the dashboard. Deliver the virus first. Finish the job. There was too much at stake. But, oh, he could taste it—the spicy taste of revenge.

He drove on at a snail's pace. Delayed gratification was good for the soul, he told himself. He looked up and saw a sign for the main train station only a few blocks away. A little further on there was an electronic sign showing that the train station parking garage was full but there was room at the nearby Parkhaus Urania. Why not just park at the airport? *Add another layer*, he told himself. The best security was layered. Flying somewhere? Park at the train station. He berated himself. *Why am I even thinking this?*

His leg was killing him from the long drive. Those blasted rods. He cursed the American, his anger intensifying along with his pain and memory. What kind of a name was Rulon Hurt?

The Reverend had offered to supply the weapon, pick him up at the airport, and drive straight to the fat man's ranch. He could be back on a plane in four hours. Back in Zurich in forty-eight max. Plenty of time. If the fat man ran again, it could take another four years to find him. The guy knew how to hide.

Helmut weighed the pros and cons. The only rational choice was to finish the job and deliver the specimens. Helmut knew that with an iron certainty. There was no other decision possible. But even in the act of reaching that conclusion, Helmut's eyes narrowed and a small smile played across his lips. He swung his car out of traffic and made an illegal U-turn back to the Urania garage.

After he parked, he walked to the main train station carrying Protis and Gyptis with one hand and dragging his roller suitcase behind him. He passed through the cavernous center of the station, weaving through the crowds toward the clock tower at the far end, then down the escalator to the lockers. At the bottom, he turned left, then left again past the rows of lockers. There were forty-eight lockers in each row, twenty-four on each side, eight stacks of three each. The lockers were big enough for a medium-sized suitcase. He found an empty one at floor level in the far corner of the last row. The bio-carrier was an easy fit.

With one hand still on the handle, he considered what he was about to do. Five days. The professor had said the viruses would last for only five days. *If I'm dead, I won't care. If I'm not dead but can't make it back, I'll have Figeli break open the locker and complete the delivery. I'm covered.*

A notice on the door said the maximum rental time was seventy-two hours. After that the contents would be taken to the luggage reclaim office. Okay, three days then. He released his grip and closed the door. From a side pocket of his suitcase, he removed twenty-four francs in coins and inserted them into the slot of locker 253. He turned the key, felt and heard a solid, reassuring click, then slipped the key into his wallet.

A train to the airport was leaving in ten minutes. He would have to hurry. He'd call Bernbailer from a pay phone at the airport after he purchased his plane ticket. And as an added precaution, he would call Figeli too and ask a small favor. Layers.

"WHAT DO YOU THINK?" Mr. Goatee asked. At first Bernbailer didn't answer. They were at the compound, sitting in the ranch house kitchen. Bernbailer had just hung up from speaking with Helmut, who was standing in line at the Zurich airport Swiss ticket counter.

"I think our problems are over," he said after a moment's reflection. "This guy is a maniac. His father fought on the eastern front and spent nine years afterwards in a Russian work camp. He's a true believer."

"Useful?"

"Very useful. Our main problem will be keeping down the body count."

"He's coming then?" Mr. Goatee asked.

"Yeah. I told you he'd call back. I know my maniacs. But he's got a deadline. He needs to be back in Zurich within three days. Five at the absolute latest. I wonder what he's up to."

"Switzerland. Didn't they supply Germany with armaments during the war?"

"Yes, and before the war as well. Neutrality has its price," Bernbailer said.

"I heard you tell him we'd supply the rifle."

"Yes. The price of our neutrality." Both Bernbailer and Goatee got a laugh out of that. The conversation then turned to the logistics of the operation and who among the men would steal the weapon and where.

In the adjoining room, Ed backed slowly away from the kitchen door. He'd heard enough.

CHAPTER 11

THE RANCH—6:00 A.M. FRIDAY

When Rulon and Yohaba walked into the kitchen that morning, Boris was sitting at the table, already dressed, and showing no signs of going home. Rulon thought about it and something inside him said to let it be, so he did.

Rulon had three theories as to why Boris was sticking around. Either it was a personal vendetta against Nazis. Or else he was waiting for Rulon to heal up a bit so he could have another go at him. Or—and this was the one that Rulon sensed on some level was the most likely, but couldn't quite get a handle on—perhaps Boris was feeling protective toward them. Or maybe just toward Yohaba.

Yohaba was beautiful, scary smart, and had a natural sexiness about her, sort of a comfortable, long-legged, jeans and tight T-shirt sexiness that was all the more attractive because she seemed unaware of the effect, preferring instead to be one of the boys whenever she was around men. Plus, she had a wild, tough, but tender demeanor that Rulon knew a lot of the rough-hewn cowboys in the area were drawn to. Now that Rulon thought about it, why should a rough-hewn Rooskie react any differently? A few times Rulon watched the two of them together. Yohaba liked practicing her Russian, but there was something in Boris's eyes. It wasn't anything sinister, judged Rulon, but the light in them whenever Yohaba walked into the room was unmistakable. On the other hand, Yohaba had that effect on just about everyone. At church and within the local ranch community, the party didn't begin until Yohaba arrived.

Standing in the kitchen now, Rulon felt the hair on the back of his neck stand up when he looked at Boris. *Could this be the thin man's revenge? Stealing Yohaba away?* Rulon's thoughts boiled over for a heated instant, but he quickly simmered down. The thin man might have known the Nazis would be at the saloon, but he couldn't have known Rulon would take Boris home in his truck. A feeling came over Rulon to be at peace about this. He looked at Boris and his heart whispered, "Friend."

Rulon went back to his room and returned with a pair of brand-new jeans he'd bought a year ago and kept meaning to return. He'd gotten the size mixed up at the store, and they were too long in the legs and too small in the waist. He tossed them to Boris and told him to try them on. If he wanted to stick around, he'd have to earn his keep. He also gave Boris a denim shirt, an old belt, and a beat-up cowboy hat. Rulon's old boots were too big, so Boris had to stick with his well-worn Nikes.

"You're a regular bronco buster," Yohaba said later when she saw Boris in his new jeans. He tipped his hat to her like a real cowboy and got a smile in return.

"Burning daylight," Rulon said. There were some strays that needed rounding up and some fence that needed fixing. Rulon and Yohaba would do it from horseback, while Boris was given a forty-five-year-old Honda 305 fitted with off-road tires.

Rulon's father went off to plow a line along the north hills for a firebreak. He'd seen how the storms were coming in and how the wind was playing. He figured there'd be some lightning strikes and fires coming from that direction.

Working together all day, there were a few laughs and lots of sweat. Rulon didn't like to talk much when working. That was usually okay with Yohaba, but now that she had Boris to talk to, she spent her time bossing him around in Russian.

Throughout the day, as they searched the gullies for strays, Rulon kept his eye on Boris whenever he was with Yohaba. A few times he saw them talking seriously together, with Yohaba acting insistent and Boris looking away.

They had lunch under an old spruce tree sitting by itself in the middle of the grasslands about eight miles from the ranch. While they ate, Boris told them about Moscow. He said that in all the time he lived there, with all the daily traffic jams, only once did anyone ever pause to let him merge in. But the thing he hated most was when Putin left work at the Kremlin and the police blocked all the streets so he'd have a clear drive home.

"The spirit of the czars lives on," Rulon said when Boris was through with his story.

"Do you think Russia will ever go right wing?" Yohaba asked.

"Yes," Boris said. "The capitalists in my country grind the faces of the people. In your country too, only Americans too stupid to see it."

"Whoa, partner," Rulon said. "Capitalism isn't so bad. Look what it's done for America. A first-world country of over three hundred million people. You can't beat that."

"Your Theodore Roosevelt put capitalists in their place. Now, in twenty-first century, capitalists have upper hand again. Free trade have downside, eh? Now they move their capital anywhere in world where labor is cheapest. Whole world now bidding for same jobs. Supply and demand. Marx got some things right. Capitalists will squeeze wages out of people like big orange juice machine. Maybe America go right-wing too."

"Ratchet down the negativity," Rulon said. "You don't like Nazis. Okay, we understand that. But now you don't like capitalists either. Come to think of it, the Communists killed some of your family, so you must hate those guys too. So what is it? Is there anyone out there you do like?" When Boris didn't answer, Rulon prodded, "Well?"

"I like Yohaba," Boris said.

"Well, she's a capitalist," Rulon replied. "So what are you? A libertarian?"

Before Boris could answer, Yohaba said facetiously, "He sounds more like a Tea Party guy to me."

"What is Tea Party?" Boris asked.

"They're guys who don't like taxes or government interfering in their lives," Yohaba said.

"Ah," Boris said. "Anarchists. No, I don't like those either."

That got everyone laughing and the conversation shifted to the weather, and then to federal grazing policies—Rulon's two favorite subjects.

Later, under a warm sun poking through clouds, Boris took a snooze against the tree. Rulon and Yohaba let him sleep and went over to check on the horses.

"The man's a Ubangi tree worshipper," Yohaba said, looking back at Boris while she brushed Mister Fuzzy.

"He said he likes you," Rulon said as he brushed Clyde.

"I caught that. Still trust him?"

"Yeah, I do. Have I ever told you? I have great instincts about these sorts of things. I think there's a reason he's here. I never felt that about the other guys. They were just punching bags. I think somehow this one's gonna help us work things out with the thin man. I see you jawing at him quite a bit. Are you working on him to help us?"

"Dang, Cowboy," Yohaba half yelled, then caught herself. She looked quickly at Boris to see if he was still asleep. "Yes, yes," she hissed. "That's exactly what we were talking about. You're never going to say anything. Let me handle this. Okay?"

"Okay," Rulon said mildly. He picked up a pinecone and threw it at Boris. "Time to saddle up," he called.

They came in at dinnertime pushing fifteen head and three calves. It had been a good day.

After dinner that night, Yohaba went looking for Rulon. She found him in the barn, helping his father rebuild the tractor carburetor.

"Boris's car is gone," she said. "Did he say anything about going somewhere?"

There were tools laid out on the hood, and Rulon was bent over inside the tractor. "No. Maybe there's a Tea Party meeting some-where," he said, his voice coming out muffled from somewhere inside the engine compartment. "Dad," he said. "Can you hold the light a little closer, please?"

His father tugged on the extension cord to get some play and moved the lamp closer.

Yohaba blew a strand of hair out of her face. "Want to bet he's paying a visit to the Nazis?"

That got Rulon's attention. He stood up, his face speckled with oil. "Let's take a break," he said to his father.

The old man switched off the torch and said, "I want to hear this."

"I think Boris is up to something," Yohaba said. "Why else would he leave and not say anything?"

"Any of the guns missing?" Rulon's father asked.

"I don't think so," Yohaba said. "But who could ever tell? We have so many."

"Is the SIG in the cabinet?" Rulon asked. "He seemed partial to the SIG."

Yohaba was only gone for a minute."SIG's still there," she said when she returned. "What do you want to do? He's a big boy; should we just forget it?"

"Better go after him," said the old man to Rulon. "He's your Rooskie."

"Yeah," Rulon said heavily. But then perking up slightly, he said to Yohaba, "Darling, run and get the checkbook while I clean up, will ya? Maybe we can kill two birds with one stone."

CHAPTER 12

An hour later, Rulon and Yohaba were overlooking the Covenant of the Chosen compound from the vantage point of the same dusty hill they'd been on the day before.

"This is too weird," Rulon said as he peered through his binoculars. It was now a little before nine, cool and dark, with a thin cloud cover shading the rising moon. Below them, eight searchlights, arranged so their beams crossed, lit a compound teeming with people.

"Kind of like a cathedral," Yohaba said. "Weird. I wonder if the effect is intentional."

Rulon estimated there were at least a hundred cars and trucks parked around the perimeter fence, with dozens more coming up the dirt road in a steady stream of headlights. Attendants in Nazi armbands directed traffic at the crossroads and organized the parking. To Rulon's eye most of the several hundred people milling around in the compound looked like civilians. The true Nazis stood out. There were about a dozen in full regalia walking purposefully around, pointing and giving orders to twice their number of white-shirted minions.

At one end of the compound was a brightly lit stage facing several hundred metal fold-up chairs arranged in rows with a wide aisle down the center. Evenly spaced around the stage were muscular members of a ten-man security detail in full black Waffen SS uniforms with black visored caps, white belts, and red armbands with a black swastika inside a white circle. They stood frozen in place, their legs spread and their arms folded behind them, grim-faced, caps pulled low, eyes straight ahead.

Technicians wearing headphones checked the sound system, the words "*Testing, one, two three*" booming over the speakers. Inside the fence along one side was a long row of tables with cakes and pies. Couples coming in from the parking lot dropped off more desserts. Separate tables held kegs of beer and urns of coffee. Banners behind the stage and over the entrance gate screamed for attention: *White power. Power of the County. Save our Racial Nation.* Arc lights and blaring music.

"Not quite Berlin 1939, but an impressive turnout," Rulon said. "Must be Hug-a-Nazi Day or something. Sort of has the feel of an open house, don't ya think?"

"Or a church social."

"What's that music?" Rulon asked. "Shouldn't they be playing 'Ride of the Valkyries'?"

"It's OI music from a group called Storkraft," Yohaba said. When Rulon gave her a look, she said, "Hey, we all lead secret lives."

Rulon shrugged. "Strength through OI. Kind of catchy. But I still prefer Wagner."

"I think Wagner's been off the hit list ever since *The Blues Brothers.* It reminds too many people of Henry Gibson flying through the air in his Pinto. Quick. Who told Gibson: 'I've always loved you'?"

"Eugene Anthony," Rulon said, without taking his eyes from the binoculars. "You're gonna have to do better than that." He handed the binoculars to Yohaba. "I don't see him. See if you can spot him."

She scanned the crowd. "That's a negative, Cowboy. But look over there." She handed the binoculars back and pointed to a cleft in the hills a hundred yards outside the fence line on the far side of the compound.

"I wonder what they're up to," Rulon said. Hunkered down in a shallow ravine out of sight from ground level were several dozen seedy-looking men drinking beer.

"I wonder whose side they're on," Yohaba said. "They're not wearing uniforms. Maybe they're protestors. Oh, this could get interesting."

"Looks like a goon squad to me," Rulon said. "We're gonna have to get inside the compound. Geez, I'm gonna kill Boris. You brought the checkbook, right?"

They slid and stumbled down the brush- and rock-strewn hill, then walked the two hundred yards to the compound where they mingled in with the throng flowing through the gate. There was a sign on either side of the entrance that read, "No Jews Allowed. Free Beer for War Veterans."

"Shouldn't we be nervous?" Yohaba asked as they jostled along with the crowd. "What if someone recognizes you?"

"I'm in stealth mode," Rulon said. "I'm activating my cloaking device now."

"Listen to me, Cowboy. There is no such thing as . . ." Yohaba made quote marks with her fingers. ". . . *stealth mode.* Not one of the guys you beat up is going to say, 'Gee, he looks like that maniac Hurt, but nah, it can't be.' This is just more of your kooky spy school nonsense."

"Hold my hand in case I totally disappear," Rulon said.

"You are Jason Bourne in a clown suit," Yohaba replied with a groan. "You are not even remotely cloakable. Besides, you look like Quasimodo with your half-closed eye. Now, can we be serious? What do we do if they spot us? I don't want to be torn apart by a mob."

"You have a lot to learn, lady," Rulon said. "This cloaking stuff is real, and the best covert operators learn to develop it. Have you ever turned because you sensed someone watching you? Well, good snipers learn how not to activate that reflex in people. Anyway, to answer your question: No. With all these people around, they won't start anything . . . I don't think."

As they pushed through the gate, a uniformed attendant greeted Yohaba and handed her a flyer. She said to Rulon, "Did you hear that? He called me 'sister.' All this religion stuff is icky. They're messing with our minds."

Once inside, Rulon angled toward the fence to scrutinize the cars and trucks parked on the other side. "A lot of out-of-state plates.

Washington, Utah, Nevada, Montana, even Ohio."

Yohaba grabbed Rulon's arm and whispered, "This is starting to feel like *Gunga Din* when Cary Grant and Sam Jaffe infiltrated the Kali cult in the temple."

"Yeah, or like Donald Sutherland in *Invasion of the Body Snatchers* when he had to pretend to be one of the pod people," Rulon replied.

Yohaba didn't respond but turned to an older couple beside her. "Hello," she said pleasantly. "Where are you from?"

The woman, long gray hair and in her mid-fifties, answered, "We're from Sandpoint, about four hundred miles north of here, darlin'." She noticed Rulon's face, flinched, and said, "Ooo. What happened to your husband?"

"Oh, he's a professional bell ringer," answered Yohaba. "Occupational hazard." The woman looked at her strangely, but Yohaba kept on cheerfully. "You've come a long way. I sure hope it's worth the trip."

"We're just curious, but, frankly, no one seems to have any answers these days." Before Yohaba could respond, the couple got caught in a human eddy and swirled away in the crowd.

Rulon and Yohaba walked past the Quonset hut and saw the door had been replaced and the metal around it bent back into shape.

"Someone's been busy," Yohaba said.

A voice came over the microphone asking everyone to please take their seats. They worked their way to a couple of empty chairs near the back.

A few minutes after they sat down, just after 9:00 p.m., Mr. Goatee, in all his fascist glory, stepped to the podium and announced over the microphone that the Reichsfuhrer would be right out. Even from the back they could tell his face was swollen. Rulon and Yohaba hunched down sheepishly. After he left the stage, they sat back up, waited, and chatted to the people around them . . . and then waited some more. After twenty minutes, the man next to Rulon huffed angrily that the dang meeting was supposed to start at nine. Still, they waited.

Around them, other people were also fidgeting at the delay, talking sharply with each other, and looking angrily at anyone in a uniform. A few raised their hands and waved over an usher to complain.

Several men started to stand, but their wives or girlfriends stopped them with a hand on their arm. A few people did get to their feet, but instantly men in uniform rushed over while motioning to a minion to bring something to drink.

Eventually, the annoyance in the audience rose to a steady buzz, and like a sea under a gathering storm, the crowd stirred in constant motion—heads turning, hands raising, people getting up only to be coaxed into sitting back down. Even the hardcore Nazis were fidgeting and stealing looks at the blockhouse where Bernbailer was presumably unavoidably delayed. Finally the door opened, but out came only Mr. Goatee. Again he strode to the podium.

"The Reichsfuhrer appreciates your patience," he said, then walked off without even an explanation for the delay.

The jaws of the audience collectively gaped open as their eyes followed him in disbelief.

A man from the third row stood and yelled, "How much longer? Hey! Hey, you! How much longer?" But Mr. Goatee jumped off the stage and disappeared through the blockhouse door without looking back.

Another man further back hollered, "Most of us have driven for hours. The guy lives a hundred feet away, for crying out loud. What's the holdup?"

A bearded man in bib overalls tried pushing his way to the stage through the line of Waffen SS guards, but they held him back and convinced him to return to his seat. Someone threw a half-filled beer cup at one of the guards.

In the second row from the back, Rulon and Yohaba watched the scene with growing fascination.

"This is all choreographed, isn't it?" asked Rulon.

"I've got the same feeling—down to the guy throwing the beer at precisely 9:30. Cowboy, it just might be these guys aren't as dumb as they look. They're playing this crowd like a banjo. Hey, isn't that your buddy over there?"

Rulon followed Yohaba's eyes and saw Ed in a white T-shirt despite the chill, standing by the beer kegs, holding a beer, and talking to three of his skinhead friends.

Rulon caught his eye and jerked his head to say "c'mon over."

Ed surreptitiously nodded back, wrapped up his conversation, and sauntered over to sit in the chair behind Rulon. He looked around, then leaned forward into the gap between the two of them.

"Man, you are loco, just plain loco, to be here," Ed said with an angry scowl on his face. "I oughtta kick your rear end." Then leaning in closer, his expression turned friendly and he said in a whisper, "How'm I doing? Do I look angry enough to you? I gotta look angry in case anyone's watching." Ed's expression turned mean again and he poked Rulon repeatedly in the shoulder as he spoke. "You'll understand if I keep a mean look on my face and act like I'm threatening you. Hey, you're pretty solid there, partner. Been working out? Gosh, dang it, I spilled my beer. Am I looking mean enough?"

"You look downright vicious to me," Rulon said dryly.

"Me too," Yohaba said, smiling. "Can you ratchet it back a little? You're scaring me."

"Sorry, ma'am," Ed said with a burp, and then with a wink he added, "It's my irrepressible Aryan heritage coming out."

"Ed," Rulon said. "If you could keep from breathing your irrepressible Aryan beer breath in our faces, I would appreciate it."

"Sorry, guys."

"So why the wait?" Rulon asked. "What's fancy britches up to?"

"Ah," Ed said. "That's the secret sauce. Can't tell you the plan without giving away state secrets. Need-to-know basis only. We've been practicing for weeks."

"Geez, Ed," Rulon said. "How'd you ever let ol' Bernbailer bamboozle you into this?"

Ed laughed and held out his hand to say "wait," while he took a long sip of beer. He wiped his mouth with the back of his sleeve. "That's not how the world works, pardner. Nobody here is bamboozled except Bernbailer. He thinks we're following him, that he's lifted us up. But it's the other way around. The boys here did the lifting, if you know what I mean. He puts into words what people here are thinking and then they let him lead. We get the governments we deserve, folks. That's the one universal rule of politics. But me, I don't believe none of it."

"If that's the way you feel," Yohaba said, "why don't you leave?"

"Me? Leave?" said Ed, waving his fist in Rulon's face and looking fierce. "No, I'd miss the weekend paintball games too much. And, besides, some of these guys are my friends. But Rulon here, he's the one who should be leaving."

"What do you mean?" Yohaba asked suddenly anxious. "Is somebody planning something?"

"I . . . I . . . I . . ." stammered Ed, ". . . didn't say nothing. Nobody trusts me to tell me anything. They just keep me around to beef up the numbers."

"Ed, you're a terrible liar," Yohaba said. "Tell us. C'mon. Rulon's got more call on your loyalty than these idiots. C'mon."

Ed stole a glance at his three friends by the beer table, who were now eyeing him suspiciously. "Rulon here's gotta watch his back," he said as he started to get up. "It's not over between him and Bernbailer, not by a long shot. He's brought in a regular goose-stepping commando from Europe somewheres just to take care of him. Made a phone call and the guy grabs the first flight over." Ed looked around. "I don't see him, but somethin's up. He didn't come for the intellectual conversation."

"Let me guess," Rulon said. "He's getting close to fifty, muscular, dresses sharp, short hair, short beard, flattened nose, walks with a limp. Am I close?"

"Do you know him?" Yohaba asked Rulon.

"Yeah," Rulon said. "The infamous Helmut von Bock."

"Name sounds right," Ed said. "The description too, except for the flattened nose. He's got a perfectly wonderful nose. But, listen, I don't think it was smart of you to come. These guys aren't the 'turn the other cheek' types. They're more the 'shoot you in the back' types, if you know what I mean. And the Kraut, he's one scary dude. Even the hard cases here shy clear of him." Ed looked over at his buddies again and didn't like what he saw. "Listen, Rule, I've gotta knock your hat off or this won't look convincing. Please can I knock your hat off?"

"No," Rulon said.

Yohaba gave Rulon an elbow in the ribs. "Let him do it. He's earned it."

"Please," Ed asked humbly.

Rulon sighed, and Ed knocked his hat off. Rulon caught it before it hit the ground.

With a final furious grimace and a wink, Ed said good-bye and went back to the beer table and his suspicious friends.

After Ed left, Yohaba put her arm around Rulon's wide shoulders and pulled herself closer. "Cowboy, can we please go to the police now? This is out of control."

"Yeah," Rulon said. "I think you're right. Tomorrow. For sure."

"Let's go, then. Let's get out of here."

"Darling, this is the safest place we can be. They wouldn't do anything here. Settle down, I want to see what happens."

For a full fifteen minutes more, the irritation, the annoyance, the growing sense of sheer outrage continued to build until finally, just when it seemed a single shout of "Let's get 'em, boys" would have sent the entire crowd, men and women, charging the stage to rip it apart with their bare hands, Bernbailer finally made his appearance.

A single spotlight picked him up as soon as he left the blockhouse, and the other spotlights went slowly dim. He was dressed in black like his guards, with the same black swastika on his left arm. The only difference was that he wore a black belt with an ornate scabbard and knife dangling on a chain. In his hand was a manila folder.

He walked to the edge of the stage, every angry eye upon him but stopped short of stepping up. Instead, he spent another full minute chatting to one of the guards while the heckling grew ever more personal and vicious and the guards had to form a cordon around him for protection. Many in the audience were involved now, either yelling something, or fuming to the people around them. Some were hit with spray from thrown cups, which only added to their irritation. Strangely, almost no one actually persisted in pushing past the guards to leave.

"I know we're being manipulated," whispered Rulon to Yohaba, "but even I'm straining to keep from running up there and slugging the guy."

Reichsfuhrer Bernbailer concluded his conversation with the guard and stepped onto the stage. But before he'd gotten halfway to the podium, he did an about face and retraced his steps back to the same guard to continue the discussion. Now the crowd was a raging beast. One particularly furious voice rang out a few rows away. Rulon turned and recognized the big mouth as one of the Nazis from the bar fight.

"Hey, I know that guy. He's a Nazi," Rulon said. "This doesn't make sense."

"Au contraire, I think it does," Yohaba said. "Don't get involved."

Now the Reichsfuhrer was back on stage, the Waffen SS squad forming a half-circle behind and beside him as he walked. When he reached the podium, he stood behind it stiff and awkward, looking not at the crowd but down, shifting his weight from foot to foot, and shuffling the papers he'd brought.

"What's he doing? What's the idiot up to?" Rulon asked out loud to no one in particular.

Yohaba looked over at him and said, "Down, boy. Just watch."

For a full thirty seconds more, an eternity in the insanity prevailing, Bernbailer quietly fussed with his papers, not even lifting his head. Finally he stopped and while still looking down, began talking, so low at first that no one could hear him. His lips moved; people leaned forward to hear. Some of the men who just a few seconds ago were screaming for blood were now yelling for the audience to hush down.

Only as the crowd fell silent did Bernbailer begin to raise his voice, still quiet at first, then rising slowly, punctuated now and again with a benign hand gesture. His voice continued to rise, and his movements grew increasingly emphatic, his hand keeping time with short downward thrusts like swinging a hammer. The crowd was completely silent; the darkness, except for the spotlight, was almost complete, like a church; the podium like an altar.

He raised one hand to heaven, a priest making an offering. The congregation was observant but not reverently so; their earlier outrage channeled in a new direction, like a stampede being turned, or like a train taking a curve too fast, bending to a new direction, the tension between the audience and speaker teetering on one wheel. Their anger mixed with wonder to be molded and worked like a lump of clay, exposed now, pliant and useful.

He grew angrier, his eyes aflame, hammering home each point with his fist, adding a flourish, jerking his hand up and outward like a music hall conductor. The crowd stirred to life. Shouts of agreement rang out as in a tent revival. His head thrashed, one finger pointing upward, the other hand still pounding out his points.

"WE BELIEVE," he roared, "in the preservation of the white race as demanded by God. WE BELIEVE our racial nation has a right and is under obligation to preserve itself and its members. WE BELIEVE there is a battle being fought this day between the children of darkness and the children of light. WE BELIEVE that the present world problems are a result of our disobedience to divine law. There are those out there who would destroy EVERYTHING you hold sacred, EVERYTHING you believe in. NOTHING that is good would survive. YOU and YOU and YOU" —pointing to people in the crowd—"your CHILDREN will be reduced to servitude. TO SERVITUDE. But, today, now, you have a choice. You can bury your head in the sand or you can STAND UP like righteous men and women and FIGHT, FIGHT, FIGHT for what you believe in as an offering to—"

Bernbailer stopped, looking puzzled, and craned his neck to see something happening behind the audience. There was a commotion by the gate and the crowd, following Bernbailer's gaze, turned as one to see. The compound lights came on.

As Rulon and Yohaba looked, Yohaba whispered, "Oh, this is too brilliant."

The goon squad they'd seen in the bushes were clustered in the back arguing loudly with the security guards.

"Jiminy Christmas," Rulon said. "I recognize some of those guys from yesterday in the trucks."

"Are you sure?" Yohaba asked. "You were pretty far away."

"I saw 'em through the scope. I know what I saw."

As they watched, Mr. Goatee strode into the argument and tried reasoning with the intruders. For his trouble, he was roughly pushed to the ground. A member of the audience helped him to his feet while Goatee's comrades continued to argue with the new arrivals.

"Right wing fanatic!" screamed one of the goons at Bernbailer. "Skinhead clown!" screamed another as he tried pushing his way through a phalanx of Nazis. He was wrestled back but struggled to break free, screaming, "Losers" and "Nazi bitter ender," and making obscene gestures through the tangle of arms.

Bernbailer shook his head sadly. "No, sir," he said into the mike. "I am not the loser, and we are not bitter. We are simply awake. Wake up, my young friends. Do not speak words you will only regret when you are older."

A guard and one of the goons got in a pushing match, and the Nazi went flying into the audience. Again, he was helped to his feet by members of the crowd. The Nazis were getting the worst of it. Now the goons spread out, trying to outflank the security. Everyone watched in silent fascination.

"We don't want any trouble," Bernbailer said. "We respect your right to express your views, but, please, no violence. There are civilians here."

His words only fueled the anger of the interlopers, who erupted in a renewed torrent of abuse. Parts of the meeting turned into a rugby scrum with the Nazis showing restraint and the hecklers straining to get past them to the stage. A goon took a swing, missed his target, and hit a bystander. The man's wife stood up and swung a purse at the assailant. She got pushed, and some of the audience joined in to help.

With a roar, the goon squad broke through the first security layer and ran down the center row, tripping over feet and accidentally knocking people out of their chairs. Men got up to defend their wives. Entire sections of the crowd were fighting back, pushing and throwing punches of their own.

Rulon watched as pockets of Nazis and civilians fought back to back against the mob trying to get to the stage. In the scuffles, women got bumped and pushed, and invariably a single Nazi would rush to their aid only to be set upon by the mob. Boyfriends and husbands bravely rose up. Punches were connecting, and a half-dozen melees broke out in front of the stage.

One huge ruffian made it all the way to the podium, only to be decked by a right uppercut from Bernbailer and sent falling backward into the first row of chairs.

"Where did that come from?" Rulon said. "Yesterday the guy couldn't punch his way out of a wet paper bag."

"Protect the women!" Bernbailer shouted, his deep voice booming over the mike. Then bellowing, "Follow me, men!" he led his SS security detail off the stage to plunge into the thickest part of the battle.

Thirty minutes later, a sweating, rumpled, exhausted Bernbailer was standing on the stage again with a microphone in his hand, finishing up his closing speech.

"And so we have come together on this day to prove symbolically that we are more than a collection of individuals striving one against another, that none of us is too proud, none of us too high, none is too rich, and none too poor, to stand together before the face of the Lord and of the world in this indissoluble, sworn community and this united nation. Thank you all for staying—from the bottom of my heart, I thank you."

Bernbailer smiled wearily and sat down on the edge of the stage, still holding the mike. He tried adjusting his jacket's torn lapel but gave up with an amused chuckle. In front of him sat over a hundred people in a makeshift semicircle of folding chairs. Behind the crowd, skinheads were picking up the other chairs and stacking them neatly in the backs of four pickup trucks. The cake tables had been overturned in the fighting. Three men worked together to hose them down and clean things up. A couple of dogs nosed around in the mess.

Rulon and Yohaba sat in the last row, hanging around to give Bernbailer the check for the tires. Bernbailer spotted them and, to Rulon's surprise, gave a friendly wave.

Rulon started to wave back and caught himself. *I will not.*

Bernbailer lowered his hand and focused again on the crowd before him. "Thank you, thank you," he said with a look of genuine gratitude. "If you think this didn't turn out the way you expected, well, you're not the only one." He fiddled with his ripped lapel again but let it flop down in an obvious show of pointlessness, getting a laugh from the crowd. "Is anyone here hurt?" he asked suddenly. "Does anyone need some help? Some ice maybe?"

Bernbailer looked around earnestly, making eye contact with everyone in the audience. "Gruppenfuhrer," he called loudly. "Bring some ice and towels. Please, everyone, raise your hand if you need anything. There's a corpsman around here somewhere, though I suspect he has his hands full right now." Another ripple of laughter from the crowd.

A few hands went up. A corpsman appeared from the wings and weaved among the chairs to their assistance. He wore an authentic WWII German corpsman's uniform complete with gray tunic and two black leather pouches on his belt.

While a half dozen of his men walked among the chairs helping people, Bernbailer told a story about a meeting he had with a special agent from the FBI's Salt Lake City Division Boise office to discuss a police harassment issue.

". . . and so he tells me that my problems were nothing compared to Martha Stewart's." People leaned forward at his words, listening intently, chuckling good-naturedly. "It turns out he was working in the FBI's Manhattan headquarters when Martha Stewart came in to be fingerprinted. He says he couldn't believe when he saw her that this was really Martha Stewart. She didn't look anything like in the magazines. She's not wearing makeup and looks like she'd just gotten off the red-eye from LA. But then again she was having a really bad day." This time real laughter. "But then after she's finger-printed the stuff they give her doesn't quite get the ink off her fingers and nobody knows what to do. And this FBI agent is still thinking this can't be Martha Stewart." Bernbailer paused.

He had them now. Everyone was smiling and into the story. "But then she pulls a lemon and a small spray bottle of seltzer water out of her purse and proceeds to scrub her fingers clean. And while she's doing this, she gives the entire office a lecture on which lemons are the best to use and which brand of seltzer water works best for clean-ing off fingerprint ink. Identity confirmed."

The audience erupted with laughter at the punch line. All the irritation at having to wait for his appearance, all the mounting frus-tration, and then the anger when the fighting broke out, all had evaporated, and what was left was a pleasant, good feeling at the feet of the Reichsfuhrer. Brothers-in-arms.

"Groan," Yohaba said. "That's a Conan O'Brien joke."

The gathering slowly broke up. Most put their names on the mailing list. Yohaba saw the middle-aged couple from Sandpoint get up to leave, and she walked over.

"Hi there," she said. "Are you both okay?"

"Oh," said the woman. "The old hubby had to defend my honor

a few times. He's my hero tonight." She hooked her arm through his and squeezed tight. He looked humbly proud.

"It was all staged, you know," Yohaba said. "Those guys that broke things up were Nazis themselves. My husband recognized some of them. They were just trying to get your sympathy."

The couple walked away unconvinced.

After the crowd had mostly dispersed, Bernbailer broke free from a small circle and walked over to Rulon and Yohaba.

"You've got a lot of hard bark on you, Mr. Hurt," said the Reverend good-naturedly. "Didn't expect to see you here today."

"Here's the check I promised," Rulon said.

Bernbailer took the check and held it up to the light. "Looks real," he said. "You're not only a man of action, Mr. Hurt—you're a man of your word."

Rulon and Yohaba started to walk away, but before they took two steps, Bernbailer asked, "What did you think of our little show tonight?"

Rulon turned and started to say something but stopped himself. He took off his cowboy hat and fussed with the sweatband. Finally, he set the hat back on his head and said, "I've seen more realistic fights on *SmackDown*. Next time you need to bring in your hired hecklers from another coven."

Bernbailer's eyes stabbed at Rulon with pure hate. "Perhaps next time I will," he said with an amused smile.

Rulon and Yohaba walked off.

As Bernbailer watched them go, a late-model Chevy pickup drove in through the gate. The driver did a double take when he saw Rulon but didn't stop. He pulled up alongside Bernbailer.

"Why didn't you call?" Helmut demanded. "I spend half the night staking out his ranch and Hurt is here all the time." He put the car in reverse. "I'll be back."

"You can't," Bernbailer said, reaching in through the window to grab the steering wheel. "Too many people saw him here. If anything happens on the way back from the meeting, they'll know it's us."

"They'll know it's you anyway," Helmut said.

"Probably. But that doesn't matter as long as I have an alibi. If you kill him now, I don't."

"Take your hand off the steering wheel," Helmut commanded, slowly enunciating each word. When Bernbailer didn't react, Helmut said, "Or after the cowboy, you're next."

Bernbailer correctly concluded that Helmut wasn't kidding and let go. "Please," the Reverend said. "I only saw them myself a few minutes ago. Please. It would destroy everything we've accomplished tonight."

Helmut did a quick calculation of plane connections, locker cleaning schedules, and virus shelf life. He turned off the engine and got out of the truck. In his hand he held a .338-378 Weatherby Magnum with a sling, artificial stock, and Shepherd PE1 scope. Perfect for elk and two-legged game.

"I can take one more day," he said and threw Bernbailer the keys. "It needs gas. Fill it up." He slung the rifle over his shoulder and walked off toward the house.

In the bedroom he'd been assigned, Helmut laid the rifle against the wall and sat down on the bed. He was dusty, tired, and fuzzy-headed from jet lag. He extended his hand. It trembled slightly. Not good for a sniper. He waggled his hand and tried again. Still no good. He stood up and looked in the dresser mirror. His eyes burned and watered from lack of sleep and from lying in the dirt for hours surrounded by pollen factories disguised as bushes and cheat grass.

He needed to get some sleep but couldn't. Jet lag. Every year it got worse. He took off his shirt and studied himself in the mirror. A thick, white scar from an old knife wound ran from right shoulder to heavily muscled pectoral. His short, pewter-colored beard hid the battle scars on his face. He looked at his hands, gnarled from a thousand fights, then cupped his face and dragged his hands slowly down his cheeks, stretching the skin. He looked in the mirror again and smirked at the sight of his only redeeming feature—a perfect, surgically constructed nose.

While he was debating whether to lie down or take a shower, a cell phone rang from inside the suitcase next to his bed. He fished phone number four out of his bag, looked at the number, and swallowed hard before answering.

"Where are you?" said an ancient, rasping voice in German.

"I'm in the US with Bernbailer. In Idaho."

"Is this a joke?"

"When did I ever joke, Father?" Helmut said. "Don't worry. The picnic basket is safe. Hold on." Helmut stood up and grabbed his wallet off the nightstand. He pinned the cell phone between his shoulder and ear and rifled through his wallet until he found the locker key. "If anything happens to me, it's in a locker in the Zurich Hauptbahnhof—253. I will be there to pick it up in twenty-four hours." Silence on the other end. "If I'm not there by this time tomorrow, then have someone break it open and get it. If it's not there, it will be in the luggage reclaim office."

"Do you have a reason for this diversion?"

"Father," Helmut said, "it's the fat American. Bernbailer found him. It has been four years. I couldn't take a chance of losing him again."

The old man exploded in fury. "You risk everything for THIS!" he shouted. "FOR A PERSONAL VENDETTA!"

While he vented, Helmut sat down on the bed, listening silently. He hated disappointing his father, but knew, after the anger always came the sorrow. At least when dealing with his only son.

A final furious rant then a long silence. Helmut's father at last spoke up again, this time quietly and sadly. "You risk much, my son, my only son. I would have sent a team in your place. I would have sent ten teams. You are my blood, my heir. A personal vendetta? Could it not have waited?"

When Helmut didn't answer, his father asked. "How long has Bernbailer known about this man?"

"He says he just found out."

"Do you believe him?"

Helmut chose his words carefully, for Bernbailer's sake. "He's been helpful."

"I'm sure he brought up the reward."

"Yes. I'll let you know when to send it to him. I'll be back in Zurich in twenty-four hours. Don't worry. But remember: 253, just in case."

"Perhaps I should send a team to get it now."

"No, without the key, you'd have to break into the locker. It's not worth the risk at this point. These are the Swiss. The package is safe. There is a deadline though. Today is Saturday. The bio-carrier can only preserve them for 120 hours. That would be roughly 6:00 a.m. Tuesday. This is very important. The specimens must be at the Boblingen lab by no later than 6:00 a.m. Tuesday, or else in a recharged bio-carrier. If I'm not there in twenty-four hours, do what you have to do."

"Vengeance consumes us both, my son. I cannot blame you for being like your father. But be careful. I had influence within the French judicial system to reduce your sentence after Marseilles, but in America I would only have bombs and blood . . . and the virus to use as a threat."

"I know."

"Yes, you know. But still you risk yourself." As he talked, the father's voice rose with pride. "You are an Aryan in every drop of your pure blood. You are invincible. Take care of your business with this cowboy, then quickly come back. Crush him, my son. Crush him with an iron heel. Do not let him live another day, then come back. I have need to lean on your strong arm and walk together again through my garden. There was a time when our people almost conquered the world. This is but a little thing. Call me again as soon as you have killed the fat American. Heil Hitler, my son."

After talking with his father, Helmut always felt uplifted, as if he could do anything. His father had that effect on people. Helmut disassembled the cell phone and went to take a shower.

CHAPTER 13

AT THE COMPOUND, 10:30 P.M.

Rulon and Yohaba trudged silently up the hill back to the truck. After a minute, Yohaba said, "You really can't change people, can you?"

She walked nimbly between the bushes, despite the steepness of the hill and three-thousand-foot altitude, her breathing only slightly elevated. Since she'd given up smoking two years ago, she'd taken up running to burn off the jitters. Rulon plodded determinedly behind her, breathing hard.

He stopped to answer and rested with his hands on his knees. "No," he gasped. "That's something they have to do themselves. What brought this up? What have I done now?"

"No, no. It's Ed. I was just thinking about him. He's a sad fellow, don't you think?"

"Yeah. I gave him a working over once in high school. Did I ever tell you that? I outweighed him by sixty pounds. Gosh, I was a jerk back then."

Yohaba said, "I thought what he said about Bernbailer was pretty insightful. That thing about Bernbailer being the one who was fooled. It made me think about Hitler. You know how people always say that Hitler and the Nazis tricked the Germans? I don't think so, I think—"

Rulon cut her off. "C'mon. We gotta keep going."

Yohaba picked up her train of thought as they started moving again. "I'll bet it was like Ed said. Hitler just told the people what they wanted to hear. Think about it. Hardly any of them were against the war when it started."

"Except Johann Elser," Rulon said.

"Who's he?"

"He was a carpenter who tried to kill Hitler in '39."

"Just like von Stauffenberg."

"No. Von Stauffenberg did it in mid '44. By then the Germans hated Hitler because he was losing, not because they disagreed."

"Wow, Cowboy, that's pretty cynical. Do you have something against Germans?"

"No. Do you?"

"No, because this Nazi thing is not about Germans. It's about people. You replicate those conditions with any group of people: bad economy, lost pride, lies up the yin-yang by a master communicator. Mix in some crackpot religious flattery, and that's what you get. It was all a plan. A lot of politicians use his methods today and people don't even realize it. Probably the politicians themselves don't even realize it."

The hill got steeper and they walked in silence until they were at the truck on the other side of the crest.

Rulon sat on the tailgate to rest, took his hat off, and wiped his brow with a bandanna. "Tyler has a professor in one of his communications classes who's published papers on Hitler. You wanna talk to him?"

"The professor, yes. Tyler, no."

"He's family, get over it. If I can handle your brother, you can handle mine."

"Mine saved our lives," Yohaba said. At her words, they both went quiet. No matter what the situation, they were always one slip of the tongue away from being back at CERN.

The seconds ticked by with their thoughts unspoken. Then, without a word, they both broke out of their reverie at the same time and smiled at each other.

Rulon said, "I want to dig into this. I want to describe to somebody what happened tonight and have them explain it. How about tomorrow?"

"It's Saturday."

"Teachers work on Saturday. I'll get the number from my brother."

"Sure. Right after you call the police. Right? The overseas Nazi? Life? Death? Remember?"

"Yes, of course. I'll call the professor right after I call the police. First thing in the morning. In fact, I'll call the police now." Rulon tried his phone but he couldn't raise a signal.

On the way home, he tried again and got through to the police dispatcher, who added his complaint to the next day's squeal sheet. She said someone would swing by tomorrow afternoon after the downtown pet parade.

"I'm surprised they're even coming," Yohaba said. "Wacko, middle-aged Nazis coming to Twin Falls to assassinate one of the ranchers. I *know* it's true, and even I find it hard to say without laughing."

Rulon next called his brother who, as expected, was sitting in a bar. The lucky part was it was a late-night social with his communications class, and his professor was sitting across the table from him. Tyler put the professor on, and Rulon explained about the event they'd just attended, telling her just enough to whet her curiosity. The professor was moderating a debate the next day on the Boise State University campus and could meet them at 7:00 a.m. in her office in the Communications Department building.

"There. Satisfied?" asked Rulon after he hung up.

When they drove into the front yard, Boris's mangled Ford Escape was back in its usual parking place. The dogs came bounding over to greet them. Rulon got out of the truck and tussled with them playfully before walking over to the SUV. He looked inside, then grimaced at Yohaba and shook his head. He leaned through the rolled-down window and came out holding up half a six-pack of beer by the plastic rings.

"At least now we know where he was," he said.

"At least he had the good sense not to bring it into the house," Yohaba replied.

The next morning, they were up by 4:30. The first thing Yohaba did after splashing some water on her face was to check her email for messages. June 4. This was the day Einstein predicted the asteroids would collide. Nothing from her grandfather. It was lunchtime in Geneva. Maybe still too early.

By five, they were pulling out of the driveway after writing a note for Rulon's father and Boris telling them they'd be back before noon. Rulon sped past the north pasture with one hand on the wheel and the other clutching one of Yohaba's massive breakfast burritos, with Yohaba snuggled up against him, listening to her iPod. Boise was a hundred and thirty miles away. Their headlights disappeared around the hills to the north just as another truck with its lights off came up the old mill road from the east.

Helmut parked the truck out of sight in a hollow, then walked with his rifle over the hill to the same small, fallen-down spruce where he'd waited the evening before. It was cold, and he was stiff and jet lagged. The borrowed parka did its job, but his shoes were the same ones he'd worn in Marseilles and their smooth soles couldn't grip the dirt and rocks. He half stumbled, half slid into position after a quarter-mile walk, lay down on his stomach, laid the barrel of the rifle across the tree trunk, and adjusted the scope. There were lights on in the house. He settled into a tolerably comfortable position three hundred yards away and waited.

After fifteen minutes, one by one the house lights went off, and the outside lights came on, followed a few ticks later by the front door opening. Helmut watched through the scope as the same old man he'd seen the day before stepped onto the porch.

The old rancher stood and stretched while the two dogs capered around him. He walked across the yard into the barn, the dogs close behind. Helmut followed him with the scope, its crosshairs held steady on a point just above his ear.

Helmut lay there in the dark and thought about the two viruses and how he had jeopardized the entire mission by coming to Idaho. And didn't care. He wondered if he'd have a problem making his plane connections back to Zurich. And didn't care. Despite his initial anger, his father understood and that was all that mattered. His father had always been there for him. Had been his guide and his strength ever since Helmut could remember. It was just him and his father now. No more mother. No other children. No grandchildren. Helmut held out his hand. Steady as a rock.

I'm a predator, he said to himself. *I have the timeless patience of the hunter*. He settled down to wait.

CHAPTER 14

Rulon pulled into the huge BSU stadium parking lot a few minutes before seven. It was nearly empty, and Rulon angled straight across the lot to a space on the side near the campus buildings.

After turning off the engine, Rulon took a deep breath. "Ah, the memories," he said. "Every time I come back I brush 'em away like flies."

"You must have been quite the campus hero with your wrestling and hammer throwing," said Yohaba.

"I guess so. But one of my strongest memories is the evening I passed my thesis defense for my communications degree and knew I was going to graduate. I walked around the campus afterward for a couple of hours soaking in all the feelings and sights, knowing I was going to miss this."

"What was your thesis on?"

"It was titled, 'How the Persuasive Property of Identification Is Used in Beer Commercials to Attract Alcoholics.' "

"Your thesis was on beer commercials!" Yohaba exclaimed sarcastically. "Wow, sounds like a tough major. What was your grade point average?"

"Groan," Rulon said. "Grade point average is not a good measure of what you learn or how smart you are. A university education is so much richer than that."

"That's wonderful," Yohaba said. "Now tell me your grade point average."

"Only small minds focus on grade point averages," continued

Rulon with dignity. "At Boise State I learned good study habits, self-discipline, and critical thinking. All invaluable traits that have served me well in my years since graduation. Plus I was a student athlete."

"You're stalling. Stomp your foot twice if it was two-something."

That did it. Through gritted teeth, Rulon said, "For your information, I had a three point seven average and carried a dual major—history and communications. And I was an academic all-American my last two years. Geez, woman. Starting extra early this morning, aren't we?"

"Oh, don't be so sensitive," Yohaba said cheerfully. "Getting personal information out of you is like pulling teeth."

Among the handful of vehicles in the lot was a white Nissan pickup ten spaces away. There was movement in the pickup, and, for the first time, they noticed there was a short, middle-aged woman inside. They stopped talking and watched as the squat, heavy, fire-plug of a woman, dressed in jeans and an orange BSU windbreaker, got out holding a cup of coffee, a purse, and a leather briefcase stuffed with papers. Once out of the car, she set her briefcase down to search her ample purse, then patted every one of her pockets until finally finding her keys. She locked the truck door and marched toward the campus.

"Sort of has the look of an anti-Nazi communications professor," Rulon said. They got out and headed after the woman, picking up their pace until they were only a few feet behind.

"Excuse me," Rulon said. "Are you by any chance Professor Freling?"

The woman whirled around, spilling half her coffee.

"Don't sneak up on me like that," she said with relief when she saw who they were, but more important, who they weren't.

Rulon noticed her free hand slowly withdrawing from inside her purse and suspected she was packing.

"You're Tyler's older brother, aren't you? And you must be Yomama."

"Umm . . . actually it's Yohaba," Rulon said. "She's Swiss."

Introductions were made as they walked past the tennis courts toward the Communications Department building on the east side of campus.

"You have to excuse me. I'm on a hair trigger these days," Freling explained as they walked. "Not a month goes by when I don't get a death threat. Ever since I've been writing articles on neo-Nazis, it's been like that."

Rulon said, "Up until a few days ago, I thought they were just a bunch of losers sitting around tattooing each other."

"It used to be like that around here," the professor agreed, "but ever since Bernbailer moved into the area, they've become more organized and deranged. They're up to something."

They reached the communications building, and Freling unlocked the front door. Her private office was at the top of a creaky flight of stairs. It was small and cramped with a single, large casement window that looked directly into a thick tree and across a grassy area to two other buildings. In the middle of the room was a worn wooden desk with an open laptop, piles of papers and a cheap roller chair. Bookshelves filled with books lined the available walls from floor to ceiling. In one corner was a glass case holding a potato the size of a football. Not the biggest potato Rulon ever saw, but impressive.

Freling removed a stack of papers and folders from two padded folding chairs and arranged the chairs in front of her desk.

Once everyone was settled, she said, "Now, tell me your story. What happened at the meeting last night?"

Yohaba looked at Rulon, and he nodded. *Go ahead*. While she described the evening, Freling scribbled furiously on a notepad, interrupting only occasionally with a question.

When Yohaba was finished, the professor looked over her notes. After a few moments, she said, "This is beautiful. This is classic Nazi event staging. Hitler believed that staging these huge events was important because it gave people a sense of community and made them feel protected."

Rulon nodded. "We suspected it was all planned. Some of the things we could figure out, other things just seemed odd, but it was clear everything had a purpose. It felt incredibly manipulative, but whatever it was, it worked."

"Yes." The professor took off her wire-framed glasses and tapped her chin absently as she rechecked her notes. Having verified her conclusion, she continued firmly. "No doubt about it. It was definitely all planned. From the searchlights forming arches all the way down to the—what did you call them—oh, yes, the goon squad. Down to the goon squad showing up. It was right out of the manual. "Let me show you."

Freling rolled a few feet to the nearest bookcase. "*Mein Kampf* wasn't completely translated into English until 1939," she said as she searched the shelves. "When it was, a genius named Kenneth Burke analyzed it from a communications perspective. Ah, here it is." She rolled back to her desk with a book and handed it to Yohaba.

"*The Philosophy of Literary Form* by Kenneth Burke," Yohaba said. "Interesting title."

"Turn to page 191, and you'll find an absolutely brilliant article," said the professor.

As Rulon looked over her shoulder, Yohaba turned the pages until she came to a chapter titled, *The Rhetoric of Hitler's Battle*.

"How fascinating," she said.

Professor Freling tapped the page with her finger. "It's all in there. Hitler was full of hate and eventually mad, but he was also a communications genius. He was so good, it was scary. But what's even scarier is that his techniques are used today and people don't even realize it."

"People don't learn, do they?" Yohaba said.

"Not true," said the professor, "but the lesson of history seems to be that every generation must learn for itself. We are all susceptible to lies artfully told. In Germany in the 1920s there were dozens of little Hitlers running around spouting folkish, racial nonsense. Why did Hitler succeed where the others failed? It was all due to superior communications. The same thing is happening today. Hitler's tricks are being used all the time."

"But if it's a known strategy, doesn't it lose its effectiveness?" Yohaba asked.

"No. Because it's magic. Burke called *Mein Kampf* the well of Nazi magic and talked about Hitler conjuring up magic with his words. Old Burke was onto something with that. Bernbailer's got a bit of the old magic himself.

"But let me walk you through what was going on last night at the"—the professor made quote marks with her fingers—" 'Covenant of the Chosen' compound. Gosh, I love that name. *Covenant of the Chosen*. Brilliant. Utterly brilliant. But I digress." She looked down at her notes. "You mentioned the searchlights giving the feel of a cathedral. Hitler's message was essentially a religious message. He knew that nothing moved people to action better than religion. When he started out in Munich, he deliberately gave lectures in dark, smoky beer halls because churches of that day were dark and smoky with incense. He was tapping into the religious feelings of his listeners. Again—the swastika? Looks a bit like a cross, wouldn't you say? No accident there either."

"And the guards referred to people as brothers and sisters," Yohaba added.

"Yes, yes. And there were lots of references to God, Israel, being chosen by God, and doing God's will. We've seen it all before with Hitler. But this Bernbailer is good. Real good. I've had my eye on him for a while. He's in tight with the real bad boys in Europe. He first popped up in Montana, then disappeared for a few years. We think he was in Germany getting his PhD in creating human misery. He came back, and now we've got him here in Idaho. Lucky us. What else do you want to know?"

"What about the goon squad?" Rulon asked.

"The goon squad—" Freling laughed out loud. "I just love that name. I'm going to use it in my next article. Anyway, the goon squad was definitely his people. Their purpose was to create a sense of identification between the Nazis and the audience. What greater bond is there between men than fighting side by side, protecting each other and their women? Brothers-in-arms and all that sort of thing. I guarantee you he's got those people in the palm of his hand now. Hitler was a master at getting the German people to identify with his cause. He knew the exact right buttons to push."

"But why the emphasis on religion?" Rulon asked. "Logically that shouldn't work. Religious people shouldn't be buying into this garbage. They're supposed to be charitable and loving."

"If you want to get masses of people to do good . . . or evil, religion is always the best card to play," the professor said. "I'm not slamming religion. I'm just saying that it's such a potent force inside people that these big movements almost always have a religious slant to them.

"It's a little complicated to explain, but when people twist religion to their own evil ends, if they're smart, they won't contradict people's beliefs as much as glide along with them. I call it communications jiu-jitsu—taking the emotion from an already strongly held belief and altering its path slightly so the same emotion adheres to a different idea.

"Let me give you an example. Why is sex used to sell so many products? Well, on one level it's used to get people's attention. Okay, that's easy to understand. But Burke would say that on a deeper level the advertisers are trying to take a person's natural sexual desire and transfer that desire to something else—to a product. Sick but true, and people fall for it all the time.

"And you saw it yourself last night. Why do you think Bernbailer kept everyone waiting so long? It was so he'd have something to work with—some emotion he could twist. He *wanted* people to be already angry when he got up to speak. And just to make sure that was the case, he had his own people sprinkled throughout the crowd shouting epithets and stirring things up. He was confident that if the anger were there, he could channel that anger and energy toward a target of his choosing. In this case, non-whites, Jewish bankers, and politicians."

"So where's the religious angle in that?" Rulon asked.

"Religion is about God but also, to a large extent, about the devil. This is where it gets interesting. Hitler's philosophy was that all the suffering of the German people was the result of a single enemy— Jewish bankers. It's not clear how much Hitler actually believed this himself, but he explained in *Mein Kampf* that it was too confusing for people to have multiple enemies. So some of his most fascinating arguments were constructed to convince people that every ill—the loss of World War I, rampant inflation, divorce, prostitution, poverty, unemployment, take your pick—were all the result of a single cause: Jewish bankers and businessmen.

"Religion already accepts the idea that the devil is the root perpetrator of all evil and temptation. If you can somehow get your audience to identify your enemy with the devil, then it becomes a relatively small matter to blame them for every evil. And, of course, with that problem solved, any excess necessary to eradicate them can be excused. After all, you're doing God's work. One of Hitler's most imaginative myths was that Satan seduced Eve in the garden and that's how Jews came about. Do you see how pulled together this is? Burke refers to this as the associative connection of ideas.

"And it gets even stranger. Hitler viewed himself as wooing the German people, much like a suitor. Satan seduces but Hitler woos. He viewed the German people as a feminine entity. And this is one reason why he never got married until hours before he died. He needed to stay single for his betrothed—the German people. He may have been mad, but he carried out the argument totally—no half measures."

"I suspect finding a scapegoat has always been part of the strategy," Yohaba said.

"Sadly, yes," replied the professor. "The more troubles and blame you can pin on your enemy, the more you don't have to take responsibility for your own failings. Republicans or Democrats, take your pick. They both do it. I don't know what your political orientation is, but it should always be a red flag when one group paints the other as the root of all evil, or when they focus on specific hot issues to deflect attention away from the real problem. Don't get me started."

"It sounds sinister," Yohaba said, "but at the end of the day, it's just words. As long as it stays that way, I guess it's relatively harmless."

"No, absolutely no," the professor said, easily diverted back to her favorite subject. "Hitler said that revolutions are made solely by the power of the spoken word, and Bernbailer, as you've seen, is quite the orator."

"What else can you tell us about Bernbailer?" Rulon asked.

"I can tell you lots of things, but first tell me why you were there. I know you're not a sympathizer." She sat back and scrutinized Rulon. "You look pretty banged up, fella. Don't tell me; you had a run-in with them."

"Maybe," Rulon said.

Yohaba groaned. "Don't even try getting information out of Rulon. He would never admit it, but he slaughtered them. The bodies were stacked up like firewood. He even threw Bernbailer into a creek."

"Oh, tell me everything that happened," Freling said gleefully. "I want to hear this. I hope your Rulon got in some good licks."

Over Rulon's protest, Yohaba told the story, starting with the massacre at the Rockin' Rooster saloon. As she spoke, Freling rocked back and forth in excitement. When Yohaba told the part about Rulon dunking Bernbailer, the professor clapped her hands with joy.

"I wish I could have been there," she said when Yohaba was through. "I'm a communications professor, but even I admit that words don't work with these guys."

"Debating doesn't work, but sometimes sharing the gospel does," Rulon said. "It's probably the only thing that has a chance."

For a moment, Yohaba and Freling were speechless in disbelief at Rulon's comment, then the professor shook her head, chuckled, and said, "The gospel preceded by a good right hook to get them in the mood to listen. The gospel according to Rulon Hurt."

"Rulon's serious," Yohaba said. "That's why he needs me around."

"Well, know this, then," the professor said. "This Bernbailer character is a murderer. Oh, yes. Not here, not in Idaho, but in Montana. He took part in killing three illegal immigrants there five years ago, before his sabbatical to Germany. Nobody could prove anything, but my sources in the movement know what happened, and they talk about it. I'm afraid, Rulon, that you're a marked man now. They're not going to stop. They don't know how. They're psychopaths."

Their discussion with Professor Freling concluded a little after eight, and after a brief tour of the campus so Rulon could brush away more flies, Rulon and Yohaba headed back to the truck. By 9:30 they were flying down highway 84 and just passing Mountain Home.

AT THAT EXACT moment, eighty-six miles away, Helmut, lying prone, stiff, and hot on the hill above the ranch, was finally at the end of his timeless hunter's patience.

"Where is he?" Helmut snarled in German. Two rabbits twenty feet away stopped nibbling a branch to look at him. "Hey, you two," Helmut yelled. "Yeah, you."

He aimed the rifle at the closest one and slowly squeezed the trigger. He came within a hair's breadth of firing then eased off. *Get a grip,* he said to himself. Instead, he reached behind him for a rock to throw. When he turned back, the rabbits were gone.

He rolled over and looked up at the sky. In four and a half hours of waiting, he had seen the old man taking off on the tractor and the big Russian getting in his SUV and driving off. But no Mr. Hurt.

Helmut looked at his hand. It was shaking again. Overhead, the sun beat down. Its warmth, coupled with his lost sleep and a new wave of jet lag, acted like a sedative. He closed his heavy eyes, fell asleep for five seconds, then lurched awake.

Willing his eyes to stay open, he rolled back onto his stomach and peered through drops of sweat into the fogged-up rifle scope. He frantically wiped the lens with his sleeve, hating Rulon Hurt more with every wipe.

"I just want to see the pink mist from a perfect head shot," he said through gritted teeth as he rubbed away.

TWENTY MILES PAST Mountain Home, Rulon and Yohaba stopped at a gas station for a six-pack of Sprite. They were back in the truck and had only gone a few miles when Yohaba received a text message on her phone. She casually scrolled through the message and then put her phone back in her purse.

After a minute staring at the landscape, she said, "Have you ever noticed how when you've got people trying to kill you that the world ending with an asteroid collision sort of dwindles in importance?"

"Darling," Rulon said dryly, with a Sprite in one hand and the other on the steering wheel, "in the history of conversations that may be one of the all-time strangest opening lines. Let me guess: you just got a message from your grandfather."

"Yeah. He's been having me work on things. You know what day today is?"

"Uh-huh."

"June 4. Leonard just wrote me to say the asteroids didn't collide after all. They came close but there was no collision. 182 Elsa is still just cruising out there. My great-great-grandfather got it wrong."

"That's great news. Wow. Einstein was wrong. We should have

a party." When Yohaba didn't react, he said, "You don't seem very excited about it."

"Oh, don't get the wrong impression. I'm glad the world's not going to end, but I am a little disappointed that he made a mistake. Somehow that seems so weird. I mean, it's not weird if I'm wrong or you're wrong, but when Einstein makes a mistake the whole world is upside down. Do you understand what I'm saying?"

"Sure," Rulon said. "We put a lot of faith in experts. Look at the economy. Almost no one saw that coming. It shakes your faith. You think there are these great superhuman people keeping the world going and, really, they're all just human like the rest of us. It's sobering."

"Yeah."

"But hey," Rulon said. "Look on the bright side. Our kids will have a planet to live on." He put his Sprite in the cup holder and pulled her close. "Gosh, you and I are going to be great parents someday. We'll have the first Olympic champion Nobel Prize winner. Do you think that's too much pressure to put on a kid?"

"No, darling. But hold me close. For some reason, I'm more scared than I was before."

SATURDAY 10:45 A.M.

They got home before lunchtime, just ahead of a dark wall of billowing clouds rolling in from the south. They passed Rulon's father on the tractor with the two dogs trailing behind. He was still out there making his firebreaks. Yohaba reached across Rulon and honked the horn. Dad gave a curt wave.

After pulling into the yard between the barn and the house, Rulon got out of the truck, stretched, and put on his hat. Yohaba came around from the other side and handed him his half-finished can of Sprite. Arm in arm, they walked toward the house. After a few steps, Rulon broke free, leaving her standing in the middle of the yard. He walked over to the fence facing the east-side hills—the same hills from where the shots had come two days before—and leaned on the top rail, scanning the landscape.

"C'mon," Yohaba said. "What're you doing? Don't just stand

there, you idiot. Someone could be out there. C'mon."

Rulon stood with one boot on the lower fence rail, not liking the situation. *They could be anywhere and we'd never see 'em.*

He spied a glint of light near the top of the hill and stiffened. Maybe the sun reflecting off some old barbed wire. Or off a telescopic sight. No way of knowing. *Hopeless,* he thought to himself. *They could take me anytime.*

He turned away and angled toward the house with his hand out for Yohaba to take. She stood ten feet away, glowering at him with her hands on her hips.

He grinned and said, "C'mon. I'm hungry. Whatcha gonna rustle me up for lunch, woman?"

She smiled back, his smile having won her over. Then still watching her face, he heard a noise like an express train roaring, followed by a massive pain above his left ear. *What the . . .*

His first thought was that someone had sneaked up behind him with a baseball bat. He saw in slow motion the air ripple little circles past Yohaba's shoulder and some dust kick up behind her. Then all his muscles seized and spasmed, and he reflexively crushed the can he was holding, erupting a heavy mist of Sprite. His arms went limp and then his legs. The can fell to the ground, crushed flat. Rulon lolled like a rag doll and hit the ground hard.

"Ouch . . ." he said, looking up unblinking into the sun. He heard Yohaba scream his name and sensed more than saw her shadow over him. He wondered if he was back in CERN. Then blackness.

HELMUT FELT THE rifle buck, saw the confirming mist, and immediately lifted his head from the scope. Rulon was on the ground, Yohaba kneeling beside him. Helmut abruptly dropped to the scope again, and rejoiced to see Yohaba with her head flung back and her mouth gaping open. Her wails never reached his ears, but he felt them. Rulon wasn't moving. Helmut replayed the scene in his head: Rulon in the crosshairs; the mist; he sways and falls like his bones have been removed. Done deal.

Helmut got up and slowly backed away. He watched, satisfied, as the old man arrived on the tractor with the dogs, ran to Rulon, then into the house. Helmut continued backing up for ten more yards before turning and running, slipping and stumbling up the hill. Near the top, he stopped to crouch behind a large mesquite bush to look back. Down in the yard, one of the dogs was barking and trying to lick Rulon's face while the girl kept pushing him away, but the other, a huge white dog, stood by Rulon, looking silently up the hill in Helmut's direction. The dog lifted its head into the breeze, and even from where he stood, Helmut could sense the dog straining to catch a scent.

Suddenly Molly took off straight across the yard toward the hill. She crossed the flatland in a dead sprint, barely slowing as the ground rose. Bounding over bushes and clawing over fallen trees and boulders, she ran to kill the predator that had attacked her flock. Helmut let the dog get to within fifty yards before he opened up. The first bullet caught Molly square in the chest sending her somersaulting. But she staggered to her feet again and kept coming. It took Helmut two more shots to finally put the dog down for good.

Yohaba, in the yard kneeling next to Rulon, and the old man, standing on the porch, both still as statues, stared up at Helmut. In the distance, a vehicle was coming fast, throwing up a plume of dust on the ranch road. Helmut lifted the riflescope to his eyes and verified that it was the Russian's beat-up SUV.

Shifting the scope, he saw Yohaba sobbing on Rulon's chest and a dark halo spreading in the dirt around Rulon's head. He smiled. For a second, he considered sticking around and taking out the Russian and maybe the girl too, but dismissed the idea as tactically unnecessary. With a mixture of certainty and satisfaction, he made a low-profile scramble up and over the hill.

Inside the truck, he mounted the rifle behind him on hooks, fastened his seat belt, and sat there for a moment holding the key in the ignition. He took in a breath and let it out slowly. *I am death,* he thought to himself before starting up the engine.

Fifteen minutes later when he hit the main highway, he turned on his cell phone and called his father with the good news, using their own coded words. While he was talking, a helicopter flew overhead heading in the direction he'd just come. Helmut twisted his head to peer up through the windshield. It was a medical helicopter. He thought, *Don't waste your time.*

THE LIFE-FLIGHT HELICOPTER arrived exactly twenty-two minutes after Rulon was shot. Rulon was alive when the chopper touched down, but near death from loss of blood. The doctor on the flight was a silver-templed colonel in the National Guard who had just returned from his third tour in Iraq. Yohaba flew with them back to the Twin Falls Magic Valley Regional Medical Center. Dad followed in the truck, and Boris drove off on an errand from Yohaba. Rulon slipped into a coma on the way, which didn't seem to worry the doctor particularly. He'd seen it all a hundred times.

Over the noise of the rotor blades, he yelled in Yohaba's ear, "You did good slowing down the blood loss. He's lost a lot of blood, but he's gonna make it. Looks worse than it is. The bullet tore a groove but didn't penetrate the skull. He's in a coma right now, which might not be a bad thing." He patted her hand. "I've seen guys much worse than this live and come out of it fine. No one's gonna die."

Yohaba smiled weakly and wiped the tears from her face. The doctor turned away to yell something to the pilot.

Yohaba picked up Rulon's hand and rubbed her cheek with it. Gripping his hand with both of hers, she leaned in close and whispered, "Don't listen to him, my love. Someone's gonna die. I promise."

CHAPTER 15

An hour after the shooting, Helmut was sitting in the compound's ranch house kitchen with Bernbailer and the Gruppenfuhrer.

"I want the rifle disassembled and the pieces thrown in a river somewhere," Helmut said to the two men across the table.

"So now you hop a plane, and we're left with the aftermath. Is that it?" Bernbailer asked.

"I'll have the reward money transferred as soon as I'm back," Helmut said, ignoring Bernbailer's question and making no apology for the mess he was leaving behind.

"Any suggestions on how we handle this?" Mr. Goatee, the Gruppenfuhrer, asked.

Ignoring his question again, Helmut said, "I'll need a ride to the airport in three hours. Right now I'm going to clean up and have a rest. Heil Hitler." He left the rifle on the table and headed for his room in the back of the house. He despised them all for their weakness and lack of initiative.

When he was gone, Mr. Goatee asked, "Do you think there will be trouble?"

"Yes," Bernbailer answered. "But nothing that will stick. Surely Hurt had a lot of enemies. I only met him a few days ago and even I wanted to kill him." After a moment of shared laughter, Bernbailer asked, "Where do you think they'll take him?"

"Even if he's dead at the scene, the procedure is to take him to St. Luke's."

"Send a man. Have him ask around. Make sure he's really dead."

HELMUT WALKED OUT onto the Joslin Field tarmac, ticket in hand, dragging his black roller suitcase behind him like an inconvenient conscience. It was late afternoon, but the hot sun still glared and glittered off the pavement. His shadow mingled with the shadows of his fellow passengers as they trudged toward the rear-engine Canadair jet poised to fly them to Salt Lake. Jostling along, head down, silent, anonymous—just another business man in a dark gray suit, traveling on a Saturday to get a jump on the competition.

For Helmut, this was the nerve-racking part. The slow, multi-phase escape through the airport wondering about all the unknowable things that might have gone wrong. Had he been set up? Perhaps betrayed deliberately or through someone's incompetence? Perhaps spotted by a hiker lost in the hills behind the ranch? He shook his head. Too many variables to track.

Choke points everywhere, even in a small airport like this. Security personnel with guns, paid to be openly suspicious. He nervously looked around for signs of surveillance or security ready to pounce. The plane loomed up ahead. He fought the urge to walk faster than the people around him.

This was the last hurdle. His phony passport had passed the test at the check-in counter. He'd gotten through security without a hitch. But always, just at this moment, just as he was boarding the plane, his mind would cast back to the movie *Midnight Express* and how the guy was tripped up at the last second by a surprise inspection aboard the airport bus.

It can blow at any seam.

The boarding steps were fifty feet away. Cell phone number five rang. Helmut reached into his jacket pocket, recognized the number, and answered as he walked.

"It's me," Bernbailer said. "Where are you?"

"I'm boarding a plane."

"He's not dead. Not even close to dead. They're wheeling him out of surgery now."

"That's impossible."

"Improbable maybe," Bernbailer said, unable to keep the smugness out of his voice. "But apparently not impossible. I've got a man at the hospital now. Will you be coming back to finish this?"

Helmut didn't immediately answer. The crowd was pressing in from all sides. "I'll be in touch," was all he could say through his anger and disbelief, before abruptly ending the call.

He was at the foot of the stairs and put away the phone. He would disassemble it once he was seated. With one hand, he clicked the latch on his luggage handle and telescoped it down flush. Trudging up the stairs with his suitcase, he considered his options.

He could come back in a week—possibly—but quickly discarded the thought: by then, there would be security around the fat American. But right now, they were focused on saving his life, might not even be a guard outside the room. If they figured out this was retaliation for his work in Marseilles, OCD would get involved, and eventually move him to a secret location. After he healed, he'd be on the run again, this time with government help. Helmut could feel the opportunity slipping away.

Helmut reached the plane door, having concluded that Mr. Hurt had way too much luck for one man. Ahead of Helmut, a brunette in her thirties was wearing a T-shirt that said "Idaho Potatoes."

What peasants, thought Helmut in disgust.

Behind him, a line of forty passengers stretched down the steps and past the wing. He stood at the top of the stairs and looked back with bitter regret. He might never get another chance like this. Helmut shook his head, bewildered and angry at his failure. But the mission for his father must come first.

There will be another time, Mr. Hurt, he said to himself, *I promise you*. He disappeared through the door.

Ten minutes later, the last of the passengers was aboard, and the plane sat motionless as the two pilots performed their final preflight checks. Two airline workers stood at the bottom of the portable stairs, waiting for the word to pull it away.

Suddenly, a man in a dark-gray suit dashed out of the plane and down the stairs, gripping a small, black suitcase and holding a cell phone to his ear. He brushed past the two startled workers and was already twenty feet away and walking swiftly toward the terminal before a steward appeared in the plane's doorway and yelled after him. The man in the suit never looked back.

"I need a small, caliber pistol with a silencer," Helmut said into the phone. "Can you get me one?"

On the other end, Bernbailer was stammering and snapping his fingers to get Mr. Goatee's attention.

"Hold on," Bernbailer said. "Quick," he said to Mr. Goatee, who was over by the sink drying dishes. "Have we got something with a silencer? A pistol. Something small."

The Gruppenfuhrer paused in his dish drying. "Frank's got an unregistered .22 with a Gemtech suppressor. That's the only thing that comes to mind right now."

Bernbailer relayed the info to Helmut, then said, "Do you want us to send someone to pick you up?"

"Yes, but not here at the airport. Too many surveillance cameras. Give me another location." Bernbailer named a restaurant in town.

"I'll take a taxi," Helmut said. "Have someone meet me there with the weapon." Helmut stepped out of the terminal into the sun and waved for a taxi. *I am death*, he thought to himself.

HELMUT GOT TO the restaurant first, figured he had some time, and went in for a cup of coffee. Thirty minutes later, his cell phone rang.

"I'm in the parking lot in a blue Chevy Tahoe," said a voice over the phone.

Five minutes later, Helmut was in the truck with his suitcase between his legs. Without saying a word, Frank, the driver, reached into the glove compartment and handed him something heavy wrapped in yellow muslin. They drove to the hospital in silence.

Frank drove down the ramp to the hospital parking garage. Helmut, always wary of surveillance cameras, obscured his face with his hand and pointed to a parking space in a camera blind spot. Frank started to pull straight in but Helmut made him turn around and back in.

"We may have to leave in a hurry," Helmut said.

"Right," Frank replied. He backed in nice and easy and turned off the engine.

"We've got a guy up there in the waiting room on the fifth floor,"

Frank said. And then he laughed. "Don't kill him by mistake."

Helmut didn't find it funny.

In his hand was a Smith & Wesson .22LR with a ten-round magazine and an anodized Gemtech suppressor with a non-galling titanium tread mount.

"It's got a real low first round pop," said Frank when he saw Helmut staring at the gun.

Helmut put the muzzle against Frank's head. "Wait here. I'll be back in ten minutes. If you're not here when I get back . . ." Helmut cocked the pistol.

"I understand, sir," Frank said. "I won't let you down."

"On second thought," Helmut said. "Give me the keys."

Frank fumbled nervously getting the keys out of the ignition. He handed over the keys, and Helmut got out, heading for the elevator. Frank watched him go with an immediate sense of relief. Tattooed Frank had spent five years in the super-max prison at Florence, Colorado, and was a predator himself—but Helmut was the bigger predator.

As soon as Helmut disappeared behind the closing elevator doors, Frank flipped down the truck's sun visor and caught the spare key as it fell.

"There's gonna be a bloodbath," he said out loud. He waited a minute more just to be sure Helmut wasn't playing any tricks, then reached across the seat, opened the passenger door, and shoved Helmut's suitcase out of the truck. He slammed the door and drove out of the garage, out of Twin Falls, out of the Magic Valley, and three hours later straight out of Idaho into Oregon.

HELMUT RODE THE elevator to the fifth floor, the pistol in his belt under his jacket. The elevator doors opened, and Helmut followed the signs to intensive care, seeing no one along the way but hearing voices from the rooms he passed. He walked into a waiting room that was otherwise empty except for a brother Nazi in jeans and a blue, long-sleeved shirt, sitting in a chair reading a newspaper. When Helmut walked in, the man dropped the paper and stood up.

"Room 508. But there's people with him. His wife, his dad. Some guys from his church. Maybe you should wait."

"Maybe you should leave," Helmut said.

The man protested, "You can't kill 'em all. If I were you I'd . . ." but something in Helmut's expression made him shut up. The man turned on his heels and left.

Once he was alone, Helmut looked around for surveillance cameras. Seeing none, he took out the pistol and chambered a round. Hiding the pistol again under his jacket, he pushed through two swinging doors and walked down the hallway past an empty nurse's station and numbered rooms 502, 504, 506 . . . walking neither fast nor slow, looking for cameras. Death inevitable. He was in no hurry. Doing his job. Culling the weak. Taking revenge. *I am death.*

He stopped in front of 508. Looked both ways. Quiet on a Saturday afternoon. Small town hospital. He pulled out the pistol, and put one hand on the handle of the partially open door. From within, he heard the soft murmur of voices. A vigil over the infirm. He slowly pushed the door open and then stepped through and closed the door behind him.

Rulon, his head bandaged like a mummy, was unconscious in the bed. There were six other people: four men, two women. One of them was the young wife sitting in a chair on the far side of the bed. Next to her sat the old man in bib overalls. At the foot of the bed was a baby-faced doctor in a white smock holding a clipboard. Nearest to Helmut was an old, bent, white-haired nurse in a white uniform and white stockings with a wrinkled white face and hideous red lipstick. Two men, furthest away, were behind the girl. They were farmers about Rulon's age, in rumpled suits—hayseeds, from the church.

Helmut put his finger to his lips: *Hush.* He motioned with the gun. *Away from the bed.* He lied with a smile. *No one will get hurt.*

If it had been one of the men to move first, Helmut would have responded appropriately, but it was the old nurse and that threw him off. With one hand, she hiked up her white skirt while the other hand flashed to her stockinged thigh. *But why?* Helmut wondered. A glimpse of leather. *Wait.* More movement. This time the girl. Her hand hidden by the bed, but her elbow rising like lifting something from the floor. The baby-faced doctor, the old man, the two men in suits—all in motion now. Too much movement. *What the . . . ?*

For a fraction of a second, there is a Mexican standoff. Five heavy-caliber pistols and the old nurse's .22 all pointed at Helmut. Helmut with his suppressed .22 pointing back. And then the first fusillade strikes, spinning him around—the old nurse in a perfect tactical position, knees bent, two-handed grip, arms extended; the old man steady, absorbing the recoil, firing with one hand; the baby-faced doctor, the two men, but especially the girl, standing now as she fires, the narrow eyes of a predator, all blasting away—and sending Helmut bouncing off the door in time to receive the second salvo.

He hits the floor as if his bones have melted, but the bullets keep coming. His body arches and jerks, his limbs flail and spasm as bullets tear through flesh and ricochet off bones. The thunder doesn't stop. Now the doctor at his side with his finger feeling for the carotid artery. The doctor yells something. Running footsteps. Helmut's eyes are open, but he does not blink and he cannot see. He pants furiously, then suddenly stops as if holding his breath. His final thought seems to him unimaginably profound: *Idaho potatoes.*

PART 2

MRS. HURT AND MR. ZOKOLOV

CHAPTER 16

MAGIC VALLEY MEDICAL CENTER
SATURDAY 3:00 P.M.

Yohaba stood over the doctor with the others and watched Helmut die. She stood there, her snub-nose Smith & Wesson .38 caliber airweight revolver hanging at her side, curious at her own reaction. Rulon was always wracked with guilt and angst after episodes of extreme violence. Almost three years after CERN and he still had the occasional nightmare. Maybe it would hit her later, but right now, looking down at Helmut, Yohaba felt . . . nothing. She lifted the gun to her face, puffed out her cheeks, and mimicked blowing smoke from the barrel like a western gunslinger. Then, from force of habit, she expertly twirled the pistol twice and in one smooth motion stuck it in her belt.

"Welcome to Idaho, my friend," she said.

Everyone in the room nodded solemnly at her words. After a few moments, they all turned away from Helmut except Yohaba and Rulon's father.

The old nurse moved off to the side, discreetly lifted her skirt, and replaced the .22 in her thigh holster. She next removed her wig, used it to rub off some of the makeup, turned to the others, and said in a deeply masculine voice, "I'll pay fifty bucks to the man who does the paperwork on this one."

"Dang," the baby-faced doctor said as he took off his white smock and threw it in a corner. "No one is going to believe this." Under his smock, he wore a white shirt, tie, and had a shiny badge on his belt.

He looked at Mr. Hurt disapprovingly. "Did anyone ever tell you it's against the law to shoot someone?" He pointed at Yohaba. "And you. I realize you are under a lot of stress. Feeling better now? What the heck were you doing with a gun? And you . . ." He looked at the two men from the church in their frumpy dark suits. He started to say something, then just waved his hands at them. "Get out of here. Just get out of here. Go. Go wait in the waiting room. Go. Take a Bible with you and read something. I'll deal with you later."

The two men looked at each other, holstered their guns, and did as they were told.

The hospital loudspeaker boomed the alarm, "Code blue to intensive care . . . Code blue to intensive care," and hospital personnel piled into the room. Thirty seconds later a crash cart pushed by a team of orderlies came barreling through the door.

Two white-smocked doctors kneeled over Helmut, yelling instructions as orderlies unloaded equipment. A well-oiled team leaping into action. Then a middle-aged doctor straightened up, murmured a few words to a colleague, received an affirmative nod in reply, and held up his hand.

"Hold it, people. It's all over but the crying." The room came to a stop. The doctor looked at the wall clock. "Time of death 3:04 p.m. Somebody write that down." Nobody moved. The doctor stood and peeled off his latex gloves. A few people starting filing out, and he prodded the rest with "Say good-bye, folks." Still, most people didn't budge.

The same doctor turned to the baby-faced man, now revealed as a gun-toting special agent. "I've never seen a guy more dead. I lost count of the bullet holes. Was all this totally necessary?"

Benjamin Drummond, OSD station chief out of Boise, replied, "It was him or us, doc. Don't give me a hard time."

The doctor shook his head in disapproval, pushed through the crowd still in the room, and left.

Suddenly, Chief Drummond was aware of his crime scene being tampered with.

"Hold it. Hold it right there," he yelled to the curious onlookers.

"Hey, don't touch that gun. This is a crime scene, everyone."

He spread his arms wide and walked forward, scooping up nurses and orderlies like a sheep dog, herding everyone away from the body and out of the room. As he moved, he called over his shoulder to Agent Wallace Burns in the white dress, sitting on a chair, rolling down his stockings, "Hey, get off your duff and help me." Then he turned to the hospital staff. "Everyone back, please. Go back to work. How about a little cooperation, please? Yes, that means even you, ma'am. There's nothing you can do here. Trust me, he's feeling no pain. This room is now off-limits."

Agent Burns flopped the wig carelessly back on his head and leaned forward wearily on his chair with his forearms on his knees. "I've got an idea about the paperwork. How about we say I shot him first and that my shot killed him, and the others were just shooting a cadaver? Can we do that? Keep this simple? Is there a law against shooting a cadaver?"

A dirty look and a well-placed epithet got Agent Burns moving. He threw down his wig and went over to help his boss.

Yohaba, still rooted in place, looked down at Helmut. Drummond put a hand on her shoulder. "I'm glad you called us. That was smart."

"Yeah," she said softly. With deadly conviction she added, "I shot him first. Dead center mass. Just like Rulon taught me."

Wallace and Ben, Rulon's two good friends from his OCD days, looked at each other, shrugged, and continued herding all the gawkers out of the room. Rulon's father and Yohaba suddenly found themselves alone.

Yohaba, still speaking softly, said, "Rulon says that in the end, all men are caught in their own snare."

"And thus he flattereth them and leadeth them along until he draggeth their souls down to hell," Rulon's father said in reply.

"What was that?" Yohaba asked.

"The rest of the scripture." Rulon's father tucked his Colt .357 Trooper back under his overalls and hooked his thumbs in his overall straps. "Seemed to fit the situation." He looked down at Helmut. "Well . . . I guess that says it all." When Yohaba didn't say anything, he figured the conversation was over, went around the bed, and resumed his vigil over Rulon.

All the commotion was now in the hallway. Yohaba crouched down to return the .38 to her ankle holster. She knew Rulon's father was watching her, but she quickly turned Helmut over and searched him anyway. She came up with a bullet-shredded passport, a wallet, a set of car keys, a ring, a parking ticket, and a brand-new Nokia cell phone miraculously untouched by the carnage. She stole a look at the doorway, then stashed what she'd taken into her two back pockets.

As she stood up, she locked eyes with Rulon's father on the other side of the bed.

"Is he the one?" the old man asked.

"Yeah," Yohaba said. "Rulon busted him up quite badly once with Freya and sent him to a hellhole prison outside of Paris. This was all about revenge."

"Marseilles?"

"Yeah. How'd you know?"

He ignored her question. Instead, he asked, "What was his name? The man who wanted to murder my son in his bed."

"Helmut von Bock," Yohaba said. "He was a Nazi."

Rulon's father came around and sat on the edge of the bed. His shoulders sagged, and he looked tired. He was quiet for a few moments, took a small breath, then said, "Did Rulon ever tell you much about his past? When he was younger, I mean."

There were voices from the hall as Wallace and Ben kept having to deal with newcomers.

"No. Not much."

"He wasn't always religious. I once had to bail him outta jail for beating a man half to death. He was a junior in high school and the man was an ex-con twice Rulon's age. Toughest man from here to Salt Lake. Rulon beat him so bad the guy left town, didn't even stay to press charges."

"Was it over a girl?"

"Hmm . . . No. A woman."

"Why are you telling me this now?" asked Yohaba softly.

"Rulon lives in two worlds. Always has. I can't figure how he keeps his balance. He's the most violently peaceful man I've ever known. I see God's hand in his life, giving him experiences, fashioning him for some purpose. When he brought you home, I wondered at first what he saw in you. But then, after a while, I saw that you were a diamond in the rough, and I knew Rulon knew what he was doing. I prayed hard about it and came to see God's hand in you two finding each other. I taught you to shoot for a reason. Felt I had to do it. Didn't know why exactly. I reckon that was part of the plan."

"I'm not religious," Yohaba said. "I go to church because of Rulon. I think you know that. Rulon and I pray every night. I'm not saying I don't believe in God. It's just that I'm not religious."

"You got something planned, don't you?" the father asked, looking down. "You and that Russian. Back at the ranch, before the chopper came, I heard you two arguing. Then he goes off like he's got an errand to run."

In three years of living on the ranch, this was the longest one-on-one conversation Yohaba and her father-in-law ever had. The father used to talk more before his mom died, Rulon said. Yohaba understood, and she loved the old man despite his reserve. She came and sat next to him on the bed. As they talked, she held Rulon's hand and absently twisted the wedding ring on his finger.

"His name is Boris. He works in their sick, violent world. Knows what these people are like. These Nazis will never stop until Rulon is dead. He told me that, and I believe him. They will be back again and again, as long as it takes." She nodded toward Helmut. "Now that their poster child is dead, they'll be parachuting in."

"Why the argument?"

"He was going to deal with them at the compound—kill them all, I think. I talked him out of it and told him when the time came we'd do together whatever needed to be done."

"Rulon would never want you to get involved."

"I know."

The old man looked down and scuffed his foot on the floor, reminding Yohaba of one of Rulon's quirky habits. "Why would the Russian get involved? I thought he came here to fight Rulon."

"He has his reasons," Yohaba said, intentionally vague.

The old man thought about that. "Does one of those reasons have a tattoo on her neck?"

"I suspect so," she said. Their eyes met. "But I can handle him." She paused. "I need him for what I have to do." When Rulon's father didn't say anything, she added, "Rulon trusted him, and that's good enough for me."

The old man started to respond but was interrupted by a commotion in the hall and Boris's voice rising above everyone else's.

"It's Boris," Yohaba said.

She dashed from the room, and immediately her voice was mixing in the conversation outside. After a minute, she returned with Boris in tow. He was wearing black jeans and a dark gray bomber jacket that said "Bronco Nation" across the back.

Boris raised his eyebrows and whistled low as he stepped around Helmut. He started to bend down over the body but Yohaba stopped him.

"I already did that." She patted the bulge in her rear pocket.

She turned to Rulon's father. "Boris says the local police are in the building. We don't have much time. We have to go. If we can get to Europe quickly, we might catch them by surprise. End this now for good."

The father asked, "Why not take this to the authorities?"

Boris's dismissive snort said it all. Yohaba interpreted. "We already did that, didn't we? And look how it turned out. It didn't stop those murderers from trying."

Yohaba had spoken sharply, and there was silence. She sighed and struggled to modify her tone. "Boris says guarding Rulon won't stop the attempts on his life. Eventually, they'll find a hole in his security. The alternative is that we keep running all our lives, but we all know Rulon would never put up with that."

Old Mr. Hurt gave no sign of agreement but, in his slow, western way, said, "Give me your gun. They'll test ballistics and match the bullets. I need to give them your gun. I'll . . ." He wrestled for an instant with his conscience. ". . . I'll tell them you couldn't stay. I won't outright lie . . . but I'll buy you some time if you can get outta here. I'll tell 'em you're grieving. Need to be alone. Everyone knows Rulon. They'll be sympathetic."

He gave Yohaba a warm, unexpected hug. "You better go, child," he whispered in her ear. She crouched down to her ankle holster, came up with the pistol, and handed it to him.

"Look," he said in mock surprise as he handled the gun with

both hands, "I've accidentally smeared your fingerprints." This was the closest thing to a joke Yohaba had ever heard him make. Then his face went hard and he looked at Boris.

"Tell me why you are doing this."

Boris said, with a slightly bemused look, "He speaks to me."

The father caught his drift and drawled, "Didn't have a reason to until now."

"What is it, old man?" Boris asked, meaning no disrespect.

"Is it because of Yohaba?"

Boris appraised Rulon's father with respect and thought carefully before answering in his deep, grinding voice. "Know this. They are my friends. I cannot separate them in my mind and call myself their friend."

The father nodded slowly as he considered Boris's answer, and he decided he liked it. He leaned back so he could regard them both. Some seconds passed before he spoke, but when he did his soft voice resonated with authority.

"Sometimes by small means, great things are brought to pass," he said, looking straight and unwavering into Boris's eyes. "Do this small thing for me. Swear to me. Swear to me that while you are together, you'll only call her Mrs. Hurt."

"Why?" Boris asked.

"As a reminder."

Boris looked at Yohaba, his face expressionless, then back to the old man. He nodded his understanding. "*Da*. I swear it."

And you," the old man said, turning to Yohaba, "swear to me—" He turned back to Boris. "What's your handle?"

Boris looked puzzled and Yohaba jumped in. "Your name."

"Zokolov," Boris said.

"Hey, that's not the name on your passport," interrupted Yohaba.

"Hush," Boris said.

"And you," the old man said back to Yohaba, "swear to me you'll only call him Mr. Zokolov."

A bewildered Yohaba looked back and forth between him and Boris, considered their solemn faces, and answered, "I swear," quickly followed by a look at Boris and "We gotta go." She leaned over Rulon and kissed him on the lips. "'Bye, my love. Wish me luck. Oh, I wish

I had more time, my love. Understand. Please understand, I do this for us."

She straightened up, wiped tears from her eyes, and faced the old rancher. "If he wakes up and I'm not here, please, help him understand. I should be back . . ." She deferred to Boris for the answer.

"In a week," Boris said, "or we'll be dead."

Yohaba nodded. "A week at most. I'll be back. I promise." She gave her father-in-law another hug.

"Come," Boris said, standing at the door. "Before the *apparatchiks* arrive."

"Now go," the old man said. "I will pray for you both."

CHAPTER 17

Twenty minutes later, Boris and Yohaba were in Boris's SUV heading back to the ranch to pack. They'd gotten past Wallace and Ben easily enough and were now driving, lost in their own thoughts. Yohaba still hadn't heard how Boris had fared on his errand. And Boris still didn't know the circumstances of Helmut's death. Yohaba broke the silence.

"Listen, Boris," she said. "I don't want you thinking Rulon's dad is weird. He means well."

"The name is Mr. Zokolov," Boris replied, looking straight ahead with two hands on the wheel and his face hard as flint.

Yohaba started to protest, but Boris cut her off. "You keep promise to old man or Rulon will be shamed of you. Me too."

Yohaba looked at Boris, trying to determine if he was serious.

While she was deciding, he said, "I am serious."

"Okay, okay, Mr. Zokolov," Yohaba said, convinced. "But tell me, is this going to be hard for you?"

"Old man not so dumb, eh. Drop it. How did fashisty die?"

"If this is going to be too hard for you, I can do this myself."

Boris reached over and grabbed Yohaba's right hand. He brought her hand to his face and smelled her fingers.

"I love smell of gunpowder on woman. You shot him. Good. Now tell me. How did it happen?"

156

"It wasn't just me."

"Tell me what happened," Boris ordered.

Yohaba told the story. When she was finished, Boris said, "Good thing I'm not there. I die. Rulon die. Maybe all die."

"Why do you say that?" Yohaba asked.

Boris took a deep breath. "Once he see me, he shoot, no hesitate. Maybe shoot everyone. Who moved first?"

"I believe it was the agent dressed as the old nurse."

Boris chuckled deep and thoughtful. "Ha. The one event he could not process fast enough."

Yohaba said, "Strange how life turns out. Who lives, who dies. It hangs on a thread, doesn't it?"

"Yes, control is illusion," Boris said. "And to survive you must learn important rule number one. I give you first lesson. Person most afraid, die first. Remember that. Must never panic, never freeze. Always do your duty."

"Rulon told me never to pull out a gun unless you intend to kill someone."

"That is second rule."

"It seems like a stupid rule to me. You pull out the gun so you *don't* have to kill someone. They see the gun and calm down, and you can control the situation."

"I will explain. Two types of people. One type, afraid for life when gun come out. They don't know you nice woman go to church on Sunday, say blessing at meal. They must kill you if they have chance, out of fear that you will kill them. Second type more dangerous. True predators, look in your eyes. If they don't see . . . see . . ." Boris searched for the right word. ". . . conviction, they smile inside. And then they attack. Understand what I'm saying? In your heart, you must be ready to kill first or don't pull gun. Gun make everyone in situation have to kill you if they get chance."

"I never looked at it that way."

"How many times you see Rulon pull gun?"

"Once. We already talked about it. That time in the Hönggerberg forest. No, wait. Three times."

"Did someone die each time?"

"Ha. No. That ruins your theory. One time Rulon thought he killed someone, but he didn't."

"What happened?" Boris asked. Yohaba briefly told him the story of the luggage store fight. When she was finished, Boris said, "Close enough. Your Rulon know rule too. How do you feel about shooting fashisty?"

"I feel fine," she said, sounding a bit surprised at her answer. "No bitter aftertaste. Am I weird?"

Boris laughed. "Probably. That is why Rulon love you."

At Boris's words, Yohaba saw Rulon again standing in the ranch yard hammer circle smiling at her, getting ready to push a big throw. Then her mind's eye shifted, and she pictured Rulon's dad on his knees by Rulon's bed praying for her and Boris.

She said, "Yeah. Now tell me what you learned from Ed. Where should we start looking?"

Boris said, "First tell me. Why you so ready to leave Rulon? Why you not more worried?"

"His father gave him a blessing," Yohaba said. "He said Rulon would turn out all right." Boris looked puzzled, so Yohaba explained what a blessing was. When Boris raised a skeptical eyebrow, she said, "I've seen it work. I don't totally get it myself, but it works."

Boris considered that for a moment, shrugged, then answered her earlier question. He related how he tracked Ed down at the video store, how angry Ed was that Rulon had been shot, how ready he was to talk. Ed told him about the overheard phone call from Zurich, Helmut's anxiety to be back in Zurich in three days or five at the latest, and Bernbailer's complicity.

When Boris was finished, Yohaba pulled Helmut's things out of her pocket and opened the passport.

"This passport is a phony," Yohaba said as she flipped through the pages. "This isn't his name. Rulon told me his real name. Helmut von Bock. Boy, what a name. Hard to say without goose-stepping."

"There was World War II German field marshal named Fedor von Bock," said Boris. "Maybe related."

Yohaba turned the last page and threw the passport down. "Wow. What a lucky dog. He's been to every place I want to visit."

She set aside the BMW keys and went through the wallet next.

A French driver's license, credit card, and several business cards in the same phony name. An old photograph of a young boy with his parents, the father sporting a Nazi armband and a Hitler mustache.

Von Bock junior never stood a chance, thought Yohaba with a sad shake of her head.

There were various receipts and a French medical insurance card. A parking ticket. Sixty-seven American dollars. Three hundred fifteen euros. Five hundred eighty Swiss francs. Yohaba went through all the pockets, opened all the flaps. The contents on her lap were the details of a person's life. Strangely empty. Somehow it was sadder than even the dead body left behind.

As a final search, she bent the empty wallet in several directions. There was resistance in one corner. She felt through the leather along the edges of a small metal object, dug deeper in one of the folds, and came out with a key. She held it up and twisted it in the light. It was short and stubby with a triangular, blue grip.

"What do you think, Mr. Zokolov?" she asked. Boris glanced over.

"Does it have a number on it?"

"Yes. 253."

"Locker key. Airport or train station. Our first lead. But maybe nothing."

"Maybe, but it's definitely a train station. There is some faded lettering on it that says SBB. The Swiss train system is called the Schweizer Bundesbahn."

"Okay, train station."

"Ed told you Helmut was in a hurry to get back to Zurich. How long can you keep things in a public locker?"

"Three days usually," Boris said.

"That's what I thought. What was Helmut's deadline again?"

"There were two," Boris said. "Three days and five days."

"Why two deadlines?" Yohaba asked.

"Perhaps two separate assignments."

"Possibly," Yohaba replied. "Odd, though. If he had a three-day deadline, why even mention the second one?"

"Maybe he was workaholic and had back-to-back assignments," Boris suggested.

"Okay," Yohaba said. "Still, why even mention the second job?"

Boris shrugged.

Yohaba told Boris about Rulon's original encounter with Helmut and the Nazis in Marseilles, and how Rulon thought it might have been drug related. They discussed flying to Marseilles but kept coming back to Zurich and the locker key. In the end, Zurich was the logical first stop, but wherever they went, there'd be some mop-up work to do later in Twin Falls.

"Omigosh," Yohaba said after they had settled on Zurich. She was holding her hands out in front of her and watching them tremble. "I'm getting the shakes now, just like Rulon does after a fight."

"Welcome to club," Boris said. "It's your body reabsorbing adrenaline. You get used to it."

After a few minutes, Yohaba calmed down enough to call information for the airline numbers and begin checking available flights.

Thirty minutes after leaving the hospital, Boris pulled into the ranch yard and parked a few feet from the porch. Yohaba got out, but instead of rushing into the house to pack, she stopped dead in her tracks and stared at the spot where Rulon had been shot. The ground was still stained with his blood.

She was starting to lose it when Boris came up from behind, grabbed her around the waist with one beefy, black-haired arm, and carried her kicking and yelling up the steps. He let go of her on the porch and kept on walking into the house without saying a word. Through her tears, she aimed a big roundhouse kick at his retreating rear-end but missed. After a few more moments of looking back over the yard, she wiped away her tears with her sleeve and followed Boris inside.

When Yohaba stepped through the door, Boris was nowhere to be seen. She could hear the floor creak and the ticking of the hall clock. With Rulon in her life, she was always surrounded with laughter and talking or the sounds of men working on things. Now the house was eerily quiet.

There was a noise from the back: Boris in his room packing. They had a plane to catch. She broke out of her reverie and went to her room to do the same.

She closed the bedroom door behind her, took Helmut's things out of her pockets, and threw them on the bed. She next did a quick tour of the room and adjacent bathroom. The bed was made, no clothes lying around, boots neatly arranged in the closet. Towels were hanging folded on the racks. Everything looked in order except for the bloody towels in the bathtub. Dad would have to deal with that. For convenience's sake, she decided to take only a small carry-on suitcase.

She packed a minimum of clothes and toiletries, making sure she left enough room for a few, more essential items. She took the desk chair over to the closet and used it as a stool from which to reach the back of the top shelf. Stepping down with a shoebox in her hand, she carried it and the chair back to the desk. She laid the shoebox on the desk, opened the lid, and took out a curious-looking pistol.

It was a CIA prototype: nonmetallic, automatic, made of a super-hard ceramic material as strong as steel. Magnetically inert and invisible to metal-detectors, the pistol was illegal. Even owning the ceramic material was illegal. Rulon told her he got it from Markus, an old boss of his at OCD. It had a seven-round magazine that loaded into the handle. When the trigger was pulled, a plastic spring drove the slide mechanism forward. This pushed a caseless ceramic bullet from the magazine into the chamber and fired it. The propellant ignited in two stages to keep the chamber pressure low so the gun didn't blow up. Even the nonmetal, caseless bullets were against the Geneva convention.

Yohaba disassembled the gun and the magazine and laid the parts in her suitcase exactly the way Rulon had shown her. Some parts flat, some on their edges. He said that though a metal detector wouldn't pick them up, a good X-ray inspector might be able to recognize the shapes if they weren't laid out just right. She also took all eight bullets out of a plastic bag and scattered them among her clothes.

She next took out of the shoebox an equally illegal Mad Dog Mirage X ceramic knife. So sharp it could cut glass and shave steel, it was safely enclosed in a Kydex acrylic polyvinyl alloy sheath. Total weight was two ounces with a three-inch blade. Again, she positioned the sheathed knife up against the side of her suitcase exactly as Rulon had shown. How he came to own it, she had no idea.

For her last item of tactical gear, Yohaba went back to the closet and removed a plain black Blade Runner bullet-stab vest. It was less than three pounds, hardly noticeable under a shirt, yet capable of protecting from punches, kicks, knife stabs or slashes, and rounds from a 9mm or even a .357 Magnum. She folded the vest and placed it on top.

Yohaba stepped back. Had she forgotten anything? She looked around the room, spied a pair of sunglasses on her bedside table, and threw them in. She asked herself again: *Have I forgotten anything?*

She went into the bathroom and looked around but got side-tracked by her image in the mirror. She studied her face closely. What had she done today, and what would she have to do over the next few days? There were faint dark circles under her eyes. Stress. She looked into her green eyes and struggled to see herself objectively. Who was this person looking back at her? Was she a killer? The thought came to her: *What e're thou art, act well thy part.* One of Rulon's favorite quotes—usually said by him to justify doing a good deed.

She pulled a small, red, heart-shaped plastic case out of the medicine cabinet, a bottle of alcohol, a tube of Neosporin, and a sewing needle. She smeared a glob of the antibiotic over and inside her left nostril. Next, the needle was rinsed under hot water and doused in alcohol. With needle in hand, and a few deep breaths, she prepared to jab the needle through the center of her nose ring scar . . . then stopped. Fearing she might ram it in too hard and puncture the septum, she looked around for something small and hard to put in her nostril to block the needle.

She rifled through the cabinet drawers and found a nail file. After thoroughly cleaning it as well, she gritted her teeth and, without hesitation, put the file in her nose as a shield and jabbed the needle through the skin. Her eyes welled with tears. Painful but done. She dabbed at the wound with a hand towel. More Neosporin inside and out. Then from out of the red case a small, tight-fitting, black-gold nose ring. She held it close to her eye and turned and studied it. A past life remembered. Another deep breath. It went in and clipped smoothly; she hadn't lost her touch. Grabbing the sides of the sink, she leaned in close to the mirror.

Welcome back, she said. She gazed at herself, not quite sure what to make of the face staring back at her. In the other room, a cell phone rang with an unfamiliar melody. Helmut's phone.

CHAPTER 18

BOBLINGEN, GERMANY, SUNDAY 12:30 A.M.
TWIN FALLS, IDAHO, SATURDAY 4:30 P.M.

Helmut was overdue. He was supposed to call before he boarded his plane in Salt Lake. It was past midnight in Germany on Sunday morning, and his father was sitting in the wood-paneled study in his home outside Boblingen. A fire crackled in the fireplace, throwing dancing shadows across the walls and the old man's face.

Gustav von Bock had served on the eastern front as a seventeen-year-old soldier in Army Group Center along with its commander, his grandfather, Field Marshal Fedor von Bock—nicknamed the Holy Fire of Küstrin for his fiery lectures in support of the Fatherland. As his grandfather's personal aide, he had participated in Operation Typhoon, the disastrous attempt to take Moscow in the winter of 1941, the coldest in fifty years, and then later experienced what was worse than the cold—the Rasputitsa, Russia's season of rain and mud.

But unlike his grandfather, who secretly hated the Nazis, Gustav was a true believer. Old, bent, bald, and shriveled, he was one of the real ones that Boris had warned about. Sitting in the shadows like a scorpion in its hole, he waited, recruited, organized, and hatched endless plots. Hitler had been too soft. He should never have allowed the Jew physicists to leave Germany during the thirties. If Germany had developed the bomb first, Europe would be a society of villages

163

and Russia a smoldering, radioactive wasteland. Chernobyl times ten thousand. Then the world would have been cowed, and German soldiers would have marched to the ends of the earth. God would have been pleased, and the posterity of those soldiers would have blessed their names forever.

But today, Gustav's son, Helmut, his only posterity, had not called.

Gustav von Bock looked small in his overlarge brown leather chair near the fire. He adjusted the thick, woolen shawl around his shoulders. Sewn into one edge of the shawl was a foot-square patch from an old gray army blanket, the last one to serve him as he retreated with his comrades back into Germany while fighting the sub-human Slavs every step of the way.

Those days still lived fresh in the old man's mind. "The greatest battles ever fought on earth," he told his followers in their basement meetings in the homes of the faithful, "and the greatest generalship of the war were to be found in the German retreat from central Russia. Betrayed by the administrators safe in their bunkers, we fought like lions because we knew we were the last line between our people and the godless hordes. We fought for our wives and our children. A man has no greater link or obligation on this earth than to his wife and children."

Yet, today, Gustav von Bock's only child did not call at the arranged time. This had never happened before.

He tightened the heavy shawl around his shoulders and snaked out a bony hand toward the bell on the nearby side table. Grasping the handle, he rang three times, the peals reverberating around the room and through the thick oaken door into the rest of the house. After a moment came footsteps.

The door opened and a middle-aged man in a red vest entered, poised and respectful.

"Klaus, the cell phone, please," said the old man. A long, wrinkled finger pointed to the phone on top of the mantle.

Klaus performed the service, inquired if anything more was needed, then retired.

Gustav knew that his son was on the last of his five cell phones. Knew he used each one only once. But this was the number he used last, so he dialed.

After six rings, the phone was answered but no one spoke. He could hear breathing, though.

"You are a woman," he said after a long silence. No response. "I hear your breathing."

More silence.

"Who are you?" he asked, curious and kind.

"Who are you?" a woman's voice asked in return. A young voice, he noted, in perfect but slightly accented German. Swiss accent. A bit guttural. Zurich. Wary but firm. Intelligent. A liberated woman. Someone with a purpose.

"I am Werner Schuman," the old man said, using the fake name he and his son had chosen. "Father of Franz-Peter Schuman. The owner of the phone you are using."

Yohaba recognized the son's name as the one on Helmut's passport.

"Who are you, Fraulein?" the old man asked pleasantly again.

"I am the killer of Helmut von Bock," Yohaba replied.

"If this is a joke, it is in very bad taste," said the old man evenly and slowly, though his heart rate jumped and his face paled. "I'm afraid that name means nothing to me. Who are you and how did you get this phone?"

Cool. Very cool, thought Yohaba. She considered his voice. *Old. About the right age. I'll bet he really is the father.*

She said, "He didn't die well. He was trying to murder an unconscious man in a hospital bed. What a coward. I wouldn't admit he was my son either."

The old man asked again, "How did you get his phone?"

Yohaba could hear the façade crumbling ever so slightly. She indulged her cruelty.

"At the end, he couldn't even whimper because his jaw had been blown away."

"You are a woman," the old, bitter Nazi said, still maintaining his control. "Forgive me, but Mr. von Bock could never be killed by a woman. The thought is absurd."

She almost had him. Just another little push. "You do know him then. I thought so. I'm suggesting a closed-casket funeral. But it's up to you."

No response from the old man.

Taking a chance, Yohaba said, "I know about Zurich and locker 253. I have the key."

Again a long pause. "What are words? Proof of nothing. You know a name. You say you have a key. If you knew what you had and whom you were speaking to, you would hang up now and run for your life. But we would still find you. If we cared enough. You have no idea what you are up against."

This was going nowhere. Yohaba decided to do away with pretense. She said, "Helmut von Bock was shot dead today at the Magic Valley Regional Medical Center in Twin Falls, Idaho. Make a phone call. Do a Google search. I don't care. I didn't count how many bullets hit him, but I'd be surprised if it was fewer than a dozen. I have his wallet, his cell phone, his locker key, passport, car keys, some silly ring with a skull and two lightning bolts on it—you name it. Short of doing a séance and bringing him back from the dead, there's not much more I can do over the phone to prove I killed him, but I'm open to suggestions."

"You know nothing, you know . . . you . . ." Helmut's father faltered over the words, suddenly convinced his son was truly dead. "What have you done to him?" snarled and spluttered the old Nazi with terrible malevolence. His words became louder and clearer, all pretense swept away. "I will find you. I will track you. If he is dead, you are dead, and your family, and everyone who aids you. I will hunt you to the ends of the earth. I will hunt you past the gates of hell. If you have children, do them a kindness. Kill them now yourself, before I get my hands on them. I will—"

Yohaba cut him off. "No, you listen to me. If you've got this thing about sons, I suggest you adopt one, because your Helmut is really and truly dead. And good riddance, I say. But you got it all wrong. You better find a bunker quick, because I'm hunting *you*."

With that, Yohaba clicked the phone off. She heard something behind her and turned around. Boris was standing in the doorway, visibly upset.

Yohaba turned away, shut down Helmut's cell phone, grabbed

the rest of Helmut's things, and stuffed the whole lot angrily into her suitcase. Job done, she paused, bent over with her hands gripping the edges of her luggage.

After a few moments of stony silence and without looking up, she said, "What is it?"

Boris said, "You like to pull tiger's tail, Mrs. Hurt? You don't like element of surprise?"

"You're not seeing the big picture, Mr. Zokolov. I just made our job easier. The entire Fourth Reich will be waiting for us in the Zurich Hauptbahnhof. The tiger will be coming to us."

Boris said, "I once hunted for Russian government department called Inspection Tiger in Primorskii Krai near Vladivostok. We hunted man-eating tigers. But someone forget to tell tigers. They hunted us too."

"I'm sure before this is over I'll have heard all your stories," Yohaba said brusquely and annoyed.

She zipped up her suitcase and set it on the floor. Her laptop was still on the desk, but she decided to leave it. The effort of picking up the suitcase had reopened the wound in her nose, and the sting of it amplified both her bad mood and her guilt at having vented her cruelty. She knew Rulon would be disappointed with her.

"Your nose ring is bleeding," Boris said.

Yohaba touched her nose and wiped away a drop of blood with her finger.

"That's the least of my problems," she said. "Come, we've got a plane to catch."

THE OLD MAN sat in the leather chair, gasping, his mouth wide open. He rolled his head from side to side and screamed from the bottom of his soul. His wrenching cries brought Klaus running down the hallway and bursting into the room just in time to hear the old man's next words.

"Dead. He is dead, Klaus. My son is dead." He buried his head in his hands and sobbed.

Klaus stood next to his master, fearing to offer comfort, not knowing what to say, while Gustav told him what happened.

"Maybe she was lying," Klaus said when the old man was done.

Gustav did not stir but looked blankly into the fire. "There could be many reasons why she had his phone."

Softly the old man said, "He was in a place called Twin Falls, Idaho. Call up the local hospitals. Call Bernbailer. See if you can find any news."

Klaus clicked his heels together and left.

Gustav von Bock had spent a lifetime making contingency plans. So he made one in case his son had truly been killed by this woman who spoke perfect German with a Zurich accent. His heart told him the woman was speaking the truth. He leaned forward and prodded the fireplace logs with a poker. Sparks sputtered and weaved glowing patterns in the air.

An hour later, Klaus reappeared hesitantly at the door. The old man sensed him standing there and understood the unsaid message.

"How did he die?"

"Multiple gunshot wounds. It was instantaneous."

"Was it a woman?"

"The details are sketchy, but, yes, there was a woman involved. The Cowboy's wife."

Von Bock considered the news for a minute. "Thank you, my friend. Losses. We have learned to live with losses in our day, haven't we? Please help me to my room. I wish to sleep for a time."

Klaus assisted the old man to his feet.

As they tottered toward the elevator, the old man said, "You will alert the Oberkommando. The mission must not be forgotten or my son would have died in vain. Our first objective will be to obtain the specimens from the locker in Zurich. Then we hunt the girl."

"Of course, mein Herr," Klaus replied. "And what about the Storm Division?"

"Yes, yes. I was coming to that. Have the Sturmabteilung assemble here in eight hours. That should be enough time."

"How many, mein Herr?"

The old man thought for a moment. "Twenty, I should think."

FIGELI LEANED AGAINST a wall on the first sub-level beneath the Zurich Hauptbahnhof, feeling unobtrusive under the low ceiling and subdued lighting. It was 4:10 a.m. on Sunday, and he was fifty feet from locker 253. During the course of his four-hour-on, four-hour-off shift, he liked to rotate among a half dozen leaning posts, all strategically chosen so as to avoid the gaze of security cameras while allowing him to keep an eye on the target row.

The Zurich police did not suffer loiterers well. Figeli knew to keep moving, changing his jacket, swapping hats, shoes, gym bags, and varying eyeglasses out of a stash of items he kept in a locker. He even made a point of continually altering his posture and gait. Figeli was no dummy. Layers.

Helmut had described this two-man assignment as only a precaution. No expected threats. Just watch the locker and make sure it wasn't tampered with. If he wasn't back in three days, verify that its contents were removed only by authorized station personnel according to normal procedures and taken directly to the luggage claim office.

Figeli looked at his watch and yawned. Guido, his partner from the Brise de Mer gang and currently asleep at the Schweizerhof hotel across from the train station, would be relieving him in fifty minutes. Crime: four percent planning, one percent terror, ninety-five percent boredom.

The crowds had been gone for hours, but still the train station was far from empty. There was a family with three young children. And a man in a military uniform. And several dozen refugees from a punk rock concert. All crossed in front of Figeli in quick succession.

There was nothing out of the ordinary until a tall old lady in a head scarf and long, tattered coat came shuffling across the floor carrying a COOP grocery bag. She staggered a little as she walked, and that caught Figeli's eye. Ever suspicious, Figeli watched her and thought: *If this is a ploy, she's good.* She weaved across his field of view and turned into the same row as Helmut's locker. *What are the odds?* thought Figeli. He pushed himself off the wall and went after her, taking a circuitous route to avoid the cameras. As he entered the row, he saw the woman trying to force a key into 253.

He hung back and watched as she swayed slightly, withdrew the key and held it close to her face, looking puzzled.

"Can I help you?" he asked from a safe distance.

She turned and saw a dark, middle-aged man, slim, short,

wearing a brown leather jacket and a gray cap. As soon as she turned her head and he saw her bleary red eyes, he suspected she'd been drinking. He took a few steps closer, and her breath removed all doubt.

"Here, let me help you," he said. He approached and pried the key from her unsteady hand. It was for locker 245—the one directly above 253. He opened the locker and returned the key. Her gratitude was profuse. She wasn't used to young Swiss men being so kind to an old Bulgarian immigrant.

Figeli went back to his post, thinking, *My good deed for the day.* Forty-five minutes later, Guido showed up to relieve him.

CHAPTER 19

IDAHO, SATURDAY, 6:00 P.M.

The manager of the Boise airport rental car company considered having Boris arrested when he first saw the condition of the Ford Escape. The bumper had been torn off somewhere in the hills and the body dinged and scratched in a dozen places. The manager walked slowly around the SUV, making little marks on a drawing on his clipboard, his lips pursing tighter with every step. Fortunately, Boris had previously purchased the premium vehicle insurance and was covered for everything but damage incurred in a war zone.

Boris and Yohaba watched the manager inspect the car and felt confident until he stuck his finger through a bullet hole in the left rear fender. "Is that a bullet hole?" he asked.

Boris and Yohaba came around the car to stare dumbly at the jagged-edged ring. But the contract specifically said "war zone" not "damages from bullets," and eventually, the manager chose the path of least paperwork, signed everything off, and they made their flight with five minutes to spare.

Three hours later they were sitting at a gate in the international terminal of San Francisco airport, waiting to board a 9:00 p.m. Lufthansa flight to Zurich. Economy had been fully booked, and Yohaba ended up having to buy two $6,000 business-class tickets. Not that Boris could have fit in an economy seat.

While they waited, a text message came in from Yohaba's grandfather.

Elsa tracking nicely. All is well. Now projected to miss earth by 37.3 million miles.

Love, Leonard.

As she was considering texting a reply with news of the shooting, boarding was announced. In the end, she couldn't find the right words and turned off her phone. What could she say to anyone that would make sense? Who besides Boris would understand why she was doing this.

"I just figured out why America have unemployment problem," Boris said once they were seated in the plane. Yohaba had the window seat and Boris the aisle. While Boris talked, Yohaba changed out of her running shoes into a pair of flip-flops for the long flight.

"America too efficient. Not enough paperwork. If America have paperwork like Russia, then everyone employed, everyone happy."

"If America had paperwork like Russia, then everyone employed but everyone alcoholic like in Russia," Yohaba said, mimicking Boris's speech pattern. Then in her natural tone she said, "But lack of paperwork doesn't mean things here are cheap. Have you given any thought to how you're going to repay me for your ticket? I suppose I could let you work it off. What's the minimum wage in Russia?"

"I work on commission with financial accelerators for body count, Mrs. Hurt," Boris said with a straight face. "But in your case, travel expenses and your previous cooking payment enough."

At his answer, she turned away, closed her eyes, and leaned her head against the window. Her eyes welled up but no tears came.

"Thank you, Mr. Zokolov," she said through the lump in her throat. "It's not about the money. I have enough. But I couldn't do this without you."

"Sleep, Mrs. Hurt," Boris said.

It was eleven hours to Munich. Yohaba was asleep before the plane took off and didn't stir again until they were over Ireland. As soon as she awoke, she wanted to plan their next steps, but Boris was watching *Madagascar 3* and made her wait.

Madagascar 3 was the last movie she and Rulon had seen together. While she waited, she worried about Rulon. Would he be the same person? Though the prognosis was good, what if he had brain damage and needed to relearn how to read, write, and walk? What would that be like? She felt an enormous weight of guilt for leaving him. And guilt about the streak of cruelty she'd displayed with the old Nazi.

What have I done? What am I doing? she asked herself.

Was she crazy to be flying to Europe to have it out with the Nazis? Probably. Then why was she doing it? She thought about CERN and the thin man's eternal revenge.

The Nazis are the same. They don't stop, she said to herself. She remembered Professor Freling's words: *They're not going to stop. They don't know how. They're psychopaths.*

Rulon frequently talked about people needing to be the drivers of their own bus, be captains of their own ship. Despite all the fights he'd been in, he never did anything out of revenge—except for the time he spun out his BMW and splashed Isabella with mud in the woods near Bergun. Yohaba chuckled as she recalled the scene. Rulon! Secretive but honest, simple but no dummy, violent but gentle. Rulon's dad was right about him. He had a combination of mutually exclusive character traits that defied explanation.

She vowed she would never let herself get caught up in the downward spiral of revenge . . . like water down a drain, leading to nowhere except the grave.

With Rulon it was always about protection. The first time she saw him use Freya, it was to protect her. The Hönggerberg forest? Again, protection. CERN? How did he ever do what he did to save her after the beating he'd taken? It was love that drove him, not revenge. As Yohaba searched her feelings, she was comforted to realize that it was love driving her too. Love for Rulon and also love for their life together. They would never have peace if they went into hiding or ran.

She'd never seen a more terrifying sight than Rulon rising off the table in room G14-b with blood running down his face and Freya in his hand. Love could be just as terrifying as anger.

Just as Yohaba made a truce with her feelings, Boris took off his earphones and retracted the movie screen back into the center console.

"Now. What is so important?" he asked.

"We need to make a plan," Yohaba said. "You're the expert. What should we do?"

"They'll be waiting for us at locker. Thank you for that."

"Beats running all over Europe looking for them," Yohaba said. "C'mon. You've been through Russian spy school." She looked at her watch. "We've got over an hour before we land. Plenty of time. C'mon, I'm taking notes."

Boris sighed. "My goal is that neither of us gets killed. What's your goal?"

"Yeah, about that. I've been having a change of heart. At first I pictured us going there and killing them all. But now I'm thinking that's not such a good idea. I just want to make it so Rulon and I don't have to run all our lives. Helmut's dead. I wish that could be the end of it."

Boris said, "It never is. But good you have senses back. This not cartoon movie. When you fly to country and kill people, you go to jail forever. Also, you make more enemies and they hunt you down forever. If that was your great plan, I would tell you find quick plane back to Idaho."

"You were singing a different tune yesterday," Yohaba said defensively.

"True. But thinking clearer now."

"So what's the plan?"

"We negotiate equitable settlement," Boris said. "But this also can be dangerous in extreme. First, we must find locker, see what's inside, then maybe we have negotiating chip."

"If there is a bomb or something radioactive in the locker, we can't let them have it. Promise me that," Yohaba said.

"We will see. But having something they want gives us leverage to arrange meeting. In the end, who lives, who dies will not be up to us. Locker will be under surveillance, but fortunately, this is Europe, not America. Not likely people have guns. Just knives maybe. Swiss gun laws very strict. Only total idiot would bring gun."

Oops, thought Yohaba.

THEY LANDED IN Zurich at 7:33 p.m. coming down through a thick cloud cover onto a tarmac dotted with puddles. As they walked off the plane, Yohaba, proud of her country's efficiency, predicted their luggage would beat them to the carousel, and it did. They collected their two small suitcases and passed through customs without incident. As soon as they were in the crowded arrivals hall, Yohaba excused herself and weaved between pockets of people toward a restroom, dragging her carry-on behind her.

Once behind a restroom stall's securely locked door, she put the toilet lid down and laid the suitcase on the flat surface. The zipper stuck, and in her exhaustion, she felt herself starting to lose it. Sleeping on a plane was not like the real thing. She took a deep breath, wiped the sweat from her brow, and tried again. After a few more tugs, the zipper finally moved freely.

She took her black leather jacket and bullet-stab vest out of the suitcase and hung them on the door hook, then rummaged through her clothes until she found the ceramic knife, the ceramic bullets, and all the pieces for the ceramic pistol. She laid everything out on her clothes and reassembled the pistol.

When finished, she pulled back the slide and squeezed the trigger. *Snap!* Everything worked. Next she assembled the magazine. Finally she took the eight bullets and one by one loaded the magazine to its full seven-round capacity. She debated what to do with the last bullet. Normally, Rulon would fully load a magazine, plus keep one bullet in the chamber for an extra round. It was less safe to carry that way, but she knew why Rulon did that. The extra bullet could be the one that saved your life.

She decided to do it Rulon's way. She inserted the magazine, chambered a round, removed the magazine, loaded the eighth bullet, then replaced the magazine. After engaging the safety, she reached behind her and tucked the pistol into her belt. The knife in its scabbard went into her back pocket. Finally, she put on the bullet-stab vest and her jacket.

When she stepped outside the restroom, Boris was waiting.

He asked, "Can we please go hunt bad guys now, Mrs. Hurt?" He stopped and looked at her. She refused to meet his gaze. "What did you do in there?" he asked.

"None of your business," Yohaba said.

"It's not cold. Why did you put sweater on beneath jacket?"

"It's not a sweater; it's a bullet-stab vest, if you must know. Rulon gave it to me for Christmas one year."

"That Rulon. He one romantic guy." Boris grinned and shook his head. "Smart guy too. But you forgot one thing."

"What's that, Mr. Zokolov?"

"Flip-flops, Mrs. Hurt? Planning on beach party? Put on shoes."

Yohaba gave Boris a cold stare. "Why?" she challenged.

"You cannot run or fight in flip-flops."

Yohaba swallowed her pride and switched back to her running shoes.

From the arrivals terminal Boris and Yohaba took the elevator downstairs and then walked through the main airport shopping area to the underground train station. On the way, they purchased two cell phone SIM cards from a SwissCom store, and from a transportation kiosk, two train tickets to the Zurich Hauptbahnhof—the main train station—with the cash she'd taken from Helmut's wallet.

"He'd want to make amends, I'm sure," Yohaba said, feeling oddly guilty for using Helmut's money.

By the escalator to the trains, Boris spied some lockers and insisted they stow their luggage even though it meant having to come back for them later. At first Yohaba protested the inefficiency, but Boris explained that the lockers at the train station were a choke point and the most likely waiting place for Helmut's homicidal friends. They needed to get off the train with their hands free.

Five minutes later, they were waiting on the train platform beneath Terminal 2 for the next train into the city. An overhead electronic board indicated an eleven-minute wait.

Sharing the platform with Boris and Yohaba were six couples, a family with two small children, four women of mixed ages, a thin, middle-aged man in a brown hooded sweatshirt, two well-dressed men in their fifties, and a small knot of people in hiking apparel.

While they were waiting, Boris sketched out the plan. It was very Russian: simple, direct, and with no squeamishness about a women's role in combat. Yohaba would be the bait.

Boris said, "The locker is most obvious choke point. Men will be watching there, but probably also at stairs and escalators and maybe at entrances."

"They'd need an army for that," Yohaba said. "There are a lot of ways to get in." She described for Boris the general layout of the station.

"Okay," he said when she was done. "But must assume every choke point covered. Here is what we do. They know about young woman with big mouth, but they don't know about me."

"Unless they called Bernbailer," Yohaba said. "Which is what I would have done."

Boris thought about that. "Yes. Small change of plan." Boris started to say something, then looked down, obviously struggling to hold his temper. He collected himself and said calmly, "I cannot tell you how much shooting mouth off to old man has complicated this." Yohaba started to explain why she'd done it, but he waved a hand and cut her off. "All that is in past. I will hang back. Maybe forty meters. More dangerous for you if you are spotted, but less chance of you being spotted if we're not together. Can you accept that? Do you trust me?"

"Yes and yes."

"You will walk through station, and we will see who follows. If we capture one of them, we can interrogate and improve our tactical intelligence." While they were talking, the S14 arrived, the doors opened, and they got in.

Fifty feet away, the middle-aged man in the brown sweatshirt spoke softly into a dangling cell phone mike.

"They just got into the third car from the front," he said. He waited a few seconds to make sure they were definitely on, then also boarded the train. "I'm in the next car down," he said. "We'll be there in eight minutes."

In the third car from the front, Boris had hold of Yohaba's arm, making her wait by the door. The other people trying to get on glared at having to walk around them.

"Wait," he said to Yohaba. Just as the doors started to close, he tightened his grip on her arm and stepped with her back onto the platform. "Quick," he said. They hid together behind one of the plat-form pillars.

"What was that all about?" Yohaba asked after the train had cleared the station.

"Staying alive," said Boris. "We had company."

"Oh, man," Yohaba gasped. "How did you know? Where were they?"

"Did you notice the man in the brown sweatshirt?"

"No. Where was he? Was he on the train?"

"Eventually, yes. But first he was on platform with us. Look, you must stop relying on me," he said angrily. "You must start using all your brain and senses and stay alert. You said Rulon taught you things about his trade. Start using them. You're smart. We have to be team and use all our wits if we are to make it."

"I'm sorry," Yohaba said. "So tell me, what did I miss?"

"It was one man on station. He didn't fit in. There was something . . ." Boris paused in midsentence as he tried to recall exactly what it was that alerted him. "Okay. The sweatshirt was too thick for weather and too bulky. It could easily conceal a weapon. And he had no suitcase."

"So? Him and ten thousand other guys. Maybe he spent all day in the mountains and just dropped a friend off at the airport."

"You are thinking like civilian. You must stop that. Now learn. He wore heavy rubber-coated sports watch, and his shoes were laced-up kind and thicker than most. Why do you think I had you change flip-flops? Same reason. Professionals need sturdy watch and heavy shoes for fighting that won't fall off."

"You spotted all that? That's amazing. Rulon had the same gift. He could walk into a room and in thirty seconds describe everyone there, what they were wearing, and if they were a threat. When he worked for OCD, he always wore loafers and fragile-looking watches. He said trained people would spot the loafers and watch and dismiss him as a noncombatant or amateur and that would give him an edge. He also used to wear a foam pillow under his jacket to make himself look fat."

"Your Rulon no dummy. I heard all the stories, talked to the survivors, and when I first meet him even I fooled. Anyway, man in sweatshirt also had earphone cords running to pocket. Could be iPod but could also be cell phone alerting others ahead. Also, he didn't rush on train. He hung back as if to confirm we really got on."

"Wow," said Yohaba. "Individually they're all meaningless, but put them together and it paints a picture."

"It was more than that. It's also way he *wasn't* looking at us. Hard to explain. You're very smart in physics," said Boris. "Think you can be smart on street."

Yohaba bristled at Boris's insinuation that she wasn't up to the task. "Listen, buster," she said, "before this is over, you'll be offering me a job in the SVR."

Boris laughed. "First must become Russian citizen. But come. Now we get rental car."

"What about the plan?" she asked.

"Plan still okay, but not from train."

They walked back into the terminal and rented a small Skoda from the Avis counter in Terminal 2. Forty-five minutes later, they were halfway to the city when Yohaba suddenly hit the dashboard with her hand.

"We forgot the luggage," she said.

Boris said angrily in Russian, "I can't be the one who does all the thinking. Get in the game, Mrs. Hurt."

As soon as the S14 had arrived at the main station, Figeli walked through the car doors in a press of people and glided casually behind some stairs. Along the platform, travelers paused politely, waiting to board while others streamed out of the doors, anxious to get home or to make another connection.

Figeli focused on the people exiting the car ahead. No giant, no girl. *Now, where did they go?* He spotted two of his team at the other end of the platform staring at him, palms up, in a pose that asked, "What's going on?" He shrugged as if to say, "Don't ask me."

The doors closed, and the train pulled out. Figeli sprinted and caught up to the car ahead to see if Boris and Yohaba were there. Gone. He slowed to a jog and stopped. Scratching his chin, he looked up and down the nearly empty platform, perplexed.

While he was trying to decide where he'd gone wrong, his two team members walked up with their hands buried deep in their windbreakers. The three argued quietly. The two men eventually turned away, muttering about goofball wogs.

Figeli resigned himself to waiting for the next train back to the airport. He looked at the electronic board, checked the next train's arrival time, and griped to himself about bullet-headed Krauts. His only chance to pick up their trail again was if they took a rental car and not a taxi or another train. It was 8:45 p.m. on Sunday. He had a six-minute wait.

Once back at the airport, Figeli raced to the car rental desks and repeated the same story at each: he was late picking up two friends who might have given up waiting and rented a car instead. He described them and even had a picture of the girl. The manager at the Avis counter recognized the couple immediately. Yes, they had been there. He was kind enough to tell Figeli the make and model of the car and the number of the space where it was parked.

"If you hurry," the manager said, "you might still catch them. They only left ten minutes ago."

Figeli was already twenty feet away and running when he yelled, "Thanks" over his shoulder. When he got to the space five minutes later, though, it was empty. He pulled out his cell phone and gasped out the information to Helmut's uncle Eduard, who was at the train station coordinating the team.

After his call, he started to run back to the train platform but, after a few steps, settled into a brisk walk instead. *I've got to quit smoking*, he told himself.

CHAPTER 20

On the way into Zurich, a lane was closed for construction, causing even the light Sunday night traffic to back up. Yohaba, the Zurich native, was driving while Boris kept his head on a swivel, looking for followers. It was 9:20 p.m.

"I was thinking," Yohaba said while stopped. It was raining lightly and the windshield wipers swished intermittently. "We shouldn't park in the station garage. We should park someplace within easy walking distance, though."

"Da," Boris said. "If this car makes it."

"Stop it. This is a fine car. Very economical. We'll park in the Urania garage. It's less than a ten-minute walk to the train station."

"Good."

"And I just thought of a safer way to get to the locker."

"Tell me," said Boris skeptically.

"I should go in without you, grab a couple of Swiss cops and take them with me. I can tell them I need to get something valuable out of a locker, but I think I'm being followed. Tell them it's probably just my imagination, would they mind coming with me, it would just take a second. And then we can call the old man on the cell phone and set up a meeting. What do you think?"

"No," Boris said firmly. "Do you not see something wrong? Stop thinking like civilian! I told you already."

Yohaba accepted his rebuke and tried seeing the situation tactically. After a minute she said, "If the police go with me and anything does happen and they end up finding out there are drugs in the locker or something worse, I'll be arrested and thrown in jail."

"Da," Boris said. "No police. Agreed?"

"Agreed," Yohaba said.

When they reached the Urania garage, Yohaba drove down the spiral ramp and easily found an empty space on the first floor, unaware that two floors below them was Helmut's BMW left behind almost three days ago. Boris had Yohaba find a space close to the exit and back in for a quick getaway.

They sat in the car for fifteen minutes while Boris went over the plan. When he was finished, Yohaba said, "When we have what's in the locker and are driving away, I'll be a lot less nervous."

"That is good mental attitude. Think about positive future. Don't focus on obstacles."

"Rulon taught me that when we went mountain biking together. If you look at a rock, you'll hit it; if you look at a cliff you'll drive over it. You need to just stay focused on the trail twenty feet ahead."

"I cannot picture Rulon on bicycle," Boris said.

"He's great on the downhills," Yohaba said. "We should go."

As they left the garage, Yohaba followed Boris's lead as he went through the same countersurveillance moves she'd seen Rulon use—waiting and watching before moving, frequent changes of direction, and casual looks in reflective surfaces to see if anyone was following.

They emerged onto the Bahnhofstrasse, one of the world's premier shopping boulevards, and turned right past closed shops toward the main train station. The rain had stopped and the intermittent lamplights threw long shadows. The street was deserted except for a single tram rumbling past them toward the lake. Looming a few blocks ahead was the Zurich Hauptbahnhof, the largest train station in Switzerland. A massive stone edifice that, thanks to Switzerland's neutrality in World War II, was unbombed and therefore still possessed of its original 1847 grandeur.

Boris noticed her breathing and speech pattern were picking up speed and said, "Inhale, count to three. Hold it, count to three. Exhale, count to three." When she looked at him, puzzled, he said, "Just do it. It will help you relax and not panic. Panic worst thing. Always do duty. Remember, first one to show fear dies."

"Rulon said that after he'd ridden bulls a few times, it took a lot to scare him."

Boris stopped in his tracks, grabbed Yohaba's arm, and made her face him. "Mrs. Hurt, do me big favor. Forget about Rulon for five minutes, please, while we try not to get killed. Okay. Focus. Please!"

"Sorry," Yohaba said. "I'm scared. I talk when I'm scared. I'll stop."

"Do your breathing."

"Yes."

When they reached the Alfred Escher fountain in the island between the Schweizerhof Hotel and the main east entrance of the station, they were in a well-lit area with swarms of people, some waiting by the taxi stand and tram stops, others entering and exiting the station's large, arched entranceway. They circled around the construction on the north side, keeping clear of entrances, mixing with the crowds, and staying away from lights as much as possible. They crossed the tram tracks at a relaxed pace and walked along the Limmat river while marking the station's many entry and exit points.

After a short block, they left the river and ventured into the commercial district on the station's west side. Half a block into the neighborhood, the bustle of the station was left behind as the streets turned dark and deserted. They walked silently along wet sidewalks for three more blocks, until they came to an alley about a hundred meters long. It bisected a long city block from one end to the other and was just wide enough for a small car. At the far end, they could see a street lamp and decided to explore.

There were a dozen back doors along its length that led to ground-floor businesses or apartment blocks. Boris tried the doorknobs as he passed each one. All were locked. Halfway along its length, the alley opened into a small courtyard with a scrubby grass patch, a small swing set, and two cement benches. They walked straight through the courtyard and continued down the alley.

When they reached the lamp at the other end, Boris looked up and down the street, then turned around and looked back the way they'd come.

"This will work," he said. "You will come around block and enter alley here. I will be waiting in a doorway in dark."

"Da," Yohaba said.

They worked their way back to the station and resumed their circumnavigation of its massive exterior until they were standing again by the fountain in front of the east entrance.

"Remember," Boris said, "no looking back. Just walk through main hall and listen to my directions. No matter what happens, you don't look back."

"Okay."

"Turn cell phone on now."

Yohaba took her cell phone with the new Swiss SIM card out of her pocket, turned it on, and put the twin earphones in her ears. Boris did the same with his.

"Now test," he said. He walked a few feet away and she spoke to him. Everything worked, and she rejoined him.

He said, "One more thing. No flying back kicks or somersaults."

"What are you talking about?" Yohaba asked, confused.

"Every woman in American spy movie does somersaults when fighting. Very stupid. Don't do it." He laughed and playfully made a huge fist and punched her lightly on the shoulder. "And don't screw up."

Yohaba smiled bravely, took a deep breath, and stepped off the sidewalk. A tram had just dropped off its passengers, and Boris watched with approval as Yohaba slowed to mix with the crowd and disappear with them into the station's entrance. Her job was to pick up a tail, then lead the man to the alley several blocks away where Boris would take over.

In all the adrenaline and drama surrounding Rulon's shooting, there had been little time to stop and think. Now as Boris watched Yohaba walk away, he almost whispered into the phone for her to come back. This was madness. But she was lost in the crowd.

The wheel turns, thought Boris fatalistically. He followed after her until he had her in sight again but stayed about forty yards behind.

As soon as Yohaba entered the station's large main hall with its expansive ceiling, Boris said into his phone mike, "Turn right. Head to north entrance." He watched her turn and walk past the cafés and small shops that lined the east wall and work her way through the flow of people coming in from the north side. He took his eye off her for a moment to check the surrounding area and immediately saw a man in a sports cap, jeans, and a blue, long-sleeved shirt casually push off a wall and walk after her. Boris's adrenaline surged and his breathing quickened.

"You have company," he said into the phone. "This happening very quickly. Now go left. Get out of there. Head for west exit."

She turned toward the west with the man in the cap only fifteen yards behind. Yohaba was halfway across the hall when Boris noticed her tail nod to his right. A man in a black windbreaker stepped from the shadows and joined the parade.

Boris said, "I'll bet you never pick up men so easily, Mrs. Hurt. Now two men following you. Leave station now through north side."

Yohaba veered sharply right, exited out the north entrance into the night, then made a sharp left. The two men quickened their pace and followed her outside.

Boris observed that they stayed together, focused hard on the girl, and never looked behind. Amateurs. Or maybe they believed the girl was alone. But how could that be? Surely the man at the airport had reported there were two of them. Boris was suddenly wary. Maybe he was wrong about the airport. He slowly turned around, half expecting to see an army of Nazis behind him. No. Just the normal throngs of travelers. Relieved, but puzzled and still worried, he stayed with the plan and followed Yohaba. The disturbing thought came to him: *Something is not right.*

Yohaba led her tails along the station's west side, crossing tram tracks, weaving through people waiting for buses, never pausing, never looking back. Boris whispered encouragement and kept her informed of what was happening behind her. The men kept pace, never attempting to close the gap and never looking back.

Boris had just dipped behind a bus stop kiosk when he saw two rough-looking men slip out of the station's west exit, hands in their pockets and eyes intent on Yohaba in her black leather jacket, jeans, and long auburn hair. He pegged them as a threat and was about to warn Yohaba when three more suspicious-looking men emerged from another exit. In the last group was a man wearing a brown hooded sweatshirt. Even from the back, Boris was sure he was the man from the airport. Now there were seven of them.

"Turn right, now," Boris said into his phone. "Don't look back.

You picked up five more admirers. I thought Zurich supposed to be safe place for young woman."

"Me too," Yohaba said in a shaky voice.

She changed her direction even as she spoke, crossed in the middle of the street, and had a row of five-story buildings on her right. The three groups of men didn't converge but continued following separately and silently after her, passing through the light of each successive street lamp into the shadows and out again.

When they were a block from the station, the two groups of two men crossed the street to be on the same side as Yohaba. The group of three stayed on the opposite side where they were but picked up the pace. Other than Yohaba, her silent followers, and a few lonely pedestrians, the streets were deserted.

Three blocks from the station, the streets were darker, emptier, quieter. A car went by, its tires hissing on the wet pavement, headlights scattering light across the puddles. Yohaba walked from street lamp to street lamp down an empty Konradstrasse. The three on the opposite side had picked up the pace and were now even with Yohaba. The four other men on her side still trailed behind, the first group of two maintaining their twenty-yard gap and the second group another twenty yards behind them. This forced Boris to fall back even more. He was now seventy yards behind Yohaba. So far, no one had made an overt threat and no one appeared to know that Boris was following.

To anyone watching, it was a normal street scene in boringly safe Zurich. But Boris knew the situation was out of control. He felt the clutch of panic in his gut. He considered ordering Yohaba back to the train station where there'd be witnesses and police, but knew her pursuers could easily cut her off on the open street. He looked for a bus or a tram that she could sprint for and hop just before the doors closed. Nothing. No sounds, no tracks, no overhead electrical bus cables. They were two blocks from the station and no bus stops. The streets were quiet except for Yohaba, her shadows, a few couples, and a few solitary figures walking dogs after the rain.

Boris had planned for one man to follow the girl. A second man added complexity but was workable. Three men was a huge problem, but seven, seven was a fatal and irretrievable miscalculation. He realized why they never turned around. They knew he was there, and he didn't matter. They knew if they focused on the girl they would either draw him out to his death or their numbers would chase him away. Either way he'd been outmaneuvered.

Boris looked behind him. Nothing suspicious. The action was all playing out in front of him. Yohaba was approaching the alley.

"Change of plan," Boris said, hoping for some brilliant idea that would save them both, but managing only an unimaginative brute force plan that had him sacrificing his life for hers. "When I say 'run' you must run with everything you have. Understand? You cannot walk around block as planned. You must run completely around block and then come through alley from other side. Don't stop running no matter what. It will be two-hundred-yard dash. I will be waiting for you somewhere in alley. Do you understand? Don't stop running. Go past me, then keep running to train station. Don't look back."

"I'm not leaving you," Yohaba said. "But I can do the rest. Lead them up the alley from the other side. Got it. I just hope they haven't recruited Usain Bolt." Boris could hear her breathing accelerate sharply as the extra adrenaline kicked in.

"Wait for signal. I will make diversion. Give you bigger head start. Get ready."

"Okay. I'm glad I changed out of the flip-flops."

Boris grunted his agreement, then looked around for something to throw. He passed a dozen bicycles in a bike rack and spotted one where a U-lock was stuck through the rear wheel and not anchored to anything solid. As quietly as possible, he picked up the loose bicycle and did a hammer thrower's spin before sending it sailing through the air.

A split second after the bicycle crashed into the middle of the street, he yelled, "NOW!" into the cell phone. All of Yohaba's pursuers turned and looked at the bike skidding toward them and didn't see Yohaba take off in a sprint.

"Hey, fashisty," Boris roared in German with a thick Russian accent. Now they all looked at him. "Why you up so late on Sunday night?"

Boris scanned the row of bicycles, found another one with a chain through its wheels but also not chained to the rack. He grabbed the chain, braced one massive foot on the wheel, and with one titanic pull ripped the chain loose through the spokes. He now had a heavy chain with a heavy-duty lock attached to it. He twirled it a few times, wrapping and unwrapping it around his burly forearm.

"Hey, fashisty. Why you not home in bed?"

While Boris distracted the Nazis, Yohaba ran for her life. Her earphones popped out of her ears after the first steps and got ripped away by her pumping arms. For a few seconds, her pursuers focused on Boris and hesitated. But then one of them turned to check on Yohaba. When he saw her running away at full speed, he yelled and chased after her, running half sideways for a few steps as he shouted orders to the others. Three of the men followed him but three stayed behind to deal with Boris. She had a fifty-yard lead, but to Boris's eye the men were clearly faster. It would be close.

The three men who faced Boris spread out as a team, flipping switchblades open as they advanced. One of them was the man with the brown sweatshirt. They were about two hundred yards from the train station. The street was deserted, apartment buildings with small, ground floor businesses on both sides, half with their lights on. The Hotel Montana across the street. The three Nazis formed a half-circle and converged on Boris. Boris swung the chain over his head and cursed them. The group hesitated. While they stood there, a doorman stuck his head out of the hotel entrance. He shouted at them and threatened to call the police. The three men hid their knives and slowly backed away.

"Some other time, Slav," snarled one of them. They continued backing up a few more steps, then broke into a run and followed their friends.

As soon as they turned the corner, Boris ran twenty yards and turned down the alley, still clutching the chain and lock. He ran as fast as he could, hoping, at any moment, to see Yohaba turn the corner ahead of him. When he hit the courtyard, he didn't stop, but thought surely he should be seeing her race up the alley by now. When she didn't appear, he got a sick feeling in his stomach. He listened now for her screams, losing hope with every step.

He was thirty yards from the end of the alley, with all hope now lost, when Yohaba suddenly appeared in a frantic sprint, taking the turn too fast and having to push off the alley wall to keep her balance and keep running. Just as she did, a man leaped for her, missed, and went sprawling. Yohaba never looked back. Head down, arms pumping, lungs searing, legs heavy, she fought to keep sprinting.

Another man skidded around the corner and leaped over his fallen comrade. Boris stopped and pressed into a doorway. Yohaba saw him and ran past, her eyes wide with fear and effort, her head back, her mouth open. She was starting to seize up badly from lactic acid, her pursuer just five yards behind and closing fast.

Just as the Nazi reached the doorway, Boris stuck out an arm like a miller's beam and clotheslined the guy right across the throat. The pursuer's head stopped, but his legs kept going, forcing him to flip ninety degrees in the air until his legs were pointing almost straight up, his body pivoting around Boris's stationary arm. He then crashed to the ground, the back of his head hitting the pavement with a sickening crack.

Yohaba pulled up and turned just in time to see the guy's head hit the ground. She jerked away at the sight.

"You killed him," she gasped between breaths, sickened at the thought. "I think you killed him." She bent over with her hands on her knees and panted for air. "There's more coming."

"Run!" Boris yelled at her, then turned to face the light at the end of the alley.

The man who had dived after Yohaba was on his feet, adjusting his cap and eyeing Boris warily. Two more men ran up, but the man with the cap held them back. Both sides stared at each other from thirty yards away, breathing hard. Then the three men who had faced Boris on the street caught up and slid to a halt by their comrades. The Nazis were now all together again. Six of them still standing.

Boris knew there was no point in running. He'd never even make it back to the center courtyard. He was quick but not fast. Out of the corner of his eye, he saw Yohaba still there. She came toward him on wobbly legs, still breathing hard, done in.

The man who had just missed tackling her was the man with the sports cap and long-sleeved shirt who had been the first to follow Yohaba in the station. Not taking his eyes off Boris, he pulled a cell phone from his pocket and made a call. He spoke, listened, then put away the phone. "Just give us the key and you can go," he said.

Boris laughed. "Yes, fashisty always keep their word."

Yohaba put a hand on his arm and whispered, "There's too many."

Boris swore. "I said you go," he said angrily. "I will stay and negotiate."

She pulled at his arm. "Maybe we can get back to the station where there are police around." The Nazi with the cap stepped forward. He looked to be in his late thirties, and had a round face and a crooked nose. It started to lightly rain again.

"Just the key." He held out his hand and advanced up the alley. The five other men hung back slightly. "You can't outrun us," he said. "You can't outfight us. Don't be stupid."

The alley was six feet wide, too narrow for more than two of them to attack at a time. Boris weighed his chances. The problem with knives was you always took a cut even if it was just on the arm. He stayed quiet. He could back up and probably keep them off for a time, but once they reached the courtyard they'd spread out and surround him. Better they fight here where it was narrow. Yohaba could get away. But then what? They'd hunt her down easily enough. She was a babe in the woods. The man said he wanted just the key, but Boris knew they wanted the girl even more.

"Hard way. Easy way. Your choice," the Nazi said as he continued to walk forward. He had his hand out, palm up. "Just the key." When after ten seconds neither Boris or Yohaba said anything, the man said, "Okay, the hard way." He reached behind his back and came out with a wicked little knife. Behind him his five buddies did the same. Boris couldn't see them clearly in the shadows, but he saw their hands move and heard the menacing click of the switchblades. The six men were now only ten yards away and advancing again.

Boris and Yohaba slowly backed up. Boris whispered to her to run, but Yohaba said no. He looked at her quickly, and she looked back defiantly.

He said, "You are idiot, Mrs. Hurt." Boris swung the chain over his head. The six men were now five yards away and stepping over their fallen comrade. One of them reached down and felt his carotid artery.

"He's dead," he said, and at his words, the situation, already filled with murderous intent, kicked up a few notches in intensity. Boris snatched a quick look behind him. The courtyard was twenty yards away.

"Go. Go now," Boris said to Yohaba. "Do what I say. Get to the airport and go home. This is over. I am sorry."

"Your planning stinks," Yohaba said. "I'm handling things next time."

Boris smiled. "Positive thinking. I like that. Now go. Time for joking over."

Boris pushed Yohaba behind him and forgot about her. He stopped, spread his legs, and seemed to fill the entire alley. His focus was on the pack in front of him. "You want key. Come and take it."

The light was behind the Nazis, and Boris couldn't see their faces clearly, just their forms moving forward in a dark, shadowy phalanx. He unwrapped the chain from around his arm and stood ready. While he was trying to decide whether or not to charge, he heard a click behind him, a strange sound that wasn't metallic. He remained focused on the men in front of him and saw them hesitate. Then from behind him Yohaba spoke.

"One step closer, and I'll drill you."

Boris dared not turn to look. He imagined her with her hand in her pocket pretending she was armed. He groaned and growled out of the side of his mouth, "I told you leave." Something came into his peripheral vision. It was Yohaba's extended hand at shoulder height, and it held a gun.

The six men were stopped in their tracks. They were close enough that Boris could see the confusion in their faces.

"That's not a gun," said the Nazi in the cap. His tone started out a little unsure but then grew in confidence and arrogance as he spoke. "You couldn't have gotten a gun through airline security and you haven't had time to procure one since you arrived in Zurich. We were watching you at the airport. You have no idea who you're up against."

Yohaba said, "This is the twenty-first century, my technology-impaired friend. I may not know what I'm up against, but I know what you're up against. This is a ceramic pistol. Airport scanners can't detect it. It fires ceramic bullets. It's even quiet. The powder fires in two stages so it won't shatter the barrel. I could shoot you now and not even wake the neighbors."

"There's no such thing. You're bluffing," the Nazi said.

"Are you sure?" Yohaba asked. "Willing to bet your life on it?"

"It's a toy gun," the man said.

"If you insist," Yohaba replied coolly. "I killed your Helmut von Frankenstein, and now I'm chasing you with a toy. If that makes sense to you, then I say take another step forward." With that, Yohaba took a step past Boris to within three yards of the men, her arm extended, the barrel of the gun pointing directly at the forehead of the guy in the cap doing the talking.

She was close enough for him to see her face, and for her to see his, but not close enough for him to grab the gun out of her hand. Boris held his breath. He dared not move. He dared not speak. He dared not even touch her to move her out of harm's way for fear of breaking the spell.

Yohaba and the Nazi leader locked eyes.

"You won't shoot," the man said, seemingly confident but now tacitly conceding that the pistol was genuine.

"Your logic is dazzlingly brilliant," Yohaba said. "I shot your buddy, there's another dead guy right behind you, but I'm not going to shoot you."

Behind the leader, one of the Nazis, a man with a tattoo on his chin, snarled, "She's bluffing." He took a step forward, but the leader held out his arm and stopped him.

The leader backed up a step with both arms extended, pushing his men back too. "Grab Ingo," he said, meaning the dead man.

The whole pack then began a wary, begrudging retreat. Two of the men grabbed Ingo under each arm and dragged him along. The leader walked backward, not taking his eyes off Yohaba.

"You haven't seen the last of us," he said, pointing at her. Then laughing smugly, he spoke to Boris. "Hey, Slav. Lucky you have your woman to do the fighting for you. Pigs." He spat, then turned and caught up with his men.

The group reached the end of the alley and turned left. Once out of sight, the leader kneeled down over Ingo and confirmed he was dead. Still kneeling and not looking up, he said to the man in the brown sweatshirt, "Follow them. Stay close. Stay in touch."

YOHABA WATCHED THEM go. She put the pistol on safe, twirled it twice in her hand, then stuck it in her belt.

"Do you play poker, Mrs. Hurt?" asked Boris once the Nazis were out of sight. "That was best bluff I ever saw."

"Why, thank you, Mr. Zokolov," she replied. "But it wasn't a bluff."

"But fashisty right. Airport security too tight. It must be toy. But that is great story about ceramic gun."

"It's not a toy," she insisted. "It's real. It's exactly what I said it was. But come on. Let's go. I'll explain later." She broke into a jog. "Man, am I sweating."

Boris caught up to her. He wrapped the chain around his hand so he could run more easily, then asked, "Where we going?"

"To the locker, of course. They'd never expect us now." Yohaba figured the six men would send for a car to pick up the body and call it a night.

Boris shrugged. Why not? His plan hadn't turned out so well.

She asked, "What do you think? Do you think that was all of them?"

"No. I think they leave some people back at train station. I think they not stupid like me. But they will not expect this. It's a good plan."

They jogged another twenty yards before Yohaba asked, "Did you mean to kill that guy?"

"No," Boris said. "But when you chase girl down alley with knife, sometimes you die."

"Yeah," Yohaba said. "Speaking of which. You won't mind if I start referring to you as Custer."

"What does that mean?"

"Custer was this American cavalry officer who attacked an Indian village in 1876, not realizing that every Indian in the world was there waiting for him. Sound familiar?"

Boris grunted. "You do realize we are followed."

Yohaba started to look back, but Boris stopped her. "Don't look. Trust me. Someone following."

"How do you know? Did you hear something?"

"No, but it's what they must do. They can't lose us now."

"Right."

CHAPTER 21

Just as they reached the end of the alley, Boris touched Yohaba's arm to stop her. He pulled a dentist's mirror out of his pocket, crept up to the end of the alley, and used the mirror to look around the corner in both directions. All clear.

"Rulon used one of those at CERN," Yohaba said. "You two are so alike, it's scary."

As soon as they left the alley and turned onto the sidewalk, Boris motioned to Yohaba to keep quiet while he pressed himself against the building, waiting to intercept whoever was following. He used the mirror again to look back down the alley. "Shhh," he said. "Someone comes."

After thirty seconds, they heard the patter of soft footsteps followed by a head poking cautiously around the corner. Boris grabbed the man by his longish black hair and smashed him against the brick wall. Boris watched him sag to the ground and then charged into the blackness of the alley. He came back a few seconds later to find Yohaba kneeling next to the man, searching him. She found a knife and a cell phone and slipped both into her jacket pocket.

"There was no one else," Boris reported. "Here, let me help you." He grabbed handfuls of sweatshirt, hauled the man easily to his feet, propped him against the wall with one meaty hand, and roughly searched him with a thoroughness that would make an airport

194

security guard blush. He took away the man's wallet and key chain, tossed both to Yohaba, and finished the search by punching his captive brutally in the stomach. The man fell to his knees, slumped to all fours, and threw up. Boris shook his head in disgust, grabbed him by his collar, and dragged him back into the alley. Yohaba followed.

Their prisoner with the brown sweatshirt was a small, dark-complexioned middle-aged man. It was Figeli.

Boris said to Yohaba, "This was same one on train."

Boris sat him up in a doorway twenty feet from the street. He slapped Figeli in the face a few times to bring him around, then crouched beside him and spoke in German, a more fluent language for him than English.

"Okay, Fashisty. I talk, you listen. Then you talk, I listen. You understand? Say yes."

Figeli mumbled something.

"Close enough," Boris said. "First question: how many are at the train station?"

Figeli mumbled a few indistinct obscenities. Boris cupped a shovel-sized hand over Figeli's mouth and gripped Figeli's thigh, searching with his fingers for the right pressure points just above the knee. Figeli's feet jerked and kicked as he frantically tried to pry Boris's hand from his leg. It was like trying to unwrap a python. After ten seconds, Boris let go and Figeli stopped flailing.

"Next time I break something," Boris said. "Understand?" Boris slowly released his grip around Figeli's mouth.

Figeli responded with a clear, high-pitched yes.

"I don't approve of torture," Yohaba said firmly from over Boris's shoulder.

"I don't either," Boris replied. "Keep watch at the end of the alley. Tell me if anyone comes."

After Yohaba left, Boris leaned in close enough for Figeli to almost suffocate in his sour sweat, humid bad breath, and merciless eyes. Boris said, "Women can be so gullible, but you're not, are you?"

Figeli, eyes wide, shook his head emphatically.

"Good," Boris said. "How many are at the train station?"

The question was barely out of Boris's mouth before Figeli answered, "Fifteen."

"Does that include the men we just dealt with?"

"Yes."

"Where are the ones at the station?"

"On the same level as the locker. Though I'm sure they moved a few to the upper level by now."

"The men you were with just now, what will they do?"

"Two will stay with the body and call for a van. The other three will likely head back to the station."

"That makes eleven total at the station if the two with the body don't make it back and I don't count you. Right?" said Boris in an ominously implied threat.

"Yes," agreed a trembling Figeli.

Boris continued. "What's in the locker? And before you answer, remember what I did to your friend."

"Drugs," Figeli lied, calculating that if he told the truth, the big Russian might kill him out of revulsion. "But listen, I am not a fascist. I'm not even German. I'm Corsican. I was hired to help. This means nothing to me but the money. If you kill me, my gang will hunt you down. It is their code. It's not worth it. I'm not worth it. They are crazy about such things."

"My gang's bigger and crazier," Boris said. "All this for some drugs in a locker? Somehow I don't believe that. That's your first lie. I'm keeping score."

"That's what they told me," Figeli said, fully alert and sweating for more reasons than the unseasonal heat. "I told you. I'm not one of them. I'm their pet froggy. Okay, I didn't believe them about the drugs, but that's what they told me."

Boris decided to deal with the lie later. He asked, "If it's so important, why not break into the locker and just take what's there?"

"We wanted to do that, but someone wants the girl very badly. The locker is supposed to be the bait to draw her out."

"Not logical. The contents don't have to be in the locker. All that is necessary is that the girl thinks something is there. I ask you one more time: why not break into the locker?"

"If she didn't show up by nine tomorrow morning, we were to break it open and remove the contents."

"Of course. But why wait until then?"

"She has the key. The lockers are alarmed. It's much easier if we have the key."

Boris considered that, and it made sense. He said, "We understand there are deadlines."

"The locker is safe for three days. Until noon tomorrow. After that the contents go to the luggage claim office for ninety days. Obviously, at that point things become more complicated if we don't have the key."

"Where were they taking it?"

"To someplace in Boblingen," Figeli said, referring to a German city a two-hour drive north of Zurich. "That's all I know. The man the girl killed was supposed to deliver it, but he went to the United States instead."

Boris knew there were other questions he should be asking, but the jet lag was slowing down his thinking.

While he was wracking his brain for something else to ask, Yohaba came back from the edge of the alley, touched his shoulder, and whispered, "Three of them just turned the corner at the end of the block. They'll be here in less than a minute. Hey, I hope you asked him where the old man lives."

Boris nodded, held his finger to his lips for Yohaba to hush, then pointed to a doorway ten feet away and motioned for her to hide.

After Yohaba slipped off, Boris leaned in close to Figeli and, bristling with menace, whispered an inch from his ear, "If they discover us, you will die first from a crushed windpipe. It's not much harder than crushing an ice cream cone. I know." Boris gripped Figeli's throat and squeezed just hard enough to reinforce the message. Figeli closed his eyes and moved his lips in silent prayer.

Yohaba flattened herself as deeply into the doorway as she could. Boris pushed further into his doorway with Figeli. After a short, tense wait, the three men on the street walked by with only a cursory glance down the alley.

Boris waited half a minute, then nodded to Yohaba to go check. She pulled out her pistol, stepped out of the doorway, and silently hugged the right-side wall all the way to the street. The Nazis had passed right to left. She held the gun with two hands, arms extended pointing to the ground, and took a deep breath, then quickly stuck her head out in the direction they'd gone. She did this several times in both directions before she gave the all clear.

Well done, thought Boris.

Focusing once more on Figeli, he asked about the old man. Figeli told him the old man's name and that he lived just outside Boblingen, Germany, in a big house on a river. When Boris didn't say anything, Figeli misunderstood his silence and burst out in a near panic that the old man was deranged, that he was the father of the Nazi the woman killed, that he would never give up looking for her even if it destroyed his life's work.

Boris had one more question. "We want to end this once and for all. Is there a way?"

"Man to man? There's only one way to end this. Give them the key and the girl," Figeli said. "They would pay you for both. Only one person wanted the American cowboy dead, and the girl shot him. Now, it's just about the key and the girl."

Boris thought about that. "Thank you. You have been useful."

Figeli looked relieved, but only for an instant, because, without warning, Boris rolled him roughly onto his stomach and sat on his upper back, crushing the wind out of him. While Figeli struggled, Boris straddled him and braced his heavily shod feet against the wall on either side of the Corsican's head. Figeli protested, but Boris stifled his feeble cries by cupping two massive hands around Figeli's jaw and then arched backwards. Figeli's eyes went wide with terror as Boris began to lean back even further in the act of snapping his neck.

In a flash, Yohaba was at Boris's side, prying his thick fingers from Figeli's face and hissing in German, "What are you doing? Are you a maniac? Let him go."

Boris relaxed and released Figeli's face. Still sitting on Figeli's back, he lifted Figeli's head by his hair, twisted it slightly so they could see each other, and said calmly, "Don't move. Stay quiet. Okay?" Figeli, gasping and choking, nodded assent. Boris released his grip and Figeli's head flopped forward.

Turning to Yohaba, Boris asked in German, "What did you think he was going to do if he caught you?"

"I know what you are getting at. But there are some things we can't do. If it happens in the course of events, that's one thing. Like that guy back there. I'm not blaming you for that. But not this. Not this way."

Boris said, "Okay, let's compromise. Let me do this one. But we'll let the next one go."

Figeli, still coughing, cocked his head slightly. "You should listen to her. I think she has a point."

Boris raised a huge hand to give him a swat, but Yohaba grabbed it on the backswing and held on. While gripping with all her might, she moved in close so her face was only inches from Boris's.

She said, "You're making jokes. You know I'm right. We'll make him promise not to ever try and hurt us again."

"I promise," Figeli said quickly. "By all the saints in heaven, I promise."

Boris looked disgusted. "Fine." With a look of resigned disappointment, he reached into his jacket pocket and pulled out a roll of duct tape. He unrolled enough tape to wrap around Figeli's head several times and tape his mouth shut. Next Figeli's hands, then his feet. Finally, he wrapped the roll a dozen times around Figeli's upper body, pinning his arms to his side. When finished, he rolled Figeli against the alley wall and stood up.

Looking down at his trussed-up captive, Boris said to Figeli in an attempt at black humor, "I hope you don't live to regret this. A snapped neck would have been quick and relatively painless. You sure you don't want to reconsider? It would just take a second."

Figeli didn't get the joke and just shook his head vigorously.

"We're doing the right thing here," Yohaba said. "Rulon would be proud of you." She started to turn away but then paused and crouched down to speak to the little Corsican. Figeli saw her tattoo and wondered if she were part of a gang.

"I'm sure you are a bad person," she said. "Maybe you've even killed people in the past. I don't know. But maybe it's just the world you grew up in, and you don't know any better." Behind her, Boris let out a huge groan and turned away. Yohaba set her jaw and carried on doggedly. "But let me tell you something, there's a special place reserved in hell for people whose hearts mercy can't touch. We're letting you go even though it's probably not the smart thing to do. Do you understand what I'm saying?" Figeli nodded. She looked into his unreadable eyes and said, "This is what mercy feels like. You should try it sometime. And another thing. I shot this maniac's son because after ambushing my husband and shooting him in the head, he came to the hospital to finish him off. I happened to be there and got off a shot first. Do you understand what I'm saying? If I hadn't shot him, he would have killed my husband. Killing him wasn't something I planned to do or wanted to do."

"Come," hissed Boris from the edge of the alley. "We're losing initiative."

"Hold your horses," she said over her shoulder. Focusing on Figeli again, she said, "The guy who died back there. Did he have a family?"

Figeli nodded.

"Children?"

Figeli nodded again.

Yohaba grimaced. "This whole business stinks. Look, I'm sorry. You weren't there, but I saw how he died. It wasn't intentional. He could have just as easily lived if he landed a little differently. It was bad luck. Do you understand?" Again, Figeli nodded. She dropped his wallet and car keys in his lap and left.

Yohaba caught up with Boris and together they turned toward the Hauptbahnhof. She looked at her watch. It was just after eleven. Trains ran all night over the weekend. There would still be people in the station. Maybe with enough witnesses around, they could pull this off without any more violence.

Boris started to say something in Russian but Yohaba cut him off.

She said, "Do you mind? I'd prefer speaking English. Something comes over you when you speak Russian. It's like you have a personality change."

"Maybe it is English that is personality change," he replied in English. "By the way, Mrs. Hurt, I was impressed that you never used my name in front of Nazis. Was that on purpose?"

"Yes, as a matter of fact, it was. I think I'm getting the hang of this spy stuff. All of Rulon's lessons are coming back to me. I find it all rather exhilarating. It's like I was born to do this."

"Don't be overconfident," Boris said harshly. "You will get us both killed. You are going through three stages of tiger hunter. First stage is fear. I liked you better when you were in stage one. You are now in stage two—cocky. Most dangerous stage. You will either get killed or almost get killed. Never fails. Probably you will get me killed too."

"I'm not getting overconfident," Yohaba said defensively. "And I'm not going through any stages."

"Yes, you are," Boris said. "It is inevitable. Come. Let us see how stupid you can be."

"Not that I care, but what's stage three?" Yohaba asked.

"If I live past tonight, I will tell you."

CHAPTER 22

ZURICH, SUNDAY, 11:05 P.M.

Boris and Yohaba walked back to the station, but instead of entering, they curled around to the north and got on a waiting #46 bus heading toward Rutihof. They got off ten minutes later at the Nordbrücke stop and walked twenty yards to the stairs leading down to the Wipkingen platform to pick up the S2 heading back to the Hauptbahnhof.

"This will catch them by surprise," Yohaba said confidently. "Trust me. They'll never expect us to come in on a train. Rulon says that it's all about getting every little edge you can to work in your favor."

Boris said dryly, "Thank you for that, Mrs. Hurt. When this is over, please write book titled *The Wit and Wisdom of Rulon Hurt* and send me copy."

Yohaba's plan was to make their approach from the train platforms below the lockers, walk quickly upstairs to 253 (barreling past anyone who stood in their way), take whatever was there, and leave. Even late on a Sunday night she counted on there being a few people around and certainly a few police. She assumed the Nazis wouldn't dare risk a major confrontation in the main station but instead would follow them outside and try funneling them to some prearranged ambush point.

Their train arrived. Boris told Yohaba to let it go and wait for the next one fourteen minutes later. Standing on the Wipkingen platform, he couldn't come up with a better plan, but peppered her with questions until they had worked out a few contingencies.

For a weapon, Boris had the chain and lock wrapped around his waist under his dark gray bomber jacket. Yohaba insisted on carrying the pistol, and though Boris argued that he should have it, he did it halfheartedly. If everything fell apart, she would need it to blast her way out.

With her back turned to the other people on the platform, she gave Boris the ceramic knife. He looked at her sharply when she handed it to him. "Nice of you to share. Could have used blade earlier." He took the knife out of its scabbard, tested the sharpness with the tip of his finger, and chuckled darkly. "Could do heart surgery with this. Might have to before night is over." He sheathed the knife and put it in his pocket.

They discussed their escape. Should they take a train out of the station and double back to the car, or should they leave the station on foot and walk straight to the garage?

"The eternal question," Yohaba said. "What do you think, Mr. Zokolov? I can go either way."

Boris thought about it and did not want to get caught on a dark street again. "We should leave by train. We must time this carefully so we don't wait long on platform after we are done."

The rain had stopped and the night was humid and pleasantly warm. Yohaba had unzipped her jacket, exposing her bullet-stab vest.

Boris said, "Zip and button jacket, Mrs. Hurt. If they see vest, they go for head shot."

Yohaba complied without comment. The S2 showed up, and they got on. It was twenty minutes to midnight, and three minutes to the Hauptbahnhof.

By midnight, the crowds in the main station had vanished and been replaced by solitary, weary citizens trudging in and out. On the first sub-level beneath the main floor, scattered travelers emerged from stairs or escalators to hurry, head down, to the train platforms at the south end. With eyes only for the large electronic board displaying the train schedules, no one made eye contact, and no one ventured into the somber, shadowy catacombs where the lockers were. If someone had, they would have seen a group of eight men huddled together and talking softly in the row containing locker 253.

"There is no such thing as a ceramic gun," said Helmut's uncle, the white-haired Eduard. "The gun powder in the bullet would blow it apart. It's simple physics. I'm afraid you let the woman make a fool of you." Eduard the Reichsleiter, a true believer, the cause's heir-apparent after Gustav, spoke pleasantly and condescendingly, which made the dressing-down even more humiliating for his subordinate. Alongside Eduard were his two personal bodyguards, both muscle-bound great-grandsons of Waffen SS heroes.

"I'm not so sure," Tilman said. He took off his cap and used it to wipe his brow. Ingo's body had been picked up, and Tilman and the remaining members of his team, except for Figeli, were together again. "Her husband worked for OCD. He could have had access to all sorts of technology we never heard of. She seemed, I don't know"—he searched for the right word—"convincing."

Eduard, looking like a professor in his brown turtleneck and brown suede jacket, continued the lesson in his slow, pedantic way, as if Tilman hadn't spoken. It was an annoying family trait. "Worst of all, you have probably scared them away. No key and no girl. Worst of both worlds. They were six feet away from you, and now they are . . . ?" Eduard let the unfinished question dangle in the dim light of the locker row.

Tilman ran his hand through his short blond hair and put his cap back on. "It was a complex situation in a densely populated neighborhood. We were in an alley where our numbers were less effective. I made an operational decision."

"I believe I asked you a question."

"I ordered the Corsican to follow them."

"And what was his report when he last called in?" Eduard asked.

Tilman looked at his watch and saw the digital display was blank, probably broken when he jumped for the girl. Annoyed, he tapped the face with his finger. With a rising sense of incompetence exposed, he inclined his head toward the man on his right. "How long has it been?"

A bald, solidly built man looked at his watch and said in a clipped, precise tone, "Over an hour, sir."

"Over an hour," Eduard repeated, pronouncing each word slowly and distinctly. Then adding with final distaste, "I see." He looked at the five members of the team. "Does anyone find this an unusually long time?"

No one answered; only Tilman maintained eye contact.

Eduard looked at each face. "Hmm?" he asked several times. "Has no one an opinion?" Receiving no answer, his expression turned serious and angry. "Oliver, Martin," he barked to two of Tilman's men. "Backtrack all the way to the alley. Find the Corsican before the police do. If he's dead, and I suspect he is, you know what to do. Call in every ten minutes. Go."

Oliver and long-haired Martin turned on their heels and left. Eduard stood at the back of the row of lockers with his bodyguards and thought about his next steps. He considered replacing Tilman as squad leader. That could wait. Upstairs he had seven more men positioned at various choke points. He needed to recall them.

"We have some work to do. First, I want—" he began, but was interrupted by a woman's voice.

"Ah, excuse me, guys, you're blocking my locker," said Yohaba casually. In her hand was a strange-looking pistol. Behind her, casually swinging a heavy-duty chain, was one of the biggest human beings Eduard had ever seen. His two bodyguards stiffened. Tilman and his men spun around, startled, unprepared. Their facial muscles flinched quirkily in their shock. Yohaba had never seen men do that before.

"Hello, Fashisty," Boris said.

Someone in the row lost bowel control.

"The restroom's over there," Yohaba said, with a casual wave of her gun.

"It's them," Tilman said over his shoulder to Eduard.

Eduard pushed his way to the front. Yohaba had stepped a few feet into the row and was holding the gun at waist level. As Eduard came forward, she snapped into a wide, bent-kneed stance and brought the pistol up to eye level in an extended two-handed grip.

"Hold it right there, grandpa."

Eduard stopped five feet away. "How nice of you to join us," he said. "Here we are searching all over for you, and you do us the honor of paying us a visit." He slowly extended his hand. "The key, please. And then you are free to go."

"Did you leave your white cane at home?" Yohaba asked. "There's a gun pointing at your head."

Eduard put his hands on his hips and laughed. "Oh, child. You are too amusing. Men, draw your weapons." Behind him, Tilman and his team cautiously pulled out their knives and flipped them open. The two bodyguards each took out a Bonowi camlock combat baton, grabbed the tip, and ratcheted their weapons out to their full, whippy, twenty-one-inch length.

Eduard laughed again. "My man, Tilman, told me about your little bluff in the alley. Nicely done, child. But, really, a ceramic pistol? Do you think we are all so easily fooled? A ceramic chamber could never withstand the pressure of the igniting gunpowder. You really must spend more time studying armament specifications. Like the Fuhrer, I have an extensive knowledge of the performance characteristics of military weapons."

"Fascinating. Are you trying to convince me or yourself?" Yohaba said.

"Tilman," Eduard said. "Please step forward and disarm this foolish girl. Then kill her."

Tilman swallowed hard and stayed rooted where he was.

"Tilman," Eduard said pleasantly. "I order you to take the toy away from the girl and kill her."

Tilman didn't move. Instead, he responded in a flat, gray voice, "I don't want to. I believe that is a real gun."

"You tell him, Tilman," Yohaba said with gusto. "Remember what I told you about the two-stage gunpowder. Don't be an idiot. Remember what they taught you in school—never change your first guess."

Eduard reached behind him with one hand and dragged Tilman forward by his belt buckle. "Captain Tilman!" Eduard said, leaning in close to Tilman's ear. "Think carefully before you answer. I am giving you a chance to redeem yourself from your debacle in the alley. Look at her. Tell me what you see?"

"A gaping gun muzzle. Looks about a 9mm."

"Get ready," Boris said to Yohaba out loud in English, not caring who heard. "Remember what your fortune cookie cowboy said about pulling guns."

Eduard looked at Yohaba and took her measure, and saw only a skinny young woman way out of her league. Just an hour ago, he had heard from Bernbailer's own lips the rest of the story about Helmut's death. Yes, the girl had been there in the hospital room, but so were two OCD agents. It wasn't clear if the girl even had a gun.

Slightly behind his back, Eduard flexed his left wrist and index finger in a peculiar way, dropping a Boker fixed-blade knife, handle first into his palm. As a diversion, he let his shoulders slump, released Tilman's belt, and appeared to concede.

Eduard said, defeated, "Men, put down your weapons and step aside. If no one will help me, I can't do this by myself." He turned his back to Yohaba and urged his men to one side for her to pass. Suddenly, he whirled with the blade in his hand, faster than the eye or the brain could follow, his brown jacket flaring as he spun. A flash of light. All eyes widened. He crossed the gap to Yohaba, knocked the outstretched gun aside with one hand, stepped in closer, and plunged the knife upwards into her stomach. His eyes went wild, crazy, and he let out a satisfying grunt. She fell backwards, breaking her fall slightly with one hand, while still holding onto the gun with the other.

Eduard's little diversion was well played. Boris was a step slow but moved forward to engage just as Eduard reared back to slash the pistol from Yohaba's outstretched hand.

A strange sound—*pffftt-pop*—echoed in the row and froze Boris in his tracks. A curious tendril of smoke rose above Eduard's head, confusing the men behind him. Eduard's legs folded, and he spun in a slow-motion corkscrew all the way to the ground. As he turned, his men saw the source of the smoke: a neat hole in his head. They stood there while their minds and senses fought to re-synch. As Eduard fell below their line of sight, they got their first look at Yohaba sitting down, pointing at them with the gun, more smoke rising from the barrel.

"Ouch!" she yelled from the ground. Then through a grimace, she blurted, "Ah . . . drop your weapons everyone. Man, that hurt. Who's next? Didn't I tell you? Two-stage ignition. Two-stage ignition. What was so hard to believe about that? Geez. No wonder you morons lost the war."

One by one, beginning with Tilman, who was closest, they all dropped their weapons. Yohaba got up slowly, in obvious pain, but made sure to keep her weapon pointing straight. Once on her feet, she motioned with the pistol toward the wall. The seven Nazis quickly complied and pressed up against one side of the lockers, leaving a clear path to 253. Yohaba stole a look at Eduard and felt nothing.

She reached into her pants pocket with her left hand, came out with a key, and held it at shoulder height. Boris grabbed it as he walked past, making sure he didn't get between the Nazis and her gun. He stepped over Eduard, then crouched beside him and searched him. He found a cell phone in the inside jacket pocket and held it up for Yohaba to see.

"Always take cell phone," he said in English. He stood up and quickly went along the line of Nazis, searching each in turn. Third man down, he found a Boker Plus Besh-Wedge neck knife hanging in a scabbard between the man's shoulder blades. He tore off the man's shirt to get at it.

"When the lady said to put the weapons down," Boris said in German as he casually flipped and caught the knife, "she meant all the weapons." He punched the man viciously in the stomach, doubling him over and dropping him to his knees. He continued searching the others. When he was finished and had collected the weapons from the floor, he had six extra phones and an assortment of knives in his pockets, and the two batons in his belt.

He headed deeper into the row, checking the locker numbers until he found 253 at the bottom near the back. He was turned away from Yohaba, so she couldn't see what he was doing but could hear the sound of a key being inserted and turned, a metal door swinging, something heavy being dragged, and finally a door closing and clicking shut. He came back and stood alongside her to face the Nazis with the thirty-pound Ermetico anodized aluminum bio-carrier in his grip.

"You should be grateful to the woman. She saved your lives," he said in German. He looked in their eyes and answered their unspoken question. "If she wasn't here to stop me, you'd all be dead." He paused and scowled. "We are going now. You will wait five minutes before you leave."

He backed away and Yohaba, still pointing the gun, followed his lead.

"Tell the old man we'll be in contact," she said as she backed up. As soon as they cleared the end of the row, Boris looked around and nodded in the direction of the escalators, and they both fled out of view.

The five Nazis all breathed a sigh of relief. The two bodyguards rushed to Eduard and rolled him over, hoping for a miracle. His wide, unblinking eyes told the story. Tilman shook a cigarette out of a crushed pack and lit up. He looked down at Eduard.

"Who's the fool now?" he asked softly.

One of the bodyguards looked up with tears in his eyes. "Shut up, you coward."

"Coward?" Tilman asked with a wry smile. "Me, a coward, when the principle dies and the bodyguards live? I think you're confusing me with someone else." Tilman got down on one knee and tenderly closed the old man's eyes. Too soft for anyone else to hear, he said, "Helmut and now Eduard. I know I should hate her. I wonder why I don't." He stood up. "Gleason," he called. A young man in a sweatshirt came over. "When we get back, find out all you can about her—the girl with the black nose ring and spider web tattoo. Find out who she's working for, who trained her. And who is her Neanderthal lover."

"Lover?" Gleason asked. "What makes you say that?"

Tilman looked down at Eduard again and became distracted. "Oh," he said after a moment. "The way he looked at her. I thought it was obvious."

Gleason asked, "Do we go after them?"

"No," Tilman said. "They'll be contacting us to make some kind of deal. Right now, my biggest problem is how to get this body out of here." He took a long drag on his cigarette and exhaled. "This place is loaded with surveillance cameras. Okay, here's the plan. We're going to need one of those garbage cans on wheels and a maintenance man's uniform. And lots of plastic." Gleason listened as Tilman described what needed to be done.

While Tilman was talking, the man with the bowel problem had been edging closer to the end of the row, intent on slipping away unobserved and finding a restroom. As he stepped clear of the row, he suddenly folded like a broken kite, went airborne, and crashed against the lockers. Everyone jumped. Tilman's burning cigarette fell from his mouth.

Boris stepped into view. He reached down, grabbed the unconscious man by his jacket collar, and flung him like a sack of oats toward his friends.

Boris said, "We will restart the clock." He made a point of looking at his watch. "Five minutes, starting now." He walked away and caught up to Yohaba waiting by the escalator with the bio-carrier.

"That should teach them patience," said Boris with a quick look over his shoulder. He stepped onto the escalator with Yohaba. "Now we should have full five minutes."

"And how would you teach them charity, Mr. Zokolov?" asked Yohaba facetiously.

"Charity not so easy. Much more painful," Boris said.

On the platform, Boris spied a garbage can and discarded all the weapons including the chain and lock. He looked at the chain wistfully before letting it slip from his hand. He'd never even gotten to use it. He kept only the cell phones and the ceramic knife. A few minutes later, the S14 to the airport pulled in and they boarded.

While they were sitting on the train staring out the window, Eduard's phone rang in Boris's pocket. Before Boris answered, he had Yohaba lean closer so she could also hear. The voice on the other end began talking immediately in German.

"We found the Corsican alive. He was wrapped up like a mummy in duct tape. He said he told them nothing about the viruses. He said they think it's drugs."

"What else?" Boris asked in his best imitation of Eduard's voice. Yohaba covered her face in embarrassment.

"Who is this?" asked Martin with the long hair.

"Insolent fool!" Boris snarled, loudly enough that a nearby passenger looked up from her magazine. "How dare you question me? You will answer the question!"

There was a long silence. Finally Martin said calmly, "Put the woman on, please."

Boris handed Yohaba the phone. "It's for you."

"Yes," Yohaba said into the phone.

Martin asked, "How did you get this phone?"

"We took it off some old guy's body."

Another long silence before Martin spoke.

"What color was his hair?"

"White."

Martin thought about it and made his decision. "Where are you? Is there anyone else around?"

"Where we are isn't important. We opened the locker, and we have the case." After a pause, she added, "It's just us. No one else is around."

Martin spoke rapidly. "In the case is a deadly virus. Some of us are not happy about that. If you're smart, you'll destroy it. But whatever you do, don't let the old man get it."

"You mean Gustav von Bock?" Yohaba asked.

Martin, surprised she knew the old man's name, hesitated and then said, "Yes."

"The case is our ticket to meet with him. We have a truce to propose."

"He's old. He's had his day. Make your peace if you can, but don't let him have the case."

"Who are you? Why are you telling us this?"

"Destroy the case," Martin said and clicked off.

Yohaba slowly handed Boris the phone.

Boris immediately began disassembling it. "We need to take the batteries and SIM cards out of phones so we can't be tracked. I don't know if they have resources to do that, but I would guess they have sympathizers in government agencies."

Yohaba said, "What if the phones are password protected? Take the batteries out and we'll never get back in, and we'll lose all the numbers." She thought for a moment. "Do all the phones, but not the old man's. As soon as I get a chance, I'll write down the numbers in his call log and contact list." Boris nodded. Then referring to Martin, Yohaba added, "Funny, just when you think you've got the good guys and bad guys all figured out, one of them pulls a stunt like that."

"Yes, he good guy for fashisty. We will kill him last." As he worked, he added, "When we get to airport we can pick up our luggage." He patted the case on his lap. "We have weapon of mass destruction. This our lucky day."

CHAPTER 23

Gustav von Bock sat in front of his fireplace, staring straight ahead, his thin white hair plastered flat. A half-empty glass of wine was in his hand, the old woolen blanket draped and rumpled around his shoulders.

Klaus entered the room, walked softly across the thick rug, and stood to the side of the brown leather chair. After a moment, the old man turned to Klaus with a drawn, ashen, black-eyed face and waved a weary hand for him to proceed. Klaus cleared his throat and told Gustav what happened at the Zurich Hauptbahnhof.

"Early victories or losses are harbingers . . . of nothing," said Gustav when Klaus was finished. "So the woman can kill. Bravo, I say to her. Bravo. Her day is coming." He did not rant and rave. After Helmut's death, he had no more tears and no more screams.

The train station was a disaster but not an irreversible one. That the woman and the Slav had risked so much was proof that they planned to use the bio-specimens to negotiate and were not planning to inform the authorities. They had risked their lives and even killed to obtain it. There was something they wanted to trade. The Cowboy's life perhaps? And, assuming they knew of the five-day shelf life, they would move quickly.

Eduard was a loss, but even with that there was an upside. Eduard had been a bitter rival within the movement. With him gone, there would no more be a house divided.

The woman would have her meeting, Gustav decided. It would be in the woods somewhere. Camouflaged sharpshooters. Silenced weapons. Graves already dug. Of the twenty men called up for this operation, fifteen had gone to the train station and, based on the girl's personal threat to Gustav, five had stayed behind at the estate to guard the old man. Even considering the lost men, there were more than enough assets to do the job properly.

Suddenly, Gustav was in a good mood. When this was done, he would finish off the Cowboy too, as a memorial to Helmut.

"Call off the hunt," Gustav said. "The girl will be contacting us soon. She will come to us."

ON THE SECOND floor of building 133 at the intersection of Einstein and Rutherford roads just a few blocks from CERN's Meyrin entrance, Leonard Steenberg paced up and down the worn, industrial-green carpet in his office.

At that exact time, Boris and Yohaba were walking across the Rudolf Brun bridge in Zurich on the way to pick up their car. They had retrieved their luggage at the airport and taken a taxi back into town. As a precaution, they had the taxi drop them off several blocks from the Parkhaus Urania. Layers.

Steenberg had been in the office all weekend double-checking the work of his colleagues from the La Silla observatory in Chile. Their initial reports had been cause for rejoicing. It had been a near thing, but 182 Elsa had not collided with another asteroid. Einstein's prediction, made shortly before his death, had been wrong.

After the miss, the observatory's staff had recalculated Elsa's path. To everyone's great relief, nothing had changed: it was still on course to miss earth by 37.3 million miles when it made its closest pass on April 2, 2029. They sent the raw data to Leonard, and he and others verified the results.

Seven hours later, another email came from Chile. As a precautionary double-check they had retaken the measurements. Apologies. They must have made an earlier mistake. Elsa was still going to miss earth, but the revised estimate was now 22.4 million miles and due to pass on April 4, 2029.

Then twenty-four hours later came the bombshell. The astronomers in Chile were quite embarrassed. It was as if the measurements were changing by the hour. But that was impossible. They had rechecked both their original and revised numbers and weren't quite sure where they went wrong. In any case, the latest measurements showed Elsa passing earth on April 10, 2029, but happily, still missing by 3.6 million miles. All was still well. Sorry.

As he read that latest email, Leonard broke into a cold sweat. Each new measurement brought Elsa closer to earth and closer to Einstein's original collision date of April 13, 2029. Steenberg and the other scientists drafted into the analysis all confirmed the original findings of the astronomers in Chile. And then they confirmed the accuracy of each succeeding list of numbers. What no one could explain was why the numbers were changing.

As Steenberg paced back and forth, he stopped for a long minute suddenly remembering, then pausing to ponder, a cryptic sentence Einstein had written on the back of one of the star field photographs he made the year before he died. It was something to do with billiards. As Steenberg recalled the words, for one intense second, he felt the speed and power of the asteroid hurtling silently through space. His world wobbled and he held both hands out to steady himself.

An idea came screaming into his head. He raced to his desk and chair, then frantically searched through his drawers until he had the photos. One by one he flipped them over until he found the one he wanted. On the back, in Einstein's hand, it read, "A slow massé shot curves sooner, even though a harder shot spins faster."

Steenberg stood and resumed his pacing. After twenty minutes, he sat down and sent an email to his colleagues at La Silla asking them to check if Elsa had a moon and if Elsa's rotational period had changed. He thought about sending a text to Yohaba but decided not to. She led a quiet life on the ranch in Idaho. Why disturb her tranquility unless it was absolutely necessary.

In the Magic Valley Regional Medical Center's intensive care unit, room 56, shooting victim Rulon Hurt opened his eyes for the first time in twenty-four hours. Something beeped on one of the room's monitors, and a few of the screen's slowly undulating lines began undulating a little less slowly. The same thing was happening on a monitor at the nurse's station.

Rulon's father, who had been dozing in the chair next to the bed, immediately snapped alert.

Rulon opened his eyes, blinked, and looked around, confused. He slowly raised one limp hand only to have it tangle in the tubes running from his nose and arms. He struggled for a few seconds, then gave up. In a voice thick and slow, he said, "Was it a buffalo stampede?"

His father said, "You got shot. Lost a lot of blood. Lucky for you it was in the head."

Rulon concentrated for a few seconds. "Yeah. Right. What time is it?"

Rulon's father looked at the clock on the wall. "A little before 5:00 p.m. Sunday."

Rulon nodded blankly, settled down into the bed, then got agitated. "Yohaba," he suddenly called. "Where's Yohaba?" The squiggly lines on the monitor jumped like bucking broncos. A pretty blonde nurse came rushing through the door. "Where's Yohaba? Where is she!" Rulon yelled louder. He pulled at the bandages around his head and tried to get up.

His father held him down and the nurse pried Rulon's hand loose from his dressings.

"She's fine, boy," his father said. "Simmer down. She got you here for heaven's sakes. You've been out for more than a day. Take it easy, she'll be back."

"Where is she?" mumbled Rulon.

"She had to go run an errand. She said to tell ya not to worry."

Rulon sank back into the bed, eyes closed, breathing hard, exhausted. "Oh, good. Did they get the guy? It was the guy from Marseilles, wasn't it?"

"Yeah," his father said.

"Please get her on the phone." Rulon was losing consciousness, his words garbled. "I need . . . talk to her . . . important."

"You need to rest," the nurse said, with one eye on Rulon and one on the monitor. "Sleep is the best medicine."

"She's with the big Russian," answered Rulon's father. Rulon didn't respond at first and the old man wondered if he heard him.

"Oh . . . good," Rulon said after a long pause. And then he was out again. The nurse stayed for a few minutes, until her pager went off. The father resumed his vigil.

BORIS AND YOHABA walked across the Rudolf Brun bridge, each lost in thought. Boris was thinking about operational details, Yohaba about the faces of all the men she had confronted that day—the ones that had died, especially the one she had killed, but also all the other men—the fear she saw, the determination, and the cruelty.

On the train going to the airport after shooting Eduard, she had felt so triumphant she was busting through her skin. But a black depression now gripped her. The combat juice draining off—what Rulon jokingly referred to as the post-combat elephant trampling.

She thought about the man she had saved from Boris in the alley. Take a life, save a life. Suddenly she was bowled over by the sacredness and sadness of life, the thoughts and vision of the last few hours swarming around her head like bats. Depression pecked at her self-confidence. *What have I done? What have I done?* She turned to Boris in agony.

Boris had been watching her. "Welcome to the club," he said when he saw her face in the lamplight. "No whining. You carry gun, you hunt men, you don't whine. You have killed two men now. One to save your husband. One to save your own life. Handle it or don't handle it. Your choice. But know this. If you don't kill them, they kill you."

Yohaba nodded and slowed down. Boris continued for a few feet before turning to see what she was doing.

"What is it?" he asked, looking around and tensing up. "Is something else wrong?"

Yohaba stopped, leaned over the bridge railing without answering, and stared down at the river. The bridge was about eighty yards long. Ten feet below her, the waters curled and frothed with reflected light from the lamps and window lights on both shores. A few hundred meters away, on opposite sides of the river, were the steeples of the Grossmunster and Fraumunster, Zurich's most famous churches.

"Can we wait here for a few minutes?" she asked. "I'm trying to figure out the meaning of life."

Boris looked up and down the street. It was empty. Surely the Nazis were off somewhere licking their wounds.

"Sure. But if you whine, I throw you in river," he said, coming back to join her. "You did good back there. You did your duty. Maybe you didn't notice, but old man very surprised when found out gun was real." Boris laughed out loud. "I will tell that story for years. Two-stage gunpowder. Even I didn't believe you. People who make that gun very smart."

Yohaba said forlornly, "Yeah, I did my duty. What a strange world you live in where your duty is to kill a person." She looked up and closed her eyes. A few drops of soft rain touched her face.

"Yes, strange," Boris agreed.

They stood together leaning over the railing. After a few minutes, Yohaba asked, "What's the third stage of tiger hunting?"

"Night still not over. I will tell you in morning."

"Tell me now," Yohaba demanded. "I'll protect you till morning. I promise."

Boris shook his head and chuckled. "Okay. Third stage is you are wiser and older. You never hunt tiger on its terms, only on yours. You are careful. Very, very careful."

"Oh," Yohaba replied. "I think I'm there now."

"Unlikely. But I was thinking about what you did back in alley," Boris said. "That was impressive, instinctive move. I thought we have fight for sure. Showing confidence, walking up to man. That was what convinced him gun was real." When Yohaba didn't say anything, Boris continued. "This is armament miracle. You don't get this at Walmart, eh? May I, please?" He held out his hand.

Yohaba took the gun out of her pocket and handed it over. Boris removed the clip and the bullet in the chamber, and inspected the pistol from every angle.

"Did you shoot it before today?" he asked.

"No," Yohaba said. "Rulon only had eight bullets, and he wasn't sure he could get more. This was to be only for emergencies."

"How did you know it works? I wouldn't trust gun I hadn't fired first."

Yohaba gave him a "you've got to be kidding" look. "Mr. Zokolov," she said, "my husband is the kind of guy who sits around at night disassembling his guns and filing down the edges on the parts. Then squirting them with a frictionless lubricant so they won't jam. Trust me, if he owns it, the gun works."

"Only used when Rulon wish to hijack plane, eh?" Boris said with a tight smile.

"Well, if he ever did that, it would be for a good cause. Is it really true you used to hunt tigers?" she asked, changing the subject. Talking about Rulon made her sad. She absently watched a half dozen black-tailed seagulls swimming in little circles below her and wished she had some bread crumbs to drop.

"Yes. Siberian tigers."

"Was it scary?"

"Not at first particularly. But it became scary."

"What happened?"

"We wounded a male tiger and he began hunting my team."

"But you had guns."

"Needed tank."

"Are tigers that dangerous?" Yohaba asked.

"You have no idea," Boris said.

"What was it like?" asked Yohaba, not wanting to talk but glad to have someone to listen to.

Boris looked around. The trams had stopped running and there was no one on the streets. A police siren sounded in the distance. "Smarter than men in some ways. More cunning. More patient. More focused."

"More cruel?" Yohaba asked.

"No, not more cruel," Boris said after a short reflection. "But more completely lethal, if that make sense. No introspection. No conscience. No hesitation. If Siberian tigers have AK-47s, they top of food chain. No joke."

"What happened to your team?"

"Out of six, two of us survived." Boris leaned his forearms on the railings. "Yuri, the leader. Small man but hard as permafrost. He used to be poacher. He wounded tiger. The fool went off by himself, and shot tiger in foot. Later we found nothing left of him but black earth where he was killed. Like fire-blackened dirt. Only one boot left and a pocket from his shirt. No limbs, no bones, nothing else. Tigers always leave limbs. But Yuri, he totally disappeared. Think about that.

"But then tiger come after rest of us. They are amazing athletes. Pavel was twenty feet up a tree. Tiger make jump, touch tree in one place, and drag him down. We measured later. One question we always have: How tiger know we were with Yuri? We weren't there when Yuri shot him. But tiger hunt us down. And only us. Once, after he kill Moshe, our guide, we follow footsteps of tiger backward and see that he pass within close distance of village and around campfires with other people and women cooking and doing laundry, but he never harm them. He looking just for us."

"How did Moshe die?"

"He was poacher too, like Yuri. Live in forest all his life. He had saying about tigers. He said tiger code was 'you touch me, I touch you.' Tiger come to his shack when Moshe not around. Tiger tear shack apart and drag mattress fifty yards away under tree and lay on it till Moshe come back. From tracks we know Moshe ten feet away before he see tiger. Same thing. Tiger drags Moshe off. He disappears except for rifle."

"He must have been daydreaming to get that close to the tiger and not see him."

"Maybe. But old poachers and ginseng hunters say tigers are invisible. When they want, they don't exist except as footprints. Think of that. More than just camouflage. It's like they have mental force field that makes you never look at them. They don't need invisible cape. If you hunt them, and they know they are hunted, you never see them until they attack. Never. No smell, no see, no hear. Just footprints. Imagine hunting invisible animal. That is what it was like."

"Do you hate them?"

Boris turned around and leaned his back against the railing.

"No, no more than I hate sea in wild storm. Moshe correct. They have code. Yuri drew first blood. Tiger justice. One time I meet tiger in Sikhoye-Alin forest without rifle. Seven yards between us. She stare and sit like queen until I look away. Truer majesty I never see before. I acknowledge it and bow to her. Then she take one step back, and I take one step back. Then she take another one. Then I take another one. Like a dance. I only do what she does. Later, local pine nut gatherers tell me I did exact right thing. Tiger take one step, you must take one. If you take two, you die. If you don't move, you die. Run and you die. It was about respect and obedience."

"How did you finally kill it?"

"You mean, male tiger? He died of hunger. We kept tracking him and pushing him; we never stopped. We hunted with lanterns at night. There was snow. He left easy tracks to follow. We didn't sleep for three days. He was wounded and couldn't hunt game. He tried circling back on us several times, but we had dogs and they warned us. It was thirty below zero. Tiger needed thirty pounds of meat a day just to live. We starved him to death."

"Rulon said that's how the Allies finally beat the German U-boats."

"Are we talking about the Great Patriotic War now?"

"Yes, if that's what you want to call World War II. Once a US destroyer found a German submarine, they kept on it until it was sunk even if it took days. They just kept following it. Harassing it with depth charges. Never giving up."

"I'm sure Churchill grateful when your husband share strategy with him."

"Don't be so prickly," Yohaba said. "I was paying you a compliment, saying you might be almost as smart as Rulon. Did you save the skin?"

"I assume we talking tigers again. Yes, and we ate the heart raw there in the forest before the carcass froze."

"Eeeewww," said Yohaba in disgust. "You could have spared me that part."

"Old poacher tell us that tiger who kills and eats man can think like a man after that."

"So do you think like a tiger now, Mr. Zokolov?"

"No, just smell like one," Boris deadpanned.

Yohaba laughed. "That's something Rulon would have said." Boris smiled at that and Yohaba jabbed him in the ribs. "He's your hero. Admit it." At that, Boris let out a booming laugh and they laughed together. The echoes skipped across the river and bounced off the buildings on both sides. Eventually the echoes faded; they grew serious again.

"Let's go," Boris said. Just as they pushed off the bridge railing and turned south toward the Urania garage, one of the two cell phones in Boris's pocket chimed. He fumbled to find it.

"Quick, get it," urged Yohaba, her eyes wide with excitement. "Do you think it's them?"

Boris pulled his personal phone out of his pocket and answered, "Yes," in Russian.

"Play chess with the czars," said a woman's voice, older, formal, also in Russian.

"Black knight to king three," Boris replied.

"Hold," the voice said. The phone line clicked several times as the call was passed along.

While Boris waited, Yohaba asked, "Who is it?"

Boris said, "Not Germans. Long story. I will tell, but now you must keep absolute quiet. Is that possible?" Yohaba glared at him in response.

On the second floor of the Kremlin, two hundred yards from Lenin's tomb, in an office with a desk, a creaky leather roller chair, and a lamp with a green shade, a light flashed on a speakerphone, and an old thin hand reached out and pushed a button.

"Begin," said a man's raspy Russian voice—ancient, soft, but penetrating.

Boris took a deep breath. Did the man never sleep? This was the fifth time Boris had either called in or been called since he began the assignment. But this was the first time he had been put through to the thin man.

"Where should I begin?" Boris asked.

"Do you have the specimens?"

"Yes. A recent development."

"Excellent. But let's not have a repeat of the Aeroflot blunders," said the thin man, referring to the KGB program in the eighties and nineties in which agents stole biological specimens and transported them back to Russia in commercial Aeroflot cockpits. At least two agents died from mishandling the pathogens. "I will want your full report. But first tell me about the Cowboy. How is he?"

"In the hospital. But he is expected to recover." The thin man made no comment.

Boris knew it was dangerous to play games with this man. Failure, while never excused, was sometimes accepted if lessons were learned. Lies and self-promotion, never. Boris turned away from Yohaba in an attempt at privacy. "I did not put him there," admitted Boris as quietly as possible so Yohaba wouldn't hear.

"Yes, I know," the old man said. "Now tell me what happened. I want every detail of your personal encounter."

After Boris finished describing the short fight, the thin man was silent. Finally he said, "How did he seem to you?"

"Excuse me," Boris said. "I don't understand."

"What was the Cowboy like? What kind of man is he?"

"He is an enemy. A lackey of the imperialists."

The old man chuckled softly. "Yes, yes, of course. But tell me. What kind of man is he?"

Boris hesitated then said, "He is a man I would not like to fight again."

"Because you respect him?" probed the old man.

Boris hesitated again. "Yes."

"He is rather a hobby of mine," said the thin man. "Did anyone tell you that?"

"Yes."

"He has managed to earn a grudging respect from all the agents I sent. You are not the first. You had never been to America. What do you think of it now?"

"Materialistic. A crumbling empire. Craven peasants fighting over money."

"Every agent we send says something like that. Six months later they apply for transfers, usually to the San Francisco office. Did you not find anything in America you could love?"

A strange question, thought Boris.

Boris had moved ten feet from Yohaba. He looked at her watching him and got a lump in his throat. There was one truth he could not tell the old man.

"I love the mountains in Idaho. It reminds me of the forests of Primorskii Krai."

"Yes, where you worked for Inspection Tiger. The mountains. Of course." Changing the subject back to a safer one for Boris, the thin man said, "This cowboy intrigues me. Three years ago he was an irritation. Today he is an enigma. We will talk again about this when you are done. But now, tell me about the Cowboy being shot. Was it our old nemesis, von Bock?"

Boris told him the abbreviated version starting with Rulon's shooting all the way up to Boris standing on a bridge in Zurich. He left out any mention of Yohaba.

"We have much catching up to do with the fashisty before the score is settled," the thin man said, referring to World War II. "But good. You have the specimens. That is crucial. I will send a team to pick them up. Where should they meet you?"

"In front of the Fraumunster," Boris said, naming the church on the south side of the Limmat.

The old man replied, "The team will be there by 6:00 p.m. tomorrow." To Boris's surprise, the thin man next asked, "What is she like? The wife, I mean. You are traveling with the wife."

"She is . . . capable," Boris said, hoping his voice did not betray him.

After his answer, the phone abruptly clicked off, the thin man moving on to another crises.

Boris put away his phone and looked at Yohaba, who was staring at him. She sounded suspicious as she said, "I loved your version of the fight with Rulon. I don't seem to remember it lasting that long."

"Allow me small concession to personal dignity, Mrs. Hurt."

"And me. I didn't hear you say a word about me. What am I on this trip? A potted plant?"

"I did you favor. Even to be noticed by this man is dangerous. If you were in stage three, you would understand."

"I'm in stage four. The stage where I'm ultra paranoid and thinking that even people I thought were my friends are turning against me. I heard every word you said. Have you been double-crossing me?"

Boris responded hard and cold, "Earlier in evening I willing to fight six fashisties so you can escape. Please rephrase, Mrs. Hurt."

Yohaba huffed a little, looking up now and again to glare at Boris.

Finally she demanded, with only slightly less suspicion, "Okay, Mr. Zokolov. What are you not telling me?"

"Many things, Mrs. Hurt. Many things. But none to your injury. Come. We have until 6:00 p.m. to make deal that will save you and beloved fortune cookie cowboy husband. I will tell you what I can, and Boris will be your hero of the Revolution again. Come. Walk."

They hurried along, dragging their suitcases. Boris walked so fast that Yohaba struggled to keep up. "Who was that on the phone?"

"My boss's boss's boss. You heard Rulon speak of thin man. That was thin man."

"Wow. Rulon talked about that guy like he's some kind of legend."

"He was legend fifty years ago. Now he giant oil spill filling every crevice in government; the only man Putin and oligarchs fear. Intelligent and immensely ruthless. Forged in ruins of Stalingrad. Unbreakable."

"Who were you calling a 'lackey of the imperialists'?"

"Rulon. But if pressed would include you too. Though maybe being Swiss, you more tool of international bankers."

"Fine. Make your little jokes. But this is not funny. You didn't sound like . . . well, the way you described everything, you made us sound like a bunch of gun-toting redneck hillbillies."

Boris looked at her blankly and gave no reply.

After a moment of silence, Yohaba said, "Let me rephrase that. I thought you liked Rulon."

"I do, but must be very careful with thin man. If I like you too much, he take me off mission. If I lie, maybe I get stationed in North Korea. If I misuse company resources or alter mission just to help you, maybe I go to prison. Or maybe for his own reasons, he decides you must die. Thin man no fool, and his word is law."

"You knew about Helmut all along."

"Yes." They reached the Parkhaus Urania and were walking up the spiral ramp to the pay station. "Listen. Don't talk. Don't judge. But you should know: we were ones who first told Bernbailer about Helmut hunting Rulon and about reward."

Yohaba stopped in her tracks. "What! You told Bernbailer? I

don't understand. Are you saying you set Rulon up? You didn't even think to warn us." Her hand moved to the pistol in her belt. Boris noticed the gesture.

"Save precious miracle bullets for enemy, Mrs. Hurt. I am not enemy."

They stood facing each other. After an awkward silence, Yohaba said, "Well, speak up, for crying out loud. Explain yourself."

Gesturing toward her hand, Boris said, "First you relax, Mrs. Hurt."

With a mild start, Yohaba realized where her hand had drifted. "Sorry."

Boris said in Russian, "This is too complex for me in English. And it's important that you understand completely. And it's important that you start acting like a big girl and not so parochial. This is business too. I am your friend, and I have risked much already by helping you. You know this is true. Yes?"

Yohaba nodded hesitantly and answered with a wary, "Yes."

"We knew Helmut von Bock was trying to secure biological weapons. We had been tracking him for three months and then lost him a week ago. We were desperate. There were many potential lives at stake. We knew he had a vendetta against Rulon and decided to use that as a way to draw von Bock out into the open again. One of our people posed as a fellow Nazi and called Bernbailer anonymously before I came to Twin Falls. He told him about Helmut's search for Rulon and the reward money.

"That is why those Nazis were in the bar the other night. I was supposed to meet them there, give them some money, and reinforce the message. But obviously the Nazis were at the bar to rob me and work me over.

"The plan was for Helmut to come for your husband, and then we would pick up the trail again, follow him back to Europe, and find the biological weapon. I planned to warn you when the time was right, but von Bock got there too soon. Nothing worked as planned except we got the specimens." Boris shook the bio-carrier for emphasis. "This is extremely important. Imagine if those madmen had some unstoppable plague and only they had the antidote. I guarantee you they would try it on Russians first. It is their way. The war has never stopped for them after the revenge we took when we followed them back into Germany."

"For some people World War II never really ended, did it?" Yohaba said.

"I fear that if some have their way, the European Union has only postponed the issue. And now with the euro weakening and Germany being pressured to pick up the pieces . . . Well, we will see."

"Wars and rumors of wars," Yohaba said. "Speaking of which, when are we going to call the old kraut and set up a meeting?"

"Not yet," Boris said. "We should wait until last minute so—"

Yohaba cut him off. "So he doesn't have time to set up a proper ambush and maybe he will be desperate and make a mistake."

"Da," Boris said. "Maybe you are now in phase 2.5."

"But how is this going to work? We can't give him the germs, and once he realizes that, we've got no bargaining chips, and he'll just come after us again."

"Think, Mrs. Hurt. The purpose of meeting is not to give him this," Boris said, meaning the anodized bio-carrier and its deadly cargo. "What is the purpose?"

Yohaba's eyes widened as she realized. "We have to kill them, don't we?"

"I don't make rules. But, yes. There is no other way." When Yohaba didn't say anything, Boris added, "Maybe you are thinking that they will just agree to forget the whole thing and then we should too. But think this through very carefully. Could we ever truly believe them? And would they ever truly believe us either? We have killed three of their people. Do you see where this is going? There is no going back from a killing. We are in it, Mrs. Hurt. You are in it. Accept it or go home now, put Rulon on a gurney, and roll him up to a cabin in your Sawtooth Mountains."

"Thank you, Mr. Zokolov," Yohaba said with a sigh and obvious sarcasm. "Perhaps after this you can become a grief counselor somewhere. Do they even have those in Russia?"

"No. We just have grief. Come. We must move."

They came to the pay station, and Boris handed Yohaba the parking ticket to pay. She took the ticket and looked at it, then flicked it a few times in her hand as she stood thinking. On a hunch, she reached into a pocket of her suitcase and pulled out the parking ticket she'd found in Helmut's wallet. She looked at both tickets. Except for the date and time, they were a match.

"Hey," she said. "What luck. Helmut von Frankenstein's car is in this garage. What do you bet it's a nicer car than ours?"

"We haven't got the keys," Boris said. Yohaba reached into the same suitcase pocket and pulled out Helmut's key ring, from which a rectangular BMW electronic key dangled enticingly. She wiggled it in front of Boris's nose. "I'll bet a good Russian like you wouldn't be caught *dead* in a high-performance *German* automobile no matter how fast it was." She could see Boris wavering. "It's fast," Yohaba said. "Probably too fast for you to handle. We'll just use the Skoda."

Boris snatched the key out of her hand. It only took ten minutes to find the car.

CHAPTER 24

Faithful Klaus looked down on the old man sleeping in his leather chair and wondered whether to wake him and usher him to bed. Klaus decided it was more merciful to leave him undisturbed.

Klaus covered the old man's legs with a heavy woolen blanket. The old man stirred but remained asleep. Klaus next reached down and unclutched the old man's right hand from a cell phone—the one he had used when last talking to Helmut; the one over which he expected the girl to call—and placed the phone on the dark wood lamp table next to the chair. He threw two more logs on the fire and prodded the coals back to life with a poker. The logs ignited and Klaus replaced the fire screen. The light from the dancing flames threw shadows across the room.

Klaus picked up an empty wine glass and quietly turned to leave, then stopped and gazed around the room. Gustav was an art collector: Prussian art, old ornate frames, martial scenes from the days of Bismarck, mustached generals on horseback, troops in formation with bayonets on their rifles and plumes on their helmets. And he was also a collector of books. The room was lined with floor-to-ceiling bookcases with leather-bound books and military atlases, books on armaments and tactics, and books on history. Entire shelves on World War II.

Klaus walked over to the bookcase nearest the large bay

windows that looked out on the gardens. He brushed his hand across a section of four hardcover books held upright by a scale model bookend of a 1929 Mercedes-Benz Nurburg limousine. These were Gustav's favorite books—a collection on alternative World War II history that depicted Germany carrying the day and the Third Reich living on.

What if Hitler had not held back the Wehrmacht at Dunkirk? What if he had not declared war on America? Under the terms of the treaty with Japan, he was under no obligation to do so if Japan was the aggressor. And, of course, what if Hitler had waited to attack Russia. Yes, the conquest of Russia was inevitable. Buy why 1941? Why not 1943, after England was conquered and America totally committed to the war in the Pacific? Why not then? And why the senseless slaughter of the Slavs after they first welcomed the Wehrmacht as liberators. And why divert Army Group Center away from Moscow during Operation Barbarossa. So close. *So close*, thought Klaus. Every disaster caused by a precipitous change in plans.

Wineglass in hand, he looked out the window and saw a man's shadow on the patio cement. He tapped on the window and a young man moved into view and waved—one of the guards. He was a friendly young man—intelligent, educated, the future of the movement. Behind Klaus the old man stirred.

"How long have I been sleeping?" asked Gustav, sensing without turning that Klaus was in the room.

"Not long enough," Klaus answered from the window. "Can I get you something?"

"Yes. The girl," Gustav said. The old man sat up straighter in his chair and rearranged the blanket on his legs. "The girl will suffice for now."

"Is she more important than the plagues?" Klaus asked.

"Yes."

"Good," Klaus said. "Revenge we can understand, but this thing with the plague . . . this some of the men don't understand."

"Some of the men, Klaus? And what about you? Do you understand?"

Klaus came over, still holding the empty wineglass, and sat on the footstool at Gustav's feet. He put his hand on the old man's knee.

"I have followed you too long, my fuhrer, to ever think of questioning you now. Tell me. What can I do for you?"

Gustav patted Klaus's hand. "My loyal Klaus. In many ways you have been a son to me . . . as much as my Helmut. You may get the car ready. I'm expecting a phone call. The girl will be calling. I'm surprised she hasn't called already."

While they were talking, there was an urgent knock on the study door.

"Come in," Klaus said.

A short, hollow-faced man entered, one of the men from the command and control center in the room down the hall. "Your son's BMW is moving."

"What do you mean?" asked Klaus, answering for Gustav.

"Helmut's BMW had a tracker attached to the frame. It's been parked in a garage near the Zurich Hauptbahnhof for three days. Now it is moving."

"Could it be the police?" Klaus asked.

"Not likely. It's moving south out of the city," answered the man.

"Could it be one of our people?" Gustav asked.

"We don't think so. Everyone is accounted for, and no one had a key. We've checked with Tilman."

"Who then?" Klaus asked. "Car thieves maybe?" For a few moments, all three were silent as they worked through the possibilities.

The hollow-faced man said, "Car thieves would be heading east." Klaus nodded agreement.

"It's them," Gustav said with quiet certainty. "She took the key from my son after he was killed."

"But how did they know where the car was parked?" Klaus asked with a rising sense of a good plan unraveling.

"I don't know. But it's them. Contact Tilman again. Tell him about the car. Tell him to get the men ready to move."

"But you were going to wait for the girl to call," said Klaus, trying to control his alarm. "Wouldn't that still be easier? Shouldn't we stay with the plan?"

"Who knows what tricks they will have for us at the rendezvous. Total surprise is better. With more time to think, they may decide to destroy the specimens. No. Surprise is best. Finally, something has gone right."

"But why would they take your son's car," Klaus asked, baffled and frustrated by this sudden change. "What if it's not them? What if the car has simply been stolen. Thieves might be taking it south to Italy as well."

"It's them!" Gustav swore, suddenly full of energy and throwing Klaus's hand off his knee. "Have the men assemble and go after them. And get the car ready now. And bring me my black cane. We have them."

YOHABA LEANED BACK against the BMW's headrest with her eyes closed. The tires screeched as Boris took a sharp turn coming through Horgen on the winding A3. Without opening her eyes, she said, "Slow down. I'm sure there are speed cameras. What's wrong with you?" She opened her eyes and turned toward Boris. "You're like a kid in a candy store. Slow down."

Boris said, "The beauty is I will never see speeding tickets; they will all go to Fashisty." Nevertheless he slowed down. They were heading toward Einsiedeln, a small town forty-five minutes from Zurich in the rolling foothills south of the lake. Close enough to Zurich for any rendezvous with the Nazis but far enough away that they could sleep in a hotel without fear of being found. It was Yohaba's idea. She had started to tell Boris how Rulon had said never to sleep in the same city where your enemies had seen you or knew you were heading, but Boris cut her off with a wave of his hand and said he would drive her to a hotel in Moscow if she could go five minutes without saying "Rulon." He was sick of hearing stories about Rulon.

Yohaba resumed her rest. After a minute, she said, "Mind if I ask you a personal question?" Boris made an untranslatable sound. Yohaba continued undeterred. "What was going through your head back in the Rocking Rooster? I mean, you speak English really well. You knew I wasn't translating what Rulon said. What did you think was going on?"

Boris cleared his throat. "I had just gotten off plane, was jet lagged, and had been drinking. English was rusty. Only your Russian made sense."

"Yeah, but you must have known something wasn't adding up. What were you thinking?"

"Was thinking you and husband had unusual communication problem. Needed to see marriage counselor."

"No, really. Tell me."

Boris asked, "Why is this important?"

Yohaba repeated, "Just tell me. It's important to me."

"I told you. It was confusing, that's all. I thought you both crazy American—what did you say before?—hillbillies." Boris stopped talking and went back to concentrating on his driving. Again the tires screeched.

"Okay. But I don't believe it. I think all that mistranslating put you on the back foot and made you lose the fight." Yohaba half rolled over on her side away from Boris. "Just follow the signs, Mr. Zokolov. I'm tired." Boris drove on, stone-faced. She said, "When we get to Einsiedeln, stop at the first decent hotel you see."

"Da," Boris said.

"One with two available rooms."

"Da, Mrs. Hurt."

Fifteen minutes later, they drove into Einsiedeln. Boris drove up the winding main street, past the small stores on both sides, to the huge Benedictine monastery in the cobblestoned square at the top of the hill. As he slowed and swung wide in front of the church to set up a U-turn, Yohaba asked him to stop in front of a white stone gazebo and the wide flat stairs leading up to the church's tall wooden doors. The twin bell towers were visible but the two massive wings and the main body of the church above the doors were obscured by scaffolding and construction netting up to a height of fifty feet. Hanging between the towers was a banner flapping in the wind announcing that the church would be closed two weeks for its annual cleaning.

"Too bad it's closed. You should see it inside," Yohaba said. "It's amazing. Colorful. Baroque. Not depressing at all. There's even a black Madonna in there from the dark ages."

"That is wonderful, Mrs. Hurt. We will come back as tourists someday and you can show me. Do you see any Fashisty following us? Have you noticed that?"

"Gosh, I wasn't even watching," Yohaba said. She swiveled in her seat to look behind and around them.

Boris shook his head in mild disgust. "Phase two."

He did a slow U-turn in the square and drove down the same street he'd come up. Yohaba turned in her seat to gaze back at the black shape of the monastery looking saggy and formless behind the construction netting. The thought struck her, *A fitting tomb for martyrs*, and she shivered.

Boris turned right at the first traffic circle and after a block passed a small hotel with a well-lit frontage. But he rejected that as being too convenient and therefore too obvious. He kept going for three more blocks until he found an even smaller hotel. He drove past and parked the car on a side street a ten-minute walk away. Layers. They walked with their luggage back to the hotel as it started to rain. Yohaba looked up, felt the drops on her cheeks, and began to cry. She wasn't even sure why and then it hit her.

"What is it?" said Boris.

Yohaba stepped into the alcove of a chocolate shop and leaned back against the door to steady herself. "Just give me a minute before we go in," she said through her tears. "This is reminding me when Rulon and I stayed at a hotel in Annecy. It had been raining that day too. It was the day Rulon killed the Serbian with that shot from the car. It was the first person he'd ever killed. He said he never wanted to step over that line, but when he had to do it to save me, he didn't hesitate. Now, in a way, I've just killed two men to save him."

Boris looked around. There were no cars; the street was empty. The rain came down harder. He crowded into the doorway with Yohaba.

"Your Spetsnaz buddies were hot on our trail," she continued, "and Rulon insisted he couldn't let me out of his sight. He is so protective. But the embarrassment at the front desk was killing him when he had to sign us into the same room."

"Why?" Boris asked.

"Because we weren't married and because he's Rulon," Yohaba said. Her voice rose with the emotions her words evoked and the effort to speak coherently through her tears. "Can't you just see the guy? Man, you should have seen him in the Hönggerberg forest.

Man, he was no one you wanted to mess with that day. He almost killed the other brother. Had the guy blubbering. And these guys were no Pilgrims. I had to pull him off. And then a few hours later, he's blushing with embarrassment in front of a hotel clerk he'd never see again. That's my guy. That's my Rulon. There's no one like him." She turned her back to Boris. "Just give me a second."

Boris had a lump in his throat. He reached out and lightly touched her hair, so lightly she didn't notice. Yohaba wiped her tears and turned back to face him. "I'm better now. Just had to get that out of my system."

They walked the rest of the way in silence. When they reached the hotel, the lobby was empty and no one was behind the registration desk. There was a small sign propped up on the desk next to a telephone with instructions to dial number nine after midnight. Yohaba dialed, and, after ten rings, a sleepy-sounding man answered saying he would be right there.

While they waited, Yohaba said, "I have a surprise for you in the morning. Rulon's got a safe-deposit box in a bank here loaded with a phony passport, money, and two pistols. I think one of them's a SIG Sauer. Does that make you happy?"

"Da, Mrs. Hurt. Would like gun very much. With two people dead, rules change. Things get rough now." A minute later he asked, "How did Rulon get passports? That's hard to do. It's not like in movies."

"Oh, he's a smart little cookie. He would claim to have misplaced one of his alter-ego passports while on an assignment, then apply for another one. Sometimes it didn't work, and they'd yell at him and cancel the passport. But sometimes, it would just slip through the cracks. He got three of them that way and stashed them in different places in case he ever had to make a quick getaway. It surprised me when he first told me. Rulon is so straightlaced about that sort of thing. But he said he was simply protecting government property—himself."

Boris laughed. "And then he puts them in safe deposit box. This Rulon guy pretty tricky for farm boy."

"That's what I've been telling you, Mr. Zokolov," Yohaba said. "He's got a stash like this in Switzerland. Another in France and I think one in the UK. He pays the banks every year and keeps the deposit boxes renewed. Costs a small fortune, but Rulon says—" Boris looked down and waved his hand to cut her off. Yohaba got the message. "My husband would never lie to you as a friend, and he'd give you the shirt off his back if you needed it, but he's nobody's fool."

"Da, da, Mrs. Hurt. Your Rulon really Vasily Zaytsev in disguise. Da, figured that out already."

"For us there was no land beyond the Volga," Yohaba said.

"What did you say?" Boris asked startled. "How did you know that? How did you know he said that?"

"Hang around Rulon long enough and you learn lots of obscure things. It's one of his favorite expressions. He said it was about having your back to the wall and fighting for your family. Remember, I told you Rulon taught at Front Sight. He admired your sniper Zaytsev, studied his World War II tactics. Knew about his favorite tactic, 'the Sixes'—three teams of two men sniping a single area. I'm telling you, I'd hate to be someone Rulon was determined to take out."

"Da," Boris agreed.

Just then a bald, grumpy hotel clerk in his midsixties came out of the elevator and walked behind the desk. They were in luck. The small eight-room hotel was empty. After they were processed and had their keys, they walked up the stairs to their adjoining rooms. Boris had asked for a 7:00 a.m. wake-up call. He weighed the advantages of getting up earlier, but after taking one look at Yohaba and seeing how tired she looked, sleep won. Sleep could be a tactical advantage for both of them.

As they said good night in front of Yohaba's door, she started crying again.

Boris hissed angrily, "Stop crying. Please no crying." He reached out an awkward hand.

She waved him off, went into her room, and closed the door behind her. Boris lingered after she left and rested his forehead against the door that separated them. On the other side, Yohaba heard the slight bump and turned around. She suspected what it was and almost opened the door to extend some comfort but stopped herself. Instead, she said through the door, "Go to bed, Mr. Zokolov.

I thought you did real good today." And then hoping to get a laugh out of him, she said, "Don't make me regret I let you come." Silence from the other side. She edged over to the door, touched it lightly, and leaned her ear close, hoping to hear the creak of the wood floor as Boris went to his room. When she didn't hear anything, she said, "I'm sorry about everything." She pressed her ear to the door and listened for a full thirty seconds. Just when she thought she must have missed his leaving, she heard him walk away. *Uh-oh*, she thought. *Trouble.*

BORIS LAY ON his bed fully clothed, his suitcase sat on the floor as open and empty as his killer's heart. *She doesn't know me*, he thought. *She doesn't know my past. What I'm capable of.* His heart beat stronger. *She trusts me.* Then he thought angrily, *She's a fool.* He lay there debating whether to take a shower or break down Yohaba's door when, like the thin edge of a wedge, the memory of his promise to Rulon's father worked its way into his consciousness. The thought came to him, *They are my friends.* After a minute, taking a shower seemed like the better idea. He got up, walked into the bathroom, and started to undress. As he placed his shirt on a hook next to the sink, he caught sight of his image in the mirror. Massive, prison-tattooed arms, and great chiseled chest muscles under a forest of black hair. *The things I've seen, the things I've done.*

In the next room, Yohaba was angry with herself for crying. Like Boris, she was also in the bathroom, the bathtub water running, steam fogging the mirror. She wiped away tears as she arranged and rearranged her toiletries on the sink counter. *Why am I so depressed? I did the right thing.* She stopped and looked at her smeared, vapory image in a bare spot she'd made with her hand. *I did my duty. Leave me alone!* She closed her eyes and took several deep breaths. *Rulon had said it was bad, but I never imagined it would be this bad.* She reached behind her and turned the hot water spigot all the way on. *A hot bath, that's the ticket.*

CHAPTER 25

Inside the nearly empty Gessnerallee garage a half mile from the main train station in Zurich, six men milled around a black Mercedes. Four more men were out of sight, two inside a nearby blue BMW, and another two inside a white panel van.

A man stood by the open trunk of the Mercedes, handing out pistols and moving quickly until he came to a Saiga-12 Kalashnikov-based 12-gauge combat shotgun with an 8-round box magazine. He pulled it out of the back of the trunk, held it up so all could see, and started to hand it to the next man in line. But Martin with the long hair jumped in quickly. "Thanks, but I'll take this one." The other man shrugged and took a Glock 17 instead.

The men outside the vehicles checked their weapons and put out their cigarettes. Despite the late hour and the losses they'd sustained, the night was not over.

Tilman left the cluster of three men he'd been chatting with to stick his head in the open door of the Mercedes. Martin was by now sitting in the front passenger seat with the shotgun between his knees.

"Where are they now?" Tilman asked.

"They're still stopped," Martin said. He focused on the tracking device monitor in his hand. "They're on the outskirts of Einsiedeln." He looked up. "I'll bet they found a hotel."

"Good. I didn't feel like driving all night."

237

Tilman pulled a Glock 19 out of its shoulder holster, removed the fifteen-round magazine, and pushed on the top bullet to test the spring. It pushed back strongly. Satisfied, he reinserted the magazine and reholstered the weapon. He pensively rubbed his bristly face with the back of his hand, then said to the assembled team, "It's time. Let's mount up."

They had started with fifteen men. Two had been killed. One was badly hurt, and on a train going home. Two were with the dead bodies on the way to a mortician known for his sympathies and discretion. Ten men total. *More than enough*, thought Tilman.

THE PHONE RANG in Gustav's study. Klaus answered, recognized the voice, and came to attention. He listened for a moment then looked at Gustav and mouthed the single word "Schmidbauer."

Gustav took a deep breath and narrowed his eyes. "Put it on speaker."

Klaus said into the phone, "I'm putting you on speakerphone. It's just me and the Reichsfuhrer in the room." He pushed the speaker button and laid the handset gently alongside the base.

"I just want a simple answer," began Schmidbauer before Gustav could say anything, the aggravation in his voice filling the room. "And don't ramble on as if you didn't hear me. And don't answer me with a question. Just tell me simply and clearly: Are you running another one of your private operations? Yes or no."

"Didn't you hear about Helmut?" Gustav asked. "What did you expect me to do? Nothing?"

Schmidbauer sighed. "Was that two or three questions? It was difficult to tell." When Gustav made no reply, Schmidbauer said, "As usual, you are psychologically incapable of speaking a simple declarative sentence."

"What did you expect?" Gustav replied.

Schmidbauer sighed again. "There's another one." In a rising temper, he said, "What did I expect? I expected you to see the big picture and support the council's strategic initiatives! I expected you to set an example of sacrifice for the greater good!"

"You rule by consent of the governed," Gustav said mildly. "Don't lose sight of *that* big picture."

Both von Bock and Schmidbauer ran their own factions within the greater movement, with Schmidbauer currently serving the rotating two-year stint as titular head of the eleven German cells, having taken over from Gustav eighteen months earlier.

Schmidbauer responded with genuine sadness, "I'm sorry about Helmut." But in a firmer, louder voice, he continued, "But I'm also tired of having this same conversation with you every three months! Have you lost any men?" When Gustav didn't answer, Schmidbauer called, "Klaus! Klaus, I know you're there. How many did you lose?"

Gustav grudgingly answered, "Two."

"Who?" When Gustav told him, Schmidbauer cursed softly. "This is a catastrophe. Eduard will be impossible to replace and Ingo Petersen was a good soldier. Are the police involved?"

"No. No police. We know how to handle these things. Bodies have been removed. Families will be taken care of. You can assure the council that we have everything under control."

"You don't sound as concerned as you should be," Schmidbauer said. "Eduard was a pillar."

"Eduard was your puppet and a divisive force. Petersen was unfortunate."

Schmidbauer said, "We earn our profits and take great risks in doing so. We expect losses when running drugs or smuggling, but not to support your personal fiefdom. Operations must be approved by the council. We take risks only to fund approved operations, not for some private enterprise. What you are doing is misappropriation of resources."

"These men are personally loyal to me," Gustav said, emphasizing the word *personally* so that Schmidbauer would be sure to grasp the implication—the threat. "They accept the risks."

"You're not hearing me!" Schmidbauer barked. "Our strength is in our secrecy. We have supporters throughout Europe in all the right places, but we will lose them all if we draw attention to ourselves and act like thugs. If your Helmut had followed the plan, he'd be alive. Left to yourself, you'd take us all down with you, old man. But hear this: before that happens I will take steps. I won't let you destroy everything we've worked for."

"No. You would destroy it a different way. Through an uncertain trumpet call. Through inaction."

Schmidbauer reflected on Gustav's words. "I just had an inspiration," he said after a brief pause. "You're up to something. I can feel it. This isn't just about revenge for Helmut. Why was everyone in Zurich in the first place?"

"You and I are running out of time," Gustav said. "The movement is breeding criminals, not patriots of the Fatherland. You and the rest of the council have become little more than a German mafia. It's time we struck a blow that will be heard. And remembered."

"There are worse things than being criminals for the cause," Schmidbauer said.

"Like what?" Gustav asked.

"Like being terrorists. Are you running an unsanctioned operation? Are you?" When Gustav didn't answer, Schmidbauer said, "Klaus, is he?"

Gustav motioned Klaus to kill the connection. Klaus gently placed the handset back in its cradle.

IN HIS PENTHOUSE study in Hamburg, Schmidbauer slammed the phone down, got out from behind his desk, and paced the floor. Thirty minutes later, he was calm again but deep in thought, standing with his hands clasped behind his back in front of his diamond-paned windows overlooking the harbor and the North Sea. Having made a decision, he rubbed the bridge of his nose and shook his head in disbelief at what he was about to do. Comforted in that he had no choice, he walked to his phone and dialed. A man answered after four rings.

"Today it seems providential . . ." Schmidbauer said.

". . . that fate should have chosen Braunau," answered the voice on the other end, continuing the words from the first line of *Mein Kampf*.

"Now listen carefully," Schmidbauer said. "It must be done by tomorrow. No later. Do you understand? Repeat."

"By tomorrow. No later," repeated the voice. Schmidbauer clicked off.

"Who was that?" asked the man, sitting next to Figeli in the white van in the Gessnerallee parking garage.

"Oh nothing," Figeli said, "I hope this mess wraps up soon. I just got another job to do."

CHAPTER 26

MONDAY, 2:05 A.M.

The Mercedes Maybach Armored 62S and its hulking chauffeur sat in the circular driveway under the arch, out of the rain. Klaus had the passenger door open and Gustav had just gotten into the passenger seat and was positioning his cane when Klaus's cell phone rang.

"Yes." Klaus listened for a minute, then said to Gustav, "It's Tilman. He didn't want to call your phone in case the girl called back. He says your son's car stopped in Einsiedeln. Probably at a hotel. He and the team could be there in less than an hour. If they can locate them, now would be a good time to finish this. He wants this sanctioned."

Gustav motioned for the phone. "Listen carefully," he said to Tilman. "Yes, of course I'm sanctioning this. Find them. Take care of the Russian. But just the Russian. I want the girl alive. Can you do that?"

"I can if she cooperates," Tilman replied. "Which is not likely to happen. She has a gun and is not afraid to use it. I can't have any more men killed. I won't ask them to take stupid chances for this. I can't."

"Is that fear I hear in your voice?"

"Probably, yes. But that doesn't matter. I'm just saying we can't play around with these two. This isn't a drug deal gone bad. These

241

people are hunting us. And they have the case. We'll be lucky to kill them and get away. If we try to take her alive, it puts us at risk. I want your permission to take her out as soon as we see her. I don't want anyone even talking to her. We see her, she dies. That's how I want to do this."

"I'm coming. Locate them. Stay with them. But don't do anything until I get there."

"How long?"

"A few hours," said Gustav. "We'll be there by six at the latest. Then we'll make our plans. We'll call again when we're almost there."

Tilman clicked off.

While Gustav was talking, Klaus had opened the rear door and gotten in. Gustav handed Klaus the phone over his shoulder and motioned the driver to proceed.

The driver was an immense, bullet-headed man wearing a brown trench coat and a black beret. He had thin lips, a flat nose, and thin, wispy eyebrows that linked above his pitiless eyes, dark and humorless orbs set in fields of soupy yellow from too many steroid injections. His fatless skin clung like cellophane to his face. As they sped off, the lamps along the driveway threw erratic shadows across his face creating a vaguely skull-like appearance.

Klaus leaned forward, rested his hand on the driver's shoulder. "Ready?"

"*Jawohl*," said Max Amann, proud grandson of another Max Amann, former head of the World War II Nazi publishing house Eher-Verlag.

CHAPTER 27

2:30 A.M.

Boris lay in bed after his shower, tossing and turning, frustrated and unable to sleep. The pillows were flat and uncomfortable so he stacked several of them and punched them furiously into shape. Still, sleep never came. After much turning and sighing, he ended up on his back with the covers thrown off, hot and sweating. The room was cramped with furniture: stuffed chair, coffee table, dresser with flat screen TV, queen-sized bed, two nightstands. Everything but a mini-bar. If there had been a mini-bar, he told himself, he would have gotten drunk: Russian drunk. *Well, maybe when this is over.*

He got up and threw on a pair of navy blue sweats and a plain white T-shirt. The ceramic knife in its scabbard he slipped into his pants pocket. The night clerk had said something about a small gym on the ground floor. Lugging the bio-carrier along with him, he went downstairs to the basement and found the gym at the end of a hall.

The door to the room was held open by a trash basket and had a sign that said "Wet Paint." There was a slight confirming odor, and Boris turned sideways to go through without touching the door-frame. The room was about thirty feet across. The equipment was along the walls—an elliptical machine, exercise bike, weight bench, and a rack of free weights—sparse but sufficient. Two walls had floor-to-ceiling mirrors, and another wall had a door in the corner labeled "closet." Boris laid the bio-carrier next to the elliptical machine and hopped on. After a few strides, the knife was jabbing him, so he took it out of his sweatpants pocket and dropped it on the carpeted floor next to the carrier. Five minutes later, he cranked the machine up to maximum resistance and immediately broke one of the arm poles. Annoyed, he took his things over to the free weights and resumed his workout. Curls, dumbbell rows, flyes, presses, all with the heaviest weight on the rack.

Twenty minutes later, Yohaba came through the doorway in a tight, gray sweat suit, saw Boris, and stopped dead in her tracks.

"I couldn't sleep either," she said.

Boris, in the middle of a set of curls with a huge weight in each hand, simply nodded. Yohaba headed for the elliptical machine.

"It's broken," grunted Boris, in between curls.

"I wonder how?" asked Yohaba with a knowing smile as she waggled the loose arm. She hopped on the exercise bike instead.

Yohaba pedaled hard for ten minutes, then settled down to a steady rate. Once her breathing had slowed, she said, "I notice you brought the case." When Boris didn't respond, she continued. "Look at it just sitting there. Aren't you even a little curious what's inside?" Her legs pumped away while she waited for his answer.

Boris, lying on his back on the weight bench, stopped in the middle of a dumbbell fly and looked at her. "No," he said. "I know what's inside." He went back to lifting.

Yohaba brushed a strand of sweaty hair out of her face. "You know what you *think* is inside." When she didn't get a reaction, she said, "Well, I guess it's not important. I suppose it's only important that they want it."

Boris didn't answer. Instead, he shifted to a new exercise, leaning on the bench with one hand, and doing one-arm rows with a seventy-pound weight.

After a minute of being ignored, Yohaba said, "C'mon, let's open it. Don't be a chicken. You know you want to. What if it's empty? We should find out now."

Boris put the weight down and sat on the bench. He leaned over with his forearms on his knees, his stone face glistening, sweat dripping from his chin. Without a word, he grabbed the bio-carrier by the handle and set it next to him on the bench. Anodized aluminum.

Two latches. He stood up and hesitated over the case. "This is stupid," he said finally.

By now Yohaba was standing next to him. "You don't know that. Every bit of intel is useful. Rulon says—"

Boris held up his hand. "Don't start," he ordered. "Don't say anything about Mr. Wonderful. I'm thinking."

Yohaba shoved him aside and knelt next to the case. "I'll handle this." She flipped one latch, then the other. "Hey," she said brightly. "It's not even locked."

Boris gripped her hand and held it on the second latch. "Carefully," he said slowly, drawing out the word.

Yohaba eased the lid up, peeked inside and started to say something, stopped suddenly, then gagged and clutched her throat. She looked up at Boris, scared, and he saw her eyes roll back into her head. He cried out, grabbed her shoulder, hurled her back, and slammed the lid shut. When he turned to face her, his expression was wild with anguish and concern.

Yohaba was on the floor, chortling at her joke, but when she saw his face her humor morphed into a sickening dismay. For in his unguarded expression, she caught a glimpse of his love for her—undisguised, plain, transparent, as readable as a billboard, and beyond his ability to pull back or disguise. In the next instant, she saw a flash of hurt race across his face like a fast-moving cloud when he realized it was a joke. With immediate, deep regret, she kicked herself. *What have I done?*

"Boris," she said, desperate to make amends for trifling with his feelings. "I'm so sorry. Please forgive me." He'd always been so stoic, unemotional, and indestructible. She saw her grave miscalculation. "I didn't understand," she pleaded. "Please. Please forgive me. It was meant to be a joke. Just a joke." She sat up straight and said firmly, "I need to get back home. I'm going back tomorrow. Rulon and I will work this out. This is it. Thank you. This is enough."

Boris slowly backed up and slumped down on the bench. As if sleepwalking, he lifted the case to his lap and opened it. "Never mind, Mrs. Hurt," he said from a thousand miles away. "It was a joke. I understand. Do not talk of leaving. We must finish this together."

He spun the case around and tilted it so she could see inside. Two hourglass-shaped metal cylinders, about ten inches tall and four inches wide, lay in twin depressions in the foam lining. Near the top of each cylinder were two small, alternately blinking green and yellow lights.

Yohaba crawled closer. "Looks official. Close it up now. It's scaring me. Some things should never be opened. I was stupid."

Boris lowered the lid. After clicking the case shut, he sat unmoving, his hands still on the latches.

Yohaba noticed him swallowing. "I won't leave you," she said. "You can be my brother. Can you think of me as your sister?"

"No." Boris rested the case on the bench and stood up.

"Can you think of me as Rulon's wife?"

"You talk too much."

From the doorway a man sneered in heavily accented English, "Can you think of her as Rulon's dead wife?"

Yohaba looked up and gasped. Boris spun around in a fighting stance. Standing in the doorway were two men holding Glock 17s.

The shorter of the two ordered, "Hands up. Behind your head." Turning to his companion he said, "See, I told you he was big."

Boris hesitated for an instant, glanced at the knife on the floor too far away, then placed his hands behind his head. Yohaba was still on her knees. She looked up into Boris's eyes. He nodded, and she followed his lead, also standing up and putting her hands behind her head. Her heart pounded in her chest. She looked at the two men, and her vision constricted down to their faces. She saw their eyes, could almost count their eyelashes. But her hearing vanished, as if she were in a soundproof bubble. She remembered Rulon and Boris both telling her not to panic, ever, but she could feel it coming on, the adrenaline playing havoc with all her senses.

Boris's words came into her mind: *The first one to feel fear dies.* She tried to control her emotions but she wanted to run. To dive through a window. To throw weights. To tear her clothes. Anything. These men had killed before. She could sense it.

"Smart for a rabbit family Kulak," said the shorter of the two men. "Every second of life is precious. Savor each one. You, Kulak, listen carefully. I want you to see it coming. That man you killed in the alley was a friend." He swore at Boris, the hatred lacing his tone like poison.

"You can't do us here," Boris said in German. "What would you do with the bodies? It would take three of you just to lift me. You'd get caught. You don't even have a silencer." The man who'd been talking was of medium height with short brown hair and a brown vest. The other man was as tall as Boris, at least six-four, blond, blue-eyed, wearing a dark-blue sports jacket.

"Wrong," said the taller man. He reached into his jacket, pulled out a long-barreled silencer and commenced screwing it onto the barrel of his Glock. "And, what luck, our cleanup crew happens to be in the neighborhood."

The shorter man said, "We could do you in the lobby while a tour bus was checking in and no one would ever know, you Tartar pig." He pointed with the gun. "Over there." Boris reached down to grab the carrier. A movement of the Glock and a curt "Leave it" stopped him in mid grasp. He and Yohaba moved to the center of the room, with Boris sliding over to edge in front of Yohaba. The shorter man said, "How noble. Look, he wants to protect the girl. Uh-uh. Stay away from her. Keep apart. Do as I say. Remember, every second is precious."

After Boris had moved a few feet away from Yohaba, the man said, "There. Much better. This reminds me of a story my great uncle once told. Back in 1945 he witnessed a massacre . . . of Jews. A hundred of them were lined up along a ditch and shot one by one. Do you know what was funny? Not one of them ran. Not even the hundredth one. They stood there like sheep and took it one by one. Why do you think that was?

Boris and Yohaba said nothing.

"Time's up. I'll tell you. They knew if they ran they'd be shot immediately. Each wanted that one more minute, that one more second of life. Strange, don't you think? But so human. So weak."

"How do you know that's what they were thinking?" Yohaba croaked, on the verge of tears.

The Nazi looked puzzled and then answered with a half shrug and a smile, "I don't know. I think my uncle asked the last one. He was a naturally curious man."

With her hands still behind her head, Yohaba started silently crying. The tears ran down her cheeks, and her shoulders shook. "I don't want to die," she sobbed. "Please. I don't want to die."

Both men burst out laughing.

Boris, with his hands still behind his head, said to her, "No, don't do this. Don't give them the satisfaction." Yohaba's sobs grew deeper. "Stop, please," Boris said. "This will not save us."

Yohaba fell to the ground on her hands and knees. "Please," she begged. She looked up at them, her eyes flooded, her face contorted with fear and panic.

"Oh, I wish I had a camera," the tall man said.

Yohaba crawled toward them, the tears flowing. Boris moved to reach for her.

"No, no. Don't stop her," said the shorter man. "We're enjoying this."

Yohaba groped and crawled her way forward. She was six feet from them when the short man said, "Close enough. Now stand up."

Yohaba crawled one final step with her arms and legs out of sync, bringing her right knee forward to catch up with her planted right hand. She lifted her face. The two men appraised her pathetic expression, glanced at each other, and laughed again.

She began to stand, to uncoil from the floor, and in her hand suddenly was the ceramic pistol, artfully retrieved from an ankle holster.

Make the first shot count, she told herself as she rose. That's what Rulon always said. Yohaba stood up tall, brought her arm up, seemingly slow only because of the effect of her adrenalized brain, and marked her target. All eyes got big. The words "do your duty" flashed through her mind, and an instant later she shot the short man in the neck. The *pfft-pop* of the two-stage gunpowder sounded in the room.

At almost point-blank range, the tall man fired at the same instant and missed her, hitting the mirror behind Boris. The man started to move, and Yohaba shot him in the shoulder, spinning him around just as he fired again.

People don't like to be shot at, Rulon always said. *Makes it hard to aim.*

Boris crossed the ten feet between him and the tall man, vaguely aware that Yohaba could shoot him by mistake. His opponent was now in openmouthed panic overload, that alternate combat dimension where you see all your plans unravel and death coming on a fast horse. His gun went off wildly—*pop, pop, pop*—just as Boris came over the top of him, grabbing his gun hand and his throat. And, for the first time, Yohaba saw Boris truly in action, war face and all. Boris had the gun and the man was bent over the elliptical machine, struggling futilely. One more *pop*. Yohaba looked away.

When she turned back, Boris was coming toward her, relief and rapture written all over his face. He crouched over the other man dying at her feet, picked up his dropped pistol, and walked back to the man he'd killed. He stood over him for a few seconds, then looked around the room. In the corner was a rack of hand towels. Walking over to the rack, he grabbed a handful of towels and did a strange thing. He wrapped a wad of towels around the unsilenced Glock, and shot the dead man in the shoulder, in the exact spot where Yohaba had hit him. Then he threw the towels down, did a quick search of the man's pockets, and was suddenly back at her side with both guns and an extra magazine.

Yohaba opened her mouth to speak, but all she could think to say was to ask stupidly, "Did the gun work?"

Boris nodded. He nudged the dying man at their feet with his foot. "Hey, why don't you run? Why are you not running?" he said.

"Stop that," Yohaba said. "It's cruel."

They stood over the man shot in the throat, watched him convulse, struggle to speak, then bleed out and lie still.

Boris bent over the body and placed the silenced gun against this man's neck.

"What are you doing?" Yohaba asked.

"Making it look like they shot each other and at the same time trying to destroy your ceramic bullets." Boris had slipped into Russian. He pulled the trigger, then went through the man's pockets and found two extra magazines. Now he had three.

Yohaba stumbled over to the bio carrier. "Oh no," she said. Boris came over and saw that a bullet had traversed lengthwise through the carrier and exited out the side.

"It could have pierced the cylinders," he said. He picked up the case and shook it. No sound of anything broken. He laid the case back on the bench and started to open the latches to check.

Yohaba stopped him with a touch on his arm. "No, don't."

Boris looked at her and saw she was shaking. "That was some act," he said, hoping to bolster her courage.

"Yeah, even fooled me," Yohaba said and burst into tears. *What is going on with me?* she yelled silently to herself. She turned away in embarrassment and took several deep breaths.

Boris stood there, the two guns in his hand, not knowing what to say. "Are you all right? You're not hurt, are you?" he blurted.

"I'm just fine, Mr. Zokolov," Yohaba said as she walked over to the towel rack and grabbed a fresh towel. "I'll be all right. I'm having a great time. You know how us girls are." She turned to face him with tears running down her cheeks. "We cry when we're happy."

"I'm happy too," Boris said in English, missing her sarcasm. "That was close one."

Yohaba dabbed at her face and came back to sit on the weight bench. When she was reasonably under control, she stood up and said through her partially controlled tears, "Mr. Zokolov, don't take this wrong, but I could sure use a hug right now." She held her arms out, looking down, and said barely audibly, "I don't know what's wrong with me. But please don't misunderstand, or Rulon will have to knock your block off."

Still clutching the Glocks, Boris took an awkward step forward and put his arms around her. "I won't, Mrs. Hurt." The contours of her face molded into his chest, and her whole body trembled as she pressed up against him.

When she was still, Yohaba said in Russian through her tears, "Oh, Boris. What am I turning into?"

"There's no crying in baseball, Mrs. Hurt."

Yohaba briefly looked up into his face, then settled back into him again, sniffled, and said, "Tom Hanks. *A League of Their Own.*"

"Da."

Boris knew there could be others in the building, knew that the two of them should be moving. Instead, he laid one pistol on the weight bench and slowly stroked Yohaba's head. His other hand, holding the silenced Glock, he stretched over Yohaba's shoulder and pointed steadily at the open door.

TILMAN LEANED AGAINST the black Mercedes, admiring the soaring cathedral. Even in the dark it exuded a sense of permanence, of indestructibility. A trait neither he nor his men possessed, he noted dryly. He dropped his cigarette butt and crushed it under his heel. "Where are they?" he asked testily. "How long does it take to check out a few hotels?"

Martin looked over. "Maybe they got lost?"

"This place is a postage stamp. How do you get lost? Call them. I want to hear their voices."

Martin hit his speed dial. The phone rang seven times before going to voice mail. He tried another number. Same thing.

"They're not picking up," he said. At those words, the nearby team members turned toward Tilman.

"I don't like it," he said. "Call Fritz and Marco." Martin called the two men posted to watch Helmut's BMW at the other end of town. After a short conversation, he clicked off. "Yes, they were there, then left to check the hotels."

Tilman thought for a moment. "This doesn't feel right. Go find them," he ordered. "Take Figeli."

Martin pushed off the Mercedes and walked over to the van. Tilman lit another cigarette and looked at his watch. Gustav von Bock was still an hour away. He heard a small commotion and saw Martin pull Figeli out of the van by his jacket. There were harsh, angry words exchanged as Figeli threw off Martin's hand. Tilman thought there was going to be a fight, but Figeli eventually smiled and shrugged, flicked his cigarette away, and marched off downhill into the town center. Martin looked at Tilman, shook his head in disgust, then followed.

Tilman looked up at the sky. It had rained off and on all night. Ten minutes ago he could see the stars; now they were gone. He thought he felt a drop and held out his hand. A minute later it started to come down hard. He got back in the car. *Nothing's going right.*

CHAPTER 28

3:20 A.M.

If you're feeling better now, you can let go of me," Yohaba said after a few silent minutes in Boris's arms. At her words, Boris released her and picked up the Glock from the bench and the knife from the floor. The front of his shirt was wet from her tears.

He asked, "Have I started to contribute yet?"

"No," Yohaba said. "Why would you even ask?"

"The tall guy."

"Him?" Yohaba was incredulous. "I shot him for you first. Where's your pride? And by the way, your plan is not going to work."

"What plan?"

"The plan where you make it look like these guys came into a hotel in Einsiedeln at three in the morning and shot themselves because . . ." She looked around the room. ". . . because one of them broke the elliptical machine, I suppose."

"Why is that, Mrs. Hurt?"

"Well, unless you want people to think they threw the bullets at each other, you're going to have to leave the two guns. I don't think you want to do that. In fact, that would be a really dumb thing to do."

Boris clamped his jaw stoically and stared straight ahead.

"Ha!" said Yohaba with a satisfied laugh. She wiped away the residue of tears from her face and red, puffy eyes. "You didn't think of that, did you, Mr. Zokolov? From now on, you have to clear all plans with me. Understood?"

Without a word, Boris grabbed the nearest dead man by the collar, dragged him over to the closet, and threw him in. He did the same with the other guy and closed the door. There was still a yard-wide bloodstain in the center of the room.

"Good luck with that," Yohaba said.

Boris pulled the elliptical machine over to cover the spot. The only other problem was the mirror with a bullet hole in the center with a half dozen six-inch cracks emanating like spokes on a wheel.

"Forget it," Yohaba said.

Boris crossed the room to the doorway, stuck his head out, and looked up and down the hall. "It's clear," he said. "Let's go. We must pack, then set fire to building."

"Are you crazy?" Yohaba asked in horror. "Don't even think it." When Boris came past her to get the bio-carrier, she saw he was smiling.

On their way out of the gym, he kicked the wastebasket aside and let the door fall shut behind them.

As they crept down the hallway to the stairs, Yohaba said softly, "Where is the night manager? Do you think they killed him? I'd like to get some of our money back. We hardly used the place."

"And don't forget, elliptical machine was broken," Boris whispered as he edged along the wall toward the stairwell door. "But don't talk so loud." He slowly pushed open the door, and they cautiously climbed up the stairs to their floor. Outside Yohaba's door, Boris took her key and made her wait outside while he checked that the room was clear. Once inside, he stayed with her while she changed in the bathroom and packed.

Boris watched her in silence until she started to throw her bullet-stab vest in the suitcase. "Put on vest," he said.

"It chafes me under the arms. Forget it."

Boris had been leaning casually against a wall. At her refusal, he pushed off and stood up straight with his feet apart. "This not a request. Put on vest."

"No. Mind your own business."

"This is my business. I may have to use you as shield. Put on vest."

Yohaba tried staring him down but finally relented and put on the vest.

They went to his room next and Yohaba sat in the bathroom while Boris changed. When he was done and packed, they went downstairs with their luggage, Boris still on high alert with the Glock in his hand.

On the way down, Yohaba said, "That incident in the gym. Just forget about it, okay? Like it never happened. Are you with me?"

"Hard to forget two dead bodies," Boris said.

"No, no, I'm talking about that thing where I let you put your arms around me. It never happened, okay? I don't want to ever discuss it. Ever."

"Da, Mrs. Hurt. We will only tell about you killing man, not about you snuggling in Boris's big chest. Save you much grief and embarrassment."

Once outside the hotel, they stood for a moment under the doorway overhang out of the rain.

Boris said, "We can't go back to car. If they found us in hotel, they must have found car. There will be men waiting."

"What do we do then?"

"Now good time to call murderous old man and set up meeting."

"Where should I tell him we'll meet?"

"Someplace unexpected."

"How about the square in front of the church?"

"Too open. Too many places they could come from. Could have sniper in room above square. Too exposed."

"The church then," Yohaba suggested. "Inside the church."

"But it's closed."

"Yeah, whatever that means in a Swiss village. I bet half the places here never lock their doors."

"There will be workers," Boris said.

"Is that a bad thing, having a few people around? But you saw the scaffolding. They'd probably be working outside."

"And monks."

"Don't tell me you're afraid of a few monks now."

"That's not what I meant," Boris said. "And you know it."

Yohaba reached over and zipped up his bomber jacket. "You're no good to me if you catch pneumonia." Neither spoke for a few seconds. Finally Yohaba said. "Maybe the church isn't so bad. They'll only be a few of us. We won't have weapons out. How long do you think it will take?"

"In and out. Just minutes, unless something goes wrong."

They discussed the pros and cons of meeting in the church as well as the options of meeting in the nearby woods, a coffee shop, the main traffic circle, and even going back to Zurich. The fact was there were no great options. Eventually the conversation swung back to the church, and they agreed.

While Boris kept watch, Yohaba pulled Helmut's phone out of her pocket, went to the call history log, and clicked on von Bock's number. She held the phone slightly away from her ear and tugged on the lapels of Boris's jacket to pull him closer so he could hear.

FROM WITHIN VON BOCK's long gray coat, Helmut's cell phone rang. "It's her," Gustav said. He took off a black glove and reached into his pocket. The armored Mercedes was still in Germany, five kilometers from the Swiss border crossing near Schaffhausen.

"Wait," he said into the phone. He reached for a cable dangling from the dashboard and plugged it into the phone. The conversation would now come over the car speakers.

"Can you hear me?" asked von Bock.

"Yes," Yohaba answered.

"Is it the child?" he asked.

"Is it the creepy old man?" Yohaba replied.

"How dare you speak to me like that, you impudent tart," Gustav said with a snarl.

"For a man your age, you are so immature," Yohaba said. "Your Jedi mind tricks will not work with me, Herr buddy."

Gustav, tired from the drive and lack of sleep, and emotionally drained from the death of his son, exploded into the phone with words of vengeful wrath.

Yohaba put the phone on mute and said to Boris, "Man, can I push this guy's buttons."

When von Bock settled down, Yohaba said, "If you promise to drop all future attempts at vengeance on my husband, me, my companion, and all our future generations of children, then I'll give you back your germ laboratory so you can destroy the world. Wait, that doesn't sound right. Hey, just what did you think we were going to accomplish with this phone call?"

Von Bock didn't immediately answer. "I want the case," he finally said. "Then I will forgive all claims against you, your husband, your posterity, etcetera, etcetera. Otherwise, I will hunt you down with every resource at my disposal. I will reach across the ocean to find you. There won't be a hole deep enough for you and your husband to hide. Is that clear enough?"

"But how do I know I can trust you?"

"I give you my word as a German officer."

Yohaba burst out laughing.

"I don't see how this can work," Yohaba said when she was serious again. "You're going to have to do better than that."

Von Bock said, "Hold on," then put the phone on mute. He turned to Klaus in the backseat. "She's right. There is nothing to negotiate."

Klaus said, "Ask her what she wants. She obviously had a plan, or she wouldn't have come all the way over here." Gustav nodded and took the phone off mute.

"What do you want? What would it take to satisfy you?" he asked.

"There is a way out of this for both of us," Yohaba, said "but I won't discuss it over the phone. We must meet face-to-face. I'll have the case with me. We can still turn this into a win-win."

"Where?" asked Gustav.

"Inside the Benedictine cathedral in Einsiedeln at 9:00 a.m."

"And you'll have the case," urged Gustav.

"Yes, yes, of course we'll have the case. This whole thing would be stupid if we didn't have the case. But just make sure you come alone."

"Will you be alone?"

"Well, no," Yohaba said. "Okay, that's not fair. I'll have my faithful Indian sidekick with me. You can bring one other guy with you. But don't bring someone as old as you; the case is pretty heavy."

"I look forward to meeting you, Fraulein."

"Sit five pews back from the front," Yohaba said. "And bring your walker and oxygen bottle so we can recognize you." She clicked off.

Yohaba put her phone away and Boris said, "You still pulling tiger's tail. Does that feel good? You think he doesn't hate you enough already?"

"The guy sets me up. He's like my straight man."

Boris asked, "What did you mean by win-win?"

"It's a common expression," Yohaba said. "It means I win double."

IN THE MERCEDES, right after Yohaba ended the call, Klaus said, "I don't see how this can work out. How can this ever become a win-win?"

"We kill them both," Gustav said. "Win-win."

IN BUILDING 133 at the Meyrin site of the huge CERN complex outside Geneva, it was 4:35 a.m., and Leonard Steenberg was sitting with his elbows on his desk and his face in his hands. In front of him his laptop screen glowed, throwing a light across his hands and torso. The room was otherwise dark. He hadn't slept for two days. He'd been exchanging increasingly frantic emails with colleagues around the world. Numbers had been checked and verified. 182 ELSA was still set to miss earth, but according to the latest numbers by only 400,000 miles. A whisker's half-width in astronomical terms. But why the worry? asked his friends in the scientific community. A miss was still a miss. None of them knew the full story about Einstein's prediction.

He lifted his head, thankful he couldn't see his haggard, worn face. The infernal asteroid kept altering course. Inexplicably. The fly-by date was now projected to be April 12, 2029. Only a day off of Einstein's projection. And the asteroid was still slowly changing course. In his gut, Steenberg had always known that his old mentor had been onto something. *That was just like him*, thought Steenberg with a surge of irritation. *Always the cat who swallowed the canary.* Never revealing anything overtly. Always wanting to dangle the evidence and let his students figure it out for themselves. *Always the professor.*

One more time, Steenberg punched in the numbers and ran

the calculations. There was always hope that someone had made a mistake.

Boris and Yohaba turned left out of the hotel doorway, away from their car. They walked silently in the dark and the rain, dragging their luggage behind them toward the first hotel they had passed earlier in the night. First came an open field with cows, then more small shops. When they arrived at the hotel, they were in luck. Despite the early hour there was an alert young man behind the desk. They booked two rooms and, again, Boris asked for a 7:00 a.m. wake-up call. The young man looked at his watch and gave them a strange look, but entered the time in his book.

As the elevator rose to the third floor, Yohaba said, "Do you realize that up until you took care of that guy in the gym, I'd been doing all the heavy lifting?"

Boris sighed. "What about guy chasing you in alley?"

"You stuck out an arm—whoop-dee-doo," Yohaba said.

"And the man I kicked by the lockers," Boris said.

"The poor guy was heading for the bathroom."

"And the guy with the duct tape in the alley?"

"He was half your size. Where's your pride?"

Boris snorted in response. The elevator door opened, and he and Yohaba got out and paused. They had asked for two rooms side by side, but the best the manager could do was give them two rooms on the same floor.

"Good night, Mr. Zokolov," Yohaba said.

"Good night, Mrs. Hurt," Boris replied. "You have made quick recovery. See you at seven." He turned left. She turned right.

ONCE IN HER room, Yohaba threw her suitcase on the fold-up luggage stand and immediately took out the pistol from behind the small of her back. She looked it over, removed the magazine, worked the slide, and replaced the magazine. Smooth. She laid the gun on the dresser. Without undressing, she stretched out on the bed with her hands behind her head and stared up at the white ceiling. As she sank into the soft mattress, she realized how tired she was. She had never felt so tired. But she couldn't sleep. Would she ever sleep again? *Maybe if I were in Rulon's arms.*

She sat up suddenly, took her cell phone out of her jacket pocket, and called Rulon's dad.

"Hey, it's me," she said when she heard his familiar but tired-sounding "Yea-hello."

"Where are you?" he asked. Rulon's father looked at his watch. It was just after lunch. He was sitting on the edge of a cot set up next to Rulon's bed.

"We're in a little town about an hour south of Zurich. How's the Cowboy?"

Rulon's father stretched his neck to peek at Rulon sleeping soundly on the hospital bed. He kept his voice down. "He's doing better. Doctor says if it weren't for the sudden blood loss, he'd be out of intensive care by now."

"Oh, I'm so happy to hear that. I've been so worried. You have no idea."

"Been awake several times. Been asking about you. When you coming home?"

"In a few days."

"The neighbors are all pitching in, keeping the ranch going, but they got their own places to tend to." In his slow Idaho drawl, he added, "There's lots of work not getting done."

"Dad!" Yohaba almost yelled in her frazzled, exhausted state. "We're trying to save the world here. Can you give me a few days?"

After a long silent moment, he said patiently, "Even if the world's gonna end, the cows still need milking."

Just then Rulon stirred and groaned. "Who's that?"

"Guess who just woke up," said Rulon's father. "Wanna talk to your husband?"

"Yes, yes, put him on."

The old man leaned over his son and placed the phone in his hand. "It's Yohaba. She wants to talk to you."

Rulon shook his head to clear it and blinked several times. "Hi, babe. Where the heck are you? Come to think of it, where the heck am I?"

"I'm in Einsiedeln, darling, and you're thankfully in a hospital where you belong. How are you? Oh, I'm so glad to hear your voice. Are you all right?"

"Doc says I'm going to be fine, but that's only if I survive the nurse they assigned me. I've nicknamed her the angel of death."

"I'm sure that's another one of your exaggerations," said Yohaba.

In a panic, Rulon said, "Sshhh . . . I think she's coming. Dad, block the door." That made Yohaba laugh and Rulon was pleased. "Anyway," he said. "I'm only slightly exaggerating. I've got to get out of this place before I see another brussel sprout. Speaking of which, there's a great chocolate shop called Goldapfel on Kronenstrasse just a few blocks from the monastery on the right as you're walking down the hill. How about picking me up some of those glazed, dark chocolate orange slices?"

Yohaba laughed again. "Oh, it's good to hear your voice, my darling. Yes, yes, I will bring you a shopping bag full of chocolate orange slices and feed them to you one at a time as soon as I'm home."

"Wait a second. You're in Switzerland? What are you doing in Switzerland?" Rulon asked, his brain slowly rousing from his drug-induced sleep.

Yohaba told him the story but played down the fights. Rulon's father stood next to the bed watching Rulon's expression. He could see Rulon stiffen at times and his eyes get wild as he listened. The father could only hear Rulon's side of the conversation, but he knew something wasn't right. At one point, Rulon raised his voice and the father laid a hand on his arm to steady him.

"How has Boris been?" asked Rulon darkly when Yohaba had finished her story. "Was this his idea?"

"No, no, darling. He's been a perfect gentlemen. And it's been all my idea. I dragged him along. He tried to talk me out of it. You were right about him from the start. He's a good guy. Don't be angry. It was the only thing I could think to do. They were going to keep coming for you—for us—until they got you."

"Put him on," Rulon ordered.

"Darling, I'm in a hotel room. He's not here, you idiot. Haven't you listened to a word I've said?"

"Just come home," Rulon urged. "Now, while you can. Don't push your luck. We can run together. They'd never find us. This is not your world. It's my world. Just come home."

"It will all be over in a few more hours. Then I'll come home. The

truth is, we can't stop. It's a thousand times worse than you think."
There was dead silence on the phone for a long moment. "Oops. I
didn't mean that the way it sounded," said Yohaba. "Oh, Cowboy,
don't be angry with me."

"I'm not angry; I'm scared. Baby, this is too crazy for words. I'm
dreaming this. Tell me I'm dreaming all this. You're a physicist, for
crying out loud. You're supposed to be smart. Dad never should have
taught you to shoot."

"And you never should have taught me all your spy-craft nonsense. Look, I'm surviving. I'm doing better than surviving. Boris
wants to make me a Russian citizen and get me a job in the SVR."

"I'll bet he does. Probably wants to get you a marriage license
too." The call was exhausting Rulon. The phone dropped from his
hand onto the bed.

His father picked up the phone and heard Yohaba say, "Darling,
now you're being ridiculous. You're not yourself. Just give me a couple
of hours. We just need to take care of a few more Nazis. Truth is,
these Nazis aren't as tough as they used to be."

"Rulon is asleep," said the father, just as Rulon raised a wobbly
hand for the phone. "No, wait, here he is again."

Rulon grabbed the phone with his last ounce of strength. "Come
home now. This is not right. You're going to get hurt like I did. Or
worse. Baby, please listen to me. Just this once, listen to me!"

Yohaba said, "You sound terrible. It will be all right. I'll call you
back in a couple of hours. I'm turning off the phone now. You taught
me that. You never want to have a phone ring in the middle of an
operation. See, I've remembered everything you've taught me. Good-
bye, darling. Love you. Love you. Good-bye."

Rulon dropped the phone and reached one arm weakly across his
body to rip the tubes out of his other arm, but his father restrained
him. Eventually Rulon gave up and lay there exhausted.

"We need a miracle, Pop," Rulon said, panting, his eyes closed.
"Yohaba needs a miracle."

CHAPTER 29

While Yohaba was talking on the phone to Rulon, Boris was in his room disassembling and cleaning the two Glocks as best he could. When finished, he sat in a chair with the two guns on his lap, facing the door.

Two hours later, he still hadn't slept. It was now five minutes until the wake-up call. Two hours of concentrated thinking and he had little to show for it. Every scenario he considered led to the same inevitable ending. He and Yohaba would get a few of them, but eventually . . . Well, when you were outnumbered like they were, there were no good scenarios. Except running away.

Boris looked at the silver bio-carrier sitting on the floor. He could see the hole at one end and wondered if anything had escaped. Maybe he was breathing something right now. Maybe he'd be dead in a week. Maybe nothing mattered.

The hotel phone rang and Boris picked up. "This is your wake-up call," said an overly cheerful recorded female voice.

AFTER THE CALL to Rulon, Yohaba sat staring out the window as the sun came up and the street below changed colors with the dawn. A new day in a Swiss village. *How beautiful*, she thought. *The things we take for granted.*

There was a knock at the door. Yohaba jumped out of her chair, almost knocking her pistol off her lap.

She stood, aimed the pistol at the middle of the door, and asked, "Who's there?"

"Groucho Marx," Boris said. "Let me in."

Yohaba unlatched the chain and flicked open the dead bolt. Boris brushed past her as she closed and locked the door behind him. He was ready to go—his luggage and the bio-carrier with him.

"There's been a change of plans," he said.

Yohaba turned to face him and saw he was peering intently out the window.

"What is it?" she asked anxiously.

"Put gun down and come here," he said. "Look outside. Tell me what you see."

Yohaba set her gun on the dresser and came over to the window. Boris stepped aside so she'd have a better view.

"I don't see anything," she said. "What am I missing?" She turned toward Boris and was startled to see him facing her with a foot-long piece of duct tape stretched between his hands. "Huh?" she managed to squeak just as he clamped the tape over her mouth.

She clawed at his hands, but he held the tape in place, then pinned her arms in a bear hug. She tried raising a knee into his groin, but he blocked it and moved in closer, pressing her into the corner. She struggled fiercely, her eyes wide with anger and confusion. She screamed, but the tape and one of Boris's huge hands muffled all sound. He half-carried, half-threw her onto the bed, then straddled her, pinning her arms to her side while he pulled a roll of duct tape out of his jacket pocket. She squirmed and tried reasoning with him through the tape, but he wound the tape several times around her head, sealing her mouth, until her muffled words were barely audible.

While she squirmed beneath him, he peeled away a longer length of tape and worked it around her body until she was trussed up like Figeli, with her arms pinned to her side. He next went to work on her kicking legs, wrapping them tight too. When he was done, he propped her up against the bed board and stood back to survey his work.

"Did you know," he said in Russian, "there's actually a class at the academy on the tactical uses of duct tape. I'm not kidding. Duct tape has revolutionized the spy game." Yohaba's face was red from her useless yelling.

"Did Rulon ever tell you about duct tape?" he asked. "Maybe he was leaving that for a more romantic moment. I'll bet Rulon can make a tactical nuclear weapon out of duct tape." Yohaba stopped thrashing and listened. "I taped your mouth shut so I wouldn't have to listen to you telling me about it."

Yohaba calmed down and tried speaking, but her words were unintelligible through the tape.

Boris continued. "You think you hate me now. But that's okay. You'll love me again later. Do you understand why I'm doing this? Just nod your head if you think you know." Yohaba shook her head furiously from side to side. "I'm saving your life, that's what I'm doing. But I want to talk to you first."

She started screaming again behind the tape, but when Boris simply paused and waited, she eventually calmed down again. Their eyes met.

"Do you think I am in love with you?" he asked. Yohaba slowly nodded.

"Well, you're right," Boris said. "And it's a bad situation because I like and respect your husband too."

Boris grabbed the chair Yohaba had been sitting on and positioned it in the corner of the room so he could see both her and through the window.

"I've got a plan. The dysfunctional side of me tells me I can't do it, and the functional side of me says I shouldn't do it. It's a very Russian situation. It's reasons like this we Russians drink so much. All the Russia experts are wrong. It has nothing to do with the winters, centuries of oppression, or Communism. We're just total idiots when it comes to love. It's why our bookshelves are filled with such depressing books. *War and Peace*, for example. Some people think it's about the Napoleonic War of 1803. Ha! How little they understand the noble Russian spirit! At its deepest level it's simply a 1,440-page metaphor for unrequited love. Tolstoy hated his own book and called it 'loathsome.' Are you following any of this?"

Boris craned his neck to look out the window. "Still no sign of our friends." He turned back to Yohaba. "I wonder if they found the bodies yet.

"I really like this arrangement. I talk, you listen. Has Rulon ever had to duct tape you? No, don't answer that question. But I need to tell you something. The truth is, I find you quite attractive. Your face is not the most beautiful I've ever seen, but it has character, and there are no bad angles. Looking up, looking down, left, right, under a cowboy hat, wrapped in duct tape, shooting someone—you still look beautiful to me."

Boris sighed. "How many days have we been together? I mean, just us. Two? Yes. I think it's two. Amazing isn't it? It feels longer." Boris let out a longer sigh. "I've got about fifteen minutes to kill before I go over to the church. I hope you have a strong bladder. You're going to be like that for a few hours at least."

Yohaba nodded.

"Good," said Boris. He looked outside again, more nervous and worked up than Yohaba had ever seen him. "There are a lot more people in this Swiss village than I would have thought. But they all seem to be heading out of town. That's good. I don't like civilians around during an operation."

Suddenly Boris stood up, filled his lungs, and stretched his arms high. "Ahhh . . . it feels so good to be speaking Russian. I sound like such a Neanderthal when I speak English. Did I ever tell you that in a previous life I was accepted at the Vladivostok State University of Economics and Service? That's the tenth best university in Russia, unless accepting me dropped them in the ranking."

He walked over to the dresser mirror and looked at himself. "I haven't shaved in two days." He glanced at Yohaba. "What do you think? I think it makes me look scarier." Boris looked in the mirror again and muttered a few choice swear words. "Sorry, Mrs. Hurt. I know you don't like swearing, but for some reason it seemed to fit the occasion."

He looked at his watch, then sat back down in the chair. "I have one more tiger story for you. Pay attention . . . and don't interrupt." He chuckled at his own joke. "If you live in tiger country and shoot at a tiger but don't kill him, he will hunt you forever. Do you see where I'm going with this?" Yohaba shook her head. Boris leaned forward and said quietly, "We can't negotiate with these people." Boris let the words sink in. "By the way, I'm taking your gun too. I'll be needing it more than you will. You'll get free. I don't know how, but you'll figure out something. You're a smart girl. Or the cleaning lady will find you. But listen, I've got a job to do, and I can't have you tagging along. You'll only get in the way."

Yohaba suddenly figured out what Boris was planning. She slowly shook her head as the realization hit her. A tear rolled free from each eye and traced a heartbroken track down her cheeks.

"I know what you're thinking," Boris said. "You're wondering if I'm ever going to write." He smiled at his joke, then continued seriously, "Do you know when I first fell in love with you?"

Yohaba shook her head again, the tears now rolling freely.

"When you were beating on me on the hill above Bernbailer's compound and ordering me to go with you to save Rulon. That's when I thought to myself, 'That's what I'm missing—the love of a good woman.' Funny, huh?"

Boris looked away, his expression unreadable. After a minute he shook his head and resumed talking. "I could duct tape you to the bed if I wanted, but that would be a waste of good tape. If you make a lot of noise, someone will hear and help you. Sure. But there'd be lots of questions and an immediate phone call to the police. You still wouldn't make it to the church on time."

He chuckled again and took the ceramic knife out of his pocket. "Listen. I'm going to put a little slit in your mouth so you won't choke to death if you should get sick, but you have to promise me you'll stay perfectly still. This thing is wicked sharp." Boris leaned over her with the knife just an inch from her face. "Do you trust me?" he asked.

Yohaba nodded. He held her head steady with one hand and gingerly sliced through layers of tape, being careful not to cut her lips.

"There. Better?" he asked.

Yohaba nodded again while looking at him through red swollen eyes.

"You understand why I had to tape you up, right?"

Yohaba nodded.

"Good. I don't want there to be any hard feelings about this. I don't want you saying bad things about me to Rulon."

Yohaba's agonized eyes answered for her.

He stood up with the bio-carrier. "Do you have money to pay for the hotel?"

Yohaba nodded.

"Good," he said. "Tell Rulon for me he's—" and Boris slipped into English "—one lucky dude. Did I say that right?"

Yohaba nodded vigorously as tears cascaded down her cheeks and over the tape covering her lower face. With one last half-smile, Boris headed for the door, palming Yohaba's ceramic pistol off the dresser as he passed.

Boris stepped out of the hotel onto a sidewalk and street still dark and puddled from the night's rain. He immediately looked to his right in the direction of the first hotel they'd visited that night. No crowds. No police vans. No crime scene tape. Either the bodies had not been found yet, or the Nazi clean-up crew had been exceptionally stealthy.

He had one hand on the case and his other hand in his jacket pocket, gripping one of the Glocks. The town was awake now. Small children wearing reflective safety vests made their way to school, and pedestrians on the sidewalk in ones and twos headed for work in one of the town's small shops or to the train station.

For the first time he looked up at the acrylic blue sky. The storm had blown itself out and the air was filled with the fresh feel of last night's rain and the scent of flowers from the fields across the road. There was also the faint, earthy smell of dirt and manure. He closed his eyes, inhaled deeply, and headed for the cathedral. He passed the town's main traffic circle and turned right up the hill, passing quaint little stores, cars streaming out of town, and a few pedestrians who stared at him suspiciously as they passed.

No wonder the crime is so low, he thought. *Everyone watches.*

The main street that branched off the traffic circle and led up to the monastery was too exposed for Boris's taste but had no side streets from which he could approach the church more discreetly. He continued walking up the gently sloping sidewalk as it curved up the hill.

The street was lined with small shops on both sides, all closed except for the cafés. He stopped to tie his shoe but really to check if he was being watched or followed. He saw men drinking their coffee and reading newspapers, and women, heads down, carrying folded umbrellas, and hurrying to work. No one suspicious. He stood and backed out of sight into the doorway of a nearby Thai restaurant and waited. No one rushed past looking for him. He waited and watched just to be sure.

YOHABA WAITED LONG enough to make sure Boris wasn't coming

back, then got to her feet and hopped around the room looking for something sharp. After a minute of fruitless searching, she sat on the bed thinking. In a flash of inspiration, she hopped into the bathroom and eased herself awkwardly into the bathtub, where, after a couple of minutes of grunting and straining, she managed to flip the drain plug lever with her foot. The hot water faucet proved more difficult to turn, but finally she succeeded. Scalding water gushed from the faucet sending her flopping out of the tub like a fish and onto the floor.

She wormed and wedged herself up against a wall until she was on her feet again. The tub slowly filled, the mirrors fogged, and the bathroom turned into a steam room. By the time the tub was three-quarters full, she had worked out a way of turning off the hot water with her feet while sitting on the toilet seat. Ten minutes later, she was able to immerse herself gingerly into the water.

BORIS WAITED IN the doorway of the restaurant for a few minutes before resuming his advance toward the twin monastery spires at the top of the hill. The church, the heart of the town with its centuries-old bones sunk deep into the earth, loomed into view. He could see the mass of the building, its long four-story wings, the scaffolding, and the tops of its tall wooden doors. Up ahead to his right were the closed-up stalls of the memorabilia merchants, and beyond them a wooded hill.

It was 7:45 a.m., just a little over an hour until the meeting with von Bock. Near the end of the street, Boris slowed his walk and edged along the buildings as inconspicuously as he could. He peeked around the corner of the last shop and almost bumped into an old woman. He mumbled an apology, but she brushed past without looking up. He looked again and in the square were parked a half dozen cars and a white panel van. There were men in two of the cars and several hard looking men smoking cigarettes leaning against the van. Off by itself was a Mercedes limousine with dark tinted windows.

Boris quickly ducked back and just as quickly retreated down the street the way he'd come, glancing frequently over his shoulder. The sidewalks were getting busier. Shopkeepers sweeping, display tables being set up. He reached the traffic circle at the bottom of the hill and turned left down a busy two-lane country road with green fields on both sides. Two hundred yards later he came to a dirt-gravel driveway that meandered up a long sloping hill past a farmhouse. It looked quiet, and Boris was sure he could work his way through this property to the woods on the south side of the church.

His shoes crunched gravel as he walked uphill in the driveway ruts, the carrier banging against his leg. A dog barked nearby, but no animal appeared. Boris passed the farmhouse without incident and came to a wood rail fence that barred his way into the forest. He fit the carrier through the gap in the fence rails, took one look around, gripped the top rail, and despite his size, nimbly hopped over.

The trees were far enough apart and the undergrowth sparse enough that he had no trouble angling in the right direction. The ground was wet but well drained. As he walked among the trees along a deer trail, he came across a snapped tree sprawled across his path. The stump was rotted and half-hollowed. It gave him an idea.

Ten minutes later he was back following the crest of the hill, and after a half-mile reached a trail that led down to a wide graveled path past a fenced meadow to the church.

Yohaba soaked forty-five minutes in the bathtub before the tape lost enough adhesiveness for her to move her arms. Dripping, hot, angry, and her skin red from heat, she awkwardly climbed out of the tub and twisted and wriggled as hard as she could to further stretch the tape. After several straining, frustrating minutes she stood panting through the hole over her mouth staring at her bedraggled self in the mirror. For a second she almost lost it and came within a hair's breadth of screaming and bouncing off the walls, but she held herself together. Summoning up an extra measure of determination, she resumed her struggles and finally gained enough play in her hands and arms to proceed with the next part of her plan.

Into the bedroom she toddled for the desk. Standing on tiptoes, she managed to swing her hand on top of the desk and crawl her fingers over to the heavy metal ashtray. She grabbed it firmly, whirled like a discus thrower as best she could and hurled it into the mirrored closet door. And missed. However, the mirror shattered nicely on her next try, leaving shards of sharp glass on the floor.

Fifteen minutes later, Yohaba was in dry clothes heading out of the room with her hair in a ponytail and an empty gym bag slung over her shoulder. In mid-stride she suddenly stopped herself. After a few seconds of vacillating between two thoughts she let out a furious "Aw, heck," and went back to get her bullet-stab vest.

THE CHURCH GROUNDS were quiet. No union workers on the scaffolding. No priests or visitors on the grounds. Boris walked through a large, cobblestoned courtyard with a tall spreading tree in the middle. One side of the yard was the long south wall of the church. Another side was a long, low building pierced by an arched tunnel that led into an extensive stable area with corrals and two barns. Through the tunnel, he could hear horses snorting and whinnying.

He walked the length of the church wall, trying every doorknob until he found one that turned. A cautious look around, a deep breath, a firm pull, and he was inside. He pressed against a cool wall and waited for his eyes to adjust to the dark. There were voices, and he quickly determined he was in a long, narrow hallway. While still holding the bio-carrier, he pulled the silenced Glock from his belt.

The sounds of the voices led him down the hallway to an open door that led into the nave, the main congregational seating, filled with rows of wooden pews. The voices were louder now but the words still unintelligible in the echoes of the cavernous church. Supporting the roof were four massive, gray stone pillars at least twenty feet across, one of which blocked the speakers from view.

Boris heard a door open somewhere down the hallway he just came from and turned toward the sound. Cautious footsteps approached, then nothing. He judged there were two men standing out of sight, waiting. He stealthily moved to the nearest pillar, pressed against it, and looked back at the door. No one appeared. Above him, light streamed in from magnificent stained-glass windows, trailing colored sunbeams across the church's brilliantly colored Baroque ceiling. He backed against the pillar and edged slowly around its circumference, pistol at the ready, eyes scanning in all directions—to the altar, to the organ loft, to the altar chamber in the back where the famous Black Madonna was housed.

He continued creeping around the pillar until he had a clear view of the entire church, including the fifth pew from the front. There sat an old man, bent with age, with thin white hair and a black coat, one hand resting on a black cane. Next to him was a middle-aged man with short, slicked-down black hair wearing a dark suit. The voices.

Boris moved around the pillar to get a better shot. The old man cocked an ear and straightened.

"Perhaps you and I should talk first," the old man said. Boris froze. "You're thinking, 'I can kill him now, one shot in his white head, shatter it to pieces. Problem solved. Once and for all.'" Boris didn't answer. "Humor me," Gustav von Bock said. "Look at your chest. Tell me what you see."

Boris slowly looked down at his chest and saw four dancing red dots. He held his hand out and one of the dots moved with it, trans-fixing his hand like a nail. He calculated the trajectory and looked up at the loft, then around the church until he identified the location of all the snipers. Behind him came footsteps.

"You will lay your weapon at your feet, or you will die here now, Slav pig," said a menacing but familiar German voice.

Boris considered his options. Von Bock was only thirty feet away, but the angle was bad. He would have to pivot around the pillar and take one step away before he could sight and squeeze. He'd be taking bullets by then. He considered taking the shot anyway but knew inside there was no chance.

And then he imagined Yohaba saying, "Rulon could do it, ya big wuss." He was a split second away from springing off the pillar when Tilman came into his peripheral vision from the left.

The German approached walking sideways, never crossing his feet, his pistol extended in front of him at shoulder height in a two-handed grip. Then long-haired Martin, the second man, came around the pillar from the other side and stuck the barrel of the Saiga shotgun squarely in Boris's neck.

"On the floor," Martin said, his words smothered in vulgarities. Boris hesitated.

"We owe you," Tilman said in Russian. "Do not provoke us."

Boris sank down, the shotgun at his neck and the red laser dots following him all the way to the floor. He released the carrier and the pistol and lay flat on his stomach on the marble with his hands behind his head. Tilman came over and kicked the pistol away. Martin searched him expertly and disarmed him of his ceramic gun, knife, and other weapons, including the duct tape.

"He's clean," yelled Martin, standing up with his hands full. He winked at Tilman and yelled even louder, "Hey, Figeli. Where are you? I've got a roll of duct tape for you."

"Get up," Tilman snapped at Boris.

Boris stood and without warning Tilman reared back and punched him in the stomach, rotating his hips at just the right moment to get all his weight into the blow. Boris hardly moved while Tilman hopped away, swearing and shaking his sprained hand.

Max Amann, every bit as big as Boris, was suddenly standing in Boris's face. "My turn," he said, but before he could swing von Bock raised his voice.

"Enough. Bring him here."

Tilman, Martin, and Max, holding the bio-carrier, escorted Boris, his hands behind his head, down a row of pews toward the main aisle. As they crossed the church, more Nazis rose from between pews and behind the other pillars. They marched Boris down the center aisle to where Gustav was waiting with Klaus.

When Boris was ten feet away, Tilman ordered, "Halt," and asked Gustav, "Where do you want him?"

"Not too close," Gustav said. "He has the look of a desperate man. One with a propensity for violence."

Tilman nudged Boris into a pew two away from Gustav. Gustav and Klaus had to half turn in their seats so they could see him.

Gustav said, "You have won the battle but lost the war. An old story. How often have we seen early victories lead to overconfidence and carelessness." Boris made no reply. "Where is the girl?" von Bock asked. "You mean nothing to me. Nothing. You can die or not die. It means nothing. Where is the girl?"

"She is on a plane back to America."

"I see. We have men watching your car, the train station, and the taxi dispatch garage. She must have walked to the airport then. Or maybe she took one of those little scooters that children push along with one foot."

The men around Gustav laughed. Behind Boris, five more armed men came walking up, three with rifles. One of them was Figeli.

Boris said to Gustav in German, "We split up in Zurich. She didn't come here with me."

"Of course she didn't. And that is why you booked two hotel rooms. Just to throw us off the track. Very clever." More laughter from the men. "But enough of this nonsense. You came here to negotiate. But, please, help me, exactly what was it you were going to negotiate with? What do you have that we want?"

"I have the biological agents."

"Correction. Max over there has the biological agents."

"Look in the case," Boris said.

"Max!" Gustav ordered.

Max put the case on the floor and unsnapped the latches. He knelt, staring into the open case for a few seconds. "It's empty," he said. "I'll get it out of him."

"That won't be necessary," Gustav said. He asked Boris, "What is your name?"

"Boris Zokolov."

"Boris Zokolav, do you know who was the greatest writer who ever lived? And please, no Soviet writers. They are simply the most longwinded."

"Franz Liebkind?" answered Boris with a straight face. One of Gustav's men got the joke and chuckled. Gustav silenced him with a wave.

"Oh, clever, Slav. Did everyone hear that? Our Slav has a sense of humor. That was an obvious reference to the character in the *Producers* who wrote 'Springtime for Hitler.' You see, Mr. Zokolav, we Aryans are not without a sense of humor ourselves. But no. The greatest writer is William Shakespeare. Yes, an Englishman. Does that surprise you?"

"Yes," said Boris. "I never expected you were literate."

Gustav closed his eyes and wearily waved a hand. "Max," he said. "Please." Max stepped into Boris's row and landed a haymaker in Boris's face. Boris shook his head to clear it and stared at Max in a cold fury. After a few seconds, he focused on Gustav again. Max stepped back into the aisle and stood at attention with his hands behind him rubbing his sore knuckles. It felt like he'd broken one of them on Boris's granite jaw.

Gustav continued, "Even if the great playwright had never written a play, he would still be considered the greatest writer of all time because of his sonnets. Consider Sonnet 29 for example: 'When in disgrace with fortune and men's eyes, I all alone beweep my outcast state, and trouble deaf heaven with my bootless cries, and look upon myself and curse my fate.'"

Boris sat, unmoved.

Gustav asked, "Do those words remind you of anyone?" When Boris didn't answer, Gustav continued, "You see, with a little imagination these words could be made to apply to you at this moment. Do you understand what I am saying, my young friend?" Gustav leaned forward and snarled, "Your fate is sealed if you don't cooperate, do you understand me? And there will be no hope from heaven for you." Composing himself, he continued, "Now tell me, what did you do with the contents of the case? We need the specimens very quickly or they will be useless. Let me assure you, we will have them or you will most definitely be cursing your fate. Do I make myself clear?"

Boris looked up at the ceiling, thinking.

Gustav said, "If you were a good spy, you would not have been caught so easily."

"True," Boris said.

Gustav said, "We will talk about the case first, and then we will talk about the girl. Look at me." Boris met his eyes. "Study my face carefully. Can you see? I will have what was in that case."

Boris looked around and counted at least a dozen armed men. He reluctantly said, "You can have the specimens. A trade for me and the girl. That is the only deal I will make."

"Deal," Gustav said without hesitation. "See? We have our priorities. Now that wasn't so hard. I am a reasonable man. Now come. Tell us where you have hidden them. Then you are free to go."

"How do I know you will keep your word?" Boris asked.

"Relax," said Gustav with a grandfatherly smile. "If you are being honest, you have nothing to worry about." And at those words, the same infamous words all interrogators use to lull their captured prisoners, Boris knew he was a dead man one way or another.

"It's not here," Boris said. "We'll have to drive."

"Tilman," Gustav said. "Have someone bring the van around."

YOHABA PACED IN front of the Credit Suisse bank on Einsiedeln's Hauptstrasse, waiting for it to open. With her gym bag slung over her shoulder, she pulled at her ponytail, trying to get out the ragged bits of adhesive. It was ten minutes until the bank opened at 9:00 a.m., and she desperately wanted a gun out of Rulon's safe deposit box.

BROTHER RALPH STOOD silently in the apse behind the altar watching the dozen men who had managed to enter the church even though the main doors were locked and the church closed for cleaning. At first he wondered if they might be part of the cleaning crew. But something in their demeanor said "don't approach." Having just come from community prayers, he wore a black, neck-to-ankle cuculla with sleeves like a judge's robe, wide and deep. His arms were folded inside his sleeves, his posture ramrod straight and still, like one of the statues that lined the inside walls of the church.

He watched as a giant in a long gray coat and an irreverent beret reared back and punched an equally big man in the face. Brother Ralph flinched at the desecration but continued merely observing until he realized, despite his weak eyes, that most of the men were holding guns. He withdrew soundlessly and exited through the sacristy.

Once he was safely out of sight of the intruders, Brother Ralph hiked up the skirt of his robes and ran outside across a small yard. Several priests and brothers communing on benches stopped in their quiet conversations to watch him run past. Brother Ralph never paused but continued running through the open door of the rectory until he reached the abbot's office. He stopped, gathered himself, and knocked. Through the opaque window he could just make out Father Jerome sitting behind his desk.

"Come in," said a half-distracted voice.

Brother Ralph opened the door and, with dignity regained and his arms once again invisible within his wide sleeves, entered the office. "There are men in the church who don't belong there."

"Perhaps they are pilgrims trying to appreciate the peace and quiet," said Father Jerome with deliberate irony, without looking up from his work.

"No, definitely not pilgrims," Brother Ralph said. "More like crusaders, I should say. One man punched another and some were carrying firearms."

That got Father Jerome's attention. Brother Ralph was not known to have a sense of humor. The abbot considered calling the police but then changed his mind. *Maybe they're the police.* "We will go look together," he said and stood up.

Brother Ralph and Father Jerome stepped out into the hall, only to find their path blocked by a dark-complexioned man in his late forties with a thin scar running from his left eye to the edge of his nose. He wore a black leather jacket, dark corduroy trousers, sturdy shoes and a heavy-duty sportsman's watch. Behind him was a younger man with sandy-colored hair almost to his collar.

"Oh, they're definitely carrying guns," the older man with the scar said in passable German. "Please," he motioned back into the office. "There's something important we need to discuss before you go out there."

The two Benedictines calmly stepped back into the center of the room. Father Jerome eyed the two men curiously. "Are you the police?"

The older man seemed to find that question amusing. "Of a sort, yes."

The old abbot walked behind his desk, sat down, and faced his two guests. Brother Ralph took up his post beside him.

The older man with the scar nodded to his companion. "Would you mind?" The younger man threw a wad of Swiss francs on the desk. The older man spoke to the monks. "In return for some compassionate service on your part, I'd like to make a donation to your beautiful church. But first, my German, as you can tell, is not so good. Do either of you by any chance speak Russian?"

CHAPTER 30

When the bank opened at 9:00 a.m., Yohaba could barely restrain herself from bursting through the doors and knocking down the man with the key. She beelined immediately to a teller, made her request, and was directed to a back office where a stylishly dressed woman in her mid-twenties verified her documents and escorted her downstairs to a curtained cubicle. The woman started to leave, and Yohaba could tell she was dying to ask about the duct tape residue on Yohaba's face and hair. But Yohaba fixed her with a glare and the woman left with her curiosity unvoiced. A few minutes later, she returned with a long, flat gray metal box.

Behind the curtain, Yohaba popped the lid and stared at its contents. Inside, in addition to a beat-up Italian passport and some Swiss money, were two pistols wrapped in felt cloth: A .45-caliber Colt Gold Cup Trophy, just like Rulon's, and a Sig Sauer. She chose the Colt. As she unwrapped it, two fully loaded magazines fell out and clattered on the table. She peeked through the curtain to see if anyone noticed, then gathered up the heavy-duty automatic and magazines and stuffed them into her bag. She couldn't think of a reason to take the money, so she left it in the box with everything else.

Once outside the bank, she lengthened her stride but didn't run, even though every instinct in her wanted to. Rulon had always said stay cool, stay relaxed, and never run to a gunfight; it throws off the aim.

INSIDE THE CHURCH, it had been eight minutes since the van was summoned, and it was overdue. Boris sat impassively next to Max, two pews behind Gustav and Klaus. Tilman and the rest of his men had their guns out and were keeping a wary eye on the hulking, sullen Russian.

Gustav said to Tilman, "Go and see what's keeping them."

Tilman started to leave but just as he stood up, the man he'd sent for the van stepped through the vestibule door in the back of the church and waved. "Van's here," Tilman said.

Gustav slapped a hand on his knee and stood up, leaning on his cane. "Come, Klaus," he said. "And you, Mr. Zokolov. Will you be so kind as to join us?"

Boris stood up, intending with the first chance he got to punch von Bock in the back of his neck and shatter his second and third vertebrae. He'd had ten minutes to come up with a plan and that was the best he could do: sucker punch von Bock from behind, then use Klaus as a human shield and hope he was thick enough to stop a few bullets. Then a side kick or two to neutralize the closest gunmen while the dead Klaus would get thrown into the knot of momentarily stunned Nazis. In the confusion, Boris would pick up a loose gun. Nazis would start falling left and right while bullets tore through Boris's clothes, missing him by a fraction. Finally it would be just him and Max left standing. There would be a climactic fight between the two of them and Boris would drive off victorious in the armored Mercedes. Max, on the floor, would lift his head for one last look and then collapse, unconscious. The Pope would come all the way from Rome to rededicate the desecrated cathedral.

Behind his impassive expression, Boris smiled to himself. He always believed in visualizing an optimistic outcome, no matter how absurd. In the end, there was just one thought sustaining him: *If I can just get close enough to the old man, maybe Yohaba can have a life . . . with the Cowboy.*

As Gustav walked past, Boris stepped quickly into the aisle to fall in behind him but was blocked by a grinning Max. "You stay with me, Zorg lover," he said. "Maybe when this is done, you and me could dance a little. Huh? Would you like to dance with Maxie? What do you say?"

Before Boris could answer, the main doors of the church opened with a bang, and everyone froze. A few swung their pistols toward the sound, but the rest were disciplined enough to not take their sights off Boris. From the rear of the church, a slow procession of black-hooded clergy advanced down the main aisle, chanting softly in Latin, their arms buried deep within the wide folds of their robes. The priests' heads were bowed in reverence, their faces above the jaw hidden in the shadow of their hoods as they came up the center aisle. The Nazis all looked at Gustav for direction.

Klaus whispered in Gustav's ear, "This is probably Matins—the morning prayers."

Gustav sighed an exasperated "what next?" Then with downward palms, he urged his men to sit and hide their weapons.

The chanting monks walked in two long lines, ten men on each side of the aisle.

Max crowded into a pew with Boris and pushed the nose of his pistol hard into Boris's side. He whispered, "Be patient. Your time is coming."

When the priest in front passed the last pew before the altar, he held up his hand and the procession stopped, each monk in position next to a row. The head priest took a step forward onto the sanctuary platform and turned to face the seated men. He stood quietly for a second with his head down and then pulled a hand out of his sleeve to make a slow, reverent sign of the cross, blessing the congregation.

In midcross he suddenly yelled, "Freeze!" and as if by magic a gun was in his other hand. He ripped off his hood, revealing a rather worldly looking monk with a scar on his face running from his left eye to the edge of his nose. In the same instant, all but two of the monks in the procession did the same thing, and then, pistols at the ready, twenty fully armed men had the drop on Gustav, Tilman, and the other eleven Nazis.

Boris slowly stood with his hands raised and Dmitri, the man with the scar, announced to everyone, "He's one of us."

Boris smiled, turned to a stunned Max, and without a word took his pistol away and punched him in the face. He surveyed the damage for a moment, then grabbed the bio-carrier and stepped past a preoccupied Max into the aisle.

Father Jerome threw off his hood and, with Brother Ralph in his wake, marched directly up to Dmitri. With righteous anger, he said, "There was to be no violence."

With a shrug Dmitri said, "There's always one guy who doesn't get the word. We'll make it right." Dmitri crooked a finger at the young, sandy-haired Russian entrusted with the money and watched with approval as his protégé sidled over without taking his gun off the Nazis. "Fedenka. Make it right with the good Father."

Fedenka and Father Jerome went off to the side to negotiate an equitable settlement.

Dmitri grinned at Boris. "The thin man thought you might need a little help." To Gustav, he said, "I was hoping you'd be dead by now."

"Hello, Dmitri. I told you before, I will outlive your boss."

"Yes, yes, I remember. You will now please shut up unless you are spoken to. I have no wish to listen to your voice." Dmitri turned away and ordered his men, "Disarm them."

While half the Russians kept their guns trained on the Germans, the other half walked between the pews patting down their captives and relieving them of their assorted pistols, knives, batons, brass knuckles, and cans of pepper spray. One of the Russians came to Martin, relieved him of his Saiga twelve-gauge combat shotgun, and held it up for all to see.

Dmitri wiggled his finger at Martin. "Bad boy."

When they were done, Dmitri said to Gustav, "I see you've been up to your old tricks again. But you've gone too far this time. You've upset the thin man."

"Then my plan was at least a partial success," Gustav said.

Before Dmitri could answer, Father Jerome walked up with a big smile on his face. Dmitri shot an annoyed glance at Fedenka, wondering how much money he'd handed over. Stifling his aggravation, he said to the priest, "You're looking happy, Father."

The priest showed Dmitri the money. "With such an amount, I could bribe the angels."

Dmitri approximated the amount of money in his hand and responded sourly with an old Charles Laughton line, "With a lesser sum, I have." Perking up, Dmitri said in German, "Father, we're leaving. Thank you for your hospitality and the Latin lesson. I hope our donation has bought us some good will in heaven." Father Jerome assured him it had and asked if his men would drape their robes over the front pew. Dmitri gave the order.

When they were done, Father Jerome asked Dmitri, "What are you going to do with them?"

"Nothing," Dmitri said. "They are free to go. As I told you, strictly speaking we're not the police."

Father Jerome nodded, then he and Brother Ralph bid their good-byes and left.

WHILE DMITRI WAS talking with Gustav and the priest, Yohaba had silently entered the side of the church with her Colt drawn and her gym bag slung across her back. She'd come in through the same unlocked door Boris had found and had crept down the same hallway. Like Boris, she too had heard voices and moved cautiously in their direction. She entered the sanctuary and, staying in the shadows, hid herself behind the same huge pillar Boris had used. She slowly edged around the marble column until she could see the front of the church.

Light streamed down from the overhead stained glass on several dozen men milling between the altar balustrade and the first few pews, many with drawn guns. She saw an old man with a cane and surmised this was von Bock. Her gaze shifted, and her heart suddenly soared as she spotted Boris in the middle of the crowd, alive and seemingly untroubled.

There was a man giving orders who looked familiar. She ducked back and pressed against the pillar. *Could it be?* she asked herself.

"Boris," she yelled with her back against the pillar. "Is everything all right?" Everyone froze but Boris.

"Yes," Boris said, his deep voice reverberating in the high-ceilinged nave.

"Who is it?" asked Dmitri as he and his men scanned the church, her echoing words hard to pinpoint.

Yohaba yelled, "That guy next to you. Ask him if was ever in a hospital in Zurich. Ask him if a guy named Rulon Hurt put him there?"

Dmitri laughed. "Tell her yes."

"Da," Boris yelled.

"Ask him if his name is Dmitri."

"Da," Boris said. "You can come out now. But people here are nervous. If you are armed, I suggest you come out with your hands empty and visible."

"Hey, I'm not a rookie," yelled Yohaba, highly insulted. She stuck Rulon's pistol in her bag and stepped out from behind the pillar with her hands in plain sight and a smile on her face. When she saw Boris, her eyes welled up and she had to stifle a cry of relief and pleasure at seeing him again, alive.

Boris, Dmitri, Dmitri's men, and the Nazis all watched as she came to them unafraid, weaving her way between the pews to meet a dozen strange men with drawn guns.

Her eyes were red and swollen from crying and lack of sleep, and her cheeks were hollow from lack of food since Rulon was shot. But something in her face was beautiful and serene, and there was still that look that asked "Are you as interesting as me?" But around the eyes and somewhere deep within the crinkles of her smile was an unmistakable hardness too that said, "If you touch me, I'll touch you." Like one of Boris's tigers.

The Russians who knew her history but were seeing her for the first time whispered among themselves: *the Cowboy's woman*. They'd heard the story of CERN. *She'd been there. A living witness. Saw the whole thing. Rulon and his hammer . . . all for her.*

The Nazis who had dealt with her in the alley and at the lockers under the Hauptbahnhof knew her as a person of consequence, a formidable adversary who had forced six of them to back off and had slain Helmut and Eduard. But up until now CERN had only been a wisp of a rumor from another service. As she walked toward them in the light, they now believed and watched her with that strange mixture of hatred and respect found only in their twisted world.

Dmitri remembered her from their meeting in her apartment and later in the hospital as he lay in bed, arms and legs splinted, a gift from Rulon, and marveled at the change in Yohaba. She'd been along for the ride back then, Rulon clearing a path for her through all the dangers of the hunt for Einstein's trunk. But now, she was clearing her own paths, keeping up with Boris, which not many in the service could do. She was more tanned, more muscular, harder. Ranch life, Dmitri surmised. He knew her story and Rulon's too. Knew what happened in CERN. But then everyone in the service knew. It was the stuff of legends.

He'd kept tabs on them the past couple of years through rumors and reports from the designated fighters who came back from Idaho after Karaoke Wednesday. Every time the same. They'd talk about Rulon with a grudging respect. But always their story came back to the tall beauty speaking Russian, sowing confusion, controlling the situation, more than holding her own, even controlling the Cowboy. Rulon's woman. How did Rulon know back then when he first found her working in a luggage store? How did he know that underneath that rough stone was such a finely shaped diamond?

And Gustav watched her too. The voice on the phone daring him, baiting him into one foolish gamble after another. Yes, he'd been right: intelligent, confident. A woman who made plans and executed. The killer of his son. He fingered the silver-knobbed head of his cane and found the small lever he was searching for that armed his triple-shot weapon.

She came up the center aisle, heading for Boris, and all the men parted for her. She passed Figeli sitting in a pew. He gave her a small smile. She acknowledged it with a dip of her head but kept walking right up to Boris. She stopped close and looked up into his face sternly without speaking.

Finally Boris said in Russian, "I love the silver tint lipstick."

"It's duct tape adhesive," Yohaba said, also in Russian. "Lasts all day."

"And I like what you've done with your hair."

"Yes. More duct tape residue. I'm sure it's considered quite chic where you come from." Around Boris, several of the men put two and two together and laughed. Yohaba jabbed Boris in the chest. "I could use a hairdresser. Guess who's paying for it." Boris looked at Dmitri and Dmitri nodded to Fedenka.

Fedenka came over and asked Yohaba, "Would a hundred francs cover it?"

Yohaba looked at him incredulously. "Yeah, if this was Berzerkistan. How about two fifty and that might not even cover the tip." Fedenka counted out the Swiss francs, and Yohaba tucked them away in her pants pocket.

She focused on Boris again. "You're still alive. And so's what's-his-name."

"Yes."

"Do any of your little schemes ever actually work out?"

"Not that I can recall," Boris said.

Yohaba leaned in closer and whispered, "We've still got a problem then."

"Yes," Boris said. "I know." They both glared at Gustav. Boris then beckoned to the Russian who had disarmed Martin and said to Yohaba, "He has your toy gun and the ceramic knife."

The man came over and handed Yohaba the knife but paused as he held out the pistol. For the first time, he looked at it closely. He stifled a question and handed it over. He also gave Boris back his duct tape.

Dmitri cleared his throat. Yohaba looked at him. "I was getting to you. How are the arms and legs? Everything back to working?"

"Yes," said Dmitri with his signature crooked smile. "But I have a little trouble these days getting through metal detectors. How is the indomitable Mr. Hurt?" Yohaba and Dmitri talked for a few minutes about Rulon and a little about CERN and what happened to Dmitri at the Desperado almost three years earlier. The Russians all edged in a little closer to hear. Even the Nazis stayed quiet to listen. Most of them knew a little Russian.

Boris listened, smiling inwardly as she told the story how he had taped her up and how she'd escaped. She got the men to laugh, even one or two of the Nazis, when she mimicked Boris by talking deeply out of the side of her mouth.

While Yohaba was speaking, von Bock pivoted a little as if to hear, trying to position for a clean shot.

Dmitri asked her about Helmut, but Yohaba wouldn't tell the story in front of the father. "We got him in a fair fight," was all she would say.

Boris noticed her eyes start to well up at the memory and to distract everyone, he said to Dmitri, "We need to get the specimens. I left them in the forest."

Dmitri told his men to get the Krauts moving. The Nazis, resigned to this defeat, stood up. There would be another time. When operating in a neutral country, casualties were accepted in the heat of battle, but neither side would execute or take prisoners, and there were never arrests. Those were the inviolate rules hammered out by the thin man with his many adversaries.

Von Bock saw his chance to shoot Yohaba slipping away. Too many men were now moving between them. He leaned into Klaus and whispered, "Max must fight the big Russian." Klaus looked puzzled and Gustav said, "Tell him. Do it now."

Klaus still looking perplexed edged into the pew behind Max. He whispered something in Max's ear. Max nodded, looked at Gustav, and grinned.

"An all-too-easy victory," Dmitri said loud enough for all to hear. "What do they say in basketball? 'A great team gets easy baskets.' Yes, this was a layup. Still, a win is a win. And this madness with the germs is stopped." He looked around at each of the Germans and none would meet his gaze. With a look of disgust, Dmitri told his men to hurry up and get the Krauts out of the church.

When it was his turn, Max filed out of his pew and stopped in front of Boris. The two men were of equal size. Scary massive. Bodies like blocks of granite. Max's face was smeared with blood from Boris's earlier punch, and the sleeve of his shirt was a bloody mess. They stared each other down for a few seconds before Max said, "We never got to dance, you and me."

Yohaba jumped in before Boris could say anything. "Great idea. I always tell Boris to dance with at least one wallflower."

Boris said nothing. He knew what was coming.

Max glared at Yohaba. "He does not need a woman to speak for him. Let him speak for himself."

"I'm his manager," Yohaba said. "If you want to dance with Boris, you have to wear a tutu."

Tilman came over and pulled on Max's arm. "Come. Let's go. It's not worth it." Max shrugged him off.

"You and me," Max said to Boris. Tilman went to intervene again, but Klaus caught his eye and warned him off.

Yohaba stepped between Max and Boris. "Okay, forget the tutu, but for obvious reasons Boris gets to lead."

Max looked at Yohaba in sheer frustrated bewilderment. "Why are you insulting me? Who are you? You are no one. You are a girl." He jabbed Boris in the chest. "What do you say? Huh?"

Boris pushed Yohaba out of the way, then jabbed Max hard in the chest in return. "Come. We dance," he said. Max yelled an insult and Boris said again, "Come."

Max stepped closer to Boris and yelled in his face. Boris stared back blankly and growled things too low for anyone but Max to hear. Meanwhile, Yohaba scampered around from one side to another, jabbing her finger in Max's face and adding more insults into the mix. By now, most of the Nazis were at the other end of the church, being herded out by the Russians. On hearing the commotion, everyone stopped and looked.

Dmitri and Tilman jumped in and pushed the two men apart. It was too late, though. Everyone's blood was up. Dmitri and Tilman conferred with the two antagonists. After a brief discussion, the four men agreed that the two champions should fight. When told the news, the men on both sides grinned and nodded in approval. Two single-combat warriors fighting for the pride of their service. For the Russians it would seal the triumph. For the Germans it offered a partial vindication. There were stone block horse stables, barns, and a garage out back. A perfect setting for a fight. A truce was called.

The Russians still kept their weapons trained on the Germans, but the Germans, no longer dour and grim, cooperated fully.

This fight would be their redemption, and the Russians were idiots to accept the challenge. Max was a known entity among the services. A formidable enforcer. He'd represented Germany in the Olympics as a heavyweight boxer and earned a reputation both before and after his amateur career as a skillful street fighter. Trained in a Burmese form of combat called Bando Thaing, he was a lethal mixture of skill and brute force. But Boris had an equally stellar reputation. This was a fight no one wanted to miss.

CHAPTER 31

Across the plaza from the church, the local people enjoying breakfast at the outdoor restaurant hardly noticed when a large group of men exited the front doors of the cathedral and circled around the side of the church toward the stables. Even the ones that did lift their heads paid no attention—just another tour group.

The Germans were in the middle and the Russians formed a three-sided box around them, weapons concealed but still at the ready. Boris, Yohaba, and Max walked together near the rear, keeping up a muttered banter of insults. Max tended toward ethnic epithets, and Boris toward threats of annihilation. Yohaba's abuse was less crude, but she infuriated Max beyond all reason with her taunting style—a machine gun delivery of snide insinuations. When at the end of a particularly maddening burst of mockery and derision Yohaba asked Max if his parents were siblings, Max lost it, and he and Boris almost went to blows right there.

Looking for an area big enough for the fight, Dmitri and Tilman finally settled on a small, weedy courtyard behind one of the barns that could only be entered through an arched tunnel and was flanked on four sides by the barn and the original stables from hundreds of years ago.

The men filed through the arched entryway into the courtyard with Gustav and Klaus in the lead and Tilman and Dmitri on either side, waving them through. When all but the last few men had entered, Dmitri looked up and saw Father Jerome fifty yards away and closing fast. Dmitri grabbed Fedenka out of the line just as he was stepping over the wooden threshold, spun him around, so he was pointed toward the priest, and said, "Make him happy."

The courtyard was a chewed-up concrete square about twenty yards on a side. Along one wall was a line of pallets stacked with cement bags. Another wall was blocked by two large dumpsters, one green, one blue, filled with the debris of construction. Under a wooden overhang that ran the length of one of the ancient stables, a few hay bales lay scattered.

Tilman and Dmitri were not strangers. They knew each other from past operations and had sat across negotiation tables on more than one occasion. They were both old hands and knew how the game was played. They made their two groups line up on opposite sides of the courtyard.

Tilman spoke to his men first, warning them to keep the peace. "It's over," he said. "They won this round. We will go home after this and regroup." Though he dared not show it, Tilman was greatly relieved that this thing with the bio-specimens had not succeeded.

When Tilman was done, Dmitri ordered his men to put away their weapons but keep them at hand. Despite the Germans being unarmed, he warned his men to remain alert for treachery. While he considered this the prudent thing to say, inwardly he knew the Germans would do nothing to jeopardize the fight taking place. They wanted to see it even more than his own men.

While Boris and Max limbered up, Dmitri and Tilman stood between the two groups, smoking cigarettes and chatting about a temporary truce they brokered two years ago over drinks in Berlin.

Max was in one corner sitting on a hay bale, getting his shoulders massaged by a short fellow Nazi, while in front of him another Nazi was angrily shaking his fist and urging him on to feats of manly valor.

Boris stood in the diagonal corner with his shirt off, bouncing on his toes and listening to Yohaba jabber away.

"Man," said Yohaba. "No matter how many times I see them, I still can't get over your tattoos. Oooh, this one is weird. And this one looks brand new. Did you stop off at a tattoo parlor after you taped

me up? I swear, there are more now than I saw last night in the gym."
She tapped his arm. "You missed a spot."

"What?" Boris said. "What are you talking about?" The adrenaline had kicked in, and he was irritable, ready to fight anything that moved.

"Don't take that tone with me," Yohaba snapped. "I'm talking about your tattoos. You missed a spot."

"Do you think I can take him?" Boris asked as he looked over Yohaba's head at Max. Some of the men had moved hay bales into place to form a rough square.

Yohaba glanced at Max. "My advice is to roll over on your back and expose your neck."

Boris broke off staring at Max to look down at Yohaba. He studied her face for a long moment. "I had to tape you up. There was no other way."

"Yeah, like I haven't heard that one before," Yohaba said. "Listen, up until now, you haven't done much. We've been through all that. You know how I feel. I'm not saying you haven't contributed, but now's your chance to show me what you've really got. If you win this, I'm thinking you don't have to repay me for your plane ticket." Yohaba looked over her shoulder at Max and shuddered. He had narrow pig eyes under thin, blond eyebrows. Cruelty drifted across the arena with the smell of manure.

"If I win, you'll owe me," Boris said.

Yohaba turned back to Boris. "Give it up, mister. How about if you don't win, you get my foot up your butt?" She stole another quick look at Max and swallowed hard. Max was a brute. His chest and arms were hairless and his muscles were bulging. Boris was no pushover, but Max looked like a homicidal maniac. She faced Boris again. "I don't want to put any pressure on you but that guy moves like a pregnant yak. He wouldn't last ten seconds with Rulon."

"You're supposed to be psyching me up, not reminding me about Mr. Wonderful," Boris said, still bouncing on his toes.

"That's what I just did. You lasted fifteen seconds with Mr. Wonderful. I'm saying you should handle this guy easily."

"If he wins, do me one thing," Boris said.

"What's that?"

"Shoot him."

"That's a given. But you're going to win."

From the middle of the ring, Dmitri waved the two fighters forward, and the buzz of conversation in the courtyard ceased. Boris and Yohaba stepped forward to meet Max and his two seconds, who were also approaching the middle of the ring, the short one trailing behind while still massaging Max's shoulders. The onlookers on both sides stood curious and quiet for a few moments. Slowly, they came to life again and began urging their fighters on in a steady, murderous patter. Max and Boris stood toe-to-toe staring into each other's eyes. Dmitri raised his hand for quiet and the place settled down. Dmitri said to Tilman, "You go first."

Tilman put one hand on each contestant's shoulder. "No weapons. No one interferes. The fight is over when one man doesn't get up. It stays here in the courtyard. Those are the only rules." Tilman saw some of his men had their cell phone cameras out and said loud enough for all to hear, "No cameras. No faces. You all know better than that."

Dmitri took over next. "Please. No one try anything. If anyone does, we end the fight and everyone loses out. You Germans: if we are attacked, we will shoot. Do you understand? As for my men, if anyone misbehaves, he will answer to me."

Dmitri took one more look around, suddenly struck with how incongruous the whole situation was. Men had died over the last few days, and there was a truce to watch a fight together. Well, he'd seen stranger things in his twenty years in the Russian foreign service. There was something about Gustav and his cane, though, that set off alarm bells in Dmitri's head. But Dmitri shrugged it off. He turned to his own men, fixing them with a final threatening glare. He next nodded to Tilman. Everyone withdrew from the ring except for Boris and Max. While still maintaining their belligerent stares, the two combatants each stepped back a few paces.

From his vantage point against a wall, Dmitri said, "Ding."

Boris and Max circled each other with their fists up. Boris had his left leg slightly forward, knee bent, in something akin to a martial arts pose. Max was more upright like a boxer. He feinted a slow, testing jab, but Boris was a foot out of range and merely slapped it aside. Max moved in and threw a heavy right, but Boris stepped back and it too landed short.

They circled each other, and Max grinned. "You can't run all day."

Boris rushed two steps closer to Max, but now the German stepped nimbly back. Boris did it again, then in a blink slid in low like a runner into second base and from a prone position between Max's legs aimed a kick straight up into Max's exposed groin. At the sickening impact, everyone in the courtyard turned away and groaned.

Max's eyes bulged like balloons and a high-pitched scream ripped from his lungs only to get cut off in midnote as Boris's heel sunk deeper with the pile-driver force of his massive leg. Max was lifted two feet off the floor, though afterward everyone agreed it was more from Max's jump reflex than from Boris's kick. His face went white, and he crumbled instantly when he came back down to earth, moaning softly. There he lay on his side in a fetal position while everyone on both sides stood in mid-pose like a video on pause.

Boris got up and walked unhurriedly around his opponent. When he got into position he wrapped his arms around Max's waist from the back, and hefted him partially up so he could lock his hands good and tight. Satisfied he had a good grip, he started to arch backward, but he stopped in midarch long enough to wink at Yohaba. Then with a mighty bellow like one of Rulon's hammer throw efforts, he continued unfolding and threw Max over his body in what Yohaba was to later report back to Rulon was a perfect Karelin reverse body lift.

Max bounced once before landing sprawled and unconscious in the dirt. Boris walked back to Yohaba and fell into place at her side.

As she handed him his shirt, she whispered, "I don't want to make a big deal about it, but you took twenty-seven seconds."

The makeshift arena was deathly quiet except for the wind blowing through the storage area above the stables.

After a few beats, Dmitri said, "Okay, let's pack it up."

The place came to life again. Three men ran to Max, whose arms and legs were moving. A good sign. One of them kneeled down, did a quick diagnosis, and quickly made a call on his cell phone.

The Russians were still on alert, but in the commotion and buzz of relief, no one was watching Yohaba's gym bag lying against a wall—except Figeli. Momentarily forgotten, he noticed the bulge of a familiar shape through the fabric. He drifted over and when no one was paying attention, picked up the bag and slung it over his shoulder. With the bag partially behind his back, he opened the zipper and rummaged around with one hand out of sight until he found Yohaba's Colt. He slipped it under his jacket, dropped the bag, and walked over to join Tilman, who was talking to Gustav and Klaus.

One by one, the Russians came over to pat Boris on the back. Boris hardly reacted and eventually the well-wishers drifted away.

When everyone was out of earshot, Boris asked Yohaba, "When did you start the clock?"

Yohaba didn't immediately answer but was watching as four men struggled to get Max on his feet. They got him a quarter of the way up before his head lolled to the side, and he slid back down again.

"At 'ding,' of course," Yohaba said.

"Did you start it at 'ding' in the Rooster?"

"There was no ding then, bright boy."

"The ding was when I threw the table against the wall. I'll bet you didn't start the clock with Rulon until we first made contact. Do you see where I'm going with this?"

"Geez, you are so immature."

Dmitri came over with a cigarette hanging out of his mouth. "That was worth the price of admission," he said cheerfully. Boris frowned at the compliment. A little embarrassed, Dmitri added, "I heard you went to fight the Cowboy. How did that turn out?"

"Differently," Boris said in a tone like slamming a door shut, and Dmitri knew not to pursue the subject.

Fedenka walked up, joined the group, and struck up a conversation with Yohaba. For Boris the conversation around him faded to an unintelligible buzz as he spied Gustav leaning on his cane beside Klaus, Tilman, and the little man he'd taped up in the alley.

Better keep an eye on the ferret, thought Boris.

Tilman was talking with Klaus, but Gustav wasn't paying attention, just staring at the ground looking tired, broken, and something else Boris couldn't read. Grief perhaps. The old man stared as if seeing the end of the road, which from his point of view was an apt description. His son dead. His great, final act of treachery thwarted. His revenge put on hold. His life . . . a waste.

Da, Boris thought, as he looked at the frail, old man. *He'll be dead in six months.*

Gustav lifted his head and seemed surprised to see Boris still there. He reached out with his cane to steady himself and began a slow walk across the yard. Boris nudged Yohaba, and she stopped talking to watch old Gustav totter toward them.

"Oh, this should be fun," she said out of the corner of her mouth. "Would this be a good time to tell him about the two Nazis in the hotel?"

Beside her, Dmitri was joking with Fedenka about giving away his salary. Across the yard, Tilman and Klaus looked up to watch Gustav, their faces equal parts curiosity and pity to see the old man so reduced. Figeli watched with interest, Yohaba's Colt .45 hanging heavy in his belt at the small of his back under his sweatshirt.

Boris was distracted and absently answered Yohaba, "They already know." He was more focused on Figeli. He saw him stiffen and come to attention as Gustav walked away. Something wasn't right.

Gustav stopped five feet away. "I guess this is good-bye," he said, then quickly but without hurrying brought his cane up and fired the first bullet at a completely surprised Yohaba.

Knocked backward by the bullet, she would have fallen if she hadn't staggered into Dmitri. Gustav then rotated the cane slightly so it pointed at Boris, who was reaching for Yohaba, not sure where the bullet had come from, thinking it was from Figeli or maybe Tilman. Yohaba, though, knew exactly what had happened and in a wild surge fought off the shock of the bullet when she saw where the cane was pointing and leaped in front of Boris.

She took the second bullet in her back and thought, *I'm dead,* just as she fell into Boris's arms.

Gustav's face contorted with hatred. Foiled at every turn by this . . . this . . . girl. Thinking faster than Boris, and faster than Dmitri and Fedenka, who were only now drawing their Grach automatics out of their shoulder holsters, Gustav wondered at first if the cane had misfired, but then he remembered the girl had been wearing a vest when she killed Eduard. He raised his cane on a line with her head only three feet away and squeezed the trigger just as Figeli's heavy slug tore through his lower spine, spoiling his aim.

Gustav's bullet missed Yohaba's head by a foot and ricocheted off the cement to clang into the green dumpster. The cane fell to the ground. Gustav collapsed on top of it, paralyzed and dying.

Figeli quickly laid Yohaba's Colt on the floor and raised his hands. Men came running back into the courtyard with weapons drawn. Klaus rushed over to tend the dying Gustav. Boris, on his knees, cradled Yohaba in his arms, not sure how bad she was hurt. The yard swirled with running men and chaotic yelling.

CHAPTER 32

Yohaba wearily pushed Boris away and rolled into a seated position, hunched over, arms resting on her bent knees. Dmitri started to ask if she was all right, but she held out her hand for him to stop talking. Boris remained on his knees, watching her, his hands out, ready to catch her if she should fall over. With her head still down, her shoulders slowly raised with a huge intake of breath, she paused, and then, balling her fists, she shouted, "Ouch!" at the top of her lungs. Then in a much softer but pained voice she repeated, "Ouch. Ouch." Sighing heavily, she slowly struggled to get up. Boris grabbed her under her armpits and pulled her to her feet.

Once up, she pushed him away and tottered over to Gustav. As she approached, Klaus looked up from his ministrations, his hands and shirt covered in blood, despair written on his face. Yohaba saw Gustav's chest rapidly rise and fall and looked down, mesmerized at the gaping exit hole in the old man's stomach. *How could he still be alive?* She stood over him and made eye contact.

"Was it worth it?" she asked. Gustav's jaw moved slightly, but whatever he was trying to say came out as an incoherent gurgle. His tear ducts seemed to be the only thing working properly. Tears streamed down his face. While Yohaba looked down at him, his breathing stopped. "I'll take that as a no," she said, turning to walk unsteadily toward her gym bag against the far wall. Boris trailed behind her, waving everyone else away.

When Yohaba picked up her bag, it felt light to her. She looked inside and saw the Colt was missing . . . and didn't care. She zipped up the bag in a daze. She'd been shot twice and thought for sure she'd been killed. But she wasn't. It was a lot to handle. Dmitri walked over, but before he could say anything, Yohaba asked him, "Who shot von Bock?"

"Figeli," Dmitri said.

"Figeli?"

Boris said, "The little guy I taped up in the alley. The one you wouldn't let me kill."

Yohaba gave a half-smile. "Well, there's a lesson for you." She looked around for Figeli. "Where is he? I want to talk to him."

The three of them walked outside, and Yohaba was surprised to see that most of the men had already left. A few of the Russians stood watch around the courtyard, but Figeli was nowhere to be found. The white van was parked by the barn to collect Gustav. There was also a BMW with heavily tinted windows. Dmitri had a hunch, walked over to the Beemer, and rapped on the front passenger window. It slid smoothly down.

"What?" Tilman asked. Dmitri looked inside and saw Figeli in the backseat.

"The girl wants to talk to him," Dmitri said. Tilman turned and said something.

The rear door opened and Figeli—small, thin, sharp face, wearing a brown sweatshirt—got out with an unlit cigarette in his hand. He walked over to Yohaba, stopping an arm's length away and to the side, keeping Yohaba between him and Boris. He wanted nothing to do with the Russian.

"Would you happen to have a light?" he asked. Yohaba noticed his hands shaking. Strangely, hers weren't.

"That will kill you someday," she said.

"Only if I live to a ripe old age," Figeli replied with a cautious eye on Yohaba's protector. "What do you want?"

"I want to say thanks. Why did you do it?"

"From you, that's the wrong question." Figeli looked at the unlit cigarette and frowned. "I was contracted to do it by someone above von Bock in the pecking order. No one agreed with this thing of the germs. Otherwise I'd be dead now."

"So what's the right question?"

"The right question is why did I do it *now*."

"Okay. I'll bite. Why now?"

"Ahh, my beautiful, young friend. It was your marvelous speech in the alley when your lover here wanted to kill me. I found it completely inspiring. Such eloquence. Such logic. Like musical pearls from heaven." Figeli put his fingertips to his lips and kissed them. "I couldn't let your golden voice be silenced forever. It would have been a terrible waste." He laughed.

"We're not lovers. Why do you say that?"

Figeli looked from her to Boris in surprise. He made a picture frame with his two hands and squinted through it at the two of them. "Smile," he said and laughed again. "I think you are only half right. Eh, Boris? What do you think? Maybe she is only half right?" He put his hands down.

Boris had his jacket slung over his arm. He went through a pocket and pulled out a roll of duct tape.

"Bye," said Figeli as soon as he saw the tape. He blew a quick kiss to Yohaba and returned to the car. Before he stepped inside, he paused. "Make sure they return your pistol." Dmitri closed the door behind Figeli, rapped twice on the hood, and the BMW drove off.

"I think they will kill him anyway," Boris said.

"I hope not," Yohaba replied.

Another BMW drove up and stopped by Dmitri. A door flew open and Dmitri looked at Boris twenty feet away. "C'mon," he said.

Boris said, "I will drive back with Yohaba."

"You can't. Give her the keys. She's a big girl. We need you to show us where you stashed the specimens." Boris ignored him, and Dmitri added, "The thin man said you are to come with us."

"Give me five minutes," Boris said.

Dmitri pulled out a pack of cigarettes. "I'll give you exactly one cigarette." He shook a cigarette loose from the pack, lit it, and took a long drag.

Boris and Yohaba faced each other. They both started to speak at once and then stopped in midsentence. "You go first," Boris said.

"You'll find a good woman someday," Yohaba said. "A beautiful Russian girl out of a catalog. A tall nuclear physicist with an

Olympic gold medal in rhythmic gymnastics." Boris looked into the distance and said nothing. Yohaba continued seriously, "You should come visit us. Come during round-up time. Rulon's brother is supposed to help, but he almost never comes. We could use you. Besides, Rulon would love to see you again. And we never did take you to church." Boris looked down at her. Yohaba wouldn't meet his eyes and started to choke up. "I wouldn't mind seeing you either."

Boris handed her the keys to Helmut's BMW. "Here."

"Keep them," Yohaba said, sniffling back a few tears. "I'm going back to the hotel to get the rest of my stuff, then I'll take the train into Zurich and pick up the rental car. They probably planted a bomb in the Beemer anyway."

"Phase three. Very good, Mrs. Hurt. I want a kiss."

"I'll bet you do," Yohaba said, thinking he was joking.

"I want a kiss."

"Well, you can forget it." Yohaba held out her hand for Boris to shake. Instead he grabbed it and pulled her closer. She looked into his eyes, and he pulled her closer again. Then he wrapped one huge arm around her and reeled her completely in. Yohaba softly said, "Stop," but didn't resist. Boris gently kissed her once on each cheek.

"See," he said. "A brotherly kiss."

"That was two kisses," said Yohaba.

"I won't forget what you did," Boris said, under his breath and serious. He rested his forehead against hers, and neither of them moved.

A half minute later, Dmitri yelled, "Time's up."

Boris let Yohaba go, and she faced him, eyes moist and red but looking strong. She wanted him to remember her strong.

"I couldn't have done this without you," she said. Boris wouldn't look at her, so she grabbed his jaw and made him face her, just like she had to do with Rulon sometimes. "We'll always be your friends."

Boris started to say something but couldn't. He swallowed hard, took on that Russian war memorial expression, and walked to the car.

CHAPTER 33

TWIN FALLS, TUESDAY, 4:00 P.M.

Yohaba came straight from the Twin Falls airport to the Magic Valley Medical Center. As she stood at the hospital entrance watching the taxi drive off, she had the strong feeling she'd been gone longer than just four days. More like four weeks. Or four lifetimes. Once again, her ceramic weapons had gotten through the security scans. Once again she was the wife of Rulon Hurt, Idaho rancher and retired OCD operative. She took a good look around. No Nazis. *Will the paranoia ever go away?* she wondered. With a sigh and a determined look, she walked through the main doors of the hospital, dragging her roller suitcase behind her.

On the elevator going up to the fifth floor, she suddenly remembered her nose ring and debated when she should take it out. She couldn't even explain to herself why she had put it back in; how would she ever explain it to Rulon? In the elevator's polished aluminum paneling, she studied her hazy, unrecognizable reflection.

She'd called Rulon once from the Zurich airport with her flight schedule, but, except to tell him she was safe and all was well, she had put off talking to him, using as an excuse that she had to run to catch the plane. On the sixteen-hour journey back to Idaho, she debated how much she would tell him and how much she would hide. Would she even mention the killings? Surely Rulon would take one look at her and know. Would he understand? Would the story hang together if she left out those parts? Rulon was a skillful interrogator. If there was a hole in a story, he'd find it. She had decided to leave out all the killings except Gustav's. That was the only one that mattered. That was the one that gave them their chance at leading a normal life.

She got out on Rulon's floor and found a restroom. All alone, standing over a sink, she looked at herself in the mirror. A haggard face and eyes with dark circles stared back at her. She touched her nose, wiggled the ring, and felt the wound reopen.

With both hands gripping the sink, she looked at herself again, then glanced down at the basin. There were three drops of blood. *One for every person I killed.* The nose ring slid easily out and got dropped in her pocket. She turned on the faucet and washed the blood away, then gathered her things and went to find Rulon.

All the nurses at the nurse's station recognized Yohaba, and after friendly greetings, one of them escorted her to Rulon's room. Walking down the hallway together, the young nurse bubbled with enthusiasm over Rulon's amazing recovery. She introduced Yohaba to the two bored-looking policemen sitting in chairs on either side of Rulon's door. They stood up and shook her hand. Yohaba went in by herself.

She quietly opened the door, and there was Rulon, alone, sitting up in bed, and looking out the window. He had a thick bandage around his head and significant discoloring around his eyes, but only a single visible tube running from his arm to a hanging intravenous bag.

He turned at the sound of the door and, despite being banged up, gave her a bright, sunny smile. "Hey, spy girl. Welcome back to heaven. Have I been praying hard for you!"

"Oh, baby," she said, "I needed everyone of them. Have I got stories for you."

Yohaba backed against the door to close it, then stood there hesitating. Rulon looked at her, puzzled, trying to read her expression, wondering why she didn't rush over.

She said in a trembling voice, "I'm so glad to see you awake. You look great. The nurses think you're an amazing patient." Inside, Yohaba's spirit was crumbling like a sand castle with the tide coming in. The words "I have murdered" echoed in her head. *I'm not the same person,* she told herself. *Rulon doesn't know me anymore. I don't know myself. I should leave him. Spare him.*

Rulon said, "They tell me I have the constitution of a water buffalo. Or was it the brain of a water buffalo? I forget." When she didn't laugh at his joke, he looked at her closely. "What's wrong, baby?"

"I've done bad things, Cowboy," she replied.

"I don't believe that," Rulon said gently. "Come. Tell me the story. Get it off your chest." He extended both arms. "It's sure good to see you, baby. Every time I see you it's like a sunrise over Redfish Lake." Yohaba rushed over, and they hugged for a solid minute.

The Covenant of the Chosen compound looked deserted except for the trucks parked along the fence. Most of the men were inside the buildings because of the heat. In the ranch house, an electric tea kettle whistled, and Mr. Goatee got up from the kitchen table to make two cups of tea, one for himself and one for the Reichsfuhrer.

Bernbailer looked up from his newspaper. "Make mine chamomile," he said.

"You got it, boss," said Mr. Goatee.

Bernbailer folded the paper, leaving the pages bent and messy, and threw the heap on the table in irritation. "I can't believe it's taken this long. What on earth is the delay? I have half a mind to fly to Switzerland and finish the job myself." The Reichsfuhrer and his second-in-command were dressed in identical brown shirts and black ties with a red swastika armband on their left arms.

"Patience, boss. Those boys know what they're doing. Give 'em a chance." Goatee set the cups down on the table and took a seat. "Be careful. It's hot."

Bernbailer got up and walked over to the cupboard. "I need something stronger." He came back with a bottle of Jack Daniels and two glasses.

Mr. Goatee looked askance at the bottle, then suddenly brightened up. "Okay, you talked me into it." Bernbailer poured them both a stiff shot.

Bernbailer quickly downed half his glass. "I was thinking. No matter how this works out, we might have to hide out for a while. Which wouldn't be a bad thing necessarily. I don't think the crew we have is cutting it. They let that Hurt fellow make a fool of them."

There was a creak in the floor and they both looked behind them.

Tall, lanky Ed Ryerson was standing in the doorway.

He said humbly, "I heard you talking. Permission to speak, sir?"

"Step forward, corporal," Mr. Goatee said. "The Reichsfuhrer always has time for one of his men."

"Thank you, sir," Ed stammered. He nervously wrung his ball cap in his hands. "I . . . I . . ."

Bernbailer gave Mr. Goatee a look that said, "See what I mean?"

Mr. Goatee said, "Calm down, Ed. We're family here. Just take your time."

Ed wrung his hat some more and couldn't seem to get the words out.

"Well, out with it, man," Bernbailer bristled. "Speak up."

"Well, sir. I couldn't help overhearing. If you're looking for a place to hide out, prison is good. You'd have three meals a day and lots of friends. The neo-Nazi gangs are real big in prison. You just don't want to go to the supermax in Colorado."

"What are you talking about?" Mr. Goatee asked. "The Reichsfuhrer is a busy man."

"I'm talking about the Supermax prison in Florence, Colorado. You should try and stay out of there if you can. Though maybe they won't give you a choice."

Bernbailer and Mr. Goatee both paused with their drinks in their hands and stared at Ed.

"It's just a suggestion," Ed said humbly. They watched as Ed tilted his jaw to speak into a microphone velcroed under his collar. "Okay. They're all yours."

To Bernbailer and his second-in-command, it seemed FBI agents were suddenly barreling in through every door, rappelling down from the ceiling vents, coming in through the windows, and bursting out of the closets. Their drinks fell out of their hands as beefy men, some in suits, some in jeans and windbreakers that said FBI across the back, slammed their faces into the table, and handcuffed their hands behind their backs. Some old, short guy in a crew cut read them their rights.

As three burly agents led the shocked men out of the kitchen, one of the agents stopped just as they passed Ed and asked him, "Where would you like us to put them, sir?"

Ed replied, "In a garbage dump. No, don't listen to me. In the van. Tell them lots of stories about prison life on the way. Make it very descriptive."

"Roger that, sir."

Ten minutes later, the men of the combined task force were scattered throughout the house looking for evidence, and Ed was in the kitchen alone. Three years of his life. A job well done. They told him he could choose his next assignment after this. He wandered out to the yard, thinking, *Corporate fat cats.*

No longer quiet, the yard was now like the infield of the Indianapolis 500. More than a dozen vehicles were parked haphazardly inside the compound, and uniformed police and more men wearing FBI windbreakers were leading prisoners to a yellow school bus parked in front of the Quonset hut. Ed had asked for forty men, and it looked like they'd brought twice that number. The bus was half full with bewildered, handcuffed Nazis, and a line of skinheads was waiting to get in. Ed could feel their eyes on him as he walked past. Bernbailer and Mr. Goatee were already gone in the van.

Efficient, thought Ed as he looked around the yard with his hands on his hips. *Just the way I like it.*

"Wow, what a story!" Rulon said when Yohaba was finished. "You must have been terrified." Though it made for a tight fit, Yohaba had crawled into the hospital bed next to Rulon as she related what happened in Switzerland. They were both munching out of a bag of glazed, chocolate-covered orange slices Yohaba had brought back from Einsiedeln.

"Yes," Yohaba said as she savored a particularly chocolaty slice. "It was like being in another dimension, just like you said."

"But just one thing," Rulon said, looking puzzled.

Oh, no, here it comes, thought Yohaba.

"Tell me again, I'm just curious: when you were in the alley, why do you think those guys backed down? It seems a little odd, doesn't it? One skinny gal and a single unarmed Russian, and all these rough, tough Nazis all back down. How many guys did you say you were facing?"

"Seven," Yohaba said, deciding to throw in the dead guy.

"And they all had knives?" Rulon asked.

"Yes," Yohaba said.

"I see. And you had to be unarmed because you'd just gotten off the plane." He cocked a skeptical eye. "This is an amazing story." At that point, Yohaba admitted that they might have had a pistol. Rulon considered that, "Yes, of course. Now it all makes sense. Yeah. Man, but it must have been tough procuring a weapon so fast after you landed. Just for fun, let's go over the timeline again."

At that point, Yohaba knew that Rulon wasn't buying a thing she was saying, so to spare the slow torture of Rulon in inquisition mode, she cut him off and confessed that she'd taken his ceramic pistol and knife. Rulon wasn't angry, but he wanted to hear the true story.

After she'd told her revised version of the confrontation in the alley, this time with the pistol playing a significant role, Rulon asked simply, "Do you have the parts with you now? I assume you disassembled it before you got on the plane. Mind if I see them?"

Yohaba got up, fished through her bag by the door, and handed the pistol parts sheepishly to Rulon.

He looked them over carefully as he assembled the pistol. "Seems to be in good shape," he said. "But there are only five bullets." He sniffed the barrel. "And this gun's been recently fired." He reached up and touched the spot where her nose ring had been. "Hey, you're bleeding a little."

With that, Yohaba broke down in tears, hopped back into bed, and told him the complete story, leaving nothing out. Rulon took it well, even though he had to make her stop a few times while he closed his eyes and regrouped.

When she was done, Rulon went back over every detail, helping her to see that it was all in self-defense. "No," he said. "Once you shot Helmut—which you had to do or I wouldn't be here—you set things in motion that had to play out." He also went over the other options she could have chosen and explained to her the problems with each one.

When he was finished, he said with conviction, "You did the right thing. I wouldn't have done things any differently. It was an incredibly difficult tactical environment. You and Boris should both be dead. They don't hand out manuals for situations like this."

At his words of understanding, Yohaba burst into tears again but then quickly pulled herself together. As he helped wipe away her tears, she said, "It's just like you said. It's an emotional roller coaster. One minute I feel high as a kite, like I can take on the world, the next moment I'm riddled with guilt and can't stop crying."

"Been there," Rulon said as he gently stroked her head. "But I don't think it's necessarily guilt. Your body produces very powerful chemicals in those situations, a bigger high than heroin I'm told. It's confusing, but the shrinks tell me it's mainly your body going into withdrawal."

They held each other, and Yohaba melted into Rulon, her arms around him and her head tucked up against his chest. After a minute, she said. "You know what was weird? You couldn't trust the bad guys to stay bad. I found out that most of them were getting ready to turn on old Gustav because of the bio-weapon thing. And that Figeli guy. Now, there's a puzzle for you."

"It's a fool that looks for logic in the chambers of the human heart," Rulon said.

She answered quietly, "George Clooney, Ulysses Everett McGill, *O Brother Where Art Thou.*" A few seconds later, she said, "Yeah, weird, isn't it?"

"But tell me," Rulon said. "Was I right about Boris or was I right?"

"You were dead right. He was amazing. He does have a code." She looked toward the window as if seeing all the way to Russia. "I told him we'd invite him back sometime."

"The guy took good care of my girl. He's welcome here anytime. He even got along with the dogs."

Yohaba took his hand. "Did your dad tell you? Helmut killed Molly."

Rulon swallowed hard before answering. "I've got a buddy just back from Afghanistan. He's got a German Shepherd war dog he wants me to have."

"You loved Molly. Why don't you just get another Great Pyrenees?"

Rulon looked up at the ceiling and didn't speak for a few seconds before answering through a tight-lipped smile. "I'll never get another Great Pyrenees. Nope. Not gonna happen." He raised Yohaba's hand to his lips and kissed it. "Let's change the subject."

Yohaba asked about Bernbailer. Rulon looked at the clock on the wall. "There's nothing to worry about. He and his motley crew are all rounded up by now and on their way to jail." He told her about Ed being an undercover agent.

"What?" she said. "You never told me that! I thought we weren't supposed to have any secrets."

"Darling. I never said no secrets. I just said I would never lie to you. I would never reveal another agent to anyone, not even you. You could slip someday and say something to someone, not even realizing what you had said and get him killed. Remember when Ed came over and warned us at the compound meeting? He was taking an incredible chance. I'll never forget that."

"Wow!" Yohaba said. "He stayed in character even knowing you knew about his undercover work. That was an Academy Award performance. But maybe if I wasn't there, he'd have acted differently."

"Even if you weren't there, even if he and I were on a mountaintop alone together a hundred miles away, he'd have stayed in character. He's done undercover work in Iraq, if you can believe that."

"Okay, I understand why you did it, but withholding information is still a form of lying."

"Yes, I definitely agree," Rulon said in a tone and a look that at first went over her head until he asked, "Mind if I see the pistol again?"

With that she socked him in the arm, and he grabbed her hand and wouldn't let go. Then he swung his other arm around her and she struggled to get away. They laughed and struggled until an old nurse stuck her head in the door and told them to knock it off.

"That was the angel of death," said Rulon in a whisper. "She secretly runs this place. Even the doctors fear her. If you don't eat all your Jell-O, she gives you a double enema."

Yohaba punched Rulon in the arm for that and they both almost busted a seam trying to keep from laughing. After they settled down, Rulon turned serious and asked Yohaba what she had learned from her whole experience.

"The quality of mercy is not strained," Yohaba said.

"Good," Rulon said. "Where would any of us be without mercy? What else?"

"Always wear a tactical vest."

"My girl," said Rulon with pride.

But then Yohaba got an introspective look on her face. "I'd lived in Switzerland all my life but didn't know about these secret little wars going on all the time between the services. It's only been a day, but I still would have thought there'd be something in the papers by now. There was a significant body count. Surely the Swiss police must have known what was going on."

Rulon smiled. "For now we see through a glass darkly."

"Does that mean there's hope you still think I'm beautiful, Cowboy?"

"I think roses are beautiful until I set 'em next to you, my love."

"So you still love me?"

"Heck yeah, darling. I love you more than my hammer."

"Even more than your gun?" Yohaba asked with affected hopefulness, teasing.

"Hmm . . . which one?" Rulon asked with a straight face.

Yohaba socked him playfully in the nose. "Be serious. I'm hurting here, in case you can't tell."

Rulon put his arm around her, kissed her, and said softly in her ear, "I love you. When I chose you, I knew there was a plan. I didn't know what it was, but I knew in time it would unfold. I think all of this—all that you went through—is for a purpose. To give you experience."

"You mean, like this was a warm-up?" Yohaba asked.

"Yeah," Rulon said.

"But it's over," Yohaba said. "The old Nazi is dead. And nobody else seemed to give a hoot about Helmut or Eduard."

"What about the guy in the alley then? Don't you think he might have a few friends or brothers somewhere?"

"Oh, I forgot about him."

"And what about the two guys in the gym?"

"Oh, I forgot about them too."

"It's not over," Rulon said. "Trust me."

EPILOGUE

In the heavily treed Yasenevo district in the southwest corner of Moscow sits the twenty-story headquarters of the Russian Foreign Intelligence service, the SVR. On the twelfth floor, on the side with a view of the nearby water park, closed for winter, the head of Directorate S, the department responsible for illegal intelligence and terror, sat in a room at the end of a fifteen-foot, fifties-era, plain wood table.

From the fifties himself, pale, bureaucratically pudgy with slack jaws and black eyes that looked as though they hadn't seen a bed in days, the director had been made personally responsible for Operation Cowboy by the thin man. Bizarre, crazy, eccentric. The orders had baffled him when he first took the position three months prior. A cowboy, a karaoke bar in the wasteland of America. A single-combat champion from the service academy. He expected to be initiated into the mysteries when he first became the director three months earlier, possibly finding out how Stalin had really died; was it naturally or was he murdered to stop the madness? Instead, the biggest surprise was the thin man's obsession with this American cowboy, sending a prize recruit every six months to a karaoke bar in Idaho. But then, when the director heard the entire story, it made a certain perverse sense. Still, an assassin would have been less trouble.

On his right was the latest academy graduate with a ticket to

Twin Falls. Yevgeny Volodin. Not as big as Boris, not as physically intimidating as Boris, the committee had tinkered again with the selection criteria, choosing this time to go with someone faster, someone with more . . . technique. Krav Maga was originally developed in Czechoslovakia in the 1930s by Jews needing to defend themselves against fascist thugs. Now it was the highly regarded self-defense form taught within the Israeli Defense Force. The pale and deadly looking Yevgeny was a master of that lethal, no-nonsense form of hand-to-hand combat.

Next to him was a short, handsome blond man, the academy vice principal. On the opposite side of the table were the last four men who had fought the Cowboy: all grim, rugged-looking men who had an aura to the discerning that said give a wide birth. At the far left, sitting rigidly upright, was Boris, looking sharp in a dark blue suit, white shirt, and light blue tie. Yevgeny needed to be prepped for his turn at the Rockin' Rooster.

Each of the four gave a stirring account of their experience, how they had Rulon on the ropes and were on their way to an easy victory, but then through some accident, an inopportune slip, a lost grip, or treachery from the Cowboy's woman, they lost. Though all four nodded corroboration with serious expressions, they inwardly suppressed laughter at each embellished story, having shared the truer but less flattering accounts only within their own select fraternity.

Yeygeny listened quietly, and to Boris's perceptive eyes, a bit smugly. Boris was the last to speak. When he was finished, the director ordered him to continue his narrative beyond what happened in the bar. Even he wanted to hear the details about Zurich, the biological specimens, and the Nazis. Boris complied but, for her protection, left out much of Yohaba's involvement, painting her as little more than a nuisance.

Boris had not spoken to Rulon or Yohaba since they last saw each other almost seven months earlier, but he had received an email from Rulon a month ago saying he was fully recovered, thanking him for watching over Yohaba, and inviting him to visit the ranch during round-up time. How Rulon had managed to get his email address, Boris had no idea. One more surprise from the unassuming cowboy.

Boris knew that as an SVR operative, all his emails were

intercepted and read by the department, and he dared not respond over his personal laptop, or even within Mother Russia. On an assignment in Madrid two weeks ago, he called the ranch from a pay phone, but no one answered.

"I take special pleasure in fighting really big men," Yevgeny said when Boris finished describing his fight with Max. Yevgeny weighed 230 pounds, had short black hair and pearly white teeth. "Really big men usually have no technique. They never needed any. Their size always won for them. When a truly skillful fighter takes them on, they wilt."

"True," Boris said.

Yevgeny stared at Boris. "Big men are slow and tire easily and usually are not too smart. The trick is to work them like bulls. Go for the knees or the groin, but keep your distance until they tire."

"A good plan," Boris said. "Sounds unbeatable."

For a long moment Yevgeny looked at Boris, puzzled, not knowing if he was being serious, then asked, "When I get to the bar, what about the Cowboy's woman? I hear she likes to interfere." Around the table, all the men who had been to the Rockin' Rooster broke into grins, except Boris.

Boris thought about the time in the hotel when she saved their lives by standing up and shooting the two armed men. "Yes. Incessantly," he said.

"Yet you took this Yohaba to Zurich with you," challenged Yevgeny.

"A big mistake," Boris said, his feelings for her like smoldering coals glowing red again at the sound of her name. "A very big mistake."

Yevgeny offered a crude suggestion as to the real reason Boris had brought Yohaba along. Everyone laughed, Boris the loudest.

When the laughter subsided, Yevgeny said, "Having a civilian with you must have slowed you down."

Boris's mind cast back to when he was waiting in the alley near the train station, sick to his stomach that the Germans had caught her, thinking she should have reached him by now. And then the sight of her tearing around the corner with a squad of Nazis hot on her tail. He said, "She was slower than a Siberian winter."

Yevgeny said, "She was supposed to be a scientist. Was she smart?"

Boris thought about the courtyard in Einsiedeln when she jumped in front of him and took the bullet. "No, quite stupid, really."

"I knew it," Yevgeny said. "Who else would marry a fat farmer from Idaho?" Everyone laughed again. Boris pounded the table he was laughing so hard.

AT 3:00 A.M. Yevgeny Volodin was at the front door of his apartment building with his key in his hand. After the meeting at the SVR headquarters, he had gone to dinner with some friends from the service. A party for his great adventure and expected victory. As he inserted the key, a huge man stepped out of the shadows into the lamplight that illuminated the doorway. A light drinker, Yevgeny had nursed a single vodka all night. He sensed the movement and quickly turned, ready for action.

"Oh, it's only you," he said when he saw Boris standing there, still in his suit but without the tie. "Why aren't you wearing a coat. It's freezing. And what are you doing here so late? Have you come to give me more advice?"

"To someone born in Siberia, this is not cold," Boris said. "And, yes, I want to give you some advice. But I first want to tell you how I think they really picked the right person this time. You have a certain indefinable quality. I have a feeling things will go differently with you."

Yevgeny turned back to the door with his key, annoyed at this nonsense from Boris. "Yes, Boris. Run along home now. I'm tired."

"Certainly. But before you fight the Cowboy, I think you and I should go a few rounds. Just to warm you up. Give you some practice. What do you say?"

"I say you're crazy," Yevgeny said. "Go home before I take you up on your offer." By now Boris was next to him and Yevgeny, suddenly wary, stepped back to put some space between them. He gave Boris a hard look and suddenly understood.

"Ding," said Boris.

Ninety seconds later, Boris had Yevgeny by the front of his jacket and was hoisting his bruised and battered opponent onto his feet.

Once he had him steady, Boris put his face up to Yevgeny's and snarled, "Look at me. Look at me. Your eyes will be swelled shut in a minute. I suggest you use them while you can." Yevgeny looked, and Boris was pleased to see fear. "Good," Boris said. "I see you got the message. The Cowboy likes to say actions speak louder than words. Should be a proverb for us Russians, don't you agree? Now listen carefully." Boris let go and Yevgeny slumped to the ground.

Boris crouched so he could be at eye level. "You will not get on the plane tomorrow. If you do, I'll be on the next one coming after you. You fell down a flight of stairs. Do you understand?" Yevgeny nodded vigorously. "Good," Boris said. "Now, here's the advice. Don't ever say anything bad again about the Cowboy's woman; you are not even to speak her name. Or I'll—" Boris had started to say "kill you" but then choked up at the thought of Yohaba's disapproval. His eyes went black and dead instead as he spoke slowly, grinding out each word. "—or I'll hurt you bad. Real, real bad. Not like this little polka we just had. Look at me. Do you understand?"

Yevgeny, eyes wide as saucers, nodded again. Boris got up and walked away through the circle of lamplight and into the shadows. Yevgeny listened to his receding footsteps and when he could no longer hear them, felt a wave of relief, then keeled over on his side.

LEONARD STEENBERG DROVE through CERN's Meyrin gate, on the outskirts of Geneva, in his Audi TT and waved at the guard. After the longest day of his life, he was on his way home. Up until a week ago, he was still convinced that 182 Elsa was going to miss the earth. After the near collision with another asteroid in June had upset Elsa's moon and somehow caused Elsa to bend course toward earth, Leonard, the ex-Jesuit scholastic, had religiously charted its progress.

Six months ago, Elsa's first change in course had happened immediately, and Leonard had gone through a five-day period when he was scared out of his mind that Einstein had been right. But the rate of change had suddenly slowed and Elsa stabilized into her new position. The crisis seemed over until a month ago when Elsa's course began shifting again. Just six days earlier, the calculated interception point with the earth had matched up perfectly with Einstein's doomsday prediction—April 13, 2029—and stayed there. In his heart of hearts, Steenberg always suspected his old mentor had been right.

He considered when he should tell Rulon and Yohaba. Switzerland was eight hours ahead of Idaho. It was after lunch there. He reached for his cell phone and was about to push their speed dial number when he stopped. It was Christmastime. Why ruin their holiday?

ABOUT THE AUTHOR

JIM WAS BORN IN BROOKLYN, NEW YORK, IN 1951. When a teenager, he moved with his family to the West Coast, settling in San Francisco for a time before moving south into Silicon Valley. After attending college, completing a church mission, and spending six years in the Marines, he found a home in the computer industry in 1978 and has worked there ever since. He has lived on three continents and done business in over forty countries, but he still counts Idaho—the home of his alma mater, Boise State University, and Rulon Hurt, his hammer-wielding cowboy—as one of his favorite places. Currently, Jim lives in Zurich, Switzerland, with his wife, Kim.

Learn more about Jim at his website, www.jimhaberkorn.com, or read his blog at jimhaberkorn.blogspot.com.

0 26575 11855 1